THE
PORTAL
The Portal Series
Book One

Richard Bowker

Cover and Book design by eBook Prep www.ebookprep.com

First Edition, November, 2013
ISBN: 978-1-61417-505-6

ePublishing Works!
www.epublishingworks.com

CHAPTER 1

People tell me I'm a pretty good writer for a kid, so I've decided to try to tell this story. Not that I'm going to show it to anyone. But if I don't write it down, maybe I'll start forgetting parts of it. Worse, I might start thinking it didn't really happen. But it did. It was as real as anything in this world, or any other world. So here goes.

My name is Larry Barnes, and I live in Glanbury, which is a small town south of Boston. I go to the Theodore Grossman Middle School, which even my parents call The Gross. When this all happened I was just starting seventh grade, and my life sucked.

Just to show you, here's the way things went on the day it began. First off, Mom woke me up with that chirpy "Rise and shine, Pumpkin!" that she knows I hate. One of the worst things about Middle School is you have to get up so early, and I've never gotten used to it. I looked over at Matthew, and of course he was still sleeping like a baby, because grammar school starts an hour later. One of the bad things about my life is that I have to share a bedroom with my kid brother. This is okay when he's asleep, but when he's awake it's just about unbearable, because he won't stop talking. It's like the Mute button in his brain is broken. And it's not as if anything he has to say is all that interesting. He'll talk for twenty minutes about, I don't know, lemonade, or water balloons, or pro wrestling. And he doesn't really need me to say anything, he's happy just to yak away by himself.

So anyway, I got up to go to the bathroom, and of course Cassie was already in there, taking one of her endless showers. Cassie's my sister. She's in high school, and she has "issues," my mother says. I say she's a jerk. She's the reason Matthew and I are stuck with each other, by the way; apparently there's some law that a teenage girl has to have her own bedroom. So I yelled at her to quit hogging the bathroom, and she yelled at me to get lost, and then Mom yelled at me to hurry up, and I was in a bad mood and I hadn't even eaten breakfast yet.

Breakfast was the usual—gulp your cereal down or you'll miss the bus. Dad had already left for work. I think he likes to get out of the house before all the yelling starts. Mom doesn't complain about him much, but I get the idea that she thinks the same thing. He's a computer programmer, and I guess he works really hard; but I don't see why he can't eat a meal or two with us once in a while.

While I was trying to get out the door Mom had something new to warn me about; she's always worried about something. "Larry, I read in the paper about a man in Rhode Island who was caught stalking kids as they walked to the bus stop. I want you to be extra careful out there."

"Mom, we're nowhere near Rhode Island."

"They're all over. You can't be too careful."

"But I'm almost a teenager."

"That's just the age these people are interested in."

Cassie came downstairs in time to hear this part of the conversation, and she said, "Don't worry, Larry, not even a dirty old man is going to be interested in you."

So I yelled at her, and she yelled at me, and then I had to run to catch the bus. I made it, but the only empty seat was right in front of Stinky Glover.

His real name is Julian, but guess why everyone calls him "Stinky". I suppose he takes a shower sometimes, but the effect must wear off before he gets out in public, because I've never been near him when he didn't smell like low tide. If there was a BO event in the Olympics, he'd get the gold medal. Oh, and also he's fat and stupid. Of course, no one would sit beside him if they could help it, but sometimes you had to sit in front of him, and that could be just as bad.

For some reason Stinky has it in for me. I really don't know why. I don't call him Stinky; I don't call him anything. "Hey, Lawrence," he whispered, leaning forward. "How's it going, Lawrence?"

Why someone named Julian would find the name Lawrence funny is beyond me, but that was Stinky for you. I ignored him.

I've seen the bullying video, of course, and heard the lectures from the school shrink, so I know all about what you're supposed to do, how you're supposed to act when someone bullies you. But the fact of the matter is, Stinky wasn't exactly a bully. He never beat me up or stole my lunch money or any of that stuff. He was just really, really annoying.

Like that morning. After he got through saying my name a bunch of times, I felt something long and wet in my ear, and heard him half giggle/half snort behind me. He'd decided to give me a Wet Willie. Can you imagine feeling Stinky Glover's finger wiggling in your ear, with Stinky Glover's spit all over it? Especially at seven o'clock in the morning, when your stomach hasn't really woken up yet. It's a wonder I didn't hurl.

I turned around. "Cut it out!" I demanded.

He grinned, and I saw specks of breakfast on his teeth. "What's the matter, Lawrence? Not having fun, Lawrence?"

So I got up to try and change my seat, and the bus driver started yelling at me.

Just great. It was a relief to actually arrive at school, where I had a chance to talk to Kevin Albright. He's my best friend, even though we're kind of different. I'm good at writing; he's better at math and science. He actually doesn't do all that well in school, mainly because it's just so boring, compared to all the stuff he finds out on his own, reading books and visiting weird web sites and doing science experiments in his basement. He likes me, I think, because I talk about more than video games and TV. Lots of kids think he's just strange.

In homeroom before "A" period I told him about Stinky.

"Stinky is an example of evolution gone wrong," Kevin said. "Darwin should apologize for coming up with people like him."

"I don't need apologies. I need to figure out what to do about him."

"Maybe you can pretend you have some kind of disease. At least that might keep him from sticking his finger in your ear."

"Stinky *is* a disease."

"Maybe you need an anti-Stinky pill. Stinkomycin."

Kevin was no help, but he was fun to talk to.

Everything went okay then until English class. I like English class. Mrs. Nathanson is an interesting teacher, and she's the one who thinks I'm a good writer. But there's just one problem: I sit next to Nora Lally. That's not bad, actually. Nora is no Stinky Glover. In fact, she's the prettiest girl in the seventh grade. She's got long black hair and bright blue eyes and this terrific smile. So what's the problem, then?

The problem is I can't bring myself to speak to her, even with her sitting right next to me. I get nervous. My throat feels funny. I can't think of anything to say. It's so stupid. I go to the school dances. I pal around with girls. No one has ever accused me of being shy. So why can't I talk to Nora Lally?

I haven't mentioned this problem to Kevin, by the way; I haven't mentioned it to anyone. It's too embarrassing.

That day was no different. Before class I could have asked her a question about the homework. I could have made some funny remark about Mrs. Nathanson—the kind I'm always making to Kevin. But I didn't. I just sat there like a dope. And Nora just ignored me, the way she always does.

So school finally got out, and wouldn't you know—Stinky got the seat next to me on the bus. The only thing worse than having Stinky sitting behind you is having him sitting next to you. Especially when you can't open the window. I felt like my elbow was sticking into a tub of rancid butter. "Hey, Lawrence! We're gonna be best buddies, right, Lawrence?" Giggle-snort, giggle-snort.

Finally I got off at my stop and walked home. I didn't notice any perverts, but then, I wasn't looking too hard. My mother was waiting for me with the usual questions. "How was school, Larry? How are things going?"

She's always interrogating me about school. I think she figures sooner or later I'll break down and admit I was doing drugs during gym class or something.

"Fine." So what was I going to say? My mom is really great and all, but she's sort of, well…*intense* is the word my father uses. I sure wasn't going to tell her about Nora Lally. And if I had told her about Stinky Glover, she would have been on the phone to the principal and probably Stinky's mom as well. There would have been letters written and meetings called and action plans developed. And I'd still have to get on the bus with Stinky.

"Are you sure?" she asked. "You look…"

"I said school was fine," I snapped at her. "I'm just a little tired," I added, trying not to be too grouchy.

"Well, you should go to bed earlier, then," she replied. "You know, Middle School can be very demanding, and children your age really need—"

"Good point," I said. "I'll really try."

She gave me another one of her searching glances, as if trying to figure out if my agreeableness was a danger sign of alcohol abuse. But I just wanted to end the inquisition. "Gotta get going on my homework," I pointed out, and she couldn't argue with that. So I headed upstairs to my room.

This was the best part of the day—before Cassie and Matthew got home and started bugging me. No yakking, no complaining. Just…silence. Too bad it wouldn't last. I didn't start my homework. Instead I lay on my bed for a while thinking about how rotten things were. How was I going to stand a whole year of this?

Finally I decided to go for a walk and try to get Stinky and Nora and everyone out of my brain.

I went back downstairs. "Goin' out!" I yelled at Mom, and I headed into the back yard before she could ask me about my homework. And then I kept on going, past the garage and the old swing set, into the woods beyond the yard.

I have to say something here about those woods. They're called conservation land. My father says it's great that we're next to conservation land, because no one can build on it and it increases the value of our property. My mom worries about Lyme disease, snakes, and poison ivy. When we were little she used to have a rule against us going into the woods, but she's kind of given up on that. It's better than playing in the street, I guess.

The thing about the woods is, if you go in far enough, you come to a bunch of falling-down old brick-and-concrete buildings. They were used by the Army during World War Two, although I don't know exactly what for. After the war the Army didn't need them anymore, so they gave the whole area to the town, which turned it into the conservation land.

It's not that easy to get to the buildings. There's an old road that runs up to them, but it's pretty wrecked by now because the town doesn't maintain it. But of course kids go there, and you see broken beer bottles and stuff scattered around. Everyone thinks the buildings are a safety hazard and should be torn down, but no one can agree who should pay for it. Mom really doesn't want me to go there, because she's certain one of the buildings will fall on me and I'll be crushed to death with no one to hear my cries for help. But she can't stop me.

I don't care about the buildings, but I do like the woods. They're dark and quiet, and there's no one to bug you. My dad has taught me the names of some of the trees and plants, so I don't feel like a dope in there. Anyway, the woods just felt like the right place to be that afternoon.

So I picked up a long stick and started whacking it against the trees as I walked. Take that, Stinky! Take that, Cassie!

I usually don't go out of earshot of the house—that's Mom's latest rule—but that day I just felt like walking. I wanted to get as far away from my life as I could. And eventually I found myself near those old army buildings.

I was a little surprised—I hadn't realized I had walked that far. But it was no big deal. It wasn't like a wall was really going to fall on me.

Then I heard a noise from inside one of the buildings.

Again, no big deal. If other kids were there, I'd just go home. Despite Mom's fears, I don't drink or anything, and I don't want to hang with the loser kids who do. So I turned around. I had only walked a few steps when I heard someone call to me. "Hey, Lawrence! Watcha doin', Lawrence?"

What was Stinky doing here?

"Wait up, Lawrence!"

I turned back. He was heading towards me. I really didn't want to deal with Stinky right then. I started to run.

Okay. Here's where it starts. I slowed down to catch my breath—I wasn't too worried about Stinky being able to catch up to me. I was in a small clearing. And I was still holding onto the stick, kind of whipping it in front of me like a sword. And I noticed something.

The end of the stick disappeared.

I don't mean that it got lost in the brush or anything like that. I mean, it was there, in mid-air, and then it wasn't. And then as I kept moving the stick, it came back again—it reappeared. I looked at the stick. It seemed okay—it wasn't broken or anything. I tried again.

Same thing.

My heart was pounding.

I dropped the stick and slowly reached forward. And my hand disappeared too. One second it was there in front of me, the next second it was gone, like it had been lopped off. But there wasn't any pain. There wasn't any pressure or resistance. It didn't feel hot or cold. It just felt—different. I took my hand back out and extended my foot. It went in, disappeared, and then I brought it back out.

I couldn't figure it out. All I could think was: This is really weird.

"Hey, Lawrence! Wait up!"

Stinky was heading towards me through the trees.

And then I had another thought: Wouldn't it be cool if I disappeared right in front of Stinky?

This was a really stupid thing to think. I admit it. My mom would have totally freaked out. I would've freaked out if I'd thought about it for another couple of seconds. But I had this cool vision in my mind of Stinky standing there with a dopey look on his face, and me standing right next to him in this zone of invisibility or whatever, laughing at him.

I sure wanted to do that.

So, like a total idiot, I stepped inside.

CHAPTER 2

I knew right away this was a big mistake. I guess I had thought it would be sort of like stepping into the other side of one of those mirrors where you can see the person looking into the mirror, but he can't see you. Cool! But why in the world did I think that? I dunno—seeing Stinky had made me stupid, I suppose. Things just aren't supposed to become invisible. I had stumbled onto something very weird—and very important. And instead of running home and getting a grownup the way I should have, I had gone ahead and stepped into it.

Well, it wasn't like one of those mirrors. Inside it was all cloudy. I thought I could make out dark shapes to my left and right, but I couldn't tell what they were. Trees? I didn't think so. I had brains enough to be scared, but here's where I made another, maybe bigger mistake: I didn't turn around right away and get out. Instead I reached out and groped through the clouds. I took a step forward. Then another. The cloudiness seemed to fade, and I was outside again. I heard noises. I looked around.

I was someplace…different.

Not entirely different. I was still in the woods, sort of—I recognized the little clearing, and the oak tree right in front of me. But Stinky was gone. And ahead of me, through the trees, were the backs of buildings. Beyond them was a street. The noises I heard were cars passing by.

What was going on?

I turned and held out my hand. It disappeared. So the thing was still there. But where was I? What had happened?

I decided to take a look around.

I guess that was one more mistake. Was I being brave? Or stupid? I don't know. Maybe I was just really confused.

I headed for the buildings.

Like I said, I was in back of them, and the first things I saw were dumpsters and parked cars. One building I recognized right away—a Jiffy Lube. But I didn't think there were any Jiffy Lubes in Glanbury. My dad always drives over to Rockford to get his oil changed. And this didn't look like the place in Rockford. It didn't look much like any regular Jiffy Lube I'd seen, actually, despite what the sign said. But I couldn't put my finger on what was different.

I walked around front, still trying to puzzle it out. The layout of the building was different from the one in Rockford, I decided. And the sign—it said something about their 16-point Signature Service. Weren't there more points than that in Jiffy Lube's Signature Service? Maybe different Jiffy Lubes had different numbers of points…I had no idea.

I looked around and saw another sign that said "Glanbury Plaza," and that was a little reassuring—except that the real Glanbury Plaza has a Stop 'n' Shop and a CVS in it, and this place didn't have either; it was just a little strip mall on a street I didn't recognize.

Next door to the Jiffy Lube was a Burger King. And that didn't look right either. It took me a minute—it really did—to figure out what was wrong.

The sign didn't say "Burger King." It said "Burger Queen."

Burger Queen?

By now I was extremely freaked out.

I looked around for other things that were out of whack. Sure enough, across the street people were lined up to get ice cream cones at a Dairy King. And the cars—they were mostly long and wide, with big fins, like the kind you see in old movies. In the Burger Queen parking lot I saw a really big one that was called a "Jupiter." I'd never heard of a Jupiter. And where were all the SUVs and Jeeps and minivans?

Finally I noticed the kids hanging around outside the Burger Queen. They were all staring at me. One of them called out, "Hey, rad gear, hombre!" At least, that's what I think he said.

I couldn't think what to reply, so I just stared back at him.

"I said, 'Nice clothes,'" the kid repeated, laughing. The other kids started laughing, too.

Well, my clothes were nice. My mom had bought me some Abercrombie cargo shorts and Old Navy t-shirts, and I was wearing brand-new back-to-school Adidas. But the kids in front of the Burger Queen—the boys were wearing tight black pants, shiny leather shoes, and actual white shirts—the kind you button up! The girls were wearing big skirts and baggy sweaters. The boys' hair was long and shaggy; the girls' hair was short and spiky. They all looked totally strange, like they were going to a costume party, although I had no idea what they were supposed to be dressed up as—some rock group?

And they were making fun of *me*!

I kept walking. I was scared, but I was also sort of fascinated. Why had Burger King changed its name? Why were people dressed funny? Those kids weren't the only ones—the men who walked by me wore suits with odd-shaped hats; the women wore long skirts and way too much makeup.

Why were some things familiar, while other things seemed so completely different? Traffic lights looked the same, for example, but crosswalks were painted in bright yellow zig-zags. I passed a Dunkin' Donuts that looked normal, but the cell phones I saw people using were enormous, the size of hardcover books.

And lots of people stared at me like I was the one wearing a costume.

Finally I wandered into a little park with winding paths and old-fashioned streetlights. Near the entrance, a man was standing on a bench and talking to a small crowd of people. I went over to listen. He was a tall and thin, with long black hair and dark, glittering eyes. He was wearing baggy brown pants and a shapeless white shirt with a necktie hanging loosely over it. His voice was soft, but it carried, and you could hear every word he was saying even from a distance:

"This world is not only stranger than you imagine, it is stranger than you can imagine. And more beautiful. And more full of love. Do not be complacent. Do not live your lives as if each day is a chore to be endured. Seek out the strangeness. Find the beauty. Feel the love."

He turned his glittering eyes on me, then, and all of a sudden he smiled, like he was sharing a joke with me. When he spoke again, it was as if he was talking to me personally.

"'Where is it?' you ask. The strangeness—the beauty—the love." He lifted up his hand. "It is here. It is in each speck of dirt, and in the worm that crawls through the dirt. It is in distant exploding suns. It is just over the horizon." And then, looking even harder at me with those dark eyes, he added, "It is in the home you left behind."

I shivered a little, then tore myself away from the guy and kept walking. He was really creepy. Nobody like that in Glanbury.

But this *was* Glanbury. I sat on a bench and thought about it.

I was apparently in Glanbury, but it wasn't anything like the Glanbury I knew. Had I stepped into some kind of time machine and ended up in the future? But why would cell phones be bigger in the future? And why would Burger King and Dairy Queen change their names? This just didn't feel like the future. Could it be the past, then? The cars and the clothes looked a little like something out of a 50s TV show, maybe…but cell phones hadn't been around that long, I was pretty sure. Maybe I should go find a newspaper and check the date.

Or maybe I should just go home.

But would I be able to get home? If the thing was a time machine, did it have a dial where you could set the date, like the car in *Back to the Future*? It hadn't really seemed like a time machine at all. So how could I be sure it would take me back where or when I had come from?

Well, it just had to. All of a sudden I really wasn't interested in this place anymore. I needed to get out of there, right away. I stood up.

And I bumped into someone. A bunch of books fell to the ground. "Sorry, sorry," I said, and bent over to pick them up.

They were textbooks—math and science. I went to hand them to the person, and I froze. It was Nora Lally.

She smiled at me and took them. "No worry," she said. "Thank you."

"It was my—I mean—sure. Sorry."

She tilted her head and looked at me as if trying to figure something out. Then she just smiled again and said, "See ya." And she walked away down the path.

I watched her go.

Nora Lally. Here, wearing a puffy skirt and white socks and shiny black shoes. Smiling at me.

I remembered to breathe. I should go after her, I thought. But she had already disappeared. And if I did go after her, what would I say?

What had I just said to her? It had been pretty stupid, right?

And then I thought: If she's here, then it can't be the past or the future. So what is it?

Didn't matter, I decided. I had to go home. With one last look down the path where Nora had walked, I turned and headed back toward the Burger Queen and the Jiffy Lube. I went past where the creepy guy had been preaching, but he was gone, and the crowd had disappeared. I wasn't interested in him now, though. So weird, I kept thinking to myself. Nora Lally—wearing clothes that the real Nora Lally wouldn't get caught dead wearing. But she had smiled at me, and she had talked to me, even if it was just a few words.

Back at the Burger Queen, the kids were still hanging in the parking lot. "Hey, there's the hombre in the short pants!" one of them called out.

"Hombre, aren't you a little old to be dressed like a baby?" another kid shouted.

"What do you need all those pockets for—your pacifiers?" a third one said.

I ignored them. I just wanted to go home.

Then the door of the Burger Queen opened, and I saw Stinky Glover come out, carrying a big bag of food. He was wearing a white shirt and black pants, too, but his shirt wasn't tucked in, and it looked like it hadn't been washed in a week.

The other kids moved away from him.

The strange thing was, with everyone yelling at me, I felt grateful to see a familiar face, even if it was Stinky Glover's.

"Hey Stinky!" I called out.

He looked up at me, and I could tell I'd made a mistake. "What did you call me?" he said.

"Uh, never mind," I replied.

"No. You called me something. What was it?"

"He called you 'Stinky'," one of the other kids told him, and they all laughed.

"That's what I thought." He put down the bag of food and started toward me.

Swell. I walked away.

"Hey! C'mere!"

I walked faster.

"We'll get him for you, Julie!" I heard one of the kids say. Julie?

I started to run—back behind the Jiffy Lube, with the gang of kids behind me. Past the dumpsters. Where was the oak tree? Where was the thing—the time machine—whatever? Was it still there? I had to find it.

"Hey, hombre! We're gonna get you! You can't run forever!"

There was the tree. I reached out my hand—and it disappeared. Thank goodness! I didn't look back at the kids behind me. I just plunged inside and hoped for the best.

CHAPTER 3

I stepped through the clouds inside the thing and out the other side.

"Hey! Where'd you go?" a voice called.

It was Stinky. My Stinky. Standing in the woods—my woods—looking puzzled.

I tried to catch my breath. "Hiding," I said. I didn't think I could be happy to see Stinky Glover, but right then I sure was.

He still looked puzzled. "Hiding where?"

I waved vaguely. "Behind a tree." I didn't want him to know about the time machine, or whatever it was. I moved quickly away from it.

He seemed to get back his Stinkiness. "Why are you hiding?" he said. "You afraid of me, Lawrence?"

I was no longer happy to see him. I didn't answer. Instead I just kept walking, back towards my house.

"Don't you like wet willies, Lawrence?" he called out.

I ignored him. This time he didn't follow me.

When I finally saw our swing set I stopped and took a deep breath. Man, that had been strange.

I ran through the yard and inside our house, and there was Mom, frowning at me. "Larry, I thought you were going to do your homework," she said.

"Mom, you wouldn't believe—" I began.

"Wouldn't believe what?"

I stared at her. "Well, uh, what a beautiful day it is," I said finally. "I just had to get some fresh air before I started my homework."

She looked at me a little funny, and then just shrugged and said, "All right, but I don't want you going too far into the woods."

"Okay, sure."

So, I didn't tell Stinky because I just don't like him. And I didn't tell Mom because I knew she'd yell at me—first, for disobeying her by going to the army buildings, and second, for doing something idiotically dangerous like actually stepping inside the invisibility thing. Maybe I should have—but you don't know my mom.

I had to tell someone, though.

I figured I could tell my dad. He wouldn't be too bothered by the disobedience thing, especially if it turned out I had made some important scientific discovery, which obviously I had. But he wasn't home from work yet.

In the meantime, I decided to call Kevin Albright. This was just the sort of thing he'd love.

I went into my dad's study and picked up the phone. That turned out to be a mistake. Cassie had arrived home while I was in the woods, and of course she was already on the extension in her room talking to one of her high-school-loser buddies. She'd been demanding her own cell phone, which had caused more eyerolling from Dad. So far, no cell phone.

"Hang up, snot-for-brains!" she screamed at me.

How creative. I banged down the receiver and waited for her to wear herself out talking about how cute her math teacher was or whatever. It took a while. For someone who is always too exhausted to do any chores, she certainly has a lot of energy when she's talking on the phone.

When she finally got off I called Kevin. "You'll never guess what just happened to me," I said.

"Want me to try?" he asked.

"Not really. Listen." And I told him about my adventure. I have to admit it sounded pretty whacked, but Kevin didn't have any problem believing me. More than that—he was ready with an explanation.

"Larry, this is so awesome," he said. "You've found a portal to another universe."

"A portal," I repeated.

"Yeah, you know, a portal—a gateway. An opening into a parallel universe. Not the future, not the past—just different."

I thought about it. "Okay, I sort of get the idea of parallel universes. But, I mean, that's just Star Trek stuff. They're not for real."

"Well, maybe," Kevin said. "But there's this theory I read about. It says that every time anyone makes a choice—you know, turn left or turn right, watch the Red Sox game or watch the Celtics, whatever, a whole other universe splits off from this one. And in that other universe, everything is exactly the same as this one, except that in one of them you changed the channel and in the other you didn't."

"But that's nuts," I protested. "That would mean there'd be, like, kazillions of universes."

"Okay, well, it's just a theory," Kevin said. "But what if it's true? Or something like it? In the place you went to, what if the guy who started Dairy Queen back whenever decided to name it "Dairy King" instead? So another universe splits off, and things go on from there. When some other guy is starting Burger King, well, in this world the 'King' part is already taken, so he names it 'Burger Queen' instead."

"Okay, but what about all the other stuff—the different clothes, the cars, a whole new Glanbury Plaza in the conservation land behind my house? All that's because somebody decided to name his business 'Dairy King'?"

"The butterfly effect," Kevin said. "You know—the idea that a butterfly flaps its wings in China and changes the weather in America. One event ends up making a big difference. Maybe the Dairy King choice wasn't when that universe split off. Maybe something else happened a whole lot earlier. Doesn't really matter. The point is, the changes just keep piling up from when it started, until finally everything is just a little bit different, or maybe a lot different, and there's no way of tracing everything back to that one little event that started it."

"But Stinky was there," I pointed out. "And Nora Lally."

"It was a different Stinky and Nora," Kevin replied. "And a different Glanbury. But not entirely different. No reason why they couldn't be there. No reason why *we* couldn't be there, for that matter."

That was a strange thought. But it made sense. Something else still didn't make sense, though. "Okay, let's say you're right, and there are all kinds of parallel universes. There's no way of traveling between them, right? No one has ever been to a parallel universe. So what's up with this—this portal? Where did it come from? How come it's back there in the woods behind my house?"

"Beats me," Kevin admitted. "Maybe it's like black holes before they got discovered. Maybe these things are all over our universe but no one has noticed them before."

"Or maybe somebody put it there," I suggested. "Aliens—like that black slab in *2001*."

"Yeah, could be."

"But the thing is, why was I the first one to find it? I know it's invisible, and it's kind of out of the way in the woods, but it's not *that* out of the way."

"Maybe you weren't, but other people kept it secret," he suggested. "Or the government took them away. Maybe it only shows up every few years—like a comet. I don't know, Larry. Anyway, when can I see it?"

"Well, I was going to show it to my dad tonight, and—"

"Larry, come on, you can't do that!"

"Why not?"

"Because once you talk to your father, the grownups'll be in charge—scientists, the army. Like in *ET*. We'll never get near the thing. This could be the most amazing thing that ever happens in our lives. You can't just give it up without doing a little exploring."

"Kevin, I almost didn't get out of that other universe," I pointed out. "What if I couldn't find the thing again? It's invisible, remember?"

"Well, we just have to be more careful. Where's your sense of adventure?"

All of a sudden Cassie was standing in the doorway of Dad's study, shooting death-rays at me with her eyes. "Are you going to be on the phone *all day*?" she demanded.

Dad says Cassie speaks in italics, and I think I know what he means. I ignored her. "Look, Kevin, I gotta go," I said. "Let me think about it."

"Please, Larry," Kevin begged. "One more time. Just one more time."

I hung up, and Cassie stomped off to make another call. Why wouldn't Dad just give in and get her a cell phone? I went upstairs to my room.

Matthew was playing my *Final Fantasy* on the Playstation.

"Matthew!" I screamed.

"Oh. Sorry," he said, as if he'd never heard the one about not messing with my stuff. Then he started talking endlessly about some video game he wanted to invent that would be way better than *Final Fantasy*.

I ignored him and lay down on my bed.

A portal to a parallel universe, practically in my backyard. That was so cool. But did I want to go back inside it? It would be fun going with Kevin. And there was Nora Lally and her smile…maybe I'd run into her again.

But what about those kids who had chased me? I could wear different clothing if I went back, so I could blend in better. And I'd stay away from Stinky—that was always a good idea.

Just once more, I thought, then I could turn it over to the grownups. Would I become famous? The First Human to Travel to Another Universe…Or would it all be top-secret, and we could never tell anyone?

Thinking about all that stuff, I kind of blew off my homework, and before I knew it, it was time for supper.

Dad sometimes doesn't make it home for supper, which drives Mom nuts, but he managed to make it tonight. Not that it helped. Family suppers are rarely very pleasant. Lately Cassie has been on some weird diet that only she understands, so she automatically hates everything Mom cooks, which gets Mom in a bad mood. And of course Matthew never shuts up, which gets the rest of us in a bad mood.

"So how was everyone's day?" Dad asked. He always asks that. And he expects an answer.

Cassie rolled her eyes. She acts like she'd rather have her fingernails pulled out than talk to any of us.

I tried to think of something, but if I wasn't going to mention the portal, what else was there? "Fine," I said—my usual answer.

"Did you practice the piano?"

That was the last thing on my mind. My parents have made me take lessons for years, but I'm still not very good. "Uh, no, not yet," I said.

"You have a lesson tomorrow afternoon," Mom pointed out.

"Okay, okay, I'll get to it."

"How about you, Matthew?" Dad said. "Anything interesting happen at school?"

That was all the opening Matthew needed. "We had gym today," he said, "but Jeremy Finkel is such a ball-hog, he only passes to Luke Kelly. Luke isn't as much of a ball-hog as Jeremy, only like maybe seventy-two percent, but he thinks he's so cool and tries to dribble through his legs, but most of the time the ball just bounces off his ankle. Anyway, I was on a team with Peter Gorman and Chet Pillogi, and we were playing this game the gym teacher made up—well, it's kind of complicated, see…"

Dad always tries to look interested when Matthew gets going, but after a few minutes of that sort of thing, even he starts to fade. I just zoned out until the usual fight started because Cassie left the table without asking to be excused, and who did she think she was? And she started screaming about how she hated this food and this family and her entire life, and why couldn't everyone just leave her alone?

When the Cassie storm blew over, Dad asked Matthew and me if we wanted to go outside and play catch after supper, but we didn't, so he just stared at his plate like we'd kicked him in the teeth. He seems to think playing catch is such a great thing, but Matthew and I don't like to play catch. It's boring. Baseball is boring. I'd actually rather practice the piano. So after supper I did, just long enough to get my parents off my back. Then I knocked off the rest of my homework, watched some TV, and went to bed.

Matthew was already in bed, but he wasn't asleep, so of course he wanted to talk. "Larry?"

"What?"

"I don't like it when we all yell at each other."

"Me neither."

"How come we can't get along better?"

"I don't know. How come you won't stop playing my videogames without permission?"

"I'll stop, really I will."

"Okay." He really meant it, too. For now.

He paused, and I thought maybe he'd given up. But then he said, "Larry?"

Give it up, I thought. "What?"

"I don't know what Cassie gets so mad about. Life is okay, don't you think?"

"If you say so, Matthew."

And that was it—at least, that's all I remember. *Life is okay*. Sometimes Matthew could be surprising.

The last thing I thought about before falling asleep was not Nora Lally's smile, but that long-haired man in the park, and the way his glittering eyes fixed on me.

This world is not only stranger than you imagine, it is stranger than you can imagine.

That portal back in the woods had certainly turned my world strange.

Eventually I drifted off to sleep, and a bunch of strange dreams. And before I knew it, it was time to get up and go to The Gross again.

CHAPTER 4

I was stuck sitting in front of Stinky again on the bus. He still seemed puzzled about what happened in the woods. "Hey," he said to me. "I wanna know how you did that."

I didn't answer.

"Come on," he said. "You were there, and then you weren't. How'd you do that?"

"Your eyes weren't fast enough to keep up with me," I answered without turning around. "Leave me alone."

And you know what? He did.

At school, Kevin came up to me in homeroom. "So what do you think, huh? Are we gonna do it?"

I was feeling a little less sure than I'd been yesterday. "I don't know, Kevin."

"Look," he said. "You don't have to go, if you're scared. Just show me where it is, and I'll go by myself."

"I'm not scared," I protested. "I'm—prudent." That's the word my mother always uses. A prudent person doesn't ride roller coasters, or pet strange dogs, or enter portals to parallel universes.

"Okay, fine, you've already been there—you can afford to be prudent," Kevin argued. "But I haven't had my chance yet. And if you don't show me the thing, I'll never have a chance."

I gave up. "All right all right," I said. "Come on over. But you gotta promise to be careful."

Kevin grinned and gave me a high-five. "Of course I'll be careful," he said. "And prudent."

School took forever. In English class, Nora just sat there next to me, and I started thinking: Wouldn't it be great to see that smile of hers again in the Burger Queen world? And there was lots of other stuff to check out. Who was president in that world? Did The Gross exist?

Did I exist? Thinking back on what happened yesterday, I wasn't really sure if Nora or Stinky had recognized me. Maybe Nora smiled at me because she knew me from school, and I looked so strange in my clothes.

What would happen if I met myself? Would we both explode or something? I should ask Kevin; he was bound to have a theory.

Anyway, the more I thought about going back there with Kevin, the more excited I got. Just be cool and don't get into any trouble, and everything would be fine.

Stinky stayed away from me on the bus ride home. I was beginning to think I had really spooked him. Anyway, when I got home, Mom was on the computer. She has a part-time job writing grant proposals for Glanbury College, and she does a lot of her work in the downstairs study. "Don't forget your piano lesson this afternoon," she said as I walked past.

I had in fact forgotten about the stupid lesson. "But Kevin is coming over," I said.

"Tell him to come tomorrow," she said. "He'll live."

Kevin would go nuts if he had to wait another day, I thought.

"What if he goes home when we have to leave?" I asked.

Mom sighed. "I suppose. But don't go disappearing in the woods."

"Huh?"

"You heard me. I want you back in the house, ready for your lesson, at quarter to four."

"Oh. Sure thing." I headed upstairs.

"And Larry—how was school?" Mom called out.

"Oh, you know. The usual."

In my room, I switched out of my cargo shorts into some regular khakis. I should have told Kevin not to wear anything weird, but it was too late now. He was probably already on his way to my house. His mother lets him ride his bike across town—without a helmet—

which is something I wouldn't even bother asking my mom to let me do.

I went downstairs to the kitchen to have some cookies and milk while I waited for him. As I ate my Oreos I started to get nervous. I didn't really like lying to my mother. And this was my last chance to back out.

I didn't have long to think about it. Kevin showed up a few minutes later, breathless and excited. "Ready?" he said.

"Want some Oreos?" I asked.

He shook his head. "Who can think about Oreos at a time like this?" he said. "Let's go."

"Okay, but we have to be back by quarter to four. I've got a piano lesson."

"Sure, fine. I've got my watch. So let's go."

Obviously Kevin didn't want to chat.

I put the milk away and we left the house. It was another beautiful day—the kind you hate to spend inside. Kevin had parked his bike by the garage. We went through the yard and into the woods. Kevin kept running on ahead of me, then waiting impatiently for me to catch up.

Kevin is shorter than I am, and he has this weird combination of freckles and black hair, which is always flopping onto his forehead. He looks younger than most seventh-graders, I think, but actually he's a couple of months older than I am. He was wearing jeans, an Old Navy t-shirt, and a Red Sox cap. I sure hoped those kids wouldn't be hanging out at the Burger Queen. "How much further?" he asked. "Are we almost there?"

"Calm down. It's near the army buildings. We're getting there."

"Okay, c'mon."

"I'm coming." In a few minutes we reached the army buildings. They looked empty—no Stinky this time. Now I had to figure out exactly where the portal was. I'd been running from Stinky—which way? It took me a couple more minutes to find the clearing and the oak tree, with Kevin making impatient noises behind me. "Over there," I said. "That's where it was." I looked around. We were alone.

Kevin took a step forward and held his hand out. He looked like he was searching for a light switch in the dark. Nothing happened at first. What if the thing had gone away? Should I be relieved or disappointed? Then he took another step, and suddenly his hand disappeared. "Awesome," he whispered.

He took his hand out, then put it back in again, just the way I had done. Then he did something I hadn't thought of—he walked around the portal with his hand outstretched, seeing how big it was. Not that big. "I think the two of us can just barely fit in it at the same time," he said. "I wonder what happens if, like, half your heart is in this world and the other half is in the other."

That made me more nervous. "Kevin, give it a rest," I said.

"All right," he said. "Just thinking out loud. It can't be man-made, right? I mean—there's no structure to it. It's not like somebody built this."

"If you say so."

"Maybe they built it in the other universe—but you said they didn't look all that advanced—they had big cell phones and everything."

"That's right. And if they built it, why would they put it, you know, behind a strip mall?"

Kevin nodded. "Could've been aliens, like you said. Or maybe it comes from some other universe altogether. What if we ended up there?"

Hard to believe, but that was the first time it occurred to me that the portal might not take us back to the world I'd visited the day before. That didn't help calm my nerves.

"This is just so great," Kevin went on, as he continued to stare at the thing—or, really, at the thin air where the thing was. "It's totally strange, but totally real." He looked at me. "You ready, Larry?"

"Well," I said, "I'm really not sure if I—"

Kevin looked at his watch. "C'mon, Larry. We don't have that long before we have to get back."

"All right, all right," I said. "I'll come."

Kevin grinned. "Attaboy."

I don't know why I agreed, really. Now that the moment had arrived, stepping back into the thing didn't seem like that great an idea. On the other hand, I pictured myself being *prudent*, hanging around in the woods like Stinky, waiting for Kevin to reappear, and the image just seemed sort of…pitiful. If Kevin was going, I had to go, too.

"So what do we do," Kevin asked. "Just walk into it?"

"Yeah. It'll be all kind of foggy, but just keep going. I think there are some sort of instruments on the sides, but I couldn't quite make them out. Just a couple of steps, and you're out the other side."

"Cool. Want me to go first?"

"Okay. I'll be right behind you."

Kevin grinned. "All right," he said. "Here goes." He stepped inside. I watched him disappear, and it really was weird, seeing him vanish right in front of me. No wonder Stinky had been so freaked. I took a deep breath, and then I followed.

I was inside the thing. Same clouds, same vague shapes off to the sides. Everything seemed kind of out of focus, like you needed special glasses to see things clearly. I blinked a few times, but nothing changed. "You there, Larry?" Kevin said.

The sound of his voice was reassuring. "Right behind you. Keep on going."

I kept my eye on Kevin's back as he moved forward.

But it was more than a couple of steps this time, and still the clouds didn't go away. Instead it started feeling cold and damp—like real fog. And then I heard shouts and what sounded like footsteps.

Uh-oh, I thought. "Um, Kevin?"

As my eyes adjusted, I could make out trees through the fog. I looked around for the dumpster, but it wasn't where it had been yesterday. Nothing was where it had been yesterday.

I saw two men coming towards us. One of them shouted at us. It sounded like Spanish, but I couldn't understand it.

"Let's go back, Kevin," I said.

But where was the portal? I had lost my bearings in the fog. The men were wearing blue uniforms and carrying rifles. They were soldiers, I realized. They raised the rifles and pointed them at us.

Kevin took off through the trees, and I followed.

I heard rifle shots and tensed, expecting a bullet in the back. But the shots missed; one of them screamed as it ricocheted off a rock or something. I was having a hard time keeping up with Kevin. A branch whacked me in the face. There was more shouting. "C'mon!" Kevin shouted back at me.

The trees petered out suddenly and we found ourselves on a road. And now we heard hoofbeats and saw a wagon bearing down on us through the fog.

"Samuel, stop!" a woman's voice called out.

The wagon slowed. We stepped back.

There were more rifle shots.

The man driving the wagon peered down at us suspiciously.

"Get in! Quickly!" the woman sitting beside him said.

We hesitated. Kevin looked at me, his eyes wide with fright.

"Now!" the man ordered. "Before the blasted Portuguese send all of us to our Maker!"

Portuguese?

More shouts, from close behind us now. We scrambled into the wagon and the man drove off. Behind us in the fog we saw the Portuguese soldiers come out of the trees and aim at us again. But the fog closed in around them before they could shoot.

I looked at Kevin again. He was shaking. I felt as if I was ready to cry.

The wagon picked up speed. And every second that passed, it took us further away from the portal, and from home.

CHAPTER 5

The wagon was piled high with clothes and furniture, which swayed as the wagon rattled along the bumpy road. Two small children—a boy and a girl—huddled in one corner, staring at us. The woman had twisted around to look at us, too. She was wearing a long coat and a bonnet. "How did you come to be in those woods, lads?" she asked. Her accent was a little strange—not quite American, not quite English.

"It's, um, a long story," I said. What was I supposed to say?

"You talk funny," the little girl piped up.

"Hush, Rachel," the mother said. "Are you from Glanbury?" she asked us.

"Yes, we are."

"Listen," Kevin interrupted, "can you stop the wagon? We have to go back."

The man pulled on the reins to slow the horse and turned around to look at us, too. "Why?" he asked.

"Their clothes are funny," the girl said.

"Could you please just stop the wagon?" Kevin pleaded.

"There's nothing to go back to," the woman explained. "The Portuguese army is destroying nigh everything. If you're separated from your parents, best stay with us till we get you to Boston. You can find them there."

"Along with everyone else in New England," the man muttered.

"Are you in the navy?" the little girl asked Kevin. She was pointing at his Old Navy t-shirt.

"What should we do?" Kevin asked me.

"I don't know. This was all your idea."

Kevin glared at me. We heard gunfire in the distance.

My parents would know what to do. But we had left them far, far behind. "We won't be able to get to it," I murmured. And then I asked the woman, "Will we be safe in Boston?"

"As safe as anywhere," she replied, "with the soldiers from New Portugal on one side of us and the Canadians on the other."

"Maybe we should go to Boston," I said to Kevin. "We can come back when—when—"

When?

"What if it's gone?" he said. "What if we can't find it?"

What if we find it, I thought, and it doesn't take us home?

"I don't know," I said. "I don't know."

Kevin slumped down in the wagon. I slumped down next to him. The man flicked the reins and the horse sped up. "I bet I know what the 'B' on your hat stands for," the little girl said to Kevin.

I thought the woman might press us about why we were in those woods, but she didn't. She and her husband started arguing about why he had waited till the last minute to leave their farm and how all their neighbors were safe in Boston by now, and here they were, barely outracing the Portuguese and endangering their children. He said he couldn't care less about their neighbors, he wasn't going to give in so easily, he just hoped the cowardly government didn't surrender without putting up a fight.

Kevin's face was scrunched up, an expression he gets when he's thinking hard. Or maybe he was just trying to keep from crying. We had screwed up so bad. This was a totally different universe. There was a Glanbury and a Boston, but who were the "New Portuguese"? And where were the cars? Where were the buildings? And now that we'd landed here, would we ever be able to get back?

The wagon continued along the road to Boston, and the gunfire faded behind us. My family drives to Boston a lot, but I didn't know exactly how far it was from Glanbury. I don't think it took very long, except when there was a lot of traffic. How long was it going to take by horse? The road wasn't that great, and we kept getting knocked around in the back of the wagon. My back hurt, and I started to get seasick.

"What time is it?" I whispered to Kevin after a while.

He looked at his watch. "Four o'clock," he said.

Late for my piano lesson. I thought about Mom, probably standing on our deck and looking out into the woods for me, worried and angry at the same time, and I got a lump in my throat. Pretty soon everyone would start looking for us, and we'd be gone—just gone, without a trace. Mom always read those stories about missing children in the paper. She'd figure this had something to do with that guy lurking by school buses in Rhode Island. But she'd never know where I went, if I was okay…

When they started searching they'd be bound to find the portal, I thought, and then they'd figure it out and come after us.

But that wouldn't work, I realized. If there were a kazillion universes, who knew which one they'd end up in?

I should never have come, I thought. How could I have been so stupid? It was all Kevin's fault…

"Larry, do you have any of those Oreos?" Kevin asked.

I shook my head, suddenly getting hungry myself. Probably no Oreos in this world, I thought. No Coke, no pizza, no Burger King—or Burger Queen.

The fog faded away as we rode. Occasionally a man on horseback passed us on the way to Boston. No one was heading in the opposite direction, south towards Glanbury. The riders would slow down and exchange news with us, then speed up until they disappeared up ahead. There were some houses along the road, and a few inns and shops that looked like they came out of an old movie. All of them appeared deserted.

We stopped once to give the horse some food and water, and we all went to the bathroom in the woods; it was gross, but the family didn't seem to mind.

"What's that?" the little boy asked, pointing at Kevin's watch.

He shrugged. "A watch," he said.

"My papa has a watch, but he keeps it in his pocket."

Kevin shrugged again.

"Don't be frightened," the boy went on. "We're going to stay with Uncle John, and he'll take care of us. He has a big house in the city, and that's where all the army is, so the Portuguese won't be able to get us."

"That's great."

The father took Kevin and me aside and spoke to us before we got back into the wagon. "I know every soul in Glanbury, and I don't know you boys," he said. "I've certainly never seen anyone wearing clothes like that, or heard an accent like that. Where are you really from? China?"

Kevin shook his head. "No, we're from America."

"Where is America?" the man asked suspiciously. "I've never heard of it."

Kevin looked at me, and I felt a little more desperate. Just how different was this world? "What—what's the name of this country?" he asked the man.

The man shook his head in astonishment. "Never heard of the like. We're in New England, lad. The United States of New England. Where's America?"

Far, far away, apparently. "Samuel, please come!" his wife called out to him from the wagon. "If we don't hurry we'll not make it to Boston by dark."

Samuel looked back at us. "I think you lads have some explaining to do, but now's not the time, I judge. Let's go, if you still want a ride to Boston."

He headed off to the wagon. "This may be our last chance," Kevin said to me. "What do you think?"

I shook my head. "It's too late, Kevin. We have to go to Boston."

Kevin didn't argue, and we silently trudged back to the wagon.

When we got in, the mother was feeding her kids apples and bread. She offered us some, and we took the food gratefully. Kevin ate his share like he didn't think he'd get another meal.

We started up again. The sun was lower in the sky now, and it was getting colder out. After a while there were more shops and houses, and a few signs of life. Dogs barked at us. On one side street I saw a bunch of hogs eating garbage in the middle of the road. Another road merged with ours, and suddenly there was traffic— more wagons carrying furniture and frightened families. Some of the wagons had a cow, a goat, or even an ox tied up behind them. Everyone was headed towards Boston.

Finally we crossed a bridge over a river, and a little ways beyond was a long high wooden fence that stretched out as far as I could see in both directions. There were slits for guns high up in the fence, I noticed. A pair of gates were open, but a group of soldiers stood by them, examining everyone before they let them pass through.

They looked like soldiers, but their uniform was different from any I had ever seen. They wore short red jackets, black pants, and metal helmets with little brims, almost like batting helmets. Each of them had a rifle slung over his arm and a pistol in his belt. When we finally reached the gates one of the soldiers came up to us. He half-saluted Samuel and said, "Name, sir?"

He had an accent that was almost English.

"Harper. Samuel Harper. That's my wife Martha."

"And where are you coming from?"

"Up from Glanbury," Samuel replied.

"Waited till the last minute, did you?"

"They were right behind us. There was some skirmishing, and I thought it best to leave. If they weren't so interested in looting, they'd be right behind us still."

"Why did you wait so long?"

"I didn't want to yield my farm to any Portuguese, I tell you that. I fired my house and barn before I left. I don't know how it got to this."

The soldier nodded and looked into the wagon. "This your family, sir?"

"Except for those two strays back there," Samuel said, meaning us. "I don't know who or what they are."

The soldier came around and took a close look at Kevin and me. "Strange outfits," he said. "And your family is where, mates?"

"Murdered," Kevin blurted out. "By the Portuguese. But we managed to escape."

Why did he say that?

"But I thought you were in the navy," the little girl objected.

"I know nothing of any murdering," Mr. Harper said.

The soldier's eyes darkened. "Well?" he demanded.

But just then another soldier called to him. "Move it along, Corporal! We'll be all night getting these people inside."

He shrugged, and stepped back. "Any disease here?" he asked loudly. "Smallpox? Diphtheria? Drikana?"

"No," Mr. Harper said. "We're all healthy, thank God."

"Pray God you stay healthy," the soldier replied. "The city is getting more crowded by the hour. There is little food, and the water is bad. You are welcome to enter, but you'll have a hard time of it. If there is a siege, conditions will get far worse. You'll have to stay in a camp."

"I have a brother in the city who will take us in," Mr. Harper said.

"Then count yourself lucky, sir. The camps'll not be pleasant places. You may pass."

Mr. Harper grunted and flicked the reins, and the horse started through the gates. "A siege," he muttered. "They want to delay as long as they can while they parley with the Europeans, as if any European has ever helped New England before. And meanwhile, all I've worked for has been destroyed."

"You needn't have set fire to the—" his wife started to say, but he quickly interrupted her.

"Better me than the Portuguese, woman. If we all did what I did, there'd be no food to sustain them, and they'd have to slink like dogs back where they came from."

I looked at the fence. Soldiers were piling up sandbags against it. Getting ready for a siege, I thought. There were sieges in plenty of video games I'd played. Sieges could last forever.

"Was your family really murdered?" the little boy asked Kevin.

Kevin shook his head. "No, but I don't think I'll ever see them again."

"Oh. That's sad."

Kevin nodded and looked away.

We were passing through a big military camp. The soldiers stared at us grimly as we went by. In the distance to our right I could see the ocean. I could smell fish and horse manure, and worse stuff. It was really getting dark now, and there weren't any street lights. I was hungry and stiff and still a little queasy from the bumpy ride. This was awful.

"Are you sure John will take us in?" Martha asked her husband.

"He'd better, hadn't he?" he replied.

"What about these boys?"

"What about them? I won't ask my brother to house and feed anyone who isn't kin, not with what's about to happen. Anyway, they haven't told the truth about anything since we met them. They can fend for themselves."

"But they're so young, Samuel."

"They're old enough to join the army, I daresay. The redbacks will need everyone they can get. They should be grateful to us. If we hadn't taken them with us, they'd be lying dead in the road by now. Or worse."

Martha gave us a look full of sympathy, but she didn't argue with her husband. The little boy said, "I'd like to join the army," but she hushed him.

My stomach started to growl.

We were past the military camp now. The road crossed some marshland, and on the other side there were a lot of shacks and tents jammed together, and some of the people in wagons got off the road to join the crowd. Was this one of the refugee camps? "Fools," Mr. Harper muttered. "Camping in the swamp. Half of them will have the flux by morning." We kept going, and after a while some of the buildings were built of brick, the road became paved with cobblestones, and there were even sidewalks.

"At last," Mr. Harper said. "Now, if I can only find the street."

The sidewalks grew crowded as we traveled further into the city. Kids younger than Kevin and me, dirty-faced and dressed in raggedy old clothes, were selling newspapers or flowers. Soldiers walked alongside women wearing too much makeup. There were lots of old people—and some not so old—holding out their hands or tin cups, begging for food or money. Policemen, dressed like the soldiers except in blue, directed traffic at every intersection. Some people on the streets rode something that looked like a bicycle with very wide wooden wheels. There were no traffic lights, and only a few dim, flickering lamps instead of street lights.

Mr. Harper made a few turns, asked directions a couple of times, and finally pulled up in front of a small house on a dark side street. A bearded man walked out of the house, holding a lantern. "Samuel," he said, "about time you came to town."

"Held out as long as I could, John," Samuel replied. "I've lost everything but what we've got in this wagon."

"I'm very sorry for that," John said, coming over to the wagon. "but of course you're welcome to stay here. Martha," he said, nodding to the woman. "And how are little Rachel and Samuel?" He reached into the wagon and patted them on the heads. Then he turned to Kevin and me with a puzzled expression. "And you are—?"

Samuel had joined his brother and was unlatching the back of the wagon. "Passers-by," he said. "Everyone had to get out or be shot. We gave them a ride, out of the goodness of our hearts."

We climbed down, followed by Martha and the children. Samuel and his brother walked back to the front of the wagon, unhitched the horse, and led it behind the house. Martha looked at us. "Will you be all right?" she asked.

I didn't know what to say. "I guess so," I said.

She reached back into the wagon and filled a small bag with apples, bread, and cheese. "Good luck," she said, handing me the bag. "I'm sorry we can't do more. It's a hard time for everyone." She turned to her kids. "Come on, children. Let's go inside."

Kevin and I watched them go into the small house. And then we were all alone on the dark street, in the strange world, and neither of us had a clue what to do next.

CHAPTER 6

We walked away from the house, eating the food in silence. I was so hungry, I forgot for a while how scared I was. But it didn't take long for the fear to return. Where would we get our next meal? Where would we sleep? Would we ever get back to the portal? Would I ever see my family again?

We didn't know where we were going. The streets were dark, and I kept tripping on the cobblestones. A dog barked at us out of an alley. There was a lump in my throat, and it kept getting bigger. From one house we passed I heard someone playing a piano, and at least that sounded familiar. But then I remembered my piano lesson, and I felt even worse.

Pretty soon Kevin and I started arguing. "This is so stupid, Kevin," I said. "Why did I let you talk me into it?"

"It's not like I twisted your arm or anything," he shot back. "I said you could stay behind, if you wanted to be *prudent*."

"I don't know why I even told you about it. I should've figured you get me into trouble, with all your theories. And why did you tell that soldier our family had been murdered by the Portuguese? He almost arrested us."

"Maybe we'd be better off if we were arrested," he pointed out. "Jail would be better than this."

We kept walking.

"You know what worries me?" Kevin asked softly after a while.

I shook my head.

"Even if we find the portal, what if we can't get back? What if it takes us to some totally different universe?"

"It took me home yesterday," I reminded him.

"Maybe you were just lucky. Maybe you go somewhere different every time you step into it."

"We'll get back," I insisted.

He didn't argue. I think he wanted to believe me. I wanted to believe myself.

It was getting cold. Neither of us had a jacket. At least neither of was wearing shorts. I was grateful when we finally made it back to the main street. With all the people around, it just seemed to feel warmer.

Now that we were out of the wagon, people were staring at us, but we were too tired and scared to care. We looked in the store windows as we walked. There was a dressmaker's shop, and a place that sold something called sundries, and a chandler, which had candles and oil lamps for sale. "No electricity, I guess," Kevin muttered. "Those streetlights are gas or something. This place is, like, two hundred years behind us." We stopped in front of a tavern called The Twin Ponies and listened to the laughter and smelled the cigar smoke and the stale beer. Someone was playing an instrument that sounded like an accordion.

"Look at this," Kevin said. He picked up a sheet of newspaper from the sidewalk in front of the tavern. It was called the *Boston Intelligencer*. It had smaller type and wider pages than in regular newspapers, and no photographs—only a couple of drawings. We read the headlines:

Portuguese, Canadians Advance on Boston
Thousands of Refugees Arrive ahead of Siege
Pres. Gardner Calls for Calm as Naval Blockade Tightens
Talks with British Continue

"It has today's date," Kevin pointed out.

"Look at the British spellings," I said. President Gardner was at pains to dispel the *rumour* that he was negotiating terms of surrender with the Canadians and Portuguese.

We couldn't make sense of a lot of what we read, but two things were clear: This place was in a whole lot of trouble, and there was plenty of disagreement about what to do about it. The paper quoted one guy as saying they should cut off all the refugees from entering the city, because there wasn't going to be enough food for everyone to survive the siege. Someone else said there was no way the city could survive the siege anyway, and the president (who apparently was in Boston) should "surrender forthwith." And the president insisted everything was going to be fine and not to worry.

"What a mess," Kevin said.

"No kidding."

A tall man wearing a round black hat and a green cape came staggering out of the tavern. He stared at us for a second and shook his head. "Strange days," he muttered, and he headed off down the street.

"So, what do you think we should do?" I asked finally. One of us had to ask the question.

"I don't know," Kevin said. "Maybe we should, you know, turn ourselves in."

"For what? We haven't done anything."

"Well, we could, like, tell the truth."

"You think they'd believe us?"

Kevin shrugged. "I guess not."

"But even if they did believe us, why would they care? They've got way more important things to think about."

"Wouldn't hurt to ask. What have we got to lose?"

We were lost on a strange world with no one to help us. There really was nothing to lose.

"I think that's a cop over there," Kevin said. "Go ask him."

The blue-jacketed policeman was across the street, standing in front of a building with his arms folded.

"Why me?" I said. "It's your idea."

"Because you're taller," Kevin answered. "He'll pay more attention to you."

Seemed like a stupid reason to me, but I was tired of arguing. We crossed the street, picking our way through the disgusting horse manure. We walked up to the cop, who stared at us suspiciously.

"Excuse me, officer," I began. My voice sounded thin and trembly in my ears. "We're not from around here, and—"

He scowled at me. "I can see that, mate."

"No, really. We're not just, you know, from another town or something. We come from a different world altogether. We'd like to, uh, speak to someone in authority."

"Of course you would," the policeman said, nodding. "And, you'd like a meal. And a nice bed to sleep on, as well. Is that it?"

I glanced at Kevin, but he didn't have anything to say.

"We're in the middle of a war, in case you didn't notice," the cop went on. "We don't feed strays. If we don't get help soon, we won't be able to feed ourselves. Now run along."

"But where?" I asked. "We don't have anyplace to stay."

He gestured off to his left. "The Fens camp is where you strays belong. Don't let us catch you stealing on the way, or you'll wish the Portuguese had caught you first. And don't be wandering the streets after curfew, either. You farmfolk—or whatever you are—aren't going to overrun this city. Understand?"

I nodded. "How far away is the camp?" I managed to ask.

He laughed. "Not far. Just follow your nose. And you might watch your step going through Cheapside—they don't take kindly to strays." Then he turned and walked away.

"Nice job," Kevin said to me. "You didn't explain anything."

"You try, if you think you can do it better."

We were silent then. We headed off in the direction the cop had pointed.

"I wonder if the Fens has anything to do with Fenway Park," Kevin said after a while.

"Who gives," I muttered.

"They probably don't even have baseball in this world," he went on.

I just looked at him. We kept walking. I was getting really tired. And I was hungry again. Would there be food in the camp? Everyone seemed worried about food.

After a while we entered what I figured was Cheapside—a nasty-looking section of town where the rickety houses were stuck close together, the street had turned into a rutted dirt path, and piles of garbage were heaped up everywhere. Follow your nose, the cop had said. There were lots of nasty-looking taverns, and people lounging in the doorways shouted insults at us as we passed. We just kept going.

Cheapside petered out after a while and we saw a bunch of buildings with soldiers guarding them. Beyond the buildings was the Fens camp.

It was much bigger than the one we'd seen from the wagon on the way into the city. It seemed to go on forever; we could see wagons and tents, smoky campfires and snorting horses. There was a rough fence around it, and at the end of the path was a gate with lamps hung on either side. A few wagons were lined up in front of the gate, waiting to enter.

"What do you think?" I asked Kevin. "Should we go inside?"

"Do we have a choice?" he replied.

Not that I could see. We got in line behind the wagons. It took a few minutes for them to enter. When we reached the gate the soldier guarding it laughed. He was short and stout and missing a couple of teeth. "Farmfolk get stranger-looking every day," he said, shaking his head. "Twenty minutes to curfew, lads."

"Can we just, like, go in?" I asked.

"You can go in, but you can't come back out—at least not till morning, and then you'll need a pass. But you'll find plenty to do inside, I daresay."

"Is there any food?"

"Not till morning, unless you want to steal some inside the camp—which I wouldn't recommend, since it'll likely get you killed. Now run along with you."

We walked through the gate into the camp. There were muddy paths of a sort, along which people had parked their wagons and set up makeshift shelters. People sat in their wagons or on chairs outside their tents, the men smoking long pipes and the women chatting with each other by the light of the campfires. One man we passed was playing a guitar while his family sang what sounded like a hymn. There were a lot of babies crying. Older kids ran around, playing tag. It didn't seem all that bad, actually, if you could get used to the smell and the mud.

We kept walking, without any idea of where to go or what to do. Kevin pointed to the guards patrolling outside the fence, rifles on their shoulders. "They're serious," he said. "Nobody's getting out of here."

Great. We were stuck inside a refugee camp. My stomach started growling and my legs started hurting. "I don't think I can walk much farther," I said. "I'm so tired I could sleep in the mud."

"We need to get blankets or something," Kevin said.

"How are we going to do that—steal them and get killed?"

He didn't answer.

"Hey there!" A thin man with long, stringy hair and a beard was standing in front of us. "Did I hear you say you needed a blanket?"

He smiled at us. His face was pock-marked, and he was missing a lot of teeth. His left eye wandered when he spoke.

Stranger danger, I thought. My mother was always talking about stranger danger. But what do you do when everyone's a stranger?

Neither of us answered, so the man kept on talking. "You boys here on your own?" We still didn't answer, so the guy just kept talking. "These are parlous times to be on your own. But I have a beautiful blanket I can let you have for a mere five shillings. Made from the finest Vermont wool. Just step over to my wagon here."

I looked at his wagon. A sad-looking donkey stood next to it, staring at us. How much was a shilling, I wondered. Didn't matter. "We don't have any money," I said.

The man's smile faded a little. "Parlous times, indeed," he said. "What about barter, then? Have you anything to trade?" He looked us over, then pointed at Kevin. "Odd-looking hat," he said. Then, "This object on your wrist—what might that be?"

"It's a watch," Kevin said.

"A watch? Strange place to have a watch. Why not keep it in your pocket? Let me take a look." He grabbed Kevin's arm. "Odd-looking watch, as well. No case, no hands on the dial. But I tell you what—I have a charitable heart, seeing you here by yourselves. I'll give you a blanket for it, and I'll throw in a pound of salted pork."

Seemed like a good deal to me, although salted pork sounded awful. But all of a sudden Kevin got a funny look on his face and pulled his arm back. "No thanks," he said.

The man's smile faded a bit more. "You lads won't get a better deal in this wretched camp," he pointed out. "Nights are growing colder, and who knows how long we'll be imprisoned here? The price of necessities will only go up."

"Sorry," Kevin said. He turned to me. "Let's go, Larry."

I was really annoyed with him. What did he want the stupid watch for? Who cared what time it was, when we were going to have to sleep in the mud?

Kevin started walking quickly back the way we'd come. "Are you nuts?" I said to him.

He shook his head. "It's not just a watch," he said. "It's a calculator. It's a timer. It's really cool."

"So what?"

"So—maybe it's worth more than a blanket in this world. Maybe *we're* worth something in this world."

"Kevin, they know how to add. They know how to tell time."

"Yeah," he said, "but they've never seen a calculator before."

"Big deal. Anyway, where are we going?"

Kevin pointed. "Back to the gate."

The gate was closing. We ran up to it and slithered through.

The soldier we had talked to before didn't look happy to see us again. "Curfew, lads," he said. "Back inside with you."

"Sir, I have a strange and wonderful invention that I'd like to share with the military leadership," Kevin said.

The soldier looked at him as if he were crazy. Farmfolk. "Let's go," he demanded. "There's a war on, and no time for foolishness."

"How much is 375 times 13?" Kevin asked.

The soldier was starting to get angry.

"Come here and see what I do," Kevin went on before he could yell at us. "This'll be interesting, I guarantee." The soldier hesitated, then leaned forward. Kevin put his watch in calculator mode, held it up so the soldier could see, then did the multiplication. "3875," he said. "See how easy that was?"

The soldier thought about it for a moment, and then said, "Can I try?"

Kevin held his arm out and showed him what to do. "I never was very good at ciphering," the soldier muttered as he hit the numbers. He grinned with delight when the answer was displayed. "Hey Caleb," he called out to a tall soldier with a scruffy beard who was guarding the gate. "Come look at this!"

Caleb took a look and had the same reaction—surprise and excitement. The next soldier who came by, though, was terrified by the watch. "This is some devilry," he muttered, glaring at Kevin like *he* was the devil.

"Now, Oliver," Caleb said to him, "it's just a toy."

Oliver shook his head. "The devil makes toys, too," he muttered, and he walked away.

"The thing is," Kevin said to Caleb, "I'd like to show this to your commanding officer. I think it might be helpful in the war. We know other stuff that might help, too."

Caleb considered, and then said, "Go find Sergeant Hornbeam, Fred. He'll be interested in this."

Fred—that was the first soldier's name—went off, and returned in a few minutes, accompanied by a large soldier with bright red hair.

He gave us the strange look we were used to by now, and then said: "Let me see the thing."

Kevin held out his arm.

Sergeant Hornbeam shook his head. "Take it off," he said.

Reluctantly Kevin took the watch off and handed it to the sergeant, who took it and studied it. Finally he let Fred show him how to use it. Then he looked at us again. "Are you Chinese?" he demanded.

"No, we're—we're farmfolk," Kevin said.

"The inscription on this object says it was made in China." He made it sound like an accusation.

"Well, uh, this is complicated," Kevin said. "It was made in China, but we didn't get it there."

"Do we look Chinese?" I asked.

Sergeant Hornbeam glared at me. "How would I know what the Chinese look like?" Then he put the watch into his pocket. "An interesting toy," he said.

"Hey," Kevin cried. "That's mine."

"I thought you wanted to contribute it to the army," the sergeant said.

"But we have to talk to somebody in charge. They'll need to know more about it."

He shrugged. "I don't see why. If Fred can use it, anyone can use it." Caleb laughed; even Fred smiled. Then the sergeant seemed to think about the situation some more. "Where are your families?" he asked.

"We're here on our own," Kevin said. "We just arrived."

The sergeant thought a bit longer, then gestured to Fred and Caleb. "Put them in the brig for the night," he said. "We'll see what the morrow brings." Then he turned to us. "Fare you well, lads," he said, and he walked away.

I looked at Kevin. The brig?

"Come on, lads," Fred said. "The brig isn't much, but it's better than the camp, I daresay."

He and Caleb led us to a long low wooden building near the camp. "Where'd you get that thing?" Fred asked. "Off a trading ship?"

"Something like that," Kevin said.

"I hear they've got all sorts of amazing inventions over in China," he went on.

"Maybe if we had the Chinese for an ally we could win this damfool war," Caleb added.

"Maybe if we had any ally at all we'd have a chance."

"What do you think Sergeant Hornbeam will do with my watch?" Kevin asked the soldiers. "We really need to get it to a general or somebody like that."

"Oh, Sarge'll do the right thing," Fred said. "Don't know if the generals will pay attention, though. They're too busy arguing with the president."

The first part of the building was the soldiers' barracks. Beds were lined up against one of the walls. A few soldiers were playing cards at a table, others were sitting on their beds cleaning their equipment. The air was so thick with tobacco smoke that I wanted to gag. Fred and Caleb led us through the barracks to a room at the back. A fat, sleepy soldier sat slumped in a chair by the door. He peered at us as we approached. "What'd they do?" he asked. "Sneak out of the camp and pinch some eggs in Cheapside?"

"If they did that, the folks in Cheapside would be happy to take care of them," Caleb said. "No, Sergeant Hornbeam wants to hold onto them. See that they have every comfort, Benjamin. They're our guests."

"No comforts to be had, I'm afraid. Odd-looking little fellows, ain't they? I like that one's hat, though." Benjamin struggled to his feet and took a key out of his pocket, which he used to unlock the door to an inner room. "Chamber pot's in the far corner," he said to us. "Try not to rouse Chester. He's only peaceable when he's sleeping."

Caleb and Fred said farewell, Benjamin locked the door behind us, and there we were in jail on our first night in the new world.

It was dark—the only light was from the small opening in the door. We heard a loud noise that we finally recognized was snoring. As our eyes adjusted to the darkness, we saw a big red-jacketed man lying with his head against the wall. Like everything in this world, it seemed, he stank.

"This is just great," I said to Kevin as we sat on the floor against the opposite wall, as far away from Chester as we could get.

"Come on, Larry, it could be worse," he replied. "This is what we were trying to do, right? Turn ourselves in. Get them to pay attention to us."

"But what happens next? What's your watch going to do for us?"

"Anyone with any brains will know there's nothing like that watch in this world," he explained. "So they'll want to talk to us, find out where we got it."

"And then what? You think they'll believe our story? You sure they won't think we're the devil, like that other soldier?"

"I dunno. But in the meantime they'll probably feed us. I've already gotten us out of the mud for tonight. It's worth a shot, Larry."

I supposed he was right. And it wasn't like I had any better ideas. Suddenly I could barely keep my eyes open. We seemed to be moderately safe for the night, except for Chester, who continued to snore loudly across the room. And there wasn't anything else we could accomplish right now except hope that Sergeant Hornbeam would do more than pocket Kevin's watch as a silly little toy. The floor wasn't going to be comfortable, but it was better than sleeping outdoors in the mud.

I thought of the couple of weeks I had spent at sleepaway camp during the summer, how homesick I'd gotten, how brave I thought I was being when I stuck it out—with a counselor sleeping in the same cabin, with my parents just a two-hour drive away and sending me letters every day. "We'll get out of this, right, Kevin?" I asked.

"Yeah. Of course we will. It's just a matter of time."

"Right." He didn't sound too sure of himself, but that was okay. I slid down to lie on the floor. "Good night, Kevin."

"Good night, Larry."

When I closed my eyes I thought of Matthew—was it really just last night?—telling me how life was really okay. Yeah, yeah, I'd thought. Would you please shut up so I can get some sleep? Now what wouldn't I give to be back in my own bed, listening to Matthew babble?

I was too tired to cry. *I miss you,* I whispered into the darkness. But there was no one there to hear me.

CHAPTER 7

When I woke up it was light out, and at first I had no clue where I was. Why wasn't I looking at the Final Fantasy poster in my bedroom? How come I was so uncomfortable? What was that weird dream I'd had? Who was that huge man glaring at me from across the room?

Chester. All the memories of yesterday came flooding back. This wasn't a dream.

I looked over at Kevin. He was still asleep.

"Boys," Chester rumbled. "I don't like boys."

"Uh, hi," I said.

Chester just shook his head and glared at me some more.

Benjamin must have heard us, because he unlocked the door and stuck his head in. "'Morning, gents," he said. "Chester, you may be excused. Go thou and sin no more."

"I'm hungry," Chester said.

Benjamin shook his head. "Not my problem, Chester. Now be off to the mess, before we become angry."

Amazingly, Chester got to his feet, dusted off his dirty red jacket, glared at me one final time, and then obediently walked out of the brig.

Benjamin then turned his attention to Kevin and me. "Sleep well, lads?"

I nodded. Kevin had awakened and was rubbing his eyes sleepily.

"Did Sergeant Hornbeam say anything about what's going to happen to us?" I asked.

"Sergeant Hornbeam is not with us at the moment. You'll need to stay here until he sends instruction."

"Any chance we could go to the mess?" I asked. "I'm pretty hungry."

"Let me see what I can do," Benjamin said, and he left, locking the door behind him.

Kevin sat up. "I dreamed that this was all a dream," he said.

"Maybe we'll wake up again, and you'll be right."

"Wouldn't that be good." He sighed. "I've gotta use that thing over there," he said, pointing to the pot in the corner of the cell. I closed my eyes while Kevin did his business.

Were there any flush toilets in this world, I wondered. Did they have toothpaste? Hot showers?

Eventually Benjamin came back with a tray of food: cups of tea and bowls of, well, mush. It could have been oatmeal, but it didn't have any milk or sugar, and it was all I could do to get a few spoonfuls down. I'd never drunk tea before, and that didn't taste much better. When I had finished trying to eat, I was as hungry as when I started. Kevin had barely touched his food either. He was looking pretty glum.

After a while Benjamin came for the trays. "Porridge not to your liking?" he asked.

"Can we go outside?" Kevin asked back. "We won't leave, I promise."

Benjamin considered. "All right. It's going to be hot—not a good day to spend in the brig. But stay right by the barracks."

We followed him out of the cell. There were only a few soldiers in the barracks, plus an old man mopping the floor. We went outside. It did feel like it was going to be a hot day. No air conditioning, I thought. No fans. I looked around. None of the buildings had been painted, and there was lumber lying around on the ground. They had been put up in a hurry, I realized.

We sat down on some boards by the entrance to the barracks and watched the wagons go by, heading for the camp.

"Maybe now's the time to leave," Kevin said.

"You mean: go back to Glanbury?"

"Yeah. We could stay off the main road and hide from the

Portuguese army. If we started now, we could probably make it by dark."

"You think the New England soldiers'd let us out that gate we went through?"

Kevin thought for a second. "I don't know. Anyway, there's got to be a way around," he decided. "They can't fence in the whole city."

"And you think the Portuguese army wouldn't shoot us if they caught us?" I said. "Or at least treat us worse than this? You think we're smart enough to find the portal without getting caught? It was your idea to do this thing with the watch, Kevin. Why don't we just see what happens?"

He didn't answer. "I wish I was in school," he said.

"I wish I had a bowl of Frosted Flakes and a big glass of orange juice."

We fell silent, and just sat there in the hot sun.

Eventually Caleb came by. "Morning, mates," he said. "Anything happen yet with your ciphering machine?"

We shook our heads. "I hope Sergeant Hornbeam hasn't forgotten about us," Kevin said.

"No, no, he wouldn't do that. He's a busy man, though. We're all busy, more's the pity. Looks like the camp'll fill up today. Have to open up another one somewhere. Never knew there was this many people in all of New England."

"Is there some way we could talk to him?" Kevin asked.

"Oh, he'll be around. Never worry, mates. Just enjoy the day."

Then he went off, and we were left to ourselves again. Soldiers came and went. Most of them knew seemed to know about us and asked about the "ciphering machine." A couple of them looked at us like we were going to put a curse on them. The sun got hotter. There was no sign of Sergeant Hornbeam.

Then a carriage pulled up in front of the barracks, and a fat officer got out. The soldiers guarding the entrance stood at attention and saluted. The officer was bald, with red cheeks and bushy gray eyebrows, and his uniform was soaked with sweat. When he saw us, he stopped. "Who the devil are you?" he demanded.

"We're waiting for Sergeant Hornbeam, sir," Kevin said. "He has a watch of mine that—"

"Oh, that nonsense. Just a gewgaw, if you ask me. Well, you can't just sit around idly all day. There's a war on, in case you haven't noticed." He turned to one of the soldiers. "Corporal—er?"

"Hennessy, sir."

"Corporal Hennessy," he repeated. "Find 'em something to do." Then he went inside the barracks and started yelling at the soldiers there about shaping up and looking sharp, there was a war on.

Corporal Hennessy looked at us. "Colonel Clarett worries that we'll forget we're at war," he said. "I think his concern is misplaced, don't you? Anyway, let's find you a chore."

We got up and went with him. "Is Colonel Clarett in charge of the camp?" Kevin asked.

The corporal nodded. "And a nasty job it is, too. No matter what you do, someone'll criticize you. Treat folks too well, you're wasting food. Treat 'em too poorly, you're starving good New England citizens. Let's just hope this doesn't last long."

"He said our watch was nonsense," Kevin went on. "Does that mean—"

"Means nothing, mate. I heard about that watch. Lucky for you Sergeant Hornbeam was on duty last night. He'll know what to do with it."

The corporal led us into another long, unpainted building behind the barracks. It had an awful stench coming out of it. "What's that smell?" Kevin asked.

The corporal gave him an odd look. "Luncheon," he said. "Have you never smelled salt pork before?"

We went inside. There was one long room, with tables and benches along the wall. There were no screens on the open windows, and flies were buzzing everywhere. A few soldiers were sitting at one of the tables and eating off tin plates. They were stabbing their meat with their knives and sticking it straight into their mouths, I noticed. Didn't they have forks here? My mother went nuts if she caught any of us putting a knife in our mouths.

We went through the room. Beyond it was a kitchen, where a shirtless, sweating man was standing over steaming pots set on woodstoves. Corporal Hennessy greeted him cheerily. "Coolest place in Boston, eh, Jonathan?"

Jonathan responded with a string of words my mother would have shot me for saying. This didn't seem to bother the corporal. "Need any help here?" he asked. "I have a couple of lads willing to pitch in."

Jonathan glanced at us and shook his head. "Try the warehouse," he said.

"Very well, then. Your loss." We went out through the kitchen and saw a much larger building surrounded by guards. Soldiers were lugging sacks out of it and loading them onto a bunch of wagons. The corporal went up to a big, bearded soldier who was supervising the loading and said, "Need a couple of extra hands, Tom?"

Tom gave us the look we were used to by now. "What are those outfits?" he asked. "Costumes for harvest festival?"

"We're, uh, not from around here," Kevin said.

"No, and you haven't done much laboring, from the look of you. Well, we can remedy that. Head on inside and grab some sacks. The camp awaits its midday meal."

"Keep 'em alive, Tom," Corporal Hennessy said. "They're guests of Colonel Clarett."

Tom just grunted.

"Fare you well, lads," the corporal said to us, and headed back to the barracks. Tom waved us inside the building.

It was filled with shelves, and on the shelves were the sacks the soldiers were loading onto the wagons. "What's in them?" Kevin asked one of the soldiers.

"Corn," he replied as he slung a sack over his shoulder. "Folks'll be mighty tired of corn before long."

I tried lifting a sack; I couldn't. Kevin was a shrimp, and he obviously wasn't going to be able to pick one up. "We'll have to do it together," I said.

"This is embarrassing," Kevin muttered.

"Just shut up and help."

So the two of us picked up a sack and staggered outside with it. Tom laughed when he saw us. "Nicely done, lads," he said as we managed to push it onto a wagon. "Heft twenty or thirty more, and you'll have it mastered."

We managed to load about half a dozen sacks before our arms turned to rubber and we had to take a break. There was a barrel of warm water in a corner, and we splashed some over us and drank what we could, but it tasted awful. "This is going to kill us," Kevin said.

"Let's just slow down. They don't seem to care what we do, as long as we don't look like we're goofing off."

We tried that, but it was still too hard. I always thought of myself as being in pretty good shape. I play soccer, and I have some ten-pound dumbbells that I work out with sometimes at home. But this was just way beyond me.

Luckily, after we'd loaded a few more sacks Tom decided there was enough food for the camp, and it was time for us all to take a break and have our own lunch. The wagons went off to the camp, and we went into the mess hall for some salt pork, boiled corn, and tea. I was hungry enough now that the food actually didn't taste too bad. I think I needed the salt after all the sweating I'd done.

While we ate we listened to the men complain. "We're soldiers, not laborers," a thin, wiry man said. "They should get the farmfolk to do this."

"They'd just stuff their pockets full of grain," the soldier sitting next to him pointed out.

"Shoot 'em if they steal. That's what'd happen to us."

"We should make 'em all soldiers," a third soldier said. "You think we can defeat the Portuguese and the Canadians with the army we've got now?"

"I hear they're signing up all the able-bodied men," the thin soldier said. "We'd be worse off if we had to take the rest of them."

"Doesn't matter who we get," yet another soldier muttered. "We've no hope of winning in any case."

That caused everyone to fall silent until Tom ordered us back to work in the warehouse. Now we had to clean up the spilled grain. This was a whole lot easier than lugging the sacks, but the heat inside the building was almost unbearable. "Wish I had a Pepsi," Kevin said.

"A Sprite."

"Dr. Pepper."

"Diet Fresca."

We came up with all the soft drink names we could think of. But we weren't going to get any. All we had was a barrel of warm water that was probably crawling with germs.

"What happens when the food runs out?" Kevin asked the thin soldier.

He shook his head. "That's when we surrender, mate. Let's hope we don't have too many die before that happens."

"How long till it's gone?"

"Don't know. Depends on how many people show up and how much they bring with 'em. Couple of months, I reckon."

That didn't sound good. Kevin was about to ask another question when we noticed Sergeant Hornbeam standing in the doorway. His red hair looked like it was on fire. "What are you boys doing?" he demanded.

"Colonel Clarett told us we had to work," I explained. "So Corporal Hennessy brought us over here."

Sergeant Hornbeam rolled his eyes. "Naturally," he muttered. "Have to put you two back in the brig," he said to us. "Come along."

I dropped my broom without a complaint. Hard to believe I'd be happy to go to jail, but I was.

"What happened with the watch, sir?" Kevin asked the sergeant as we headed back to the barracks. "Did you show it to anyone?"

Sergeant Hornbeam didn't bother to answer. He was walking so fast, it was hard to keep up.

"Please don't just hold onto it," Kevin persisted. "It's more than a toy."

"Still don't understand how you boys got hold of that thing," the sergeant said.

"Well, it's complicated, sir," Kevin began. But Sergeant Hornbeam waved him silent. We had reached the barracks, and he started shouting for Benjamin, who came waddling in, stuffing his shirt into his pants.

"Sorry, Sergeant," he said. "Making a visit to the outhouse."

"Kindly lock these two up once again," Sergeant Hornbeam ordered him. "And this time don't let 'em out on anyone's word except mine."

"What about the colonel, Sergeant?"

The sergeant muttered something under his breath, then turned and strode out of the barracks without answering.

Benjamin turned to us. "Sorry, lads. What was it you did, anyway?"

"Nothing, really," I said.

He shrugged and ushered us back into the cell, locking the door behind us. It was still empty. I slumped back down on the floor, and Kevin slumped next to me.

"This is good," he said.

"Good not to be hauling sacks of grain," I agreed.

"Yeah, but good because Hornbeam thinks we're so important he has to keep us locked up."

"If you say so. I just wish something would happen."

"Yeah, I know. I was thinking," he went on. "Remember how Stinky Glover and Nora Lally showed up in that other world? I wonder if people from our world are here, too."

"This place is a whole lot different than our world," I pointed out.

"I know, but it's not totally different. There's still a Glanbury, still a Boston. So it's a possibility, right? What if our families were living in Glanbury? What if they're in that camp over there right now?"

I closed my eyes and felt a lump rising in my throat. "You know what, Kevin? I don't really want to think about that."

"Yeah," he said softly, "I guess you're right."

We must have fallen asleep then, because the next thing I knew, a loud voice was shouting, "Wake up, dammit, don't you know there's a war on?"

I opened my eyes and saw Colonel Clarett standing over us. Behind him was Benjamin, holding a lantern and yawning.

"Come on, come on," the colonel said. "We don't have all night."

I struggled to my feet, and then helped Kevin up.

"That's it, then," the colonel said. "Let's go."

We followed him out of the cell.

"It's all nonsense," he told us, "but there you have it. The enemy's at our gates, and they're interested in gewgaws." He led us to a room in a corner of the barracks. "My own office," he muttered. "And where do I go meanwhile?"

He opened the door, and we went inside. A tall, black-haired man in a uniform was standing behind a desk.

"Here they are, Lieutenant," Colonel Clarett said. "And much luck may you have of 'em. If you want my opinion, they're a pair of thieves, and that's that. Look at the hat on the little one," he said, gesturing at Kevin's Red Sox cap as if its existence proved he was a criminal.

"Thank you, Colonel," the lieutenant said.

Colonel Clarett looked like he wanted to stay, but the lieutenant was obviously waiting for him to leave, so he turned and walked out, slamming the door behind him.

The lieutenant smiled at us. "Now," he said, "I think it's time for a little chat."

CHAPTER 8

The lieutenant gestured for us to sit. Colonel Clarett outranked him, I guess, but the lieutenant sure looked more like an officer. He was young and handsome, and his red jacket and black pants were spotless and unwrinkled, despite the heat. The colonel's office was a mess, with papers stacked everywhere and five or six long pipes lying in a jumble on his desk next to an oil lamp. Like the rest of the barracks, the room stank of tobacco smoke. The lieutenant stared at us for a few seconds, and he seemed to take in everything about us—what we were wearing, how we sat—everything. Then he sat down, too.

"My name is Carmody," he said. "Lieutenant William Carmody. And to whom have I the honor of speaking?"

We managed to tell him our names.

"Pleased to meet you." His accent was more cultured-sounding than the colonel's or any of the other soldiers we had met. It wasn't quite British, but it was, well, different—sort of like those actors in old-time movies. He pronounced "lieutenant" in the British way: "leftenant."

He cleared a space on the desk—he didn't look pleased to have to touch the colonel's pipes—and then he took a blue cloth out of one of his pockets. He unwrapped the cloth and took Kevin's watch out of it. He laid the watch carefully on the desk. "And this remarkable device belongs to—?"

"It's mine," Kevin said.

"And you obtained it where?"

Kevin glanced at me. "Well, that's a long story," he said.

Lieutenant Carmody shrugged. "I'm in no hurry."

Kevin and I hadn't really talked about this. Should we tell the truth about where we'd come from? That was the whole point of Kevin's plan. But now that the time had come, it didn't seem like that great an idea. No one was going to believe us—least of all this guy, with his icy stare.

But what else could we do?

"We're not from here," I said. "Not from…this world."

"*This world*," Lieutenant Carmody repeated, as if to make sure he had heard correctly.

I wasn't going to be able to do it. I looked back at Kevin. This was his idea. He didn't look any more eager to tell the story than me, but he did. "See, it's like this," he said. "I know it's going to sound crazy, but: There are lots of universes. This is just one of them. We come from a different universe—it's kind of the same, but not exactly. There's a Boston in it, there's a Canada, and so on, but there's no United States of New England, and no New Portugal. And our science is way more advanced than yours. By accident we stepped into this, uh, this thing that brought us to your universe. Like a portal, a gateway between universes. This happened yesterday, in Glanbury—our version of Glanbury. Anyway, now we're stuck here because we can't get back to Glanbury, because of the war and all. So the watch—it was just something I was wearing when this happened. In our world it's no big deal, something even a kid would wear. But here it seems pretty important, so we thought we'd, you know, show it to people."

Kevin fell silent. I thought he did a pretty good job, but Lieutenant Carmody hadn't changed expression. I couldn't tell if he thought we were crazy, or what. He picked up what looked like a long pencil and made a few notes on an unlined, yellowish sheet of paper. I could hear a clock ticking in the silence. A bead of sweat fell down my face, but I didn't wipe it away.

"What's a 'kid'?" he asked finally.

"It's, you know, a child," Kevin said. "Someone who isn't an adult. That's a word back home."

"Your accent is rather strange. That's how you speak, wherever it is you come from?"

Kevin nodded. "It's the same language, just a little different. Like everything else."

He gestured at our clothes. "And those strange garments—that's what you wear…?"

"We just happened to have these clothes on when we went through the portal," Kevin said. "It's all an accident, see. We don't want to be here. We just want to go home."

There were tears in Kevin's eyes now, but the lieutenant didn't seem to be moved. "Let's try again," he said. "You found this thing or stole it. The question is where, or from whom."

"No, we didn't," I protested. "What Kevin said is true."

"You're stowaways or cabin-boys on a ship that managed to run the blockade," he said. "Where is that ship now? Where did it sail from? China?"

"No, sir," I repeated. "I've never been on a ship in my life."

"This so-called portal—it's in Glanbury, you say? Did anyone see you come out of it?"

"No—well, there were some Portuguese soldiers who started shooting at us. A family picked us up on the road afterwards."

"Their name?"

I tried to remember—they had given it to the guard at the city gate. "Harper, I think. Samuel and Martha Harper."

He made another note. "And are they in the Fens camp?"

I shook my head. "They're staying with his brother somewhere in the city."

"And have you told this story to the Harpers or any of the soldiers here?"

"No. We figured no one would believe us."

"A reasonable assumption. And a prudent course of action. There are those willing to see the hand of the devil in everything, especially in these dark days." He fell silent again and stared at us some more. Then he said: "Tell me more about this world you claim to live in."

That perked Kevin up. He started talking about cars and computers and airplanes and telephones, all the stuff we took for granted back home. And he mentioned bombs and missiles and grenades, too.

The lieutenant didn't interrupt, and his expression never changed. He jotted down a few notes, especially when Kevin talked about weapons. When Kevin ran out of steam, he spoke again. "Do you know how to manufacture one of these?" he asked, pointing to the watch.

"Well, no, of course not," Kevin said. "We just buy them. Big companies make them."

"You're only a kid," the lieutenant said.

"Right."

"What about the theory behind it? Do you understand how it works?"

"Not exactly. Maybe a little bit."

"What about 'telephones' or those flying machines—what did you call them?"

"Airplanes."

"Airplanes. Can you explain how they work?"

"Not really," Kevin admitted.

The lieutenant looked at me, and I shook my head.

"If we managed to return you to this 'portal,'" he went on, "could you obtain more of these ciphering machines? Or could you bring us back 'rocket-propelled grenades' or 'submachine guns' or the like?"

Kevin shook his head. "No, I don't think so. I mean, we're not even sure we can get back home through the portal. If we do get back, I don't know if we can return here. The portal isn't really part of our world—it's not like airplanes and stuff. We don't know have any idea what it is or how it works—maybe it's from some other universe."

Lieutenant Carmody sat back in his chair suddenly and put his pencil down, as if we had tired him out. He pressed his palms together and held them in front of his chin. "What is it that you want me to do with you?" he asked quietly.

"Well, we figured we might be able to help," Kevin said. "You know, with the war."

"How, exactly?"

"Maybe we know stuff you can use."

"Enlighten me. What 'stuff' do you know that can help us win the war?"

Kevin looked at me for help. I didn't know what to say. "Stuff about science," he said, kind of desperately. "Stuff about the way the world works that you don't understand yet. I don't know exactly what, but if we think about it, maybe we can come up with something, okay? I mean, what have you got to lose?"

Lieutenant Carmody stared at him. "What do you mean, 'okay'?" he asked finally.

For some reason that was too much for Kevin. He started to cry.

"'All right,'" I whispered. "It means, 'all right.'" I put my hand on Kevin's shoulder.

The lieutenant lowered his hands to the desk and waited for Kevin to calm down. Then he said, "Let's go for a ride, shall we?"

We left Colonel Clarett's office. Outside the barracks was a fancy-looking carriage, the closed-in kind, with actual windows. A soldier standing next to it saluted Lieutenant Carmody and opened the door for him. "Back to headquarters, Peter," the lieutenant said.

The three of us climbed inside, and Peter got up front to drive. I wanted to ask what was going to happen next, but the lieutenant didn't look like he wanted to talk. Kevin still seemed pretty depressed. He just stared out the window as we made our way through Cheapside, then back downtown, where we saw more traffic and beggars and men wearing round hats and capes. We went along the waterfront, where I could make out the masts of ships in the harbor and along the docks. Finally we stopped at a large gate, and the soldiers guarding it quickly opened it for us. We went through it into a broad courtyard with big brick buildings on all sides. We came to a stop in front of the building at the far end of the courtyard.

Peter opened the door for us again, while a kid our age came up and took the reins of the horses. Lieutenant Carmody got out, and we followed him inside the building. Soldiers standing guard at the entrance saluted as he walked past them.

Inside the building was a large hall with paintings of soldiers hung on the walls and a big flag in the center—blue, white, and red vertical stripes. The flag of New England, I guessed. We went quickly through the hall and along a corridor. Finally the lieutenant stopped and knocked on a door. "Carmody," he called out in a loud voice.

"Come," replied a voice from inside.

He opened the door, and we saw a large, dark room, with a high ceiling and big draperies covering the windows. Like every room in this world, it stank of smoke. A gray-haired soldier sat behind a big desk, chewing on an unlit cigar and looking at a map. The lieutenant saluted, and the man gave a half-wave in return. His uniform was unbuttoned, rumpled, and stained, but when he raised his eyes and stared at us I knew this guy wasn't another Colonel Clarett; he was a general, and an important one. I figured he was the head of the whole army, and it turned out I was right.

I thought Lieutenant Carmody had a cold stare, but the general's gaze was even harder and colder; it seemed to suck the breath right out of me. It made me want to run and hide. Kevin and I stood on the other side of the desk from him and waited.

"These are the ones?" he asked Lieutenant Carmody.

"Yes, sir."

"Strange clothing too, eh? Let me see the thing again." The lieutenant went over, took out the watch, unwrapped it, and handed it to him. The general squinted at it and punched in a few numbers. "Fascinating. But not much use to us, is it?"

"Might speed up artillery calculations."

"That won't win the war," the general muttered. "And what's their story? Where did they get the thing?"

The lieutenant took a long look at us. "Sir, they claim to have, er, arrived here accidentally from another world, similar to ours but much more advanced. On their world, this is simply an inexpensive timepiece that one of them happened to be wearing."

He paused, and everyone was silent. "Of course. Yes," the general said finally. "Why didn't I think of that?"

Lieutenant Carmody gave a few more details from Kevin's story. At the end the general rolled his eyes. "And do you believe this tale, lieutenant?" he asked.

"Sir, I don't know. But as we discussed, this object is far beyond our ability to manufacture. Or the ability of anyone else, for that matter, including the Chinese."

"We knew that already, Lieutenant. I sent you to form an opinion. Are they telling the truth?"

For the first time Lieutenant Carmody looked uncomfortable. "It seems absurd, but…I can come up with no other satisfactory explanation. The accents, the clothes, the device…And the story itself. It's a tale beyond the ability of mere boys to concoct. In my opinion."

"Hmmph," the general muttered. He returned his gaze to us. "What does the 'B' on that strange hat of yours stand for?" he asked Kevin suddenly.

"For—for Boston," Kevin replied. He sounded as scared of the general as I felt. "It's a baseball cap."

"And what is 'baseball'? Some sort of game?"

"Yes, sir. It's a sport. Teams from different cities play it—Boston, New York...It's like cricket, I think. Maybe you play cricket here?"

The general ignored Kevin's question. "Sit, both of you," he ordered. "Now, explain the rules of baseball. Tell me everything you know about it."

I was grateful to be able to sit down. And Kevin looked really happy to be able to talk about baseball. "Well," he said. "there are nine men on a side, and the field is set up with three bases and what you call home plate..." He went over the rules, then he started in on how the major leagues were set up and the history of the game. He explained how you figured out an earned run average and slugging percentage and stuff like that. It was really boring if you ask me, but the general paid close attention.

"Enough," he ordered finally. "A strange game, indeed. I think it's time for a drink, Lieutenant," he said.

The lieutenant went to a cabinet and got a bottle out of it. He poured some dark brown liquid into a glass and handed it to the general, who gulped. "Feel free, Lieutenant," he said, gesturing at the bottle, but Carmody shook his head.

The general poured more liquor into the glass. "Earned run average," he muttered.

The rest of us waited.

"We are not mystics, Lieutenant," he said. "We are not philosophers. We are soldiers. We do not always need to understand; but we do need to act."

"Yes, sir."

"If we don't win this war," he went on, "President Gardner may survive as a puppet of the Canadians and the Portuguese, at least until they can figure out how to carve the nation up. You and I, Lieutenant, will most assuredly not survive. Can these boys help us win this war?"

"I don't know, sir."

The general eyed him. "Not the right answer," he said.

"Sir, if we believe them, they're too young to understand what they know about—airplanes, telephones, that sort of thing. But such things wouldn't help us in any case. We don't have the time or anything like the capability to reproduce them. But I have a suggestion."

"Yes?"

"Send them to Alexander Palmer. Have him find out what they do understand, and whether we can take advantage of it."

"Palmer? He thinks we're all idiots."

"Just the president, sir."

"Well, he thinks the war is a disaster."

"Yes, but that doesn't mean he wants to lose it. Imagine if Harvard College were to be turned into the University of Southern Canada."

The general poured himself another drink. "Airplanes," he muttered. "Telephones. Wouldn't it be nice? What do you imagine His Excellency would think of all this?"

"President Gardner would think it's insane. It would give him an excuse to fire you if he found out you were wasting time on it."

The general nodded. "Precisely. Palmer's still over in Cambridge?"

"I believe so. Holding out till the last minute, I suppose. Rather stubborn."

"Bring them to him. See if he'll help. But for God's sake keep it secret."

"Yes, sir."

The general pointed his cigar at us. "On-base percentage," he said, as if he were accusing us of something. Then he picked up the watch and handed it back to Lieutenant Carmody.

The lieutenant led us out of the room—which was a good thing, because I was about to hurl from the stench and the tension. We walked quickly back out into the courtyard. The night had gotten cooler, thank goodness. "I'll wager you lads are hungry," he said. "Let's see what we can find to eat."

He was sure right about us being hungry. We followed him into another building across the courtyard, then through a door labeled "Officers' Mess." He roused a private who was dozing in a chair in the corner of the room, and in a few minutes we were served roast beef, bread, and milk by candlelight. The milk was pretty warm, but other than that the meal was fabulous.

"I believe General Aldridge likes you boys," Lieutenant Carmody said as we ate. You could've fooled me. "I wasn't at all sure how he'd react to your story."

"Who's Alexander Palmer?" Kevin asked.

"An old professor of mine from college. Often rather ill-tempered, but the smartest man I know. I think he'll enjoy this challenge."

"Are you going to take us to him now?" I asked.

"Rather late for that, I'm afraid. Let's find you some accommodations here for the night and pay him a visit tomorrow."

The building we were in also turned out to be the officers' quarters. When we were finished eating, the lieutenant brought us to a tiny, hot room in the attic. There was nothing in it but a couple of thin mattresses on the floor, an oil lamp on a rickety table, and a chamber pot in the corner. "This is where our servants usually sleep," he explained. "Except they're now on active service in the army, and we have to fend for ourselves. I'll fetch you in the morning."

"Thank you, sir," I said.

He gave us a wave and left.

Kevin and I sat down on the mattresses. "A good meal and a better place to sleep," he said. "Progress, huh?"

"Kevin, how are we going to help them win the war?"

He shook his head. "I don't know, Larry. But we should be able to think of something."

"What if we can't?"

"I don't know," he repeated. And then he said, "I'm sorry, Larry. This is all my fault."

That's what I thought yesterday when we first ended up in this mess, but I remembered the way Kevin broke down earlier as Lieutenant Carmody gave him a hard time, and I changed my mind. "No, it's not," I said. "We both screwed up. Anyway, we'll be okay."

"*Okay*," he said. "Funny how they don't know that word. Anyway, I sure hope you're right." He stretched out on his mattress. "Good night, Larry."

"Good night, Kevin." I lay down on my mattress and closed my eyes. My muscles ached from all the lifting I'd done. It had been a long day. At home, they were probably still searching for us. Maybe they'd found the portal by now and were trying to figure it out. How many worlds would they have to visit before they discovered this one? How long would they keep looking?

Meanwhile, what was tomorrow going to bring for Kevin and me?

I fell asleep with my mind full of questions.

CHAPTER 9

Peter, Lieutenant Carmody's driver, came for us the next morning, just as we were waking up. He was a big man with long, bushy sideburns and a large mustache. "The Lieutenant would like for you to come to his quarters," he explained. He talked slowly, as if he wasn't sure we could understand him.

We followed him down a couple of floors and along a short corridor, until we reached a door with Lieutenant Carmody's name on it. Peter rapped on the door and opened it without waiting for an answer. We all went in.

The lieutenant's room was large, with a bed, a desk, and a comfortable-looking chair, in which he was sitting. There was a rug on the floor and curtains on the window. On the desk was a vase with a single flower in it. The place looked pretty homey after where we'd slept the last two nights.

The lieutenant got up from the chair and greeted us. Like yesterday, his uniform was crisp and clean. He wrinkled his nose when he got a whiff of us. "Peter, I believe we'll have to get these lads washed," he said. "Then let's have them put on their new clothes." He pointed to the bed, where a couple of outfits were laid out—dark pants, shapeless shirts, and clunky shoes. They weren't much to look at, but that was okay by me; it would be good not to have people staring at us anymore. "Bring their clothes back here, Peter," he went on. "I'll hold on to them. Lads, I'll meet you in the mess."

"Yes, sir," Peter said. "Grab the clothes, lads, and follow me."

We went downstairs and out a back door, into an enclosed area next to the stables. Laundry hung on lines, and there were buckets filled with water sitting on wood stoves that were tended by an enormous woman with sweat pouring off her. Next to the stoves were tables with towels and big blocks of yellow soap on them. A few soldiers were standing at the tables and pouring water over themselves.

"Grab a bucket, lads, and go to it," Peter said. And to the woman he said, "Bessy, we need to get these lads cleaned up." I was a little embarrassed about taking my clothes off in front of the woman, but there was nothing to be done about it. Anyway, it felt good to wash. "Hand those clothes over when you're ready," he ordered us.

We did as we were told. Peter was intrigued by our boxers—it turned out that only rich people wore underwear here—but he was totally fascinated by the zippers on our pants. We showed him how they worked, and he couldn't stop zipping and unzipping. "How the devil does it do that?" he asked.

It was something else we couldn't exactly explain.

My new shirt didn't fit very well. The pants were itchy, especially with nothing on underneath them. The shoes were incredibly heavy compared to my sneakers. "You look terrible," Kevin said.

"So do you."

But at least we were reasonably clean.

Peter brought us to the mess, where Lieutenant Carmody had breakfast waiting for us—porridge and tea again, but also scrambled eggs, which tasted great. The lieutenant nodded his approval at our outfits. "You look like you're just off the farm. And you smell much better. Now finish up. We have to get you over to Cambridge."

After we were done, he hurried us out to the courtyard, where Peter was waiting with the carriage. The three of us got in, and we rattled off over the cobblestones. The streets were filled with horses and carriages and big wagons and those strange-looking bicycles, not to mention a hog or two and some nasty dogs. Lieutenant Carmody tapped his fingers impatiently as we made our way through the noise and the traffic. "You'd think it was life as usual in the city," he said. "More refugees adding to the confusion, I suppose. It'll be midday before we get to Harvard."

"We have Harvard in our world," I said. "My father went there."

Lieutenant Carmody gave me a look, as if he still wasn't ready to believe this stuff about parallel universes. "What does your father do?" he asked.

"He's a computer programmer."

"And what is that?"

"Well, he writes software programs that, um, make computers work."

The lieutenant shook his head. "Software?" he asked. "Programs?"

I tried, but I couldn't make sense of it for him; finally he waved me silent in frustration and turned away to stare out the window at the traffic.

Finally we reached a river. I guessed it was the Charles River, which separates Boston from Cambridge, but it didn't look anything like the Charles in our world, which always seemed pretty peaceful and calm when we drove by, with joggers and rollerbladers whizzing around its banks, and lots of little sailboats out on the water. This version of the Charles didn't have much in the way of banks, with trees and bushes up to its edge, and only a couple of rowboats making their way towards the other shore. The bridge we crossed was small and rickety, and I got a little scared that if the horse became excited he could crash through the railing and send us all down into the water. But we made it across okay, and then we were in Cambridge and traveling along the Massachusetts Road, the lieutenant informed us.

Cambridge wasn't anything like our version either, of course. We passed by the usual farms and small shops; when we reached the part where the college was, the houses got nicer, and some of the buildings were pretty impressive, but there was nothing like the craziness of Harvard Square, which my dad brought us to a couple of times. In fact, the place looked pretty deserted, especially compared to Boston.

"That's where I lived when I attended Harvard," Lieutenant Carmody said, pointing to a large brick building. It was exactly the sort of thing my dad said when he brought us to Harvard Square. Big whoop, Cassie would reply, and she wouldn't even look at his dorm.

"Where is everyone?" Kevin asked.

"The students are all in the army," the lieutenant replied. "And most of the townspeople have retreated across the river into Boston.

Cambridge will not be defensible if the Canadians choose to advance on it. And they will advance before long."

"Why is Professor Palmer still here?"

"Because he's a contrary old sod," the lieutenant muttered. I didn't exactly understand the words, but I got the idea.

We kept going, and eventually Peter pulled up in front of a big white house down a dirt lane. We got out, and the lieutenant went over and knocked on the door, but there was no answer. He shook his head and walked around back. We followed him.

In front of a red barn a gray-haired man with a small beard was tossing apples into what I figured was a cider press. My family went apple-picking a couple of times, and they'd had gizmos like it in the orchards. We approached. "Good morning, Professor," the lieutenant called out.

The professor looked up. "Ah, William," he replied. "Nice to see you." He didn't seem at all surprised. "Don't you have a war to fight?"

"Ninety percent of war is preparation."

"So you're preparing?"

"You might say so."

Professor Palmer glanced at us with little interest. "And who are these fellows?" he asked.

Lieutenant Carmody introduced us. The professor gave us a brief nod and offered us a cup of cider. It was delicious.

"Don't you have friends to stay with in Boston?" the lieutenant asked him. "I can't imagine you'd enjoy having the Canadians show up at your doorstep one morning to take you prisoner."

"I have every confidence that President Gardner will find a way to make this entire unpleasant episode go away," Professor Palmer replied, and I was pretty sure he was being sarcastic. "He's still talking to the British, isn't he?"

"Yes, but there's that little matter of the naval blockade to deal with. The British ambassador can agree to whatever we want, but he still has to find a way to inform Parliament of the agreement. And as to whether they would accept his recommendations..." The lieutenant shrugged. "We don't have as many friends in London as we used to."

"William, I was having a very pleasant morning here, and now you've gone and ruined it," the professor said. "Are you telling me

His Excellency doesn't have a plan to extricate us from this disastrous situation he has allowed to develop?"

The lieutenant smiled. "Like you, I have every confidence in His Excellency."

"Pah." The professor spat on the ground. "Now, there must be a reason for visiting me with these young men in tow."

"Indeed. We have something to show you, professor, and a story to tell."

Lieutenant Carmody took out the watch and handed it to the professor, who studied it while we waited. He didn't touch any of the buttons at first, just turning the thing over in his hands. Then Kevin showed him how to use it. After that the professor sat down on a tree stump and started playing with it. "Square roots," he muttered. "To eight decimal places. Remarkable." He stood up finally. "And what is the story you have to tell, William?" he asked.

"It's a very strange one—if you choose to believe it." We all sat down, and he repeated what we had told him, the way he had to General Aldridge.

The professor scratched his head and stared at us as he listened. "Do you remember your philosophy courses, William?" he asked when Carmody was finished.

The lieutenant smiled. "How could I forget them?"

"Do you recall the discussion of Occam's Razor?"

"The principle of parsimony," he replied. "The simplest explanation is generally the best."

The professor nodded. "Such a pity you chose soldiering instead of the groves of Academe, William. You were one of our brightest students. So, can we not apply Occam's Razor here? Why postulate an infinitude of universes and the like? Can't we explain the current situation by suggesting that two boys with active imaginations have somehow come upon a device from China—amazing though it is— and concocted a silly story to go with it?"

"We could," the lieutenant agreed. "Except that, if you're right, they have concocted a better story than any I've ever heard."

"And there's zippers, begging your pardon, sir," Peter said. I had forgotten about Peter. He was tending his horses by a water pump, close enough to overhear the conversation. "On their pants, sir." And he described that other miraculous invention, which apparently he couldn't get out of his head. "You don't need buttons on your fly," he explained. "The thing just goes up and down, smooth as you like."

The professor stared at us some more.

"Ask them about baseball," the lieutenant urged. "General Aldridge was much impressed with the little one's discussion of a sport on his world."

Professor Palmer raised an eyebrow. "Solomon is not a fool like our president," he said, "but he is also not a philosopher. Well, I suppose it wouldn't hurt to catechize them."

So he began asking us questions—not about baseball, thank goodness, but about everything else on our world—politics and history and science and religion and lots more. For the first time we got to explain about America. We talked about how it became the most powerful country in the world. We talked about watching TV and playing video games and surfing the net. We talked about men landing on the moon, which got the professor to raise his eyebrow again. I described how I had touched a moon rock when my family visited the Air and Space Museum in Washington. That seemed to astound him more than anything else we said.

Like the lieutenant, the professor pressed us for explanations that we just couldn't give. I mean, I have some vague idea of how a car works. You put gas in the tank, you turn the key, you move the thing so it points to "D", you step on the accelerator…But to explain it so that it made sense to someone who has never heard of a car—I couldn't do it. Kevin was a little better, because he read so much and liked to do science experiments and stuff, but even he didn't make a lot of sense when the professor really pushed him.

After a while I figured we were screwing up pretty badly, and I started to get depressed. We'd been better off with Kevin explaining earned run averages to General Aldridge. Finally the professor stopped his questions and poured everyone more cider. Then he looked at Lieutenant Carmody. "What do you want from me, William?" he asked softly.

"We're at war, Professor," the lieutenant replied. "Our nation's survival is in jeopardy."

"You expect these boys to conjure weapons for you?"

"I want whatever they can give us."

Professor Palmer looked away. "Another world," he murmured. "A thousand wonders to explore. And what do we seek? Better ways of killing."

The lieutenant gestured towards the professor's house. "Everything you have," he said, "—your life itself—is being protected by a few thousand soldiers, with dwindling supplies and little hope of reinforcement. We don't have time to explore wonders; we need to survive."

"They're just boys," the professor pointed out. "Obviously they don't understand—"

"And that's why I've come to you," the lieutenant interrupted. "They know things but don't understand them. You don't know, but you can understand. Together, perhaps you can come up with something."

"You're asking for a miracle."

"Well, why not? If these boys are to be believed, their very presence here is a miracle."

"How long do we have?" the professor asked.

The lieutenant shrugged. "We assume the enemy will lay siege to the city before the final attack. If so, we can hold out a couple of months. By winter it will be hopeless. But the president will likely surrender long before that. And the terms will not be favorable."

The professor shook his head sadly. "How did it come to this?"

"That's for others to work out," the lieutenant replied. "Soldiers simply fight the war they are given."

"That's why you should be more than a soldier, William. But in the meantime, what is your plan?"

"The boys will stay here with you," he said. "We need to keep this secret, not least because of how the president might react if he found out. While they're here, you learn what you can from them. Whatever might help us. I'll return to check on your progress."

"And if there's nothing?"

"Then there's nothing. You will have listened to some entertaining stories while you wait for the Canadians to arrive, and the rest of us will march resolutely towards our fate."

The professor looked at Kevin and me, and I could tell he didn't like the idea of having us move in with him. "I'm an old man," he started to say, "and—"

"Nonsense," Lieutenant Carmody interrupted. "This is the opportunity of a lifetime, and you know it. You are the best person in New England for the task, and you know that as well. Don't lose the opportunity just because you're set in your ways."

"I suppose," the professor said finally, as if he was agreeing to have his foot amputated or something. "Very well."

Lieutenant Carmody nodded in satisfaction and immediately stood up. "Excellent." He turned to us. "I trust you lads will do your best. There is much at stake here."

"Yes, sir," we both replied.

"Good." He shook hands with Professor Palmer, then motioned to Peter to get the carriage ready. In a couple of minutes they were clattering off down the lane, and we were alone with the professor.

It was very quiet. Kevin and I stood by the cider press, waiting.

"Well, then," the professor said. "I suppose—I suppose you're hungry."

I wasn't, actually, but we both nodded.

"So perhaps we should dine?"

"Okay," I said.

"Pardon me?"

That word again. "I mean sure. Fine."

"Well, then," he murmured again, and he started off towards the house.

Kevin and I looked at each other. "Weird," Kevin whispered. And we followed him inside.

CHAPTER 10

"My housekeeper left to join her daughter's family in Boston," Professor Palmer explained, "but I'm used to fending for myself. Kindly have a seat."

The kitchen was large and sunny, with a big open fireplace along the inside wall. We sat in a couple of straight-backed wooden chairs in a corner and watched him putter for a while in silence. When he was done, we helped him bring the food into the dining room, which was small and dark and kind of stuffy. We ate cold roast chicken, and it was just about the best chicken I'd ever tasted. I was beginning to get the idea that food here was either terrible or delicious. Like the soldiers in the mess hall, he ate with his knife. His fork only had two prongs, and he used it just to hold down the meat while he cut it. Weird.

"Before long, meals like this will be but a memory," the professor said. "We must enjoy them while we can."

"Yes, sir," I replied. "It's very good."

"Yes. Well." He paused, then fell silent and looked down at his plate. He seemed to be having difficulty starting up a conversation with us.

"Do you believe us?" Kevin asked.

He looked up and blinked rapidly. "You know, I want very much to believe you," he replied. "Knowledge is so hard to come by—in many ways we have learned little—and forgotten much—since the ancient Greeks. The idea that somewhere, somehow, another turn was taken, and so much more has been discovered and accomplished—it is deeply exciting. But then, there is still Occam's razor."

"We're telling the truth," I said. "We're not smart enough to make up all this stuff."

The professor nodded. "That is actually the most powerful argument in your favor. Your theory, though—that we live our lives countless times, in countless different worlds—simply doesn't feel real. It is the stuff of fantastical late-night conversations in college common rooms, after too many glasses of port. Lieutenant Carmody wants weapons. I want to understand what is real."

"We don't drink port," I pointed out.

That got him to laugh. "Let us begin, then," he said. "Remove these plates, and I'll find some paper."

We cleared the table while the professor got some of that odd-looking yellowish paper that the lieutenant had used, and one of those strange, long pencils. And we started telling our story once again.

It didn't go all that well. Professor Palmer took a lot of notes and asked a lot of questions, but we had the same problem we had before. Like the lieutenant said, we knew things, but we didn't understand them. And the professor was mostly interested in the portal and how that worked and what it meant to philosophy and religion and stuff, and there we couldn't help him at all. After a while he began to look unhappy and distracted, like he was getting tired of listening to us.

Finally we took a break, and he showed us his house and where we'd be sleeping. For a famous professor, his house wasn't all that big—I think people in this world were used to a lot less space than in ours. Across from the dining room was a small room he called the "parlor," which was mostly filled up with a piano. That reminded me again of the piano lesson I had missed, which wasn't good. Next to the parlor was a tiny study crammed with books. There was a narrow staircase leading to the second floor, which had one good-sized bedroom and one small one. We were bringing up sheets and blankets to the small bedroom when we noticed a couple of paintings in the hall—one was of a little boy in short pants, the other of a black-haired woman with a sad smile sitting in a chair and holding a fan. Kevin asked the professor who they were. He looked like he didn't want to answer, and then he said softly, "My wife and son."

"Where are they?" Kevin asked. "Are they—?"

He shrugged. "They died many years ago."

"How did they die?"

I thought that was kind of a pushy question. The professor again looked like this wasn't something he wanted to talk about, but he said, "In an outbreak of the smallpox." He gazed at the painting of the child. "It occurred shortly after Seth's portrait was completed."

"Smallpox?" Kevin said. "I'm pretty sure that's totally cured in our world."

The professor turned and glared at Kevin. "Do not trifle with me, boy!" he shot back angrily.

Kevin retreated a step. I think he was afraid the professor was going to hit him. "I didn't mean to—" he said. "I mean, I'm sorry, if you don't want to talk about it…"

"How was it cured?" he demanded. "Or is that something else you don't understand?"

"I'm pretty sure they came up with, you know, a vaccine."

"No, I don't know. What is a 'vaccine'?" he demanded.

This time Kevin had an explanation. "It's like when you give someone a tiny bit of a disease, with a shot or something. Not enough to make them sick, but it gives them immunity when they come in contact with the disease for real."

"What do you mean, 'immunity'?"

"You know, when you don't get a disease, because your body has built up a resistance to the germs."

The professor shook his head, still not getting it. "And what are 'germs'?" he asked.

Kevin looked at me like, *Can you believe this?* "They're tiny, um, organisms that can make you sick," he said. "Different kinds of germs give you different illnesses. They're really small—you can only see them with a powerful microscope. Do you have microscopes in this world?"

Professor Palmer continued to stare at Kevin. Then I noticed that his dark eyes were filled with tears. "So many people have died of smallpox," he said. "And you tell me they could have been saved?"

"We've cured a lot of diseases," Kevin said.

"What about…drikana?"

Kevin looked at me. I shook my head. The name was kind of familiar, but I couldn't place it. "Never heard of it," I said.

"Me neither."

"No matter, I suppose," the professor said softly. "No matter."

But that conversation did matter. It seemed to change the way Professor Palmer acted toward us. He never really said that he believed us instead of Occam's razor or whatever, but it was just more or less assumed. It was more than that, though—before, it had been like what we were telling him was just a puzzle he was trying to figure out. Now, it was different. Now, it was sort of personal. We weren't going to bring his wife and son back, but maybe we really could help.

After supper we all sat in the parlor and talked more about his world. Professor Palmer was eager to give us his opinions about it. He seemed a little lonely, with the college closed and the town deserted and nobody to lecture to, and we were the best audience he was going to get.

"This war need never have happened," he said, "except that those purblind fools in Boston were certain it wouldn't happen. They assumed the Canadians and New Portuguese hated each other more than they hated us, and would never be able to unite against us no matter how much we provoked them. Perhaps fifty years ago that was true. But times have changed. They realized that they needn't be friends to be allies, and we were in no position to defend ourselves on two fronts. So they attacked, and we have been fighting for our lives ever since."

I remembered the newspaper we'd read and the soldiers' talk. "Why hasn't England helped?" I asked.

"Because we asked too late. And because England has more than enough problems of its own fighting the Franco-Prussian alliance. And there continue to be those who never wanted us to become independent of England, and would be happy to see us fail."

"Sir," Kevin said, "would you mind—we still don't understand what's going on here. We know about Canada, but what happened to America—you know, what we call this place? And in our world, the Spanish came here first from Europe. Portugal didn't have a whole lot to do with the New World, that I remember. We think something must have changed way back in your history, to make things end up so different."

The professor nodded. "All right. The theory makes sense. Let's see if we can find out."

It didn't take that long. You wouldn't have to have paid much attention in history class to figure out what the difference was, once you started looking for it.

In this world, Christopher Columbus didn't discover America. Professor Palmer had never heard of the guy.

What we learned in school was that the Portuguese, under Prince Henry the Navigator, wanted to find a trade route to India, so they explored south along the coast of Africa, until they rounded the Cape of Good Hope and sailed north through the Indian Ocean. They weren't interested in sailing west across the Atlantic, maybe because they knew more about geography than Columbus and realized they'd have to travel a whole lot further than he thought to reach India.

So in our world Columbus went off and sold Spain on his idea, and that's why Spain reached the New World first, why it became a huge empire, at least for a while, why Balboa discovered the Pacific and Cortez conquered Mexico and all that stuff. And America got named almost by accident when a mapmaker decided a guy named Amerigo Vespucci deserved some credit for his explorations.

That was us.

In Professor Palmer's world, the Portuguese did sail west and discover the New World. It wasn't even Columbus's idea; he never entered the picture. It was Portugal, not Spain, that got all the silver and gold. It was Portugal that became the big empire, with Spain just another loser country in Europe.

France still explored and settled what would become Canada, and England colonized the eastern part of "America." But the British colonies never expanded the way they did in our world. They stayed along the Atlantic coast, hemmed in by the Portuguese, the Canadians, and the Indians. And that's the way it stayed.

Professor Palmer showed us a map that night. New England was a lot bigger than it was in our world—it looked like it included New York and Pennsylvania—but New Portugal was huge; it extended all the way from, like, Virginia, west to what's Texas in our world, then south through Mexico and into South America. Canada was big, too, stretching down into the Midwest. On the map New England looked like this little stone stuck between two huge boulders.

How could it avoid getting crushed?

Well, things weren't always quite as bad as they looked on the map. New Portugal was too big, too spread out to be much of a nation. It was more like a bunch of half-independent states, usually at war with each other. And Canada had mostly been friendly with New England and an enemy of New Portugal.

But right now England was busy fighting a war against France and Prussia (which was sort of like our Germany), so it couldn't do much to help with the defense of its former colony. Canada and New Portugal saw this as an opportunity to carve up the little nation between them. New England had been trying to extend its borders by skirmishing with both countries, and that gave them the reason they needed to invade.

It all seemed so strange, so different, as we talked about it. There had been no American Revolution, no Civil War. New England had stayed part of the British Empire until 1925. Slavery ended there when it ended in the rest of the Empire, in the 1830's, although it still existed on a small scale in some areas of New Portugal. The whole western part of the continent remained largely unexplored and was inhabited mostly by Indians (who were called by their tribal names, because no one ever thought they came from India).

Some people were just as famous in this world as they were in ours—Beethoven, for example. But many either hadn't existed or, if they did, never became well-known. Shakespeare had died young and was remembered for just a couple of poems. Mozart, Van Gogh, Mark Twain—who were they? Professor Palmer had never heard of them, and lots of others we mentioned.

And where were all the inventions, the medicines, the discoveries? Why was this world, like, two hundred years behind ours?

The answer became obvious to Professor Palmer as we talked. "You told me this afternoon that you had never heard of drikana," he said. "That may explain a great deal."

"What is it?" I asked.

"A horrible disease—worse even than smallpox or consumption. A person afflicted with drikana has uncontrollable vomiting and diarrhea. It is as if everything in his body is trying to escape from it as quickly as possible. Most people die within two days of the disease's onset. It is also highly contagious. If it shows up in a city, it will kill a third of the inhabitants in a month."

Kevin and I looked at each other. I remembered where I'd heard the word before. "A soldier asked us about drikana when we were coming into Boston," I recalled.

Professor Palmer nodded. "They would need to be vigilant to keep the disease from entering. An outbreak would be devastating, with the city so crowded with refugees."

"Drikana sounds kind of like Ebola," Kevin said. "That's a deadly virus from Africa."

"And what is a 'virus'?" the professor asked.

Kevin tried his best to explain. "Kind of like germs, I think, only it's harder to come up with medicines for a virus. I think."

"There is no cure for drikana," the professor noted. "Early settlers in the New World were the first to come down with it. 'Drikana' was the name of a native tribe near the site of the first outbreak. Unfortunately the survivors returned to Portugal and brought the disease with them. It devastated Europe, and five hundred years later it still devastates us. For a few years it seems to lie dormant, until people begin to hope that it is finally gone—but always there is a new outbreak, just as devastating as the last.

"Surely that accounts for the difference between our worlds," he went on. "How many geniuses has the disease claimed before they could make their discoveries? How much time and effort have we spent in dealing with it that we could have spent in the search for knowledge?" He looked pained again, as he had when talking about the death of his wife and son. "And how many lives have we wasted fighting useless wars like this one?" he murmured.

"Well, it's not like there are no wars in our world," Kevin pointed out. And we talked about the Civil War and the World Wars and Iraq, the concentration camps and the A-bomb and chemical weapons. I don't think it made the professor feel much better.

"Knowledge doesn't bring wisdom, certainly," he said. "No reason to assume otherwise. More advanced weapons just allow you to kill each other more efficiently. Still, a world without drikana, with smallpox cured…I daresay most people would make the trade."

I know I would have.

"Well," he said, "this is the world we have, and we must make the best of it. Time for bed. Tomorrow we will set to work again."

We went up to our room, and for the first time in this world we had clean sheets and soft pillows. The mattresses were lumpy and, of course, we still had to pee in a pot or go outside to what the professor called the "privy." But we weren't complaining.

"Drikana," Kevin whispered in the darkness, as if trying out the disease's name.

"Drikana," I repeated, lying on my bed and staring up at the ceiling.

"Some little germ somewhere, can't even see it, and it wipes out half the world, sets progress back centuries."

"Do you think we'll come down with it?" I asked.

"Maybe the worst danger in this world isn't the Portuguese or the Canadians," he replied, not quite answering my question.

"Have you ever been in the hospital?"

"Just to the emergency room once," he said, "when I broke my thumb."

"I don't even know if they have hospitals here."

"If they do, doesn't sound like they'd be much use."

I fell silent, thinking about how safe I'd always felt at home. My mom was crazy about safety, but even if she weren't, there were doctors and ambulances and firemen and policemen around...Bad things happened, sure, but they had never happened to me. And it had never really occurred to me that they could happen to me, maybe just because Mom was always so worried. With her protecting me, what could go wrong?

Drikana.

Kevin was silent. I listened to my heart beating in the quiet room. I have to rely on myself now, I thought. Grow up. There just wasn't any choice. No use feeling sorry for myself; no use thinking about the past, my home and family and what I could have done to not get into this mess. No use hoping they'd find the portal and find this world and magically save me. A germ or a virus or whatever could kill me tomorrow, but I couldn't worry about that. I could only do my best, and try to stay alive.

CHAPTER 11

Professor Palmer was pretty gruff, and he got angry with us a lot, especially in the first couple of days. He expected us to do our share of chores, and we weren't very good at them. At home I'd have to clean my room and wash the car and stuff like that, but I sure didn't have to sweep up horse poop or empty chamber pots or feed garbage to pigs. I mowed lawns at home, but with a power mower, not a scythe—I didn't even know what a scythe was; Mom would have had a stroke if she'd seen me with one of them in my hands.

"Your utter incompetence is proof of something," the professor said, shaking his head at us as Kevin and I tried to put a saddle onto Susie, his friendly old horse.

But we kind of got used to his style after a while. He was never mean to us; he just hadn't dealt much with kids, especially incompetent kids. And we got better at our chores, at least some of them.

Life at the professor's house was actually pretty pleasant, except for our homesickness, and the occasional distant sound of gunfire, which reminded us that before very long this was going to end and we'd have to move back into the crowded city for the final siege. Some things took getting used to, though.

The smells, for one. Not just the barnyard smells—the chickens and the pigs and Susie—and the smell of the privy behind the house. But the people smells. Taking a bath was a big deal. Washing clothes was a big deal—and Kevin and I only had one set of clothes to wash. So we all kind of stank, at least until I got used to it.

The isolation was another big difference. We didn't have a clue what was going on with the war, and there really wasn't any way to find out, unless we rode into Boston. Were the Canadians heading into Cambridge? Was England going to save us? Professor Palmer didn't seem too bothered about the lack of news, but it really bugged Kevin and me.

Part of the isolation was the silence. When the gunfire stopped, there wasn't much sound at all—just birds twittering, the wind rustling leaves, hens clucking in the barnyard. No traffic noise, no airplanes, not even the hum of a refrigerator. It was kind of spooky.

And of course there wasn't much to do. We couldn't talk to the professor or do chores all the time, so we had to entertain ourselves. The professor had plenty of books, and we tried reading them. We skipped the philosophy stuff, but some of the novels were okay, although they always had lots of words we didn't understand and scenes that didn't make any sense because we didn't know enough about this world's history or geography or whatever. Kevin liked to play chess with the professor, who was delighted to have an opponent.

I actually ended up spending a lot of time playing the piano, which Professor Palmer also enjoyed. His piano had a tinnier sound than I was used to, and not as many keys, but the basic instrument was the same. The professor didn't know any of the songs I knew, so it was cool when I came up with something that he liked. One of his favorites was "Take Me Out to the Ballgame."

He had some sheet music, and I managed to learn a few of the songs from his world, too. There was one we all liked with a sad melody and strange words:

Wanly I wandered
  Through the world far and wide
  Seeking some solace
  For dreams that had died

Long did I linger
  In an alien land
  Till tears finally left me
  As I stood on the strand...

I played that song so often that it felt like it was part of my fingers.

Anyway, our job was to try to figure out how we could help New England win the war. So we talked a lot about weapons. They knew about rifles and gunpowder in this world, as we had found out right away, and they used cannons. But they didn't have anything more sophisticated than that. We tried to think of stuff from our world they might be able to use—something short of nuclear bombs and that sort of thing. I came up with hand grenades, and the professor made some notes as I described them. Kevin remembered about landmines, although neither of us was exactly sure how they worked. The professor winced and made a lot more notes. It was obvious that he wasn't enjoying this. "Demanding that young boys think about such things," he sighed. "It is deeply depressing."

Kevin and I didn't really mind. We didn't want to make the professor feel bad, but this was kind of interesting. "It's all about winning the war," Kevin pointed out. "Like the lieutenant said."

"Yes, I'm sure," the professor said, shaking his head. "At such a cost, though."

Lieutenant Carmody showed up after a few days, on horseback instead of being driven by Peter. "You boys are looking well," he said when he saw us. "And professor, how are you getting along with these lads?"

"They're excellent company," the professor replied. "Our task, however, is not a pleasant one."

"I'm not aware of anyone who thinks that war is pleasant," the lieutenant said. "But tell me what you've come up with."

We sat by the barn as we had before, and Professor Palmer talked about landmines and such. Lieutenant Carmody didn't look especially impressed. "These devices have been tried already," he said. "The French in particular have worked on them: *fougasses*, they're called. They've never been effective. The problem is keeping the gunpowder dry—once it gets moist, the fougasse won't explode. How does your world deal with that problem?" he asked us.

We didn't have a clue. "I don't think they're even made from gunpowder anymore," Kevin said. "They probably have dynamite in them or something."

"And what is 'dynamite'?"

There was that question again. Yet another word that was so familiar to us and totally strange to them. But, as usual, the concept behind the word wasn't quite familiar enough. Neither of us could tell the lieutenant what exactly dynamite was.

"All right," he said after we'd talked about weapons for a while longer. "I need more, I'm afraid. Professor, perhaps you've been focusing too much on the obvious. Let's try again. But time runs short. The Portuguese have reached the fortifications south of the city, and for all intents and purposes the siege has begun."

"How much longer do we have, William?" the professor asked.

"I don't know. I'll return in a few days, and we'll discuss the situation then. Keep working."

Professor Palmer didn't look happy after the lieutenant had left. "William's right, of course," he muttered. "Perhaps we must simplify. Get back to first principles."

"You mean like gravity?" Kevin asked.

I half-expected the professor to say: *And what is gravity?* But it turned out Sir Isaac Newton had lived in this world, and they knew about gravity and the laws of motion and all that stuff. "Perhaps gravity," he replied. "Or something equally basic. I don't know. Perhaps we should just talk."

He seemed kind of discouraged. I think his heart really wasn't in it. But then that night Kevin came up with something, just sitting in front of the big kitchen fireplace and watching the smoke go up the chimney.

"Hot-air balloons!" he exclaimed.

Professor Palmer looked at him, and then asked the usual question. "And what is a hot-air balloon?"

"My parents gave me a ride in one once as a birthday present," Kevin said. Not the kind of present my mother would ever have given me. "Hot air rises—you know that, right? Because heating the air makes it expand and become lighter. As it expands, it can push things up." He crumpled up a piece of paper and threw it onto the fire. A few of the ashes rose up the chimney along with the smoke. "So with hot-air balloons," he went on, "you have this huge, like, spherical cloth, and there's a flame underneath it so you can heat the air inside the sphere. And there's this big wicker basket attached where people can stand, and it rises with the balloon. If you want the make the balloon go higher or lower, you adjust the flame. It's really cool."

The professor looked puzzled. "Cool? How can the flame be cool?"

Kevin shook his head and explained what cool meant.

"Well then, yes," the professor said, "I agree that it is really 'cool.'" He stroked his beard, then started peppering Kevin with questions. "Can you steer a balloon?"

"A little bit. You have to catch air currents going one way or another. Someone went around the world in a balloon, I think."

"What is the balloon made out of?"

"I'm not sure. Nylon or something—you probably don't have any of that."

"Silk!" I put in, happy to be able to contribute. "In the old days they used silk. I remember seeing a show about balloons on the History Channel. The North used them in the Civil War to check out enemy positions. They were attached to the ground with a long rope so they wouldn't float away."

Professor Palmer took a pencil and started sketching what a balloon looked like. "There are clearly some practical issues here," he said, "but yes, this is interesting. We'll see what William has to say."

So that was pretty good. And another idea came the next afternoon, as we sat on the front porch during a thunderstorm. We started talking about electricity. There hadn't been a Benjamin Franklin in this world, but they did understand lightning; they just hadn't made much use of what they knew about electricity. We had already talked about electrical power and electric lights, but we hadn't talked about the basics. Now we started describing some of the experiments we did in science class, and that got Professor Palmer scribbling furiously. "Yes, of course," he said. "Storing and controlling it. What were the words again?"

"Batteries?" Kevin said. "Generators?"

"Yes, yes. And the electricity runs along wires…"

"I don't know how they work," I said, "but I think there are electric fences—to keep animals in. The cow or whatever touches the fence and gets a shock, and that teaches him to stay away from the fence."

"Electric fences," the professor said. "Remarkable. If they keep animals in, would they keep soldiers out?"

"I don't see why not. But you need to generate the power."

"Yes, of course."

More writing, as the rain came pouring down. I thought of the people in the camp, with only the shelter of their wagons. We've been very lucky, I thought. I wondered if our luck would hold.

Maybe Lieutenant Carmody would send us back to the camp when he'd gotten whatever he could out of us. Or maybe the Portuguese and Canadians would attack tomorrow, and then what? Even if New England somehow won the war, what would happen to us next month, next year, if we couldn't find the portal, and we ended up stuck here forever?

A couple of days later Lieutenant Carmody returned, looking preoccupied and worried. This time we sat around the dining room table, and Professor Palmer brought out his notes and drawings. As usual, the lieutenant listened carefully, then asked a lot of tough questions. I couldn't tell if he was happy with what we had come up with or disgusted with the time he had wasted on us. After a while he simply nodded and said, "Right. Let's go back to Boston."

"Why the devil do we have to go to Boston?" the professor asked.

"To talk to General Aldridge. He's at the fortifications in Brighton. Along the River Road past the new refugee camp."

"Does that mean you like our ideas?" I asked.

"That means General Aldridge won't chew my head off for wasting his time on them. Now let's go, if you please. There's a war on, as one of our more discerning senior officers likes to point out."

Professor Palmer didn't act pleased, though. "I don't see why Aldridge can't come here," he grumbled. Secretly, though, I think he was kind of relieved. He went and changed into a white shirt and a long gray coat, and then we went outside, hitched up Susie to his carriage, and headed off to Boston, with Lieutenant Carmody leading the way on his horse. The professor's carriage wasn't as fancy as the one Peter drove; it was open and smaller, and a whole lot bouncier as we went over the bumps and ruts of the Massachusetts Road. But it was kind of fun to be going somewhere for a change.

Like the lieutenant said, there was another camp now along the Charles, just past the bridge. We saw hundreds of people there as we passed by. "Poor wretches," the professor muttered. "Things get worse by the day."

Eventually the river bent away from us to the right, and that's where the fortifications started. Looking at them got the professor muttering some more. "How do they expect to keep the enemy out with earthworks and palisades?"

They really didn't appear all that impressive. Maybe I'd seen too many movies, but it seemed like any good-sized army should have been able to overrun those pointed stakes and piles of dirt. After a while we reached an area where the fortifications were still being constructed, and I spotted General Aldridge talking to a bunch of other officers. He looked even sloppier than he had the other time I'd seen him. He hadn't shaved in a while, and a small unlit cigar was clenched between his teeth, just like it had been the first time we met him.

We pulled up next to him and got out of the carriage. "What a colossal waste of time, Solomon," Professor Palmer said to him. "Why don't we invite the Canadians over, hand them the keys to the city, and be done with it?"

"Good afternoon to you too, Alexander," General Aldridge replied. He looked at us. "Runs, er, struck in," he said to Kevin.

"Runs batted in," Kevin corrected him.

The general nodded. "Of course. Certainly. How could I forget?" Then he turned to Lieutenant Carmody. "Well, Lieutenant, I suppose you have your reasons for subjecting me to this paragon of courtesy?" he asked, gesturing at the professor.

"Sir, can you spare a few moments?" the lieutenant replied.

The general waved the other officers away and had an orderly produce a few chairs for us. When we had sat down, the lieutenant continued. "They have a couple of ideas, sir, that it would be well for us to consider." And he started talking about some of the things we had come up with—mostly the balloons and the electric fences. Professor Palmer and Kevin and I jumped in with comments and corrections while the general listened in silence.

"Balloons," he murmured when we were done. He made it sound like a word in a foreign language—which, I guess, it sort of was. "Electricity. And we have no idea if any of this will work?"

"The ideas have a sound theoretical basis," the professor replied. "As for their practical application, that is a question of time and resources."

"We have precious little of either," the general pointed out.

"Then we should start preparing for the surrender ceremony instead," Professor Palmer said. "President Gardner is very good at ceremonies. I'm sure it will be memorable."

That got a laugh out of General Aldridge. "What is it that you need?" he asked.

"Silk, and lots of it," the professor replied. "Copper wire—even more of that. Experienced carpenters, machinists, seamstresses, and blacksmiths. Munitions experts. Sir Henry Bolles. James Carlton—I believe he's staying at the Somerset Club. Professor Harold Foster—he's probably drunk in a ditch somewhere, but no one knows more about electricity. We will need open land. And we will need to be left alone."

The general lifted an eyebrow. "Are you sure that's all?" he asked. "How about some gold ingots? Perhaps a shipload of molasses? A deserted island in the West Indies?"

"Most amusing," the professor replied. "It may in fact not be all. But it is a start."

The general took the cigar out of his mouth and looked at Lieutenant Carmody. "Well?"

"The landmines and grenades and the like—I'm dubious that we can accomplish much with them," he replied. "I'm intrigued by the reconnaissance potential of these balloons. As for the electric fences, they would of course have some tactical value, depending on how powerful they can be made. But there's more, sir."

"What's that?"

"Surprise. Terror. Dismay. Some of the soldiers who saw that lad's watch thought it was the work of the devil. What will our enemies think if they see flying devices used against them? They may think: If we can do these things, what other wonders do we have in store? What will that do to their morale, their will to defeat us?"

The general nodded slowly. "Yes, it's always good to have the devil on your side," he said. "It will be difficult to keep this secret from the president, I fear."

"Undoubtedly. He need not make the connection with the boys, though, if that's your concern."

"I suppose." General Aldridge sat there for a moment, staring into space. Then suddenly he flung his cigar onto the ground and stood up. "Lieutenant, get them what they need," he ordered. "Let's make this happen, and the president be damned."

Lieutenant Carmody leaped to his feet. "Yes, sir."

The general looked at the professor and the two of us and shook his head. "An odd crew to entrust with the future of our nation. But beggars can't be choosers. Fare you well."

He turned and walked back to the fortifications.

"Well, then," the lieutenant said to us. "I believe we have some work to do."

CHAPTER 12

Things changed once the meeting with General Aldridge was over. We all went back to army headquarters, and Lieutenant Carmody and Professor Palmer had a long meeting to figure out what they needed to do. Kevin and I just hung around in the courtyard, wondering what was going to happen next.

"They wouldn't just get rid of us now, would they?" Kevin asked.

"No way. We're too valuable."

"Why? They've got what they need from us."

"But they'll want more, won't they?" I pointed out. "I think we'll be okay."

Kevin didn't look reassured. Luckily, Peter came along and made us forget about our problems for a while. "How are your zippers, mates?" he asked us, grinning.

"Don't have 'em anymore," I replied. "It's hard getting used to these buttons."

"I bet it is. The lieutenant is very interested in you lads, you know."

Peter pronounced the word "loo-tenant."

"What do you think of Lieutenant Carmody?" Kevin asked.

"Oh, he's a good enough sort," Peter replied. "Plenty ambitious. I expect he'll be president one of these days, assuming we still have a president, so you want to stay downwind of him."

I didn't know exactly what that meant, but I think I got the idea. The lieutenant and Professor Palmer came out a little while later, looking serious. "Lots to be done, lads," Lieutenant Carmody said. "You'll stay the night here and return to Cambridge in the morning. Be sure to remain quiet about where you come from. No tales of portals and alternate universes and such. If it comes up, say you were cabin boys on a pirate ship that visited China. People will believe anything about China. Is that clear?"

"Yes, sir," I said.

"Will we be doing anything to help?" Kevin asked.

"Of course you will," Professor Palmer replied. "We just have to get organized first." He seemed to understand that we were worried. "If we actually manage to win this dreadful war, lads," he pointed out, "you'll be heroes."

That was a good thought, although it wasn't clear how we'd be heroes if we were supposed to keep everything secret. Anyway, we went back to the hot attic room where we had spent the night before meeting Professor Palmer for the first time, and we waited for the professor and the lieutenant to do their business in the city. Early the next morning we returned to Cambridge with the professor. In the barn, the chickens and the pigs were hungry and the cow needed milking, and it almost (but not really) felt like we were coming home.

We took over the cricket fields at Harvard for our work. Lieutenant Carmody was worried about the Canadians pushing into Cambridge unexpectedly, but here we had the space and the privacy we needed, so he decided to take the risk. Equipment and people started arriving almost immediately, and the professor spent a lot of time talking with the experts he'd brought in to help. Most of them started out pretty dubious about the whole thing, but his reputation kept them at it.

The balloons turned out to be the most straightforward thing we attempted. It was easy enough to start with toy models and then get bigger as people started to understand the idea. One tricky part was figuring out the right way to control heating the air to make the balloons rise. That was pretty much a matter of trial and error. Another problem was creating the big wicker baskets, which involved finding willow trees and reeds in the city. To obtain the silk for the full-size balloons they held a drive to get all the upper-class ladies in the city to hand over their old dresses, telling them they were for bandages. The results looked kind of strange, but they worked.

The electricity business was harder. It was a good thing Kevin had been paying attention when Mrs. DiGenova did the electricity unit in the fifth grade—of course, that was the sort of thing Kevin liked. I remembered about copper being a good conductor, but I had sure forgotten about zinc in batteries, and I had also forgotten how you could transform the energy in, like, waterfalls or even pedaling bikes into electricity.

Luckily, they found Professor Foster—the guy Professor Palmer thought would be drunk in a ditch somewhere. I don't know if he was an alcoholic, but he was really strange. He was very tall, with frizzy brown hair and the palest skin I'd ever seen. Someone called him a walking mushroom, and that seemed like a pretty good description. But the big thing was, he loved electricity. It seemed to him to be the most wonderful, mysterious thing in creation. Lieutenant Carmody didn't want us talking to most of the people who were involved in the projects, but he agreed to let Professor Foster meet with us.

We described batteries to him and he seemed to catch on immediately. "Yes, yes, an array of capacitors!" he shouted. "Leyden jars connected in parallel!"

I had no idea what he was talking about. He brought Professor Palmer, Lieutenant Carmody, Kevin, and me to his laboratory, which was located in a shed behind his house in Cambridge. It was a dusty place filled with pieces of metal, wires, and bottles of chemicals. He showed us a jar lined with foil. At the top of the jar was a ball connected to a shaft. "Do you see?" he said. "You use the ball of sulfur to rotate the shaft like so—"

"—and the electrical charge builds up in the foil," Kevin said.

"Exactly!" Professor Foster exclaimed. "What a brilliant boy!" He turned to the lieutenant. "Would you like to touch the foil?"

Lieutenant Carmody didn't appear eager to do it, but he reached his hand into the jar and, sure enough, got a shock.

"You see, the current moved from the foil to your hand," the professor explained.

"I built one of these in my basement," Kevin said while the lieutenant rubbed his hand.

"Remarkable! Stupendous!"

"Can we kill people with this?" the lieutenant asked.

That shut everyone up for a minute.

"Lightning kills," Professor Foster said finally, in a much lower tone. "We cannot capture the power of lightning."

"But these boys—"

"All I know about is the electric fence," I said. "The electricity runs along the wires and just gives you a shock if you touch it." But I really wasn't so sure about that. I thought about the electric fence in *Jurassic Park* and how powerful it was. Could they do something like that here?

"An electric fence would be a sight better than Aldridge's foolish mounds of earth and pointed sticks," Professor Palmer pointed out to the lieutenant.

"It all depends on the charge we can build up, store in the battery—what an evocative name!—and then transmit along the wire," Professor Foster said. He absently turned the shaft in the jar. "Copper and zinc," he muttered, "copper and zinc…There are practical difficulties, I suppose."

"We have six weeks," the lieutenant said. "Eight at the outside. Any longer than that, and your work will be useless."

This seemed to fluster him completely. "Oh, my. I don't see how…well, perhaps…"

The lieutenant looked at Professor Palmer.

"I will work with Bartholomew," the professor said. "If it can be done, we will do it."

Lieutenant Carmody nodded, satisfied. "Let's get started, then."

Professor Palmer explained to us about his friend later, when we were back home for the night. "Electricity has never been taken seriously, I fear. I have seen those jars used as an entertainment at parties—young ladies think it quite daring to put their hands inside and receive a shock. So Bartholomew's interest in electricity has always seemed bizarre, almost amusing, to most people. To have it become part of the effort to win the war—well, it's a bit much for him to take in."

He set up the chess board to play Kevin. I sat down at the piano and started playing "Take Me Out to the Ballgame".

"Do you think we we'll be able to win the war?" Kevin asked.

"I'm not a soldier, thank God," the professor replied. "I have no idea what it will take to win militarily. But I do know that we cannot win if we lack the will—if we believe the cause is hopeless and victory impossible. That is the current situation, thanks to our president's ineptitude. Right now it is just a matter of counting out the days to our defeat and hoping it will be as painless as possible. But defeat is never entirely painless. Speaking of defeat, I would be paying particular attention to your rook, if I were you."

"But that could be changing, right?" Kevin asked. "I mean, the attitude."

"Let us hope so. Let us hope."

"Larry, do you notice how we're saying 'we' now?" Kevin asked me that night in our room.

"Huh?"

"When we talk about this place—about New England. Used to be we'd say, 'Are you going to win?' Now it's, 'Are we going to win?'"

I thought about that. "You're right," I said. "We're part of it now."

"Not that I'm not thinking about home, you know?" he went on. "It's just—we're here. This is it."

"When the war is over," I said, "all we have to do is go back to Glanbury and find the portal."

"Yeah. If we survive. If we're not, like, sold into slavery or something."

"We'll survive. We'll win. We'll get back there."

"Yeah, I know."

Home. I realized I hadn't been thinking about it as much lately. My fights with Cassie, my annoyance with Matthew and Mom and Stinky Glover…all that stuff was starting to seem kind of far away now. We had a war to win. And in the meantime, I was getting used to going to the privy, to lighting candles and oil lamps, to living without TV, even to eating watery porridge and salt pork.

Home.

I fell asleep on my lumpy mattress, and my dreams were strange and confused.

After a few weeks General Aldridge came to Cambridge to check on our progress. The hot-air balloons were going well. We had a small prototype that was tethered to the cricket field by a fifty-foot rope. It looked kind of goofy, stitched together out of all those different-colored dresses, but it worked. The general peered up at it as it floated above him. "People can fly in that contraption?" he asked.

"After a fashion," Lieutenant Carmody replied.

The general laughed. "If that doesn't scare the Portuguese, nothing will."

As Lieutenant Carmody had expected, we had been less successful with the stuff we were trying to do with gunpowder. Nobody had a solution for the moisture problem, least of all Kevin and me. General Aldridge talked with the munitions guys, and then said, "No sense wasting time. Pack up and return to your units."

Then there was electricity. Professor Foster had moved his equipment from his shed to a larger building near the cricket fields. He was so excited to be explaining his work that he was practically bouncing off the walls. "The electrical fluid moves along the wire," he said, showing the apparatus he had set up. "The side that gains fluid acquires a vitreous charge. The side that loses fluid acquires a resinous charge. According to my calculations, the force between the charge varies inversely as the square of the distance. So it follows that—"

"Touch the wire," Lieutenant Carmody said.

General Aldridge looked at him. "What?"

"Touch the wire, sir," the lieutenant repeated.

The general hesitated, and then reached out and grabbed the wire. "Drat, that smarts!" he shouted, jumping back and glaring at the lieutenant.

Professor Foster clapped his hands in glee. "You see?" he said. "You see? A fundamental force of the universe, under our control. Isn't it marvelous?"

That started a barrage of questions from the general. How much electricity could you store? How far would it travel along the wire? What happened if the wire broke? Professor Foster answered as well as he could.

"That's good," General Aldridge said finally. "That's very good. Lieutenant, we need to talk about deployment."

"Yes, sir."

We all walked out of the building. I was pretty happy. Professor Foster looked like he was about to levitate with joy.

Outside, a soldier in a fancy red-and-gold uniform was waiting on a large black horse. He was wearing a big hat with an even bigger white plume on top. When he saw us he dismounted, stuck the hat under his left arm, and saluted the general. "Message, sir," he said. "The honor of a reply is requested."

General Aldridge didn't look happy. Neither did the lieutenant. The soldier took a letter out of his pocket and handed it to the general. He broke the seal, opened it, and studied it for a moment before handing it back. "All right," he muttered.

The soldier hesitated. "Is that your answer, sir?"

"Of course it is, you dimwit," the general exploded. "Now begone!"

The soldier hastily got back onto his horse and rode off.

"Er, bad news?" Professor Foster asked.

General Aldridge glared at him for a moment, and then shrugged. "Depends on one's point of view, I suppose," he said. "My presence is required at Coolidge Palace."

"Well, uh, that doesn't sound—"

"Gardner knows," Professor Palmer said.

General Aldridge nodded. "Yes, apparently he knows."

"But surely he can't complain about—"

"You're invited as well," the general said. "And the boys. He knows about the boys. He wants all work stopped until he's met them." He looked at us. "You're in luck, lads," he said. "You're about to meet His Excellency, the President of the United States of New England."

CHAPTER 13

"The man's an idiot," Professor Palmer said. "We won't go."

General Aldridge scratched his chin. "I may have my disagreements with the president, but I fear he's no idiot. In any case, you have no choice. This wasn't an invitation, Alexander; it was a summons."

"Why can't we just bring him out here and show him what we've accomplished?" Kevin asked.

"One must first persuade him that it's worth the trip," the general replied. "Lieutenant, see that they get to the palace. If Professor Palmer gives you any trouble, arrest him or something. I'll follow along presently."

"Yes, sir." Lieutenant Carmody turned to us. "Let's go, then, shall we?"

The lieutenant didn't have his carriage, so we all piled into Professor Palmer's. He decided we needed to improve our appearance, so we stopped back at the house, cleaned up, and borrowed a couple of the professor's dressy white shirts. They were about the right size for me, but way too big for Kevin. Lieutenant Carmody thought it was an improvement, though.

The professor, meanwhile, was still in a snit. "Everything is wasted—science, planning, courage—without political wisdom," he said.

"We elected the president," Lieutenant Carmody pointed out.

"Not with my vote. He promised us a stronger New England. And now with his reckless adventurism he has all but destroyed it."

The lieutenant wasn't interested in what the professor had to say about President Gardner. He just wanted to get us to Coolidge Palace. Once we had changed, we got back in the carriage and hurried off to Boston.

It was twilight by the time we crossed the bridge into the city. Things were looking worse. Many of the trees I had seen there on the trip to Cambridge had been chopped down—for firewood, I guess; the smoke from the fires in the refugee camp stung my eyes. The smell of sewage was almost unbearable. There were fewer people on the streets, but those who were out looked tired and hungry. More than one of them rushed up to the carriage with hands outstretched, begging for food. We didn't stop.

In our world, I'd gone into Boston a couple of times to visit the Massachusetts State House, a big brick building with a gold dome at the top of Beacon Hill. Here, there was more than one hill in the center of the city, and the president lived in a mansion at the top of the middle hill. This was Coolidge Palace—named, I found out, after the first president of New England, Sir Calvin Coolidge. I remembered him as a not-so-important president in our world, so that struck me as really strange. But I didn't say anything about it.

We drove up to the front gate, which was guarded by stern-looking soldiers with those silly plumes in their hats. Lieutenant Carmody got out of the carriage and talked to one of them, who came up and looked at us suspiciously. He wrote down our names, then opened the gates and let us through.

It was like going through the portal again—this time entering a serene, lovely world where nothing was out of place. As we drove up the gravel drive to the large granite building we saw one groundskeeper sweeping leaves off the immaculate lawn, another trimming a bush that was so perfectly shaped it looked artificial.

"No refugees allowed near Coolidge Palace," Professor Palmer muttered. "Wouldn't do."

At the front steps a groom took Professor Palmer's carriage, and then a tall man in a bright green suit wearing a long white wig escorted us up the steps and opened the door for us. I thought I caught him sneering at Kevin and me, in our crufty pants and shoes, but I couldn't be sure. This was the first time I'd ever seen anyone in a wig for real, and I almost burst out laughing. He led us along a couple of corridors lined with portraits of people I didn't recognize, and finally deposited us in a small room whose walls were painted with scenes of pretty shepherdesses tending flocks of sheep. He instructed us to wait there until summoned, and then he left.

"Waste of time," the professor said.

Lieutenant Carmody gave us instructions about how to act in front of the president. Give a small bow when you're introduced, speak only when spoken to, throw in lots of Your Excellency's. He looked like he was right at home in the palace.

Eventually the guy in the green suit led in General Aldridge. He had shaved and put on a clean uniform, although the way he wore it, it still managed to look rumpled. At least he wasn't chewing on a cigar. He sat in one of the overstuffed armchairs and folded his arms. "His Excellency is dining this evening with the British ambassador and friends," he said. "I expect that we are the entertainment."

"What's the game?" Lieutenant Carmody asked. "Is he trying to embarrass you?"

"Perhaps. Show that he's still in charge."

"He could simply discharge you."

"At the risk of having half his cabinet resign," General Aldridge pointed out. "Lord Percival would certainly object, as would some of the others. At any rate, the president can't afford a political crisis now. And he can't afford to make me too angry."

Professor Palmer seemed to pick up on this. "The soldiers respect you, Solomon," he said, "and they don't respect Gardner. They'll follow you, if you decide to—"

The general raised a hand. "Rebellion is not an option," he replied in a stern voice.

"But surrender is?"

"None of us can guarantee victory," the general replied. "Even with electricity on our side."

"How do you think the president found out about us?" Kevin asked.

"The president has spies everywhere, and there are many people working on our projects. Apparently Cambridge wasn't far enough away to keep them secret from him. I didn't really think it would be. As for you boys—it isn't clear what he knows about you, other than your existence. So I think we should just find out."

We fell silent and waited some more. Night fell, and I got hungry. I started to wonder if this was some kind of punishment, and we weren't really going to see anybody after all. Then at last the guy in the green suit returned, and we walked down another fancy corridor. He opened a set of big double doors, and we were ushered into the presence of the president of New England.

General Aldridge went in first, and the rest of us followed. We were in a large dining room with high ceilings and walls covered with more portraits of men wearing wigs. A bunch of people were seated at a long table, eating dinner. My stomach growled as I caught the aroma of roast beef. A fat, red-faced man sat at the head of the table, digging into his food like he was afraid any minute the Portuguese would swoop down and grab it away from him. He was wearing a black coat, a white ruffled shirt, and a short wig. Sweat poured down his face. When he noticed us he waved a fork at General Aldridge. "Solomon," he said, "I hear these boys are your new military advisers." He had a strange, high-pitched voice.

The remark didn't seem very funny to me, but the men and women at the table gave it a big laugh. Most of the men wore black suits, like the president. The women wore fancy gowns and lots of jewelry; their hair was piled up so high on top of their heads I thought they might lose their balance.

General Aldridge smiled and bowed. "Your Excellency," he said, "nowadays I take advice wherever I can get it."

"Odd you can't get good advice from your highly trained staff. You've met the Earl of Chatham, Solomon?"

The general bowed to the guy on the president's right, a short man with huge ears that stuck out from his wig. "Mr. Ambassador, good to see you again."

The earl nodded back with a little smile. He didn't seem to be enjoying himself.

"You," the president said, pointing his fork at Kevin, "where are you from, boy?"

Kevin remembered to bow; I'm not sure I would have. "From Glanbury, Your Excellency," he said.

The president chuckled. "Glanbury? When has anything useful come out of that godforsaken village?" More laughter from the table. The president speared a hunk of roast beef and stuck it into his mouth, looking satisfied with himself. "And you are full of advice for General Aldridge?"

"Not really, Your Excellency. We're just staying with Professor Palmer."

"I hear differently," the president replied. "I am told there are very strange doings over in Cambridge."

"We are attempting to develop—" General Aldridge began.

"I know exactly what you're attempting to do," the president interrupted. "We're besieged by our enemies, winter is setting in, and you're devoting precious time and manpower to projects suggested to you by ten-year-olds?"

I wanted to yell at him that Kevin and I were both teenagers, practically, but I managed to restrain myself.

"Come and see for yourself, Your Excellency," the general offered calmly.

President Gardner waved away the suggestion and speared another hunk of roast beef with his knife. "Mr. Ambassador," he said, turning to the earl next to him. "What is the message you delivered to me today, smuggled in from your superiors in London at great risk?"

The earl shifted in his seat and looked uncomfortable. "Excellency," he said, "I think it more suitable for—"

"Come, Cecil, we are all friends here," the president insisted.

People around the table grew quiet.

"Sir," the earl began, "His Majesty's government regret that they will be unable to provide assistance to your nation in its current difficulty. Unfortunately, the demands of the war in Europe preclude—"

"Thank you, Cecil, we all understand about the demands of war," the president said. He motioned to a servant to refill his glass with wine. The earl looked down at his plate.

"Sir," General Aldridge said to the president, "this is unhappy news. But it simply means that we have all the more reason to press ahead with our efforts."

"It means what I say it means," the president retorted. And he stuffed a large chunk of beef into his mouth. I looked at General Aldridge. He had turned red. I imagined it was all he could do to keep his temper. I had no idea how Professor Palmer was keeping his.

I looked back at the president, and his face was red, too. Then he stood up. One hand reached for his throat, the other reached for his wine, but knocked it over. He tried to say something, but nothing came out.

He was choking on his meat.

The people at the table started shouting out instructions. One of the servants came over and pounded the president on the back. Didn't help. His eyes were bulging now, and his face was the color of a rotten tomato. He gestured wildly, hitting one of the servants who was trying to loosen his collar.

That's when I figured I should do something.

Mom made me take a first aid course in fifth grade. It had never come in handy till that instant.

I went up behind the president—no one seemed to notice me. He was doubled over now, still clutching at his throat. I shoved a lady out of the way, then wrapped my arms around him, put my hands together, and pushed up on his chest.

The first push didn't work. I could feel people grabbing at me now, trying to pull me away, but I managed to try again. And this time the piece of meat popped out of the president's mouth.

People dragged me away from him then, and I didn't see what happened next. I was afraid some security guy was going to shoot me, but eventually they let me go and then got out of the way, and President Gardner stood facing me. His face was still red and splotchy, but at least he didn't look like he was going to keel over. At least he was breathing.

"You were the one?" he demanded. "You saved me?"

I nodded.

"How did you learn how that—that thing you just did?"

"We know how to do a few things in Glanbury," I said. "Your Excellency."

Kind of a wisecrack, I know, but he had made a wisecrack about my home town. He stared at me, and I wondered if he was going to have me beheaded or something. And then he threw his head back and laughed. "Very well, then," he said. "Your village is apparently not as benighted as I had imagined." He picked up a glass of wine. "A toast—to Glanbury!"

That kind of broke the tension. The president ordered places to be set for all of us, so we got to eat some of that roast beef. Which was good, because I was just about starving at that point. The servants offered to pour us wine, but Kevin and I asked for milk instead. General Aldridge ate, but he still didn't look happy. Professor Palmer asked me about what I'd done. "Is that something from your world?"

"Uh-huh," I said. "It's called the Heimlich maneuver. I guess you haven't figured it out here."

"Indeed. I wonder if it will change his attitude towards us."

"Can't hurt," Lieutenant Carmody replied. "You know, General Aldridge is right: he's not as incompetent as you think, Professor. He took some gambles during his presidency and lost. But some would say the gambles had to be made, if New England were to survive."

This was more of an opinion than we usually heard the lieutenant offer. But Professor Palmer wasn't buying it. "A real leader would not be locked up behind palace gates," he said, "swilling wine while his countrymen starve."

The lieutenant shrugged. "He has just seen his last gamble fail—reason enough to seek solace. And in any case, little would change if the wine were not drunk."

After the meal was over we got another summons from the green-suited butler. The president wanted to see us all privately. The butler brought us to a big office with lots of bookcases and a fire blazing in a marble fireplace. "Now we'll get down to business," General Aldridge murmured. Lieutenant Carmody, Kevin, and I stayed in the back of the room, while the general and the professor sat in a couple of chairs next to the fire. Eventually the president showed up, followed by a couple of the guys who had been at the dinner. One was tall, dark-haired, and a little stoop-shouldered, as if he had gone through too many doorways that were too small for him. The other one was shorter, with a narrow face and bright eyes; he had taken his wig off, so you could see there were just a few wisps of gray hair on the top of his head. "Vice President Boatner and the Foreign Minister, Lord Percival," Lieutenant Carmody whispered to us.

General Aldridge and Professor Palmer stood as the others entered. "Oh, sit down, sit down," the president said, and he himself sank into one of the chairs by the fire. He looked really tired. The vice president and the foreign minister sat on either side of him. "Anyone care for a brandy?" he asked.

No one did. He sighed and waved the butler out of the room.

"So, would you care to explain about these boys, General?" the president said. "I have heard that they are the spawn of Satan. Seems rather unlikely, from the look of 'em, but what do I know?"

"Nothing as interesting as that, I fear," General Aldridge replied. "They were impressed onto a pirate ship a couple of years ago and spent a good deal of time in China. On the return voyage they escaped and made their way back home to Glanbury, but the Portuguese had overrun the place, so they had to flee to Boston. They are bright lads and picked up a good deal of useful knowledge in the Orient. We are merely trying to take advantage of it amid our current difficulties."

I was impressed by how smoothly the general could lie; he was very convincing. The president shifted in his chair and stared at Kevin and me. "They look no more like pirates than they do the spawn of Satan," he remarked. "But your story is somewhat more plausible, I suppose. Now please tell us what is going on over there in Cambridge."

So General Aldridge went through it all, with some help from Professor Palmer. The president folded his hands over his big belly and closed his eyes. I thought he might be falling asleep, but he opened his eyes every once in a while to ask a good question. The foreign minister asked questions, too, but the vice president stayed silent. The president especially liked the idea of balloons. "Imagine being able to simply float away from this siege," he murmured. "How delightful."

"Nevertheless," the vice president said suddenly, "you should end all this nonsense immediately."

"May I ask why, Randolph?" the general said.

"Because our only hope is in negotiating with the enemy, and if they find out what you are doing, it will simply make the negotiations more difficult."

"Why so? If they find out, I suggest it will incline them to negotiate more seriously, realizing how difficult we are going to make it for them to defeat us."

"It will more likely incline them to end negotiations altogether and attack immediately, before you have a chance to complete your little science experiments."

"They are far more than science experiments," Professor Palmer replied hotly. "They have the capacity to revolutionize the way we conduct warfare."

"We have neither the men nor the munitions to defeat this enemy, now that the British have abandoned us," the vice president insisted. "To believe anything else is arrant nonsense."

The president looked over at the foreign minister. "Benjamin, what say you? Might as well get everyone into the fray."

"Well of course you know I disagree with Randolph," Lord Percival began. He had the most British accent of anyone I'd met so far, except the Earl of Chatham. "We're in a dire situation, I won't deny it. But if the Canadians and Portuguese believe they have such a decisive advantage as Randolph describes, why haven't they attacked already, instead of sitting outside our gates and waiting for us to crumble? They have as much to fear from a long siege as we do. Their supply lines are hopelessly extended, so they have to live off the land—but what supplies will be left for them, by January? And of course the Portuguese soldiers aren't used to the cold, and neither Portuguese nor Canadians are eager to be here in the first place. Their armies may simply melt away if they don't make a decisive move soon.

"Now we have these new developments from Solomon. I say, let them continue. They may be enough to alter the balance. I don't know. If the enemy do find out about them, that's all to the good, in my judgment. Let the enemy worry that they've got in deeper than they'd prepared for. Let them realize that the price for this adventure may be far greater than they are willing to pay."

"Bosh," the vice president retorted. "We all know this will be finished well before January. They are waiting for the moment of maximum preparedness on their side, maximum vulnerability on ours. Then they will strike. And nothing that General Aldridge is doing or can do will change the outcome. We need to negotiate now, and hope we escape with our lives."

President Gardner raised a hand, and everyone fell silent. "You see how clear my advisers make things for me," he said. "Ah, well." He turned to the vice president. "Randolph, make contact with the enemy tomorrow. We begin negotiations for surrender."

The vice president bowed, looking satisfied. "Very well, Your Excellency."

"But Your Excellency—" Professor Palmer began.

The president glared at him, and he fell silent. "Solomon," he said to General Aldridge, "in the meantime, please continue your 'science experiments,' as Randolph calls them. I see no good reason not to continue preparing for the final battle, even if it may not occur."

The general bowed slightly in turn. "Thank you, sir."

The president waved his hand at us. "All right then, you may all go." Everyone got up to leave. As I was headed for the door the president pointed at me. "You, stay a moment, if you please."

I looked at Lieutenant Carmody, who grinned and gave me a little shove back towards the president.

"Sit," the president ordered when everyone was gone.

I sat down next to him.

"Your name?"

"Larry Barnes, Your Excellency."

"Master Barnes, would you like a cigar or a glass of brandy?"

"Uh, no thank you, Your Excellency."

"Odd. I'd think a pirate boy would have developed a taste for tobacco and spirits."

"I'm still a little young, Your Excellency."

"Yes, I suppose so." He leaned back in his chair. "Tell me about China, Master Barnes. I've always had an interest in the place, but I've met so few who have actually travelled there."

Great, I thought. I'm supposed to lie to the president. "Well, it's really…different. Lots of people. In some ways they're, uh, pretty advanced."

"Yes, the electricity, and the—what was it?—the balloons. What else?"

What else? I tried to think what else. "Like, toilets," I said. I explained about flush toilets. That was pretty good. Then I brought up bicycles, because I'd seen a TV show about how everyone in China rides a bicycle. I'd seen a few here, but they were really primitive-looking. Then the president asked me what they ate in China, and I had a good answer for that, too, because we ate Chinese food at home a lot.

President Gardner looked kind of puzzled after a while. "Well, you do seem to know something about China," he said. "It must feel strange to be back here in New England."

"Pretty strange," I agreed. "But I'm getting used to it."

"Yes. Good. Well, I want to thank you for saving my life, Master Barnes. Very fortuitous that you were here tonight."

"My pleasure, Your Excellency."

The president stood, and we shook hands. "Are you sure you wouldn't like a cigar?" he asked.

I was sure.

Outside, General Aldridge had already left, but Lieutenant Carmody, Professor Palmer, and Kevin were waiting for me, eager to know what happened. "We talked about China," I said.

"He doesn't believe our story," the lieutenant remarked.

"Maybe he's not so sure now. I was pretty convincing."

"Good lad," the professor said.

"Too late to return to Cambridge, I'm afraid," the lieutenant said. "Let's go to the barracks. Then back to work in the morning. The stakes are only getting higher."

Kevin and I returned to our old room in the attic. "More interesting than The Gross, huh?" I said, feeling pretty good about my meeting with the president.

"Yeah, but I'd still rather be home."

I lay down on the thin mattress. Kevin was right, of course. But still…it wasn't everyday you save the president's life, and he offers you brandy and a cigar. And that sure beat having to deal with Stinky Glover and your stupid sister.

CHAPTER 14

We returned to Cambridge the next day, and work started up again. Everyone had rumors to spread: that the president was making plans to surrender, that General Aldridge was going to seize power from the president, that the people in the camps were going to riot, break out, and try to take over the government, that the Canadians were about to attack Cambridge…

It was hard to concentrate, but Lieutenant Carmody kept the pressure on. "Work as if your lives depend on it," he told people. "Because they do."

Professor Foster was scared to death of the lieutenant. He was happy to talk about electricity and give little demonstrations for people, but he got very nervous when he actually had to accomplish anything. I got the impression he was drinking heavily. So Professor Palmer spent a lot of time working with him, making sure that he stayed focused on getting things done.

The balloons worked pretty well, except for one thing: they didn't stay up long. It turned out the hot air leaked out of the silk too quickly. Kevin and I didn't know anything about that. Finally someone figured out that they should sort of coat the silk with linseed oil, and that did a good job of stopping up the leaks. People started going up in them, and they were really excited when they came back down. "The grandeur of God's creation is laid out before you," one of them said.

Lieutenant Carmody just wanted to know if they could see the Canadians with their spyglasses.

Kevin and I got to go up, and he had a lot more fun than I did. "This is so cool!" he shouted, as we looked out over the farms and the church steeples and the houses and the distant river. I decided maybe I was afraid of heights.

And then we got the word: the New England troops were retreating from Cambridge. We were going to have to leave too. "Where will we have the space to do our work in Boston?" Professor Palmer wanted to know.

"Only one place with enough room right now," Lieutenant Carmody replied. "The grounds of Coolidge Palace."

"His Excellency doesn't object?"

"He does not. Which isn't to say we won't be capitulating to the enemy tomorrow. Let's get everything packed up. We don't have much time."

"William, Harvest Day is in two days," the professor pointed out. "It would be—well, I would like to celebrate it at home."

"A bit of a risk, Professor."

"I know. But it's important to me."

The lieutenant considered. "Very well," he said, "the troops are scheduled to leave the morning after Harvest Day, unless the Canadians attack first. Be prepared to go with them; otherwise, we'll be unable to guarantee your safety on this side of the river."

Harvest Day. One more thing that was different about this world: the holidays. No trick-or-treating on Halloween. No Thanksgiving at all. They didn't have anything like the customs we had on Christmas, and most people didn't even celebrate it. Harvest Day took place in late October, and it was kind of like Thanksgiving; you ate food you had grown on your farm and celebrated your good fortune in making it through another year.

Needless to say, people weren't feeling very fortunate on this particular Harvest Day. The guys we worked with were mostly soldiers, and they still had enough to eat, but civilians were starting to go hungry in the city, and the food situation was only going to get worse while the siege lasted. People had started to sneak over into Cambridge and break into houses looking for anything they could eat or sell, and the military had had to seal off the bridges trying to keep everyone out. It was getting nasty.

So Professor Palmer wanted to celebrate one last Harvest Day at his home, knowing that it might be a long time, if ever, before he got back there again. And it was really nice that he wanted us to share the holiday with him. Kevin and I spent the day before helping him pack up his important books and papers and loading them into the carriage. We didn't want any part of slaughtering one of the pigs, but he insisted. "If you want to eat the meal, lads, you have to help prepare it." He pointed out that we would have to leave the pigs behind, and either Canadians or wolves would kill them eventually. That didn't make murdering the poor thing any less gross, though. It was a lot more fun churning the butter and baking the apple pie and the bread.

On Harvest Day itself we could hear artillery fire in the distance, and that didn't help the celebration. The reality of having to leave this place had set in, and it wasn't making any of us happy.

The professor began the big meal with a prayer of thanks, but as we ate he got off onto a topic that didn't make us any happier. "It occurs to me," he said, "that if the theory you boys propose is correct, and there are an infinite number of universes, that means there are some in which war doesn't exist, in which people have managed to find a way to live in peace and harmony with one another."

"That's not our universe for sure," Kevin said. "But I guess you're right."

"It's hard to imagine, is it not?" the professor went on. "Once I got used to the idea of a world like yours, I had only a little difficulty in imagining the wonders it might contain—airplanes and automobiles and computers and so on. But imagining a world without war, without hatred, without these endless disputes over who owns each little plot of land…My mind cannot comprehend such a place."

"At least you can't blow the whole planet up, like we can," I pointed out.

"I suppose one should be grateful for that. But I'm sure that someday even we will be able to unlock the secrets behind such weapons. And then…" the professor shrugged. "Perhaps we will find the wisdom to refrain from using them."

But he didn't sound hopeful.

We ate till we were more than full, and then we sat on the professor's front porch and watched the sun set, glowing purple and gold over the horizon. The artillery fire had stopped, and we put aside all depressing thoughts. I still missed my own family and my own world, of course, but I remember wishing that I could hold onto that moment forever, feeling peaceful and well-fed and at least moderately safe in the middle of the war and the hunger and the uncertainty.

But the moment didn't last. That was the night that Kevin got sick.

At first I thought it was part of a nightmare. We went to bed early, knowing we had to leave by dawn. I dreamt I was up in a balloon and the tether had broken. I had no idea how to steer or how to land. Below me, people were calling out instructions, but I couldn't make out what they were saying. I was floating higher and higher into the clouds, more scared than I'd ever been in my life, when finally I managed to make out Kevin's voice, calling faintly to me from far below. "Larry, Larry..."

"Kevin!" I called back, and I fought my way through the clouds until I opened my eyes.

...and realized I was lying on my bed. I sighed with relief, until I heard Kevin call my name again in a faint voice.

"What is it?" I whispered.

"Larry, I don't feel so good," he said weakly. "Could you get the professor?"

I got up and looked at Kevin in the moonlight. He was sweating, even though it was cold in the room, and his eyes glittered. He looked frightened. I felt his forehead; it was burning hot. "Be right back," I said. I went and roused Professor Palmer. When we got back to the room, Kevin was on his knees, throwing up into the chamber pot.

"Get a bucket of water and a cloth, Larry," the professor ordered. "Quickly."

I rushed downstairs to the kitchen, and all I could think was *drikana*.

No cure. You feel like you're vomiting your entire insides out. You die within a couple of days.

No cure.

If there was any immunity to drikana—or any other diseases in this world—Kevin and I didn't have it.

When I got back to the room with the cloth, Kevin was in bed again, shivering. The professor was leaning over him. He took the cloth from me and put it over Kevin's forehead.

"Is he going to be all right?" I asked.

The professor looked up at me. "I don't know, Larry," he said softly. "I don't know if any of us is going to be all right."

"Is it—is it—?" I couldn't bring myself to say its name.

The professor nodded. "I think so, yes."

"I want to go home," Kevin moaned. "I want my mom."

"It's all right, Kevin," I said. "It's all right."

"Please let me go home. Please."

I was scared out of my mind. "What do we do, Professor?" I asked. "Can we help him?"

He handed me the cloth. "Keep him cool, Larry," he said. "I'll be right back."

Aspirin, I thought. Tylenol. Motrin. There was none of that stuff in this world. Just a wet cloth on the forehead for someone who was burning up with fever. Kevin threw up some more, and the stench was bad, but I couldn't leave him. After a couple of minutes the professor returned, and he was carrying a basin and a scalpel. "What are you going to do?" I demanded.

"I have to bleed him, Larry. It is the only way to evacuate the noxious humors."

"No!" I screamed. "That's nuts!"

He hesitated. "It's the standard treatment," he said.

"I don't care. They stopped bleeding people, like, hundreds of years ago. It doesn't work. It's just a superstition."

"Larry," he said, "you have to trust me. You don't have this disease in your world. We've lived with it for five hundred years."

"And you haven't cured it. You don't know a thing about it. You don't know a thing about medicine. You're not bleeding Kevin."

I don't know how I got the nerve to stand up to him—the famous Harvard professor—but I did. He wasn't going to touch my friend with that scalpel.

We stared at each other for a minute, and then Professor Palmer put the scalpel and basin down. And somehow I knew what he was thinking: smallpox. Vaccinations. Our world could have saved his wife and son. We knew more than he did.

"Thank you, sir," I said.

"Let us pray that you are right, Larry," he replied. "In any event, we must keep him clean and cool. If he can sleep, that would be best. The crisis will be over, one way or the other, within forty-eight hours."

"There's no other medicine we can give him?"

The professor shook his head. "None that have any efficacy. In any case, his stomach cannot tolerate anything. He may be able to sip water, that's all."

In our world, Kevin would have been in an ambulance by now, heading for a hospital. Here, even if there were a hospital around somewhere, the trip in the professor's carriage over the bumpy roads would have killed him. I was going to have to take care of him, along with the professor. I was going to have to help him live.

I guess that was the worst night of my life—worse, even, than that first night in this world, back in the brig with Chester. To see Kevin suffer, and not be able to do anything about it…The vomiting continued, and then the diarrhea started, and a little while later convulsions…Before long Kevin wasn't begging to go home, he was begging to die. "Please, Larry, please! Stop the pain! Stop the pain!"

I held his hand. "You're going to make it, Kevin! You will!" And I was thinking: *Don't leave me alone here, Kevin. I need you!*

After that he must have been delirious, because what he was saying didn't make any sense at all. And then he was too weak to say anything.

I must have fallen asleep eventually, because when I opened my eyes it was gray outside. I was kneeling next to Kevin, and his hand was lying on my arm. His eyes were closed. At first I thought he might be dead, but then I could see his chest go up and down, just a little bit, and I relaxed. He was sleeping, and that was good.

I heard a banging sound coming from outside, so I went downstairs to investigate.

The professor was on the front porch, nailing something onto one of the white columns. "Is Kevin still asleep?" he asked.

"Uh-huh. What are you doing?" I asked.

He motioned to me to take a look. It was a big red "C" painted on a board. "A notice of claustration," he said.

"What's that?"

"It tells the world there is a drikana patient inside. By law and custom, no one can leave this place for seven days."

So, *claustration* was their word for "quarantine." Seven days, I thought. "But the Canadians are coming!" I said. "We were supposed to leave this morning."

"We can't go anywhere now, I'm afraid."

"We'll be trapped," I said. "They'll take us prisoner."

"Larry, we can only hope that is the worst that happens to us."

I shuddered. The professor finished putting up the sign, and we went inside. He had already made some tea, so we had a cup by the fireplace. "So what happens next?" I asked him.

"When Kevin awakens, the vomiting will likely start all over again," he replied. "If it's worse, it'll continue to get worse, and he will probably die by nightfall. If it's better, not so intense, that's a good sign, and he may survive. If he's still alive tomorrow, that's a very good sign."

"What are his odds?"

"Half the people who come down with the disease die of it. The odds are a little better if you are young and healthy."

So, fifty-fifty. Some hope for Kevin. But then there was the question that had been lurking in my mind, too scary to ask. Now it was time to ask it. "What about—what about us? Are we going to come down with the disease?"

"I don't know, Larry. I've been around the disease many times but never contracted it. Perhaps for some reason I have that immunity you talk about. As for you—who knows? I wish I could give you a better answer, but I can't."

"But we've already been exposed, right? If we're going to get it, we're going to get it."

"That's right. There's nothing we can do about it at this point."

"What does it feel like, when it starts?"

"They say it starts with dizziness, like the world won't stop spinning around you. And then you become nauseated and feverish. And finally the vomiting begins."

I closed my eyes. Did I feel dizzy? I didn't think so. Were there germs already inside me, getting ready to kill me? There was no way of telling. I opened my eyes. The professor was looking at me. He reached over and put a hand on my shoulder. "I'm sorry, Larry," he said. And then I buried my face in his chest and started to cry.

* * *

Later in the morning Lieutenant Carmody showed up. He called to us from the path leading up to the house. When the professor and I went out on the porch, he said, "It's Kevin, then?" He stayed on his horse and didn't come any closer. He had seen the sign.

"It is Kevin," the professor replied. "Last night."

"Does he still live?"

"Yes, thank God."

"I am sorry indeed to hear of this, Professor," the lieutenant said. "We can't protect you, you understand. The last troops retreat over the bridge by noon. We were getting worried when you didn't come. But we can't delay. The Canadians are no more than a mile away."

"I understand the situation," Professor Palmer replied.

"If you can, use your fireplace only at night," the lieutenant advised. "They'll see the smoke during the day."

"Yes, I hadn't thought of that."

"If you hear the enemy approach, get out as quickly as you can, before they see you. They'll probably fire the house when they notice the sign, and not bother looking inside. They'll want nothing to do with drikana."

"Of course," the professor said. "That makes sense."

"Why don't we just take down the sign?" I asked the professor.

He shook his head. "It's not done, lad. It's just not done."

"One more thing," Lieutenant Carmody said. "Perhaps I needn't say this, but I fear it's my duty. Do not try to reach Boston before the end of the claustration. Important as you are, and as much as I respect and admire you, the law cannot be broken, especially now. Orders will be issued to shoot you on sight until the week has passed."

"I would do the same myself, William," the professor replied.

The lieutenant nodded. "It's an ill time for us all. Fare you well, then. And may God have mercy on the three of you."

Then he rode off, leaving us utterly alone.

Upstairs, Kevin started to moan.

CHAPTER 15

We went back inside to take care of Kevin. He was sitting on the edge of the bed, pale and shivering, trying to throw up. "Am I dying?" he managed to whisper.

"You are very ill, Kevin," the professor replied, "but we will take care of you."

I wrapped a blanket around him.

Was he better? Worse? I changed my mind every few minutes, and finally decided he was about the same. Which meant he still had a chance. "Larry, what did I do to deserve this?" he whispered as he lay back, gasping, after one long stretch over the chamber pot.

"Hang in there, Kev," I told him.

"I just want to go to school. I just want to be with my family."

"It'll be all right."

"This is awful. They'll never know what happened to me. I'll die, and—" He started to cough, and then he began retching again. He was right. It was awful.

In the middle of the afternoon he drifted off to sleep again. I was exhausted. Just sitting was a strain.

"Go to my room and rest," the professor urged me. "I'll take care of Kevin."

I didn't want to leave him, but I wasn't doing much good sitting there, so I went across the hall and lay down on the professor's bed. I probably fell asleep right away. This time I didn't dream of balloon rides. I dreamed of stepping into the portal and, instead of finding a new world, this one started spinning around me. I got dizzier and dizzier, and I realized: the germs have got me. Drikana. I'm going to die. And I thought: I hate this world, I hate this world…

I opened my eyes. The room was dark. I blinked and shook my head. Was I dizzy? Was I dying?

No, it was just a dream. I was hungry. I had to pee. But I felt okay. I got up and went back across the hall. Kevin was still asleep. The professor was reading a book by candlelight.

"This is good, right?" I asked him. "I mean, that he can sleep?"

"It is good."

"And if he makes it through the night…?"

"That will be a very good sign. But there's nothing certain about the course of the disease, Larry. Even if Kevin survives the first two days, he will still be very weak. Often victims succumb to another disease that overtakes them in their weakened state. In rare cases, the drikana returns, and that is certain death."

"I just want to be able to hope," I said.

"So do I, Larry. So do I."

We heard the sound of gunfire in the distance. I noticed that the curtain was drawn. "We'll have to be careful about candles and lamps at night," I remarked.

The professor nodded. "It's lucky we're not on a main thoroughfare," he said. "But our situation is still perilous."

"How are we going to get to Boston after the claustration is over?"

The professor put down the book and rubbed his eyes. "Let us survive these first few days," he said. "There'll be time to decide what we do after that."

So we took turns watching Kevin through the night. He woke up after a while, and the professor tried feeding him a little broth, but he couldn't keep it down. I read to him, and he seemed to like that, but he was too weak to pay much attention. I wasn't very sleepy, so I just kept on reading, even after Kevin had closed his eyes and fallen back asleep. I was too worried to just sit there and think. Was I dizzy yet? What would I do if Kevin died? What would happen if the Canadians showed up? It was probably better not to think about those things. But it was hard to avoid, sitting in the dark bedroom in the middle of the night with your friend maybe dying next to you.

Finally I nodded off again. When I woke up, it was light out. The professor was sitting in his chair, asleep. I looked over at Kevin. He was awake. "This sucks, you know that, Larry?" he said.

I could have kissed him.

"Am I gonna be all right?" he asked.

"Of course you are."

His voice was weak, he was too exhausted to move very much, and he had no appetite, but he was definitely better. "You are a strong young man," the professor pronounced after he had examined Kevin. In private, he told me that Kevin still wasn't out of danger, but I don't think I really believed him. Kevin was okay, and the professor and I were still okay, and drikana wasn't going to defeat us.

By the end of the day we could feed Kevin some broth. By the next morning he wanted to know what was going on—weren't we supposed to leave Cambridge? Where were the Canadians? Professor Palmer explained to him about claustration, and how we'd had to stay behind.

"You mean this is, like, enemy territory now? And we're stuck here?"

"We haven't seen any Canadians yet, but yes, I expect they have taken over Cambridge by now."

Kevin thought this over. "And you stayed behind to save me," he said.

The professor put on his gruff voice. "We really had no choice, you see. The entire household must be claustrated when any inhabitant falls ill with the disease. It's the law."

"All right," Kevin replied. "But, thanks just the same. I'd be dead without you."

The professor nodded. "Of course, of course." Then he turned away, and I think maybe his eyes were moist.

So then it was a question of getting Kevin stronger and hoping the Canadians didn't notice us until the seven days were up. No fire during the day, no matter how cold it got; candlelight only behind thick curtains at night. We went outside as little as possible—to visit the privy, to take care of the animals. Once I was out in the barn, and I heard the sound of wagon wheels and soldiers' voices, not that far away, and I prayed the animals would keep quiet until they passed. Lieutenant Carmody's warning kept buzzing around in my brain— when they saw the claustration sign they wouldn't take us prisoner, they'd simply burn us up. Could there be a worse death? The sounds faded eventually, and we were still safe.

Eventually we began talking about our escape. "Anything we attempt will be dangerous," the professor explained, "but it should not be impossible to get to Boston. I have lived here much of my life, and I know the back roads well. On a clear night we should be able to reach the river without going near the Massachusetts Road— I have sketched out a route already. The Canadians won't be patrolling these roads, I think—their enemy is ahead of them, not behind them."

"But what happens when we reach the river?" I asked. "How do we get across?"

"The Canadians won't have had time to build up positions along the entire length of the Charles, even if that is their strategy," the professor replied. "They're probably massed on either side of the road. We'll need to work our way upriver. I know an inlet where Harvard keeps a small boathouse for its students. If we're lucky, it will have escaped the enemy's notice, and we can get a boat there and row across to the Boston side."

"Will Kevin be strong enough to travel like this?"

"We don't leave until Kevin is ready. He can ride in the back of the carriage, but it will surely be a bumpy trip."

"I can make it," Kevin said.

The professor shook his head. "Not until the seven days are up, at the earliest."

I thought of the lieutenant's final warning: We'd be shot if we showed up in Boston before those seven days. People didn't fool around here when it came to drikana.

Kevin had a question, too. "What happens to Susie?"

"We'll have to leave Susie at the boathouse," the professor replied. "It can't be helped, I'm afraid."

That was just awful. The professor's horse was like part of the family. But there was nothing we could say. It was clear we couldn't get her across the river.

So we took care of Kevin, and we waited.

The seventh night was clear and cold. Kevin was still very weak, but eager to leave. "I'm ready," he insisted. "Let's get out of here."

Professor Palmer was hesitant. "A day or two more would do you a world of good," he said.

"Every day we're here makes it more dangerous for all of us," Kevin replied. Couldn't argue with that. So the professor agreed: it was time to go.

There were things to be done first. We burned all Kevin's bedclothes—a requirement at the end of claustration. Professor Palmer took down the sign; that was a big relief. We unloaded the books and papers we had so carefully put into the professor's carriage a week ago; we weren't going to row them across the river. It seemed like way more than a week had gone by since we had packed the carriage, since that happy Harvest Day. If the professor was sad that we had to leave all his stuff behind, he didn't let on. Then we hitched up Susie, who seemed plenty surprised to have to go to work at this time of night. Last of all, we brought Kevin out and made him as comfortable as we could in the back of the carriage.

"Ready?" Professor Palmer asked.

"Ready."

We headed off. I took one look back at the house, wondering if I'd ever see it again. Then we turned a corner, and it disappeared.

The night was quiet, and we seemed to make a huge amount of noise as we clopped along in the moonlight. Leaves floated down from the trees like small dark ghosts. I thought of the pretend scariness of Halloween, and how different this was. The enemy was out there somewhere, ready to kill us.

Susie seemed confused about where we were heading; this certainly wasn't one of her regular routes. The professor led us through little lanes and narrow paths, staying away from the main roads. Sometimes it looked like there wasn't a path at all, and we were cutting across a meadow or through someone's backyard. We didn't see or hear anyone else; the town seemed entirely deserted.

"You okay, Kev?" I whispered to him after we went over a big bump.

"Hangin' in there," he replied, but he didn't sound all that great. "You know what I miss this time of year?"

"What's that?"

"The World Series. I wonder if the Red Sox—"

"Save the baseball talk for General Aldridge, Kevin."

"Not much farther to go," the professor said.

We made one final turn, and then I could see the rippling of water in the distance and the outline of a long, dark structure. "The boathouse," he whispered. We had made it!

We pulled up in front of the building. "Quickly," the professor said, getting down from the carriage. "Larry, bring the lantern. We may have to risk a light inside."

I turned to get the lantern. And that's when I heard the voice.

"Stop right there! Turn around and get down! Both of you, raise your hands where I can see 'em."

I turned, my heart pounding, and saw the shape of a man aiming a rifle at me. I did as I was told.

"Laurent," he called out. "Wake up and give us some light if you please."

He had one of those French-Canadian accents. In a few seconds a second soldier appeared out of the boathouse; he lit a lantern and held it up.

Both of the men had long hair and beards. The one with the rifle was big and burly; Laurent was smaller, and looked nervous. They were wearing dirty gray uniforms with the jackets unbuttoned.

"Put the lantern down and search them for weapons," the burly soldier ordered Laurent. He seemed to be the boss.

Laurent came over and patted us down. "Trying to get to Boston, eh?" the other soldier asked meanwhile.

We didn't reply.

"They don't look like spies, Robert," Laurent said when he was done. He pronounced it "Row-bare."

"And what exactly do spies look like?" Robert snapped. "Do they wear red uniforms with 'New England' written on the sleeves?"

"We're not spies," the professor said. "We're merely residents of Cambridge who delayed in evacuating."

"Well, you delayed too long," Robert said. "This is Canadian territory now. D'ye think we're too stupid to guard this boathouse?"

"Shall we shoot them, Robert?" Laurent asked.

Robert looked annoyed. "No, fool, we bring them to headquarters and have them interrogated. Even if they're not spies, they may have valuable information. Get some rope and tie them up."

"Where's the rope?"

Robert muttered what sounded like a French swear under his breath. "Hold the rifle and give me the lantern," he said. "If either of them moves, shoot them both."

"But I thought you said—"

Robert said the French word louder, then grabbed the lantern from Laurent and went back into the boat house. The professor and I stayed where we were. Laurent aimed the rifle at us in the moonlight.

And that's when Kevin moved in the back of the carriage.

"What's that?" Laurent demanded.

"That," said the professor, "is our drikana patient."

"Mon Dieu!" Laurent whispered, and he shifted the rifle and blessed himself. "Robert!" he called out. "Robert!"

Robert came back out of the boathouse a moment later, carrying another rifle along with the lantern. "What the devil is it?" he demanded, when he saw that neither of us had moved.

"D-drikana," Laurent said, pointing to the carriage. "In the back."

Robert went over to the carriage, shined the lantern inside, and saw Kevin lying down amid pillows and blankets.

"We were under claustration," the professor said. "That's why we were delayed in leaving."

Why is he telling them about that? I wondered. They'll want nothing to do with drikana, Lieutenant Carmody had said. They'd just burn us alive.

"Now let's shoot them," Laurent begged, proving my point.

"If you shoot us," the professor pointed out, "you'll have to bury us."

Robert backed away from the carriage. "How do we know it's drikana?" he said.

"Why else would we stay behind enemy lines instead of leaving with everyone else?" the professor replied.

"Please let's shoot them," Laurent said.

"Shut up!" Robert ordered him. "The claustration, it is over?" he asked the professor.

"It ended tonight. And now you can kill us and deal with our bodies, or you can let us row our patient over to the city."

So then I understood what the professor was up to. The best solution for the Canadians was to let us go and bring the disease across the river into Boston. Let New England deal with us.

Robert got the point. "The boy is definitely ill," he said. "Could be consumption, I suppose."

"Could be," the professor agreed. "But it's drikana."

Laurent looked very unhappy. "My sister died of it," he said.

"It is not a pleasant disease."

"Laurent, get a boat out for 'em," Robert ordered. "They're going to Boston."

Laurent didn't have to be told twice. He ran back into the boathouse, and soon after that we could hear him dragging a boat out into the water.

"This gun will be trained on you as you cross," Robert said to us. "If I see you turning back, you'll all be dead before you reach the shore."

"We understand," the professor replied. "Believe me, we have no desire to return to Cambridge."

Robert motioned with the rifle. "Get the boy," he ordered.

We put our hands down—my arms were really tired—and went to get Kevin. "Sorry," he said.

"Sorry for what?" I replied. "Come on, Kev. Let's get into the boat."

The professor and I half-carried Kevin along a narrow path to the dock, where the boat was waiting. Laurent was standing as far away from us as he could on the dock. We arranged Kevin in the boat as well as possible, but he looked pretty uncomfortable. "We need the blankets," Professor Palmer said to Laurent, and he motioned with the rifle to go back and get them. "Larry, you stay with Kevin," the professor said.

"Say goodbye to Susie for us," I said.

He patted me on the head and then returned to the carriage. "That was a smart move by the professor," Kevin said while we waited.

"I bet he planned it all along, and just didn't want to tell us."

He returned in a minute with the blankets and pillows. "Can you row?" he asked me.

"A little." Thank goodness I had taken lessons at camp last summer.

"We'll take turns. You begin."

Robert was on the dock now, too. "To Boston," he reminded us. "Return, and you die."

I picked up the oars, fit them into the oarlocks, and moved us away from the dock. "So far so good," I said.

"Indeed," the professor replied. "Unfortunately, now it begins to be really dangerous."

Why? I didn't want to ask. I focused on getting us out of the inlet and onto the river. I was pretty rusty at rowing, but I got the hang of it back quickly. The dock was out of sight once we were on the river, and I wondered how the Canadian soldiers were going to track us. Had Robert just been bluffing? The river was calm; its surface was like glass in the moonlight. There were just a few dim lights on either shore. And there wasn't a sound except for the swooshing of the oars. It felt incredibly peaceful.

When we were about in the middle of the river, the professor said, "I'll take over now."

"I'm not tired," I said. "I can make it the whole way."

"Larry, let me take over," he repeated. "I want you to get down in the bottom of the boat with Kevin."

"Why?"

"Because I expect the New England soldiers will start shooting at us any moment now."

"Huh? But the claustration is over! We're okay."

After a few weeks with us, the professor didn't need a translation of "okay". "They don't know who we are," he said. "They just see a boat heading toward them from enemy territory. They're first instinct will be to shoot at it. Now do as I say and get down with Kevin."

I didn't really have a choice. I awkwardly switched positions with the professor, and then scrunched down next to Kevin. "Scary, huh?" I said.

"Wouldn't it be great just to feel safe again?" he replied.

"Not gonna happen anytime soon."

We approached the Boston shore. The professor was a pretty good rower, for someone his age. "Won't be long now," he muttered. And then he shouted, "This is Alexander Palmer! Let us come ashore!"

He barely got the second sentence out when the guns started firing. The sound was like a punch in the stomach. The bullets sprayed the water around us. One of them nicked an oarlock. Kevin and I huddled together.

"Alexander Palmer!" the professor repeated at the top of his lungs. "I'm Professor Alexander Palmer! Don't shoot! Let us come ashore!"

There was a pause. "You all right?" I asked the professor.

"Yes, yes. But their aim will get better as we get closer." He shouted out his name again, and then added: "We are friends of Lieutenant William Carmody. We have no weapons."

They fired a couple more shots at us, and then I heard a shout from the shore that I couldn't understand. But the shooting stopped after that, and we continued to make our way toward Boston. I sat up a little, and I saw a lantern ahead of us. "Over here," a voice called out. "Stay in the boat."

We eased up to the bank. A squad of soldiers approached, with rifles aimed at us. "You have the drikana patient with you?" one of them demanded.

"We do," Professor Palmer replied.

The soldier came up to the boat. He was a short, plump lieutenant, and he carried a pistol instead of a rifle.

"He is much improved," the professor said. "And the claustration is complete."

The lieutenant peered in at Kevin. "Hi," Kevin said.

"Sergeant," the lieutenant called out. "Have you found the order from headquarters?"

"Yes, sir," one of the other soldiers replied.

"What time does it expire?"

"Midnight, sir."

The lieutenant took out his watch and made a big deal of checking it. What a jerk, I thought. We hadn't left Cambridge till after midnight. Obviously the time was up. "Very well," he said. "I don't approve, but the order is clear. Sergeant, find a wagon and get these people to hospital without delay. And keep everyone away from them."

"Yes, sir." The sergeant headed off away from the bank.

The lieutenant turned back to us. "Can he walk?"

"We can help him," Professor Palmer replied.

"Follow the sergeant up the path. Don't touch anyone. Don't talk to anyone."

"Let's go, lads," the professor said without replying to the lieutenant.

The lieutenant stepped back away from us as we got out of the boat. "Corporal," he said to another soldier, "burn the boat and everything in it."

"Welcome back to Boston, eh?" the professor said to us as we headed towards the path leading away from the river, and all the soldiers shrank back.

"Could have been worse," I said.

"Indeed it could," the professor replied. "Indeed it could."

CHAPTER 16

That nighttime journey from Cambridge back to Boston was the second time we had been shot at in this world. It wouldn't be the last.

Except for blue-uniformed policemen carrying nightsticks, the streets of Boston were deserted as we headed for the hospital. The policemen eyed our wagon as we raced past them, but no one tried to stop us. I think the sergeant would've shot anyone who tried.

Within a few minutes he pulled up in front of a large brick building with a sign in front that said Massachusetts General Hospital. "Wait here," the sergeant ordered us. He got down from the wagon and went inside. A few minutes later he returned with a couple of people carrying a stretcher. They lifted Kevin out of the wagon and onto the stretcher. The professor and I followed along as they brought him inside. We never saw the sergeant again.

The building didn't smell like hospitals in our world. It stank. And it was dark, with just an occasional oil lamp lighting the corridors, and not all that clean. Somewhere a woman was screaming in pain. As we walked, a bearded guy who was apparently a doctor started questioning us about Kevin's drikana. When had the symptoms appeared? Who had been present at the onset? How had we treated the illness? He wasn't happy to learn that we hadn't bled Kevin. "The height of folly," he said.

"Except that the patient still lives," Professor Palmer growled.

We passed through a door with a red "C" on it, and then into a small room with no furniture except for a bed, a chair, a little table with a candle on it, and a chamber pot. There was one small, barred window. Kevin was put into the bed, and the doctor examined the three of us. It turned out that the professor had been nicked in the shoulder by a bullet back on the river and hadn't said anything about it. The doctor bandaged him up, but other than the bullet wound he couldn't find anything wrong with us.

"You will be examined further in the morning," he said. "In the meantime, none of you is to leave this room."

"In the meantime," the professor said, "we demand that you send a message to Lieutenant William Carmody, chief of staff to General Solomon Aldridge, informing him of our presence here. Also, send word immediately to my old friend Doctor George Dreier, who is the president of this august institution. Tell him that Professor Alexander Palmer has taken up residence in his hospital and would like to chat about the accommodations. And bring us some food; we've had a taxing night."

The doctor didn't look too happy about getting those orders. He simply nodded and left without a word. We were by ourselves finally. And safe. The professor sat back in his chair and closed his eyes. "A little too much excitement for someone my age, lads," he said.

"Are we going to be stuck here?" I asked.

"I'm afraid Kevin may be in hospital for a while," he replied. "Even though the claustration is officially over, they'll want to be especially careful that he doesn't suffer a relapse. A drikana outbreak in the city would be just too devastating to contemplate. As for us— I expect we'll be able to leave once they've poked at us enough to be assured we don't have the disease."

I noticed that Kevin had already fallen asleep. "Will we be able to visit him?" I asked. "He's going to get awfully lonely in here. This place is creepy."

"That should be possible, Larry. I'll talk to Doctor Dreier."

I decided I was getting pretty tired, too. I closed my eyes. "You were really brave on the river, Professor," I said.

"One becomes brave when one has no other choice," he replied. "Now we can all relax a little." And that's the last thing I remembered until I opened my eyes and saw Lieutenant Carmody standing in the room.

"Very glad to find you have all survived," he said. "I'm informed you're all in reasonably good health as well, thank God." Gray light shone through the small window. I figured it was about dawn. As usual, the lieutenant was freshly shaved, and his uniform was gleaming.

"You might have asked your sentries on the shore to refrain from shooting at us," the professor replied. "I received a welcoming present in the shoulder from one of them."

"We did send out an order, actually, but unfortunately orders from headquarters do not always reach the men in the field. And if they do, all too often they're ignored or forgotten."

"No wonder we're losing this war," the professor muttered. "Anyway, what have we been missing in the past week?"

"We are established on the grounds of the palace, and progress continues, although Professor Foster's behavior has left something to be desired. He has not taken your absence well."

"I'll take care of Benjamin. How are negotiations with the enemy progressing?"

"Vice President Boatner and Lord Percival ably represent our interests," the lieutenant replied. "Unfortunately, the enemy seems to think there is little to negotiate. 'Unconditional surrender or death' would be a reasonable summary of their position."

"Not especially conducive to a diplomatic solution. And the situation in the city?"

"Not pleasant, I'm afraid," the lieutenant replied. "There is a strict curfew in force, dusk to dawn, and we've had to divert soldiers to help the police maintain order. So far things are relatively calm, but I wouldn't want to guess how much longer they will remain so. People are cold and hungry and frightened, and there is little hope that their situation will improve."

The curfew helped explain why the streets had been so deserted last night, I figured.

"At any rate," the lieutenant went on, "I'm delighted you made it to Boston safely, and we'd like to get you back to work as soon as possible."

"Yes," the professor said. "We may need a dispensation from Doctor Dreier to get Larry and me out of here, however."

"I'm sure he'll listen to reason."

They went off to find the doctor, and I stayed behind with Kevin. There was a loaf of bread and a pot of tea on a table next to Kevin's bed. The bread was stale, though, and the tea was cold. Kevin woke up while I was trying to swallow a few bites. I gave him some bread and explained what was going on.

"You mean I'm gonna be stuck in this place by myself?" he asked.

"Looks like it. But I'll come and visit you as often as they'll let me."

"Thanks," Kevin said. "They really don't mess around with this disease, do they?"

I shook my head. "Look at the bars on that window over there. I bet they're to keep drikana patients from escaping."

"I can see why they're scared," Kevin said. "I wouldn't wish this disease on my worst enemy. Still, it's gonna be really boring in here."

"Yeah, but it's better than most of the alternatives."

"No kidding."

Lieutenant Carmody and Professor Palmer returned then with sort of good news. The doctor had no objection to the professor and me leaving, but Kevin had to stay in the hospital for at least a couple more weeks. "He is also very interested in some of the medical theories I have picked up from you boys," the professor said. "An extraordinarily open-minded man, for a doctor. Larry, let's go. Kevin, we'll be back to visit. I'll see if I can find a chess set and some books to keep you entertained."

It felt awful leaving Kevin behind, but there was nothing we could do about it. We went outside, and Peter was waiting there with the lieutenant's carriage. It was good to see him again. He brought us straight to Coolidge Palace, and we got out to inspect the work going on. I just kind of tagged along, actually; there wasn't a lot I could help with at this point.

The balloons looked pretty much ready to use, now that people had figured out how to stop the leaks. They were still experimenting with the best way of heating the air, but that seemed like a detail. Folks had seen the balloons flying over the palace grounds and had gotten very excited. "Airships," they called them.

Professor Foster was very proud of his electric fence, but there was concern about how much power his batteries could generate, and what distance the fence would be able to cover. Professor Palmer questioned him sharply, and as usual he got confused and defensive. "It will work," he insisted. "You can count on me. You can count on electricity."

No one looked convinced.

Lieutenant Carmody left Professor Palmer in charge after a while and returned to headquarters. I hung around all day, doing whatever people asked me to, and in the evening the professor and I went to headquarters too. He was pretty tired. I figured his shoulder was bothering him, but he wouldn't admit it. "There is much still to be done, and precious little time," he said. "I fear I won't be able to visit Kevin as often as I'd like."

"I can go by myself," I pointed out.

"Traveling through the city alone will be quite dangerous," he responded.

"I survived drikana and the Canadians," I said. "Not much is going to scare me anymore."

That brought a smile to his face. "Good point," he admitted. "But courage doesn't keep you safe. We should talk to Lieutenant Carmody. Perhaps Peter can drive you."

We found the lieutenant in his room. He was okay with having Peter drive me once in a while, but not every day. "I'm sorry that Kevin is in hospital," he said, "but winning the war must take precedence."

"I worry about Larry on the city streets by himself," the professor said.

The lieutenant considered. "We could give him a military pass," he said. "That might keep him out of trouble if the police pick him up after curfew."

"That's better than nothing, I suppose."

So I got a pass, and they found me a beat-up winter coat that looked like it would be even more useful. It was definitely getting colder now. I couldn't imagine how people in the camps would survive, once winter really set in. On the other hand, everyone expected the war to be over before that happened.

The next morning Peter drove me to the hospital. It was near the river, down the hill from Coolidge Palace. I brought along a couple of books, a deck of cards, and a chess set that the professor had borrowed from a colonel who was too busy to use it. The streets were still crowded during the day, but it was hard to go a block without people running up to the carriage begging for food. The restaurants were all closed, I noticed, and there were armed guards outside the few grocery stores that were still open.

Kevin was overjoyed to see me. "This place is horrible," he said. "There's nothing to do, no one to talk to. They just bring you a lousy meal every once in a while and empty your chamber pot and then disappear. And that doctor with the beard is still mad that you guys didn't bleed me."

"And no TV," I pointed out.

Kevin sighed. "No TV. No nothing."

So we played chess (I lost every game), and we played cards, and we talked—about this world and our world, sort of all mixed in together. I had to go after a couple of hours, but I came back the next day, and the next, and every day after that.

A couple of times I had to walk, but that was okay. I was familiar with the route, and I always got back to headquarters well before the dusk curfew. Nobody bothered me, although I saw a fight or two and some people trying to break into a store. Professor Palmer started to worry less about me—not that he had much time to worry, with all the stuff he was supervising at Coolidge Palace. At the officer's mess, the food got skimpier and skimpier. Standing in line to wash up in the morning, I overheard the officers worrying that the situation couldn't last much longer. Even Bessy, the huge woman who brought out the hot water, was starting to look thin.

As for Kevin—physically he kept getting better, although he too looked thin. His mental state was another story. He had too much time to think, and the more he thought, the unhappier he got. It was the same old stuff: we wouldn't find the portal, we'd never get home, we'd be stuck here forever. But now it all seemed more real to him. "We're going to die here," he said one day. "Next week or in, like, sixty years, it's gonna happen."

"If we can just get back to Glanbury—"

"But we might not even be able to do that," he pointed out, "if New England loses the war."

"We won't lose."

But Kevin was too depressed to be convinced. "Larry," he said, "remember that first day, sitting in the brig? Remember how we wondered if our families were in the camp?"

"Yeah, I guess so. You were the one who was wondering."

"Well, I still am. I was thinking: If we can't get back home, maybe at least we can find another version of our families here."

"That'd be creepy," I said. "What if you met yourself?"

"That wouldn't be creepy. It'd be cool."

I thought about it. Hadn't I wondered if I existed in the Burger Queen world? But still..."I know Stinky Glover was in the Burger Queen world, and Nora Lally," I said. "But this world split off from ours hundreds of years ago. What are the odds they'd be here?"

"Beethoven lived in this world," Kevin pointed out. "And look at Calvin Coolidge, for crying out loud. If there was a Calvin Coolidge here, why can't there be an Albright family and a Barnes family?"

"Well, Glanbury's just a small farming town. There can't be anywhere near as many people living there in this world as in ours. I mean, think about it. The right people have to fall in love and get married, generation after generation, every since the two universes split off. Even if it's possible that our families are here, what are the odds?"

"I don't know," Kevin said. "But I think you should go look for them."

"You want me to go to the Fens camp? That's nuts!"

"Why?"

"Things are getting scary out there, Kevin. Professor Palmer is worried about me even coming to the hospital. And the camps are a whole lot worse. They won't let anyone out anymore, and people inside are getting desperate. I was talking to a couple of soldiers at headquarters, and they said they wouldn't go into the camp with anything less than a platoon."

Kevin considered. "I can't make you go," he said. "But what if they're in the camp? What if Cassie and Matthew and your Mom and Dad are just a couple of miles away from here?"

"Come on, Kevin, they're not the same people. Even if they have the same DNA or whatever, all their experiences are different. So they'd be different."

"Maybe you wouldn't be that different—how do you know?"

"What do we have in common? Farming? Smallpox? Drikana?"

Kevin seemed to lose his energy all of a sudden. Maybe it was my mentioning his disease. "Suit yourself," he said, lying back on his pillow. "I'll go myself when I get sprung from here."

"Look, I'll think about it, okay?"

"Okay," he replied. "Thanks, Larry." He didn't sound like he meant it.

But I did think about it. I had to admit I was curious, but was I curious enough to walk through Cheapside and talk my way into the camp? If I got in, could I get back out? I had my pass, but how much good was that going to do? I guess I was braver than I used to be, but going to the camp really seemed stupid.

When I visited Kevin the next day, he didn't bring it up, but I could tell he was still thinking about it too. And he was still depressed about being in the hospital, and in this world.

Walking back to headquarters afterwards, I saw a woman begging outside a tavern, with a child Matthew's age by her side. They were both wearing rags, basically. The mother looked desperate, and the child looked like he was too tired and hungry to care what happened to him. There were lots of beggars now, and most people just walked past them.

I didn't have anything to give her, but she started me thinking about my own mother. If she was in the camp, how could she stand it? At home she was worried about perverts from Rhode Island getting hold of us. What would she do if there was real danger all around her?

And then I thought: What if I could help her? Bring her food, maybe even get her out of the camp.

I got excited thinking about this, and it took me a while to realize that something weird was happening. I had slipped from imagining my real mother being in the camp to thinking about my "other" mother—the one from this world.

And it didn't seem to make any difference. I had been arguing with Kevin that the Emma Barnes in this world would be a different person from my Emma Barnes. Now I had fallen into thinking the opposite: She was my mom, no matter where she was.

Did I believe that?

I guess I sort of did. And if so, why didn't I agree with Kevin? Why wasn't I itching to go find my family?

The more I thought about it, the more I wanted to do just that.

I imagine this was the process Kevin had gone through, lying there in his hospital bed with nothing to do but think. Practically everything about this world was different and strange. But if we could find our families...well, they might be different, but I was pretty sure they wouldn't be strange. There would be some way in which my mom was still my mom, my dad was still my dad.

If they were here.

I lay awake that night in my cold attic room thinking about it some more. In the morning I was still thinking about it as I washed up outside, and then ate a hard biscuit and some thin porridge in the mess. I went over to Coolidge Palace with Professor Palmer, but I didn't say anything about going to the Fens camp; he would've gone nuts. It turned out he didn't even want me to visit Kevin anymore.

"But I haven't had any problems at all going to the hospital," I pointed out.

"Yes, but it keeps getting worse in the city," he responded. "I hear there was a riot at Dock Square yesterday."

"I don't go anywhere near Dock Square. And Kevin is expecting me."

He just shook his head. "I can't allow it, Larry," he said. "Things are just too dangerous, and you are too valuable to us. If Peter could take you, then wait and bring you back, that would be acceptable. But Lieutenant Carmody can't spare him any longer."

This wasn't good. Especially since I didn't feel very valuable. On the palace grounds I mostly just hung around and got in the way. Professor Palmer was usually in meetings or supervising something. Once I saw President Gardner, along with Vice President Boatner and Lord Percival, but he barely nodded to me. The three of them looked pretty tired. I heard that the Portuguese and Canadian diplomats were meeting with them off and on, but no one had any idea how the negotiations were coming. For all any of us knew, the war could be over at any minute, with New England surrendering and all our efforts wasted.

After lunch I decided that I couldn't stand it, so I just wandered away. The soldiers with the big plumed hats at the gate knew me, and they let me out without a problem.

I was fine as I walked through the heart of the city, but I began to get nervous as I came to Cheapside. When Kevin and I had walked through it before, it had been nighttime, and we hadn't really seen just how run-down the place was, with its narrow dirt lanes and wretched shacks. No more hogs snuffling around in the alleys, though—they'd all been eaten long ago, I supposed. And no more music and laughter from inside the saloons. The only people I saw were hunched in doorways, and they stared at me suspiciously. I began to be conscious of my warm coat, which had looked pretty shabby when the lieutenant had first handed it to me. But I thought: these people don't have enough energy to attack me.

At last I made it through Cheapside and reached the military buildings outside the camp. It felt strange to see them again, after so much had happened.

Near the barracks I spotted Chester, the guy who was in the brig with us. He was digging a big hole in the ground with some other soldiers. "Graves," he said when he saw me. "Need lots of graves."

I shuddered and hurried on.

There seemed to be a lot more soldiers guarding the camp, and the fence looked higher and sturdier. I searched for a familiar face, and finally I spotted one. "Caleb!" I called out.

He was standing in front of the barracks, talking to some other soldiers. His beard was scruffier than I remember and, like everyone, he looked thinner. He glanced over when I called his name and smiled. "Hello, mate!" he said. "What brings you back here? I hear you was involved in that secret business at the Palace."

"I got the day off. I was wondering—can I get into the camp?"

"Now why would you want to do that, mate?" he asked. "It's nasty in there. Everyone who's inside just wants to get out."

"I'm looking for a friend."

He shook his head. "Know where he's camped?"

"Not really."

"Then you'll not have much luck, I fear."

"But I need to try," I said, starting to feel desperate.

Caleb shrugged. "Suit yourself. Let's go find Sergeant Hornbeam. Easy enough to get in, I suppose. The trick is getting back out. Used to be folks could wander outside, as long as they came back before curfew. Those days are gone now. Too many people, not enough of anything else."

He brought me inside the barracks to a little office next to Colonel Clarett's—the one where I had first met Lieutenant Carmody. Sergeant Hornbeam was sitting there writing on a sheet of paper.

"Sergeant, look who's come back to visit!" Caleb said.

The sergeant looked up at me. If I was expected him to be happy to see me, I was mistaken. He just seemed puzzled and maybe a little annoyed. "What are you doing here?" he demanded.

"He wants to go visiting in the camp," Caleb said.

"By yourself? Is Lieutenant Carmody with you?"

"No, uh, just me. But I've got a pass from him."

I dug it out and gave it to him. He studied it. "Odd," he muttered, then handed the pass back to me. "Hold onto it," he said. "But take my advice and don't go into the camp."

"I'll be careful," I promised.

He shook his head. "We only go in there to cart out the dead now. But suit yourself. Show the pass to get back out. If there's a problem, tell the guards to find me."

"Yes, sir. Thank you, sir."

He waved me away, and Caleb escorted me out of the barracks.

"So," Caleb said as we walked over to the camp gates, "what does headquarters have up its sleeve? Flying airships, that's what Fred heard. Hundreds of feet above Coolidge Palace."

"I can't really talk about it, Caleb."

"Could you just tell me if there's *something*, mate? Folks is getting mighty nervous, I don't mind telling you. There's also rumors that the president's going to surrender by week's end. So are we fighting, or are we giving up? It'd be good to know what's what."

"I don't know about surrendering," I said. "But I know they're working on some things at Coolidge Palace, and I'm pretty sure they're going to help."

"As long as they're still trying, that's a good sign. Here you go, mate."

We had reached the main gates. There were several soldiers standing guard. A crowd of people on the other side of the fence was yelling at one of them, demanding to be let out. The guards just ignored them.

"This here is Larry from headquarters, Sergeant," Caleb said to the soldier in charge. "He's to be let in and out of the camp, though why he wants to go in there is beyond me."

"He'll learn soon enough," the sergeant replied with a shrug. "Take a couple of men and go to the side gate. Fix bayonets, in case you have to clear a path."

"Right." Caleb found a couple of his friends, and we went along the fence till we reached another gate, also heavily guarded, but with only a few people on the other side. Caleb and the guards put their bayonets on, then unlocked the gate and pretty much shoved me inside, while pushing back the people who lunged forward, trying to get out.

"Thanks, Caleb!" I shouted as I made my way through the people.

"Fare you well, mate!" he said. "And be careful!"

And there I was, back inside the camp.

CHAPTER 17

"**H**elp me, help me, I'm dying!"

An old man was kneeling on the ground by the gate. He grabbed my leg and wouldn't let go.

The other people ignored him. His eyes were watery; he didn't have any teeth. His whole body was shaking.

"I'm sorry," I said. "There's nothing—"

"I have no one," he said. "I can't make it to the food line. Please help, else I'll die."

"I'm sorry," I repeated. "I don't…I can't…" I pulled away from him; he wasn't strong enough to stop me.

Maybe this was a big mistake, I thought.

My next thought was: It really stinks in here.

I moved away from the gate and looked around. I thought the place had been crowded before, but now there were people everywhere, jammed together for as far as I could see alongside the narrow dirt paths. All the animals were gone, too, except for some sad-looking horses and donkeys. I remembered the cows and goats and oxen tied to the wagons that people were driving into the city the day Kevin and I arrived. Eaten by now, I figured, or dead of starvation.

I started walking. That first night, things had been kind of mellow in the camp: people singing, kids playing, old men smoking pipes in front of fires…Now all the mellowness was gone. People were mostly just sitting down, on the ground or in their wagons, wrapped in blankets, staring at nothing with dead eyes. A lot of the men were holding rifles in their laps. With soldiers afraid to enter the camp, I guess I understood why. There were lots of people walking along the paths, too; some of them looked pretty scary, like they'd kill you if they thought you had a loaf of bread on you. I really didn't feel like asking anyone if they knew a Barnes family from Glanbury. Just looking at people made me nervous.

So I walked. And I thought: How am I going to find anyone in this huge, crowded place? What if I don't recognize my family? What if my father has a beard, or Cassie has a different hairstyle, or they're all so bundled up that I walk right past them?

I wandered around for a long time until I started to get tired. I stopped at an intersection of two paths and tried to decide what to do. Should I just give up? I couldn't stay here forever. I still had a long walk back through Cheapside to headquarters.

I realized that I had a lump in my throat. Now that I was here, now that I'd taken the risk and gotten myself in trouble with Professor Palmer and Lieutenant Carmody, I really didn't want this to be a waste of time. I really wanted to find my family, or Kevin's family, or *someone*. Mostly I wanted my original idea to come true—I wanted to help my mother.

Then I saw a fight break out. "You filthy picker!" someone shouted. And two kids my age were dragging another kid down to the ground, where they started punching and kicking him.

I started to turn away. Not my problem, like the old man by the gate. But no one else was breaking up the fight, and it looked like the kid on the ground was going to get killed.

Something made me go over there. "Hey!" I shouted, and I dragged one of the kids away from the fight. He was short but tough-looking. He glared at me. "What's your problem, mate?" he demanded.

Meanwhile the kid they were beating up managed to scramble to his feet. He looked at me for a second, and then started to run away. The other kid took off after him. The tough-looking kid broke away from my grasp and punched me in the stomach. I gasped for breath and my legs buckled; he really knew how to punch. But he didn't stay to punch me again; instead, he turned and ran after the other kids.

When I managed to catch my breath I started running after all of them. Because the kid they had been beating up was Stinky Glover.

Not as fat as in our world, but I'd recognize that face anywhere.

I couldn't find them, though. They were lost in the maze of paths. I kept going until I was sure it was useless, and then I stopped to catch my breath again.

A picker. That was slang in this world for a thief. It figured that Stinky would be a picker.

I had lost him, and that was bad. But still, I was excited. If Stinky was here, then Kevin was right. Why couldn't my family or his family be here too? I just had to keep looking.

But where? Just wandering around wasn't working. There had to be a better way.

In the distance I saw people lined up. For food? The privies? I went over to the line. Everyone had a bucket. They were waiting for water, I realized.

The line moved fairly quickly. I walked alongside, trying to glance at the people in it. As usual, they looked back at me suspiciously. Who was I? Was I going to cut in front of them? I didn't recognize anyone. At the front of the line was a little stream that went through a corner of the camp. People were filling their buckets from the stream. There were plenty of soldiers there to keep the line orderly. I recognized one of them—he had been loading the sacks of grain that wicked hot first day. He nodded to me. "What're you doing here, mate?" he asked.

"Just looking for someone."

"Most everyone passes by here sooner or later. No lack of water at least. And it's not giving everyone the flux the way it did back in September. Still not the cleanest stream in the world, y'understand."

Mr. Harper had mentioned the flux. I figured it was something like diarrhea. "What happens when the stream freezes?" I asked.

"Ah. None of us'll be here by that time, I trust. If we are, there'll be worse things to worry about than the flux."

He fell silent, and I studied the people in line. Even though it only took a few seconds to fill your buckets, the line stretched out a long ways. If it was this bad getting water, I wondered what it was like getting food—if there still was any food. People probably spent a lot of their day just standing in line.

I stuck my hands in my armpits to keep them warm. Sometimes I'd walk up and down the line. Sometimes I sat on a tree stump nearby. Occasionally there was a fight when someone tried to cut into the line, and the soldiers would move quickly to break it up. But for the most part people just shuffled along in silence waiting their turn. A lot of them looked too tired to fight, or to care about anything.

At some point I noticed a distant booming. Artillery, I decided. Had the final battle started? The booming quickly became constant. An old woman standing in line started to weep.

It was getting late. I wasn't going to make it back to headquarters before curfew. I had my pass, but that wasn't going to do much good if some policeman decided to shoot me. And how much trouble was I going to be in if I did make it back? I was afraid to leave, though. If I left, would I ever be able to return?

I was getting hungry. And thirsty, watching all that water go by. I must've stopped paying attention for a while. I know I was feeling sorry for myself, even with these people all around me who were a lot worse off than I was, even with Kevin lying bored to death in the hospital. So I didn't see her until she had already gone to the river and filled her buckets.

Long black hair, shining blue eyes—I knew it was her, even wearing a long skirt and a shapeless jacket. Even looking exhausted and worried.

My first response was the same one I felt in English class, in the cafeteria, in the world neither of us inhabited now. I couldn't say anything to her. I was just too shy. She had already gone past me when I got over it. Things had changed. This was important.

"Nora!" I called out.

She just kept walking.

I went after her. "Nora?" I repeated when I had caught up to her.

There was no recognition, just puzzlement and suspicion, in those blue eyes. "My name's not Nora," she said, and my heart sank.

CHAPTER 18

I tried one last time. "You're not Nora Lally?"

She looked puzzled. "I'm Sarah Lally," she said, "Not Nora."

"From Glanbury?" I asked.

"Yes." She put her buckets down. "Your accent—are you from these parts? Do I know you?"

Same person, different first name. I felt a tremendous sense of relief. It made sense, right? They had old-fashioned names here. They wouldn't necessarily be called the same thing as in our world.

I didn't know how to answer her question. It's me, Larry, I wanted to say. From English class? I gave that oral report on Mark Twain last year, and you laughed a couple of times—remember? "No, I guess you don't know me," I managed to say.

"But how do you know my surname?"

For all the time I'd spent thinking about meeting someone in the camp, I hadn't really come up with the right answer for that sort of question. Should I tell her the truth? If not, what story could I possibly come up with? I decided to do what Kevin and I had done with the Harpers—just ignore the hard questions. So instead I just asked my own. "I wonder, Sarah—do you know the Barnes family?"

A wagon came lumbering down the path, and we had to get out of the way. My heart was pounding as I waited for her response. "Of course I know the Barnes family," she said. "They have the farm over next to the Johnson's. Do you know them, too?"

"Yeah, I—I'm related. Are they here by any chance, in the camp? I've been looking for them."

Sarah nodded. "Mostly all of us are here, sad to say."

Finally. I thought I was going to explode from excitement. "Do you know where they are? Could you—would you take me to them? I'd be really grateful."

"Surely." She stared at me. "You do look like a Barnes, I believe. What's your name?"

"Larry. Larry, uh, Palmer."

"Larry." She smiled. "Pleased to meet you, Larry." She held out her hand, and I shook it. It was the first time I'd ever touched Nora—I mean, Sarah. Her hands were rough and chafed. This was way different from going to school at The Gross.

"Can I help you with those buckets?" I asked.

She looked down at them and sighed. "That would be very kind of you," she said. "I tire so much more easily nowadays. We can drop them off with my family, and then I'll take you to the Barneses."

I picked up one of the buckets, and we started walking. "What part of the camp does your family live in?" Sarah asked.

"I'm not staying in the camp. We live in the city."

She looked at me. "I don't understand," she said. "Then why are you here?"

"I wanted to find them—the Barneses. We've never met."

"But I thought you were related."

This was already getting complicated. "It's a long story," I said, hoping that Sarah didn't ask to hear it.

Luckily she didn't. Instead she started asking me about how things were going in the city. Did we have enough to eat? Was there a lot of robbery and looting? What news had I heard about the war? The distant booming seemed louder now. Were we fighting the enemy at last?

I told her what I knew, which was a lot more than she did. But I couldn't exactly make her feel optimistic about the war.

"I know we're not supposed to say this, but I think it would be better if we surrendered, don't you?" she said. "My father has joined the army—all the men have gone. It would be wonderful if he didn't have to fight. At least we'd be safe, and we could leave this wretched camp and go back home."

"Sure, if the Portuguese let people go home," I said.

"You think they'd take our farm?"

"I don't know. If we surrender, what's to stop them from taking everything?"

"Oh my," she murmured. "That's very true."

It certainly was easy to talk to Sarah. Why had I been so frightened of Nora back at school? Not that it mattered anymore.

"Well, here's our little home of the moment," Sarah said. It was the usual—a wagon, a sickly-looking horse, a makeshift tent. A couple of kids were playing next to the wagon. One of them had a cricket bat and was trying to whack the other one. We set the buckets down. "Jared, Thomas, stop that," she ordered them. "Where's Mother?"

"In the food line," one of them replied. The other one stuck his tongue out at her.

"Charming," she said. "Larry, let's go find your relatives. You two, mind you don't upset the buckets. And don't kill each other."

My relatives. Sarah said it so casually, like visiting them was something we did every day. "Are they near here?" I asked.

"Not far. We Glanbury folks tried to stay close together. It's all so different and frightening in the camp—it's good to have familiar faces."

That reminded me of Kevin and his family. "Is there an Albright family here?"

"I don't know anyone of that name. Are they from Glanbury?"

"I think so," I said. "Is it possible they live in Glanbury and you haven't heard of them?"

Sarah shook her head. "It's such a small town. Everyone knows everyone else."

Poor Kevin. He wasn't going to want to hear that. We started walking. "Do you see the Barnes family much?"

"Jared and Thomas play with their boy. But there's no one my age in the family."

"How many children do they have?"

Sarah gave me another look. She was probably thinking: If they're my relatives, how come I didn't know how many children they had? But she answered my question. "They have the boy—Matthew—and Cassandra. She's a couple of years older than me."

Cassandra? What kind of name was that? Cassie's real name in our world was Catherine. Was she called Cassie here?

But that didn't matter. The big news was: no Larry. That made things less complicated—the universe wasn't going to explode—but I guess I was sort of disappointed. "And Mr. Barnes—is he in the army, like your father?" I asked.

"Oh, yes. Look, there they are."

I looked. Another wagon, another tent made out of ragged sheets and blankets, another horse who looked ready to keel over at any second. There was also a small, smoky fire, over which a girl sat hunched, looking tired and gloomy. A boy was climbing up the side of the wagon, chattering to no one in particular. And there was a woman telling him to get down this instant, he was going to hurt himself.

I was home.

Sarah and I walked over to them. The girl—my sister—looked up. "Hello, Cassie," Sarah said.

So she was called Cassie, just like in my world. She just stared at Sarah and said nothing.

Sarah kept talking. "This is Larry Palmer," she said. "He is, um, a relative of yours?"

Cassie turned her gaze to me without much interest and shrugged. "I don't know him."

Then my mother turned around. She looked older. Her hair had streaks of gray, and her eyes had little wrinkles around them. But she was my mom, no doubt about it, and my heart leaped when I saw her face. She, too, stared at me—a very different stare from Cassie's.

I wanted to run into her arms, but I held back. "Your name is Larry—Lawrence?" she whispered.

Her voice sent chills down my spine.

"Yes," I managed to say. "Larry Palmer."

"Who's that?" Matthew called out from the top of the wagon. "Hello, I'm Matthew Barnes. Are you from Glanbury? That's where we're from. My pa's in the army, and he's going to fight the Portuguese. I wish I could fight them. Are you old enough to be a soldier?"

"Be silent, Matthew," my mother said, without taking her eyes off me. Her gaze felt awfully strange. Almost unbearably strange. It was as if, somehow, she recognized me.

"Palmer," she said finally. "I don't recognize the name. You say you're related to us, Larry?"

"I think so." I'd been trying to come up with a story. "My mother—she died of smallpox when I was little—but she said once that she was related to the Clement family." That was my Mom's maiden name. "And a girl from the Clement family had married a man named Barnes from Glanbury."

"What was your mother's name?" Mom asked. "How was she related to the Clements?"

"Her name was Annie," I said. I was making this up as I went along. "I really don't remember how she was related. The story just kind of stuck in my mind for some reason. So I thought—I thought I'd see if I could find you here in the camp."

"He lives in the city," Sarah said. "He came here specially to look for you."

That got Cassie's attention. "You came here, and you didn't actually have to?" she asked. "That's the foolishest thing I ever heard of."

"Mind your manners, Cassandra," Mom said.

"Can you get us out of here?" Cassie asked me. "Can we stay with you?"

I'd have liked to, but there was no way I was going to be able to pull that off. "No, I'm sorry," I replied. "No one's allowed out now."

Cassie turned away, no longer interested in me. But Mom—that was how I thought of her already—still was. I was afraid she was going to keep on quizzing me about my story, but she didn't. "I don't recall any relative of mine named Annie," she said. "Probably a second cousin or some such. But no matter. You're very welcome, of course. I wish we had something to offer you, but you see how things are here."

"Why not offer him tea in the parlor?" Cassie muttered.

"That's okay—I mean, that's fine," I said, ignoring Cassie. "Maybe we can just talk."

"Well, I have to go back," Sarah said, "before Jared and Thomas maim each other. It was a pleasure to meet you, Larry. Perhaps we'll meet again."

She really seemed to mean it. "Thanks for everything," I said.

Sarah smiled and gave a little curtsy.

"It's getting dark," Mom said to me. "Won't you be out after curfew? And the artillery—"

"I'll be all right," I assured her. "The police just make sure you're on your way home."

Mom looked doubtful, but clearly she wanted me to stay. I sat down by the fire with her. Cassie looked at me the way she always did—like she couldn't believe she had to put up with my existence. Matthew climbed down from the wagon and started peppering me with questions. Mom mostly just gazed at me with that kind of puzzled look she'd had when she first heard my name.

I pretended I was Professor Palmer's son, but I tried not to say too much, afraid I'd start getting confused with the stuff I had to make up. I was pretty sure Cassie didn't believe me, although I had no idea why she thought I'd be lying. Probably she couldn't believe she was related to someone who was a professor at Harvard. Eventually I got the conversation off of me and onto their lives.

"We're just farmfolk, as they call us in the city," Mom said. "Nothing special. Though I wonder if we'll ever see our farm again."

Cassie looked disgusted. "Fine with me if we don't," she replied. She hated farm work, I was sure. I figured she wanted to move to the city, wear a wig and a fancy dress, and go to dinner parties at Coolidge Palace.

"Please don't say that, Cassandra," Mom said softly. "The farm is all we have in this world."

Cassie looked glumly into the fire and pulled her shawl more tightly around her. "Then we don't have anything," she said. "You think we're actually going to win this war? You think we'll actually be able to go back to our farm, as if nothing happened?"

"Pa is going to whip those Portuguese!" Matthew said. "You wait and see! We'll be back home by New Year's."

"Do you go to school, Matthew?" I asked.

Matthew looked delighted. "Not any more!"

Mom shook her head. "We keep talking about setting up some kind of schooling in the camp. We shouldn't just let the children run wild, day after day."

"You should let me join the army, like Pa," Matthew said. "I can help. Can't help anyone if all I'm doing is learning how to read and cipher."

"The army doesn't need little boys," Mom said.

"It needs something," Cassie muttered.

"I think the army will have some surprises for the Portuguese and the Canadians," I said.

"Oh, I do hope you're right," Mom said.

"What about the airships?" Matthew said. "Lots of people have seen them in the city. Above the palace, they say. Have you seen them, Larry?"

"Yes," I said. "I have."

"Are they big?"

"They're pretty big."

"I'll bet we can shoot cannonballs right down on the enemy from the air. The Portuguese won't have a chance!"

Mom was clutching a handkerchief and twisting it tightly. To keep from crying, I realized. She was worrying about Dad, but she didn't like to cry in front of her children. Just like Mom in my world. Everything about their lives had been different, I thought. But at bottom, they were entirely the same. "Is Mr. Barnes able to visit you here?" I asked.

"Just a couple of times," she said. "They're very busy with their training and building the fortifications and such. He's not really a soldier, you know. It's just that they need every man they can get."

"I'm sure he'll be fine."

"If something happens," she said, twisting the handkerchief, "we may never find out. Things are so upside-down."

Matthew reached over and patted her hand. Even Cassie looked sympathetic. "Pa's a dead shot," she said. "And he knows how to take care of himself."

"Yes, yes he does."

We were silent for a while, and then I asked more questions, learned a little more about them. Matthew helped a lot on the farm. He knew how to ride and shoot and fish. Mom sewed the family's clothes and cooked and worked in the fields during planting and harvest seasons. Cassie said everything was boring and she was going to get a job in the city just as soon as she could, if by some miracle we won the war. On Sundays they all went to church in their wagon; their horse's name was Gretel. Occasionally there was a dance in the church hall on Saturday night. There were lots of parties around Harvest Day. Their life had been quiet and happy, until the war.

I didn't notice how dark it was getting until Matthew spoke up. "If we don't get in the food line soon, we'll not have supper," he pointed out.

"I did it this morning," Cassie was quick to say.

"Of course," Mom said. "It's my turn. Larry, you really should be going."

"I know." The sun had set, and the curfew would be starting soon. But I didn't want to leave. It had been so long since I'd heard Matthew babble or seen Cassie sulk...

"Come with me, Larry," Mom said. "Just for a minute. Cassie, watch your brother."

We got up and headed for the food line. "They say it can't last," Mom said to me. "A few days more at most. Too many people, too little food, and the soldiers are needed for fighting, not for guarding us."

"I'm sure you'll be all right."

"Some people are going mad from the wait and the hardship," she went on. "Cassie is very unhappy."

Cassie is always unhappy, I wanted to tell her. "I think we've got a good shot at winning," I said, desperate to make her feel better.

We reached the food distribution area. There were several long lines heading towards a big wooden building much like the one where I'd helped to load the sacks of grain so long ago; soldiers were everywhere, carrying rifles. They looked like they were more than willing to use them. We got into one of the lines.

"Larry, how old are you?" Mom asked.

She was staring at me the way she had when I first showed up. "Almost thirteen," I said.

"Almost thirteen," she repeated, and she nodded, as if this was the answer she had expected. "Larry, Lawrence. This is very strange. You see, we had—we had a little baby. We named him Lawrence, too. He died of a fever when he was two months old. He would have been exactly your age, if he had lived."

I shivered, and not from the cold.

A tear leaked out of her eye. "He was so brave, but he just couldn't hold on. This world was too harsh for him. And to think: he could be just like you today."

So, that's what had happened to me in this universe: dead when I was just a baby. My family had never gotten to know me. "I'm very sorry," I managed to say. "It's...it's a big coincidence."

Mom touched my arm, which was something she did when she got really emotional. "I know it will be hard, Larry, but if you can...please come back and visit us again. It's like you...you fill up an empty space in my heart."

"I'll be back," I said. "Tomorrow."

"Thank you." She squeezed my arm. "Thank you, Larry. Of course, if you can't make it, I understand. You should really stay at home, of course. The city is so dangerous. But maybe later, if things work out, you could come visit us in Glanbury."

"Sure. I'll do that too."

She smiled at me. "Now you should go."

She looked so frail, yet so brave, standing in that long line, with her shawl wrapped around her. I couldn't stand the idea that she had to face this camp without Dad, when I could be here to help her. But she was right; it was time to go.

She leaned over and kissed my forehead, and then I left her there in the line.

I made my way back to the side gate where they'd let me in. The old man was gone, but a few people were still there, begging to be let out. The guards were different from the ones who'd been there earlier. I showed my pass to one of them. "Sergeant Hornbeam said you'd let me out if I showed you this," I said.

The guard took the pass and studied it, the way the sergeant had. "You can leave," he said, "but I don't know where you can go. It's after curfew."

"I know," I replied. "I just need to get back to army headquarters."

He just shook his head. "Well, good luck to you."

Once again the guards fixed bayonets to keep the other people from charging the gate, and they let me out.

It was dark and cold, and I had a long way to go. The artillery hadn't let up. But I didn't really care. I felt so different. I felt as if everything had changed.

My family was here. I had found them. Even if they were farmfolk, they weren't really that different from the family I had left behind.

I had gotten used to not thinking about my family—it was too painful. But now I couldn't help but think about them—at least, this world's version of them. I would steal some food from the mess for them, I thought. Maybe I could find them some warm clothes, too. If Lieutenant Carmody tried to stop me from coming back, I'd just run away.

I passed by the barracks; there were a few soldiers outside it; they glanced at me as I passed by, but no one spoke to me, no one mentioned the curfew. The hole Chester had been digging was filled up now. It looked sinister in the darkness.

I hurried through Cheapside. The streets were deserted.

Kevin was probably worried about me, but I couldn't get to the hospital tonight. Maybe tomorrow. He'd be disappointed that there weren't any Albrights, but that couldn't be helped.

What if the battle had started? Could I get back to the camp? What would happen to Kevin?

My mind just kept racing. I didn't even notice how hungry and tired I was. I didn't notice that my stomach still hurt from where that kid had punched me. And I wasn't even particularly scared—I was just too excited.

I noticed a few people, hurrying like me along the streets, staying in the shadows. There weren't any carriages or wagons. And I didn't see any policemen. I recalled the first night Kevin and I had spent in this world. We were so scared, but the streets had been busy and full of life. Would they ever be like that again?

I almost made it back to headquarters before I ran into the cop. He saw me from across the street and yelled at me to stop. I thought about running, but he took out his pistol and aimed it at me, and I figured I shouldn't take the risk. He came over and grabbed me by the collar. He was big and stupid-looking, and he sure was angry. "What are you doin', sneakin' around after curfew?" he demanded. "Shoot on sight, those are the orders. Want me to shoot you, you little sneak?"

"Officer," I said, "I have a pass and—"

"I don't care about your pass. There's no passes for curfew, those are the orders." He started shaking me. What was he so angry about?

Just then a carriage came around the corner at top speed. The policeman started yelling at the driver, who came to a stop next to us.

It was Peter.

"It's curfew," the policeman screamed at him, waving his pistol. "Get down from there."

"This is official army business, mate," Peter said. "Let the boy go and everyone'll be happy."

"Those aren't the orders," the policeman replied. "No exceptions to curfew—those are the orders!"

Peter calmly picked up a rifle and aimed it at him. "I'd hate to have to blow a hole in your stomach, mate," he said, "but I need that boy."

The policeman looked outraged, and for a second I thought he was actually going to try to shoot Peter with his pistol. But he thought better of it and let me go. I scrambled up onto the bench next to Peter. "This isn't right," the policeman pointed out. "You have a curfew, you got to—"

But I didn't hear the rest as the horses clattered off down the street. "Thanks, Peter," I said.

"Been looking all over for you, mate," he said. "Thought you might be at the hospital, but you weren't."

"Sorry," I said. I noticed we were heading away from headquarters. "What's going on?"

"Oh, nothing much," Peter replied. "Just that the President of New England wants to have a chat with you."

CHAPTER 19

The carriage raced through the deserted streets towards Coolidge Palace. "What do you mean?" I asked Peter. "Chat about what?"

"Wouldn't know," Peter replied. "The president doesn't tell me what's on his mind."

"Are people mad at me?"

Peter chuckled. "I imagine they've more important things to be worrying about, lad."

We reached the palace in no time. The guards let our carriage through the gates, and we raced up the long drive to the front steps. There was still a lot of activity on the palace grounds, I noticed.

"Hurry, lad," Peter said when the carriage stopped. I got down from the bench and ran up the steps. A green-coated butler wearing a wig opened the door for me.

Lieutenant Carmody was standing in the entrance hall, looking seriously annoyed. "Where did you get to?" he demanded.

"Well, uh, I—"

"Never mind. Let's go." He headed off down a long hallway to the president's office. Another butler bowed and let us in.

President Gardner was seated by the fire, along with General Aldridge, Professor Palmer, Vice President Boatner, and the foreign minister, Lord Percival. The president wasn't wearing his wig; he looked tired. "Ah, you've brought Master Barnes," he said when we entered. "Excellent. Have a seat. General Aldridge was just finishing one of his gloomy reports."

We bowed and sat down. The warmth of the fire felt great after being outside all day.

"The Canadian artillery pieces on the Cambridge side of the Charles are firing almost continuously," General Aldridge said. "Damage is light so far except in the refugee camp by the river. The goal, presumably, is to create confusion and panic prior to the main assault."

"And the Portuguese?"

"A similar strategy south of the city, except the firing is more intermittent. They may be conserving their ammunition."

"And the balloons?" the president asked. "The electricity? All this work taking place on my back lawn—where are we with it?"

General Aldridge turned to Professor Palmer. "Professor?"

"Four balloons are in use at strategic points around the city, Your Excellency," he said. "Two more are being completed tonight. The balloons are tethered, with ropes sufficiently long that soldiers in the balloons will be able to easily view the enemy's troop dispositions by telescope. We have developed a semaphore signaling system that allows them to send the information back to the soldiers on the ground, so that they can adjust our own deployments of artillery and troops."

"Can't the enemy just train their fire on the balloons and shoot them down?" Vice President Boatner asked. He looked as glum as he had the first time I saw him.

"The balloons are out of range of enemy artillery. They'll be safe."

"What about wind, snow, ice?" the president asked.

Professor Palmer nodded. "Weather is a concern, Excellency, particularly wind. But on calm days, the balloons will be effective."

"One might say that the balloons have already served their purpose," Lord Percival pointed out. "The enemy negotiators have seen the balloons floating over the palace. And that has provoked a change in their attitude."

The president raised a hand. "We will get to that," he said. "First I want to hear about the electrified fences."

Professor Palmer spoke up again. "We have had some difficulty getting the batteries to hold sufficient charge," he said. "We've tried generating the electricity directly, but—"

"Yes, yes," the president interrupted. "These details are fascinating, I'm sure, but we need to know the consequences. What can we do now?"

"We have fences that can be deployed across a limited area," the professor replied. "The shorter the fence, the more significant the shock it will impart."

"The plan is to expose gaps in the fortifications that will be filled by the fences," General Aldridge explained. "We hope the enemy will choose to attack in these gaps and be thrown into confusion by the shocks they receive. We may also be able to inflict some injuries."

"That's all very well," the vice president responded, "but neither these fences nor the balloons give us a decisive military advantage. We are still besieged by enemy forces that far outnumber our own. Our citizens are dying of disease and starvation, and looting and riots are widespread. The refugee camps are about to explode. The chaos and suffering will only increase if the siege continues.

"Lord Percival is correct, however: our bargaining position has improved somewhat. At our negotiating session today, the enemy made what they termed their final offer: to let us maintain a civilian administration in New England as long as we disband our army and acknowledge the co-sovereignty of Canada and New Portugal. This seems to me to be a far better outcome than we could have hoped for a month ago. We would be foolish not to take it, and instead risk the future of our nation on a battle we have no hope of winning."

"Solomon, when do you expect the battle?" the president asked.

"Not likely to be tomorrow," General Aldridge replied. "But no more than a day or two after that. We assume the attacks will be coordinated. The Portuguese are still moving troops up towards the fortifications. Once they're in place, they won't delay further."

That shut everyone up for a minute. Then President Gardner looked at me. "Master Barnes, what do you hear?" he asked. "Do the people in the city want us to surrender, or fight?"

I thought. How could I summarize what I had heard in the camp? Sarah Lally was all for surrender. Matthew was all for fighting. Mom longed to go back to the farm and have Dad be safe. "I think people just want it to be over, Your Excellency," I said. "Whatever you do, do it soon."

That brought nods from everyone.

"Might I add one more thing?" Professor Palmer said. "Obviously we have not achieved everything we would have liked with electricity. But we have a new understanding of its power. If we can continue to work on it, I believe its potential is limitless."

President Gardner's eyes rested on me for a moment before he replied. "We would need our independence in order to reap the rewards of such work," he remarked.

"That is correct."

Vice President Boatner looked like he was going to say something, but instead he folded his arms and stared into the fire. A clock in the corner of the room struck the hour. We waited.

The president turned to the vice president and Lord Percival. "Reject the enemy's final offer," he instructed them. "Break off negotiations, and escort the diplomats back to the front lines. We have nothing left to say to those who would destroy us. Solomon," he said, turning to General Aldridge, "do what you have to do, and quickly. We will show them what New Englanders are made of."

General Aldridge stood up and bowed. "Thank you, Excellency."

I expected the vice president to say something, but he simply shrugged. He seemed to know there was no point in arguing. We all got up, bowed, and left the room. The meeting was over; the decision had been made.

"Never thought I'd see the day," Professor Palmer said as we walked down the corridor away from the office. "His Excellency showing some gumption."

The vice president stopped us at the front door of the palace. "If we can help in any way," he said to General Aldridge, "let us know. All our lives are in your hands." He didn't seem happy about it.

The general nodded. "Thank you, Randolph. The first thing you can do is pray for us."

We hurried out into the night and heard the sounds of the artillery once again. "William, Alexander, come with me," General Aldridge said to the lieutenant and the professor. "There is much to be done. Larry, you can return to headquarters."

"And stay there," Lieutenant Carmody ordered. "I don't know what you've been up to, but you're too important to be wandering around the city." He signaled to Peter to take me.

Instead of getting into the carriage, I climbed up next to Peter once again. "Any news?" he asked as we headed out of the palace grounds.

"We're going to fight," I replied.

He didn't seem surprised. "There'll be many of us dead before the week is out, then," he said. He didn't look awfully upset about it. It was just a statement of fact.

"Aren't you scared?" I asked.

He shrugged. "I try not to think about it," he said. "This battle's been coming for such a long time. So we'll all just do our duty when it finally arrives."

We weren't stopped on the way to headquarters. "Thanks, Peter," I said when he dropped me off in the courtyard.

"Don't be wandering around the city, lad," he advised me. "The lieutenant's right. The situation is dangerous enough—don't go looking for trouble."

I went directly to the mess—I was starving. All they could give me was the usual: salt pork, stale bread, and tea. It would have to do. Then I went up to my room, too tired to think, but knowing I had a huge decision to make. Was I going to disobey Lieutenant Carmody and return to the camp?

I put out the lamp and dropped down onto my lumpy mattress.

When I closed my eyes, I saw my mother—tired and worried, just trying keep her family alive in that awful camp. Dad wasn't around, Cassie was about to go off the deep end. It was so familiar, but so much worse than anything in our safe world.

I had to go back, I decided. No matter what. I had to help her.

But how?

CHAPTER 20

I awoke the next morning in the cold attic room. I could hear the artillery still booming away in the distance.

I went downstairs and out into the washyard to splash some water on myself, then over to the mess for another meager meal. Word of President Gardner's decision had gotten around. A few officers were excited about the upcoming battle; most of them just seemed resigned.

Lieutenant Carmody wasn't in the mess, but Professor Palmer was. He started in on me right away. "I'm most concerned about what you did yesterday afternoon, Larry—going off like that against my wishes. Really, there is too much at stake here for such behavior to be tolerated."

I felt guilty, but I didn't want to lie to him. Anyway, I couldn't hold it in. "I found my family," I said.

He stared at me. "Your family?"

"In the Fens camp," I said. "Not the people from my world, but the same people from this world—you know what I mean. My mother and my sister and brother are in the camp. My father's in the army."

"You went to the Fens camp by yourself?"

"I had to. Kevin and I talked about it and—I had to find out if they were here." I could feel my eyes start to tear up. "I know it was dangerous, but this was maybe my only chance."

The professor shook his head. "I understand. It must be very emotional for you, Larry. But you can't risk this sort of thing—not now. There'll be time after the battle."

"After the battle we may all be dead," I pointed out.

He put his hands to his face and rubbed his eyes. Suddenly I noticed how tired he looked. He had been working awfully hard— and it hadn't been that long since the night when he'd been shot as we rowed across the Charles. "We may all be dead very soon," he agreed. "But we must proceed under the assumption that we will survive. There is really nothing else we can do. Come with me to Coolidge Palace, Larry. It's the best—and safest—place for you."

I didn't want to hurt him. I didn't want to be a burden. So I just said, "Okay."

"Thank you, Larry," he said. He asked a few questions about my family, but I could tell he had too many other things on his mind. We finished our breakfast in silence.

Pretty soon after that Peter drove us over to the palace. Everyone was busy packing up the remaining equipment, and I did what I could to help. Lieutenant Carmody was there for a while; I saw him stare at me once or twice, but he didn't say anything. Professor Foster left in a wagon with some of the electrical equipment soon after we arrived; he looked really nervous.

The artillery hadn't let up, and there was a haze of smoke over the city. It's going to happen, I thought. The president isn't going to surrender. The battle is coming.

I couldn't stop thinking about my family. What was going on in the camp? Were they safe? Were they hungry? What would happen when the battle started?

Professor Palmer wanted me to stay at the palace. But how could I? It was okay while I had something to do, but now I was just hanging around. Was I going to stay here straight through the battle? Then what? I went looking for Professor Palmer, but he wasn't around. "Heard he went off to some big strategy meeting," a soldier told me.

I wandered over to the kitchen. One benefit of working on the palace grounds was that there was still lots of food to eat. Not as good as the roast beef we'd had the first time we were here, back when I'd saved the president's life, but way better than what you'd get anywhere else in the city. Everyone else seemed to have already eaten, and the kitchen was pretty deserted. There was leftover chicken and roast potatoes, though, and they tasted unbelievable.

And that's when I made my decision. It wasn't really conscious. I just found myself walking over to the chef, pointing to the leftovers, and saying, "Could you put some of that food in a sack for me? I'm supposed to bring it back to the soldiers—a few of them are too busy to come over here, and they're getting hungry."

The chef wasn't pleased about having all those soldiers dirtying up her kitchen and eating her food. She was a fussy lady with gray hair and a French accent. She just shook her head at my request. "I'm glad this nonsense is finally ending," she muttered. "I cook for aristocrats, not common soldiers."

"Yes, ma'am," I replied. "Not much longer, I've heard. But your food has certainly been wonderful."

She brightened at the compliment. "You've not had the chance to sample my cuisine when we haven't had these annoying shortages," she pointed out.

Lots of people were dying because of those annoying shortages, of course, but I wasn't going to mention that. "I'm sure the food would be even more wonderful then," I said.

She nodded in full agreement and pulled a sack out of a drawer. "Will this be enough?" she asked, shoveling in the rest of the pan.

"Yes, ma'am, That'll do. And thank you very much."

"Come back when this wretched war is over," she said. "My stuffed pheasant is beyond compare."

"I'll certainly do that," I replied as I hurried out of the kitchen.

I stuffed the sack down the front of my coat and headed for the palace gate. Would the guards let me out? Maybe Lieutenant Carmody had left orders not to. Maybe I was a prisoner here. Well, then, I'd have to figure out how to escape. I was feeling really guilty—about lying to get the food, about letting Professor Palmer down. But I just couldn't help it. I had to get to my family.

The guards at the gate still wore those weird-looking tall hats with the plumes on them and stood at attention, hardly even blinking. There were more of them than usual, maybe because there were more people than usual outside. Begging to get in to see the president. Begging for food.

Would they be able to smell what was in the sack? I could get torn limb from limb if people realized what I was carrying.

"Good morning," I said to one of the guards. "Can you let me out? I have to get back to headquarters."

He stared down at me. "Why don't you wait for a wagon?" he asked. "They're arriving and departing all the time."

"I'm supposed to go now." More lying.

He shrugged and opened the gate for me. The people outside surged forward, and I pushed through them, just like yesterday at the camp. They ignored me. If they smelled the chicken, maybe they thought they were hallucinating.

I headed off for the camp.

I felt weird. I had really done it. Just like that, I had left. And I wasn't going back. Lieutenant Carmody, Professor Palmer, General Aldridge—they'd all be mad at me. I probably couldn't make them understand. They'd done a lot for me, but I was alone. I had lost my family and my world. I wasn't sure I'd ever get my world back, but I knew where Mom and Cassie and Matthew were. And I had to be there too.

Then I stopped. I had forgotten about Kevin. He must have been going nuts, all alone in the hospital. I needed to bring him along with me, I decided. Of course, maybe he wouldn't want to go; it wasn't his family, after all. But I was pretty sure he would—anything was better than staying in that room by himself. So I veered off and headed towards Mass General.

The haze of smoke got thicker as I approached the hospital. It was close to the Charles—but not that close, I thought, suddenly worried. The Canadian artillery couldn't reach it—right? I hurried down the long empty street leading to the hospital. More smoke. The artillery kept getting louder. I was really scared now.

I got as close as I could. The hospital was on fire. Horse-drawn fire trucks surrounded the building, and men were shooting streams of water into it. Didn't look like they were doing much good. I heard people screaming and weeping. Some were lying on the ground, others just wandered around in a daze. "What happened?" I asked a doctor who was treating a little girl with a long gash on her face.

He glared at me. "What d'you think happened?" he demanded.

"The survivors—where will they go?"

He waved vaguely. He looked exhausted. "Everywhere. Nowhere," he said. "What does it matter?" He went back to bandaging the girl.

I walked around and around the building, looking for Kevin. I saw lots of stuff that I'll never forget—people bleeding, people dying—but I didn't see him. Finally I sat down on the cobblestones and put my head in my hands. My throat was raw from the smoke. My stomach still hurt from where I'd been punched yesterday. But I didn't really notice. People were dying all around me, and Kevin was gone.

I needed my mother.

I got up after a while and trudged away from the burning building. It took me a long time to get to the camp. I was kind of in a daze. Poor Kevin. First drikana, and now…He could still be alive, of course, but what if he was burned, or hurt—what if he was dying all by himself in this alien world? I saw a couple of balloons floating above the city, and they reminded me of Kevin getting the idea for them as we sat by the professor's fireplace. He deserved better.

Cheapside was quiet. Some people were sitting on their steps, smoking long pipes, and children were running around in the lanes. It seemed strange that kids would actually be playing on a day like today, but what did I know? I wasn't a kid anymore. No one bothered me, and the sack of food stayed safe inside my coat.

Outside the camp, things were grim. Chester and his friends were digging another big hole next to the one I'd seen yesterday. By the barracks, soldiers were silently cleaning their weapons. Sergeant Hornbeam spotted me, and he seemed angry. "What are you doing here?" he demanded.

"I'm—I'm visiting someone."

"Don't you know there's a war on?" he said, sounding like Colonel Clarett.

Usually Sergeant Hornbeam scared me, but right now I didn't feel like being a nice little boy. "Look," I said, "all I want is to go into the camp. Can I do that or not?"

He raised an eyebrow, and then muttered, "I can't stop you," and he turned away.

I walked up to the main gate. There were several empty wagons lined up there, and lots of soldiers, rifles at the ready. Inside the gate was an even bigger crowd of people than I'd seen yesterday. "What's the bloody point of aiming those guns at us?" one old man shouted at the soldiers. "Why don't you go and fight the real enemy!"

Caleb was one of the soldiers being shouted at. He shook his head when he saw me. "Not a good day to be visitin', mate," he said.

"Lots of angry people inside. Must not have got a good night's sleep."

"I know," I said. "I'll be careful."

"Come on, then." We headed over to the side gate. "What's the news from headquarters?" he asked.

"We're going to fight," I said. "Tomorrow, probably, or the next day."

He nodded. "That's what we heard. Won't be soon enough, for my taste. Now be careful in there, lad. People aren't just angry, some of 'em are a bit crazy."

Once again the guards opened the gate with bayonets fixed and I pushed my way through the crowd, making sure the sack didn't fall out from inside my coat.

Caleb was right. Things were falling apart in the camp. I passed by several fistfights; no one seemed interested in stopping them. Some old guy who was either drunk or crazy just stood in the middle of a path, howling at the top of his lungs. And here and there a corpse lay on the ground, its face covered with a sheet or a scrap of clothing.

It took me a while to find my family in the chaos, but finally I spotted their wagon. As I approached it, I saw a red-coated soldier standing next to my mother. My first thought was: Is she in trouble? Then I recognized the soldier. It was my father.

Mom's face lit up when she saw me, and she pointed me out to Dad.

"Larry," she said. "It's so wonderful you came back."

"Good afternoon, Mrs. Barnes." I was so relieved to be here I wanted to hug her. And Dad.

"This is Mr. Barnes," she said, pointing to Dad. "He's just—just here for a short while. On leave, before the battle." She looked like she'd been crying, I noticed. "Henry, this is the boy I was telling you about."

My father extended a hand. "A pleasure, lad."

I shook his hand. Like Mom, he looked different in this world. He was wearing a bushy mustache. He was thin, and his hair was streaked with gray. And the uniform looked so strange on him; he had never been a soldier, and he hated guns. But it was Dad all right.

He gave me a long look. "Mrs. Barnes was talking about you," he said. "She mentioned what a strange coincidence it was, your age and first name and all," he said.

"Yes, sir." He seemed almost suspicious of me, like he thought I was up to something.

"I was afraid you wouldn't return," Mom said, "with the bombardment starting. It's so dangerous now."

"I promised to come back," I pointed out. I motioned to the makeshift tent that was attached to the wagon. "Let's go in there," I said. "I've got something to show you."

We crawled inside. Matthew and Cassie were already in there. "Hi, Larry!" Matthew called out. He was spinning a little wooden top. "Did you see the airships in the sky?"

"I sure did," I replied. "They call them 'balloons.'"

"That's a funny name. Pa says we're doing some other things to beat the enemy, right, Pa?"

"That's right, Matthew."

Cassie was just sitting in a corner with her shawl wrapped around her, shivering, and rocking back and forth a little. Her eyes were dead; she didn't even seem irritated when she saw me. She looked awful—not sick, just awful.

I pulled out the sack of food. "It's not much," I said, "but it's more than you've been getting here."

Everyone's eyes widened. "Oh, you dear boy," Mom murmured.

"This is extremely good of you, Larry," my father said.

"I promised I'd do it," I said.

"Where in the world did you get chicken and potatoes?" he asked as Mom passed out the food.

"My father—he got some extra rations at headquarters."

"Really? That's hard to believe." He raised an eyebrow and smiled, and it was just like we were back at home, and I had said something he thought was kind of funny, although I didn't know why. He didn't laugh much, but he was always acting amused, like the rest of us were putting on a play just for him. It drove Cassie nuts.

Matthew was excited. "This is the best food I've had in months!" he said. "Thanks, Larry!" Cassie took her share and started gobbling it down, but she didn't say anything.

Dad refused to take any. "We still get our rations," he said.

"You need to keep your strength up," Mom pointed out.

"I'm fine, Emma," he replied. "Larry, why don't you and I go outside and give them a little more space to eat."

We scrambled out of the tent and stood by the wagon. "Mrs. Barnes has told me a lot about you, Larry," he said. "You've made a deep impression on her."

"She's a very nice woman," I replied.

"You believe you're related to her?"

"Possibly, sir."

"How is that, exactly? Emma wasn't very clear about it."

"I'm not really sure," I replied. I tried to remember exactly what I'd said to her yesterday, so I could repeat the story. I did my best. He pressed me on the details, and I don't think I did a very good job of answering him. He still seemed a little suspicious of me, even though I'd brought them the food—or maybe it was because I brought the food, without a good explanation. Or maybe he was just curious. He liked things to be logical, to make sense. And my story didn't quite make sense.

But he let it go finally. Logically, what reason did I have to be lying? "I am very grateful to you for the food, Larry," he said, changing the subject. "It grieves me that I can eat so well and sleep in a cot while my family has to live like this." He gestured at the tent and the wagon. "It grieves me to be away from them."

"Yes, sir. But you've got to do it."

He nodded. "Yes, of course. I fear, though—" He looked away and didn't finish the sentence.

"I think we've got a good shot at winning," I said. "These balloons—"

"Ah, the airships," he replied. "Matthew is so excited by them. But they're nowhere near as useful as people hope. I've heard they'll be used for surveillance of the enemy, nothing more."

"But that's something," I pointed out. He could be a drag sometimes, telling us not to get our hopes up when we entered a contest or whatever. Just giving you kids a reality check, he'd say. But lots of times we didn't want a reality check.

"It is something, of course," he admitted. "We'll find out soon enough what difference they'll make."

"Where are you stationed?" I asked.

"On the Charles," he said. "Preparing to fight the Canadians. My captain gave some of us with families in the camps a few hours' leave to go and see them. Very decent of him."

"The battle is coming," I said.

He nodded. "Yes," he replied quietly. "It is coming."

And some of you will never see your families again, I thought.

Matthew came bounding out of the tent then, and Dad turned his attention away from me. Mom came out a couple of minutes later; Cassie stayed inside.

Mom looked worried, of course—she had plenty of reason to be worried, with her husband going off to battle. But what worried her most now was Cassie. She made Dad go back into the tent to talk to her. "The strain is too much for the poor girl," she said to no one in particular. "It's such a difficult time."

"She'll be fine," I said, knowing she wouldn't be. Cassie would always find a way to feel bad. And Dad wouldn't be able to talk her out of it. He always tried to be logical with her, and he could never get it through his head that Cassie didn't have any use for his logic. It just made her angrier, because she thought he was talking down to her. Sure enough, I could hear her squawking after a minute: "You don't know what I've been through. You don't understand, you've never understood..." The same old stuff, only she said it with the almost-British accent people had in this world.

I heard Dad's voice, too low for us to make out the words, and then Cassie again, this time in a tone I'd never heard before—beyond anger, beyond despair: "Please, Papa, please take me with you. Please get me out of here, I have to get out of here. Papa, please..."

And then she was sobbing, and I knew Dad had his arms around her, trying to calm her down. And I knew he wasn't going to succeed.

"Why is Cassie the only one complaining?" Matthew wanted to know.

Mom just shook her head.

Eventually Dad came out, looking as worried as Mom. "Emma—" he said, and sort of shrugged. "It's hard on all of us."

"I know, Henry. I know."

"Private Barnes!" someone shouted from the path. It was a sergeant, with a couple of soldiers alongside him. "It's time!"

"One moment," Dad replied. He turned back to us.

"So soon, Henry?" Mom said.

"I'm sorry."

Matthew hugged him and started to cry. "Please, Papa, stay!" he sobbed. Mom touched Dad's arm, in that way she had. I stayed back by the wagon; I wasn't part of this.

When Dad had finished saying goodbye to Matthew and Mom, he ducked into the tent and said something to Cassie. I don't think he got any response. Then he came over and shook my hand. "Thank you again, Larry," he said.

"Please be careful, sir," I replied.

"I will."

Then I blurted out, "I'll take care of your family."

He looked puzzled. "That's very kind of you," he said, "but you've got your own family."

I couldn't think of anything I could say to that. Dad kissed Mom and Matthew one last time, and then left us.

The day suddenly seemed a lot colder.

"It'll be all right," Mom murmured. "Everything will be all right."

Matthew cried for a while. Mom put her arm around him, and he leaned close to her, but eventually he got over it and moved away. That was how Matthew was. Cassie stayed inside the tent. Mom looked really upset. The distant artillery never stopped. We talked for a while about the war and conditions in the city. I told her about the fire at the hospital, and she was horrified. "Those poor people. Is nowhere safe?" And then she started in: "You should go home, Larry. It was wonderful of you to come and bring that food, but it's late already."

How could I tell her that I didn't have a home anymore? I hadn't thought this part through. "Well," I said, "I was thinking of staying here and helping you out."

She gave me a long, puzzled stare. "You can't do that, Larry," she said. "You have to go home. You have to be safe. How can you think about leaving your father?"

"No, it's all right," I insisted. "He's really busy helping out with the war. He doesn't pay much attention to me."

"I'd like Larry to stay," Matthew piped up.

Mom shook her head, almost violently. She wasn't buying it. "Larry, you must go," she said, in that tone she gets when she's really serious and we've gone too far. "Now."

I thought about telling her the truth. But that was stupid—she wouldn't believe me. I could just stay somewhere else in the camp—she couldn't make me leave—but that wasn't the point. The point was to be with my family. I felt an awful emptiness come over me. Kevin was gone. Professor Palmer would probably be so angry that he wouldn't want me anymore. And now Mom didn't want me either. I thought: She's not my real mom. This isn't the real Matthew. But I didn't believe that anymore.

I was all alone in this stupid world. "Please let me stay," I whispered.

Tears came into her eyes then. She reached for Matthew and pulled him close to her. "You have to go home, Larry," she whispered back. "You have to go home. After the war, come visit us. You'll always be welcome."

I didn't move for a while, and then I slowly got up from the ground. Matthew was crying again. I gave him a long hug. I hesitated, then looked into the tent. Cassie was huddled in a corner, staring at me. "Take me with you," she begged in a hollow voice.

She looked scary. She looked insane. I couldn't help feeling sorry for her. But there was nothing I could do. "I'm sorry, Cassie," I said. "I can't."

Her eyes turned away from me then, and she started silently rocking once more.

Outside the tent, Mom was waiting for me, her face wet with tears. "I'll visit you," I said. "I promise." She hugged me then, and I didn't want to leave her embrace. I remember once when I was a little kid and I got separated from her at the mall, and I felt so scared and lost, and suddenly I saw her, frantically looking for me by the escalator. I raced to her and jumped up into her arms, and I felt so safe there, I never wanted to be anyplace else. That was kind of how I felt there in the camp.

But Mom pushed me away finally. "Please go, Larry," she said, "before it's too late."

And so I walked away.

I don't know what I was thinking. Maybe I was beyond thinking. I made my way through the crowded, stinking camp to the main gate. I had to fight my way through the crowd, but when I got to the front I didn't recognize any of the guards, and none of them looked like they wanted to hear my story or look at my pass. Off to my right people were throwing things at the guards, who just stood motionless at the fence, their rifles at the ready. Everyone was shouting.

"Let's go!" someone yelled. "They can't stop us all!"

There was more shouting, and people started pushing against me. I could see the guards just a few feet away, and their eyes were half-scared, half-angry. Even if one of them recognized me, he couldn't have done anything to help me at this point. I felt like I was going to get trampled to death, like at one of those soccer games in South America.

And then I heard gunshots, and the shouting turned to screaming, and people were running every which way. I fell to the ground, and someone kicked me, but I didn't get trampled. I could smell gunpowder in the air, and someone near me was groaning, and a woman was calling out, "Help me! Help me!"

I was scared I'd be shot if I got up, so I stayed where I was. I heard someone shouting out orders, and the gates opened. A bunch of soldiers rushed in, and one of them hoisted me to my feet.

"I think you've outworn your welcome here, lad," he said, shaking his head.

It was Sergeant Hornbeam.

"Yes, sir," I said. "I'm just leaving."

"See that you don't return. This won't be the last of it. The night is going to be long and deadly."

"Yes, sir."

The crowd had mostly moved back. Some of the soldiers aimed their rifles at them while others collected the wounded and the dead. Sergeant Hornbeam gestured at the gate; I walked out.

It was only after I was outside the camp that I could think about what had happened. I had been in a battle—soldiers fighting their own people. I was lucky to be alive.

I was trembling and out of breath. My ribs were sore where I'd been kicked. Two soldiers hurried past me, carrying the corpse of an old woman on a stretcher. Five minutes ago she had been alive, probably screaming at the soldiers along with everyone else. Or maybe she had just been trapped in the crowd. And now she'd be dumped in one of those graves that Chester was digging. No one would ever know what happened to her.

And what was I supposed to do?

I headed off, trudging slowly through the deepening darkness. Past the barracks and the other army buildings and on into Cheapside. Going where? To do what?

I don't think I even noticed the footsteps behind me. What did I care? Then I heard the voice, loud and mocking, almost at my shoulder.

"Nice coat, mate!"

CHAPTER 21

I turned. There were three of them—short, scrawny kids, about my age probably, dressed in ragged shirts and pants. They quickly surrounded me.

"Where you headed, mate?"

"We've seen you before passin' through Cheapside, haven't we?"

"Comin' from the camp? How'd you get out?"

I tried to push past them, but they closed in on me. The thing I remember most about them were their eyes. They were wild and fearless. They didn't have anything to lose. I put my fists up, ready to defend myself. Not much point in that, it turned out, because the kid behind me cut my legs out from under me and I fell to the ground. Then the three of them were on top of me, pulling my coat off while I tried to push them away. They were small, but they were strong. One of them held my legs while the other two wrestled with the coat. I didn't have a chance. They had it off me inside a minute, and then they glared down at me.

"Got a little spunk in you, don't you, mate?"

"This is our turf, and you don't pass through without payin' the toll."

"Reckon you'll have to be punished for breaking the rules."

One of them picked up a rock and grinned. I squirmed, but there was no way I could break free.

"Hey!" I heard someone shout, and a rock went whizzing past. "Let 'im go."

The kids looked back. "None of your concern, mate!" one of them called out. "Now shove."

"Shove yourself. He's a friend of mine." Another rock went by.

The kids looked at each other. "You can have your friend," the one holding the rock said. "He's not worth dross. But we keep the coat. We're off, mates."

They let go of me and disappeared down an alley. I sat up and looked at the person who had saved me. He was walking towards me with a rock in each hand.

It was Stinky Glover.

"Hey, mate, I think I actually do know you," he said as he came up to me.

"There were some kids chasing you in the camp yesterday," I said. I was gasping a little, trying to catch my breath.

"That's right, I remember. You did a good deed for me. I made up that 'friend' bit, but looks like I was right."

"Thanks for getting those kids off me," I said.

He helped me up. I felt a little bruised, but otherwise okay. "Dangerous place to be by yourself," he replied. "Name's Julian Glover. What's yours?"

"Palmer. Larry Palmer. So, what are you doing outside the camp, Julian?" I asked. It was going to be really hard not to call him "Stinky."

"I could ask you the same thing, Lawrence," he said. "I make myself useful to the soldiers. They want something from the city, they can send me, 'cause they know I'll come back. Beats sitting around all day in the camp doing nothing, and they'll give me a hunk of meat or a hardtack biscuit for my troubles. I've got no family, so I have to fend for myself."

"No family?" I asked. "You're here alone?"

"Well, I'm 'prenticed to a blacksmith, but I've pretty much run off from him since we got to the camp. With no smithing to be done, I'm not earning my keep, so he doesn't care. What about you? How'd you end up here?"

I told Stinky the story I had made up. I figured it would get him interested, and it did.

"The Barnes family?" he said. "From Glanbury? I'm from

Glanbury. I know the Barneses. Nice people. Well, Cassie can be a trial."

"I know what you mean."

"But still—maybe we'll run into each other after all this."

"That would be great. Anyway, thanks again. I don't know what they would have done to me if—"

Stinky waved me silent. "We're even. So, you headed home?"

"Yeah, I guess so."

"You guess so? Where else'd you be going? Anyway, mind if I tag along? It's dangerous out here by yourself."

The last thing I wanted right now was for Stinky Glover to be tagging along with me. "No, that's all right, uh, Julian. Curfew's coming pretty soon. You better get back to the camp."

Stinky looked sort of disappointed. "You sure? It's no bother. I can sleep in an alleyway as well as in that camp."

"No, really. Thanks for the help, but I'll be fine."

He stared at me, and then shrugged. "Suit yourself, Lawrence. And good luck."

"Thanks, Julian."

He turned away and headed back towards the camp.

I shivered—from the cold, and from fear. I was alone again in Cheapside. I started walking quickly towards the center of the city.

It was odd about Stinky, I thought. He didn't look all that fat in this world—but then, it was hard to be fat after a couple of months in that camp. He probably stank, but it was hard to tell, because everyone sort of stank in this world, and I'd gotten used to it. But the main thing was, he could've just left me to get beaten up—what did it matter to him? But he didn't. Maybe he wasn't so bad; maybe this world brought out some different qualities in him.

I saw a policeman, who stopped and stared at me suspiciously. It wasn't quite sundown, but it was close. Did the curfew really matter, with the battle about to begin, with hospitals on fire and the camps ready to explode? I remembered that my pass was in my coat. Not that it had helped with that cop last night. But losing it made me feel a little more lonely, a little more abandoned. I was just another homeless kid wandering through the city.

I was downtown now, near where Kevin and I had been that first night when we'd asked another cop for help. There were people still out on the streets, but they all look tired and worried. A lot of the stores were boarded up. I passed by a small park. In it, a man was standing on a platform, talking to a small crowd.

Not talking, I realized after a moment—preaching.

Somehow I knew who it was, even standing outside the park, without being able to hear or see him clearly. I went into the park and stood at the edge of the crowd.

It was him. The guy from the Burger Queen world, with the black beard and fierce, dark eyes. The guy who had talked about the beauty in each speck of dirt. And in the home you left behind.

He wasn't wearing a robe this time, just a rumpled jacket and pair of pants. As before, he spoke softly, but you could understand every word he said. He was talking about suffering.

"Yes, you have suffered, you continue to suffer, but you must not let your suffering define or diminish you. You are so much more than that. The suffering diminishes you only if you let it diminish you. Even in suffering there is beauty, there is hope, there is love. More than that. In suffering lies the chance for redemption, and even the chance for greatness. How can you know what is in you unless you have struggled, unless you have been asked to do more than you thought you were capable of doing? Little consolation, perhaps, when there is not enough to eat and the enemy knocks upon our gates. But it is true nonetheless."

Someone shouted at him from the crowd, "We need food, not words!"

"What a fool!" an old man called out.

"Listen to the man!" a woman scolded him. "Let him speak."

"There's been too much talk!"

And then it seemed like he was staring straight at me as he went on, ignoring the crowd's taunts. "Our journey through life is harsh, and dangerous, and filled with sorrow and disappointment," he said. "We say to ourselves, I just can't take any more. And yet there is more to be borne. And it is only by enduring the pain that we can see the beauty."

"I'll show you pain!" someone shouted.

"It is only by living in doubt that we can find certainty."

"See the beauty in this!" the heckler said, and flung a rock at him. It hit him in the shoulder, but he didn't seem to notice.

"It is only by setting out that we can finally return home," the preacher concluded.

Then there were more rocks thrown, and fistfights broke out, and everyone was shouting. I made my way through the crowd to the preacher, who was sitting on the ground rubbing his temple.

"Are you all right?" I asked.

He looked up at me. "I'm okay," he said. "But you look cold."

Okay. He had said *okay*. "Who are you?" I demanded.

"Just a stranger passing through," he said. "Maybe I should have passed through a little faster," he added, wiping some blood onto his pants.

"No, I saw you—in that other world. What's going on? Do you know me or something? How come you know the word 'okay'?"

He shrugged. "Excellent questions. But weren't you listening? It's only by living in doubt—"

"Tell me!" I screamed at him.

His dark, glittering eyes looked a little doubtful then. "I'm sorry," he said softly. "This whole thing has been entirely my fault. I wish I could—"

"Hey you!" a voice behind me said. I turned. It was the cop I had run into the night before. He didn't look happy to see me. "What are you doing here?"

"Listen," I said, "could you just wait a sec—"

"Why are you causing trouble? Now get home before I tag you."

I didn't know what tagging was, but I supposed I didn't want it to happen to me. I turned back to the preacher—but he was gone. Vanished.

Except for his jacket, which lay on the ground at my feet. A parting gift? I picked it up.

"Did you hear me?" the cop demanded.

"Fine," I said, without looking at him. "I'm leaving."

I put the jacket on and ran out of the park, hoping to find the preacher. But there was no trace of him. I stopped to catch my breath finally in the middle of a street. I checked the pockets of his jacket; they were empty.

So who was he? Was he from another universe? My universe? Had he come here in the portal? Why? What did he mean when he said that the whole thing had been entirely his fault? What whole thing?

He hadn't answered any of my questions, and I had a whole lot more to ask him if I ever saw him again. But what were the odds of that?

I started walking. Suddenly I was so tired I could barely stand up. I knew what I was going to have to do: go back to headquarters. The lieutenant or the professor might yell at me, but they weren't going to throw me out, they weren't going to let me starve. Besides, they had more important things to worry about right now than me. And they might know what happened to Kevin.

So that's where I headed, my mind filled with the preacher and my family and Kevin and Stinky Glover and the corpse of the old woman. I felt overwhelmed; and the battle hadn't even started yet.

The streets got more and more deserted as I walked, except for soldiers galloping by on horseback. I saw a few policemen, but they ignored me. I got the feeling that everyone was starting to hunker down to wait for the battle.

Headquarters, when I finally reached it, was anything but deserted. Soldiers rushed in and out of the courtyard; wagons were being packed; officers were conferring with each other. No one took any special notice of me.

I was surprised to see Corporal Hennessy there; the last time I had seen him, he had brought Kevin and me over to haul bags of grain in the food warehouse. It seemed so long ago. He nodded to me. "Almost time, eh, mate?" he said.

"That's what I've heard," I replied. "What's going to happen to the camp?"

"Don't know. They've already pulled a lot of us out. Not much point in guarding it now, is there?"

I thought about the old woman. How many others were being killed as they tried to escape? "Why don't they tell the people in the camp? Why don't they just open the gates and let them go?"

The corporal shrugged. "Because war's a bloody mess. If you spend your time trying to find sense in it you'll go mad."

That sounded about right. "Well, good luck," I said.

He nodded. "Good luck to you, mate. And to all of us, because we'll surely need it."

I went inside to the mess. It was almost empty, but a grouchy cook got me the usual salt pork and stale bread, which I wolfed down like it was Harvest dinner. Then I went upstairs to my room.

I could hear muffled sobs while I was still on the stairs. I have never been so happy to hear someone crying.

I rushed into the room. Kevin was lying on his cot, his face buried in a pillow.

"Hey, Kev," I said, and I put my hand on his shoulder.

He turned over, and his face lit up. "Larry!" he said. "Am I glad to see you." He sat up, and we hugged for a long time.

"I went to the hospital this afternoon," I said. "I thought maybe you were—"

"I know, I know. A cannonball hit the main building and set the place on fire. Everyone was screaming to get out. It would've been easy for me if they didn't have those bars on my windows. So instead I had to go out into the corridor, and there was smoke everywhere, so I could barely see. But then a nurse grabbed me, and we found a door and got out just before the whole place collapsed. They could really use some of those red Exit signs, you know?"

"Sure. What happened then?"

"Well, I tried to help out for a while, but there really wasn't much I could do. There wasn't much anyone could do. It was awful, Larry. All these people were injured and dying—and the doctors were basically helpless."

"Yeah, I saw some of that."

"So finally I just headed back here," Kevin went on. "I'd been in that hospital long enough anyway. I feel fine. There wasn't much of anyone around, but then I ran into Peter, and he told me you'd disappeared and Lieutenant Carmody was really angry. So then I started to get worried. You hadn't been to the hospital for a couple of days, and I thought: what if you're dead? What am I gonna do here by myself? When it got dark and you still weren't back, I guess I got pretty upset."

"Sorry I haven't been around, Kevin," I said. "But see, I found my family. In the camp, just like you said. Plus Stinky Glover, and Nora Lally, except her name's Sarah here."

"Hey, that's great, Larry," Kevin said. Then he paused. "What about—you know—my family?"

I shook my head. "I didn't find them. I don't think they live in Glanbury. But they could be somewhere else—who knows?"

He sighed. "Well, maybe it doesn't matter so much. At least there's someone here from our world." He didn't sound convinced that it didn't matter. "Tell me what happened," he said.

So I told him everything. About finding my family, about how I was dead in this world, about how my father was in the army and Cassie was pretty nuts, about the meeting with the president, and

Stinky helping me fight those kids in Cheapside. And about the strange preacher in the park.

"I guess you've been busy." Kevin said when I finished. "What do you think that meant—the preacher apologizing to you?"

"No clue. No clue how he recognized me, either. But I think—I think he's like us. From our world, or maybe from another world."

Kevin was silent for a while. Then he said, "So, what do we do?"

"I don't know. Go to sleep, I guess. I'm wasted."

"But tomorrow. After we wake up."

"I want—I want to help my family," I said.

"Everyone says the battle is going to start tomorrow," Kevin pointed out.

"I know. But you can't believe how awful it is in that camp now. People are dying all over the place."

"So how are you going to help your family?"

"I don't know—bring them more food, maybe. Help them get back to Glanbury, if that's possible."

"If we get to Glanbury, we can find the portal," Kevin pointed out.

I hadn't thought about the portal in days. "Yeah," I said. "If we can get there."

"Talking to Peter today got me worried," he went on. "It sounds to me like Lieutenant Carmody doesn't want to let us go home. We've been too valuable."

"But we've told them everything we know."

"Not really. I mean—they've focused on this short-term stuff, just trying to win the war, right? But if they do win, maybe they'll start paying attention to other stuff. Like medicine. That Doctor Dreier who runs the hospital—I guess Professor Palmer talked to him, because he was in to see me a couple of times, and he was really interested in germs and viruses and smallpox and so on. I bet we could help them a lot with that."

I thought of the way Professor Palmer and then that other doctor had wanted to bleed Kevin. "It's not right," I said. "We helped them. They should let us go home."

"I know. But that's not the way the lieutenant thinks."

"So what are you saying?"

"I'm saying we should get out of here. First thing tomorrow morning. See if we can make it to Glanbury."

The idea was scary, but it was what I wanted to do. "We have to go to the camp first and find my family," I said.

"Okay. We're going to have to wait till after the battle anyway to head south."

So we had a plan, sort of. And we had each other again—which was more than I'd expected an hour ago. I blew the candle out, and we lay down on our cots to go to sleep. I was really tired, but my mind kept on racing. "Kevin," I said, "if we find the portal, do you think it'll bring us home?"

"Sure," he replied. "It has to."

I thought about what the preacher had said: *It is only by setting out that you can finally return home.* Had he been talking to me? Well, it looked like I was going to try to follow his advice.

"You want to know something funny, Larry?" Kevin asked after a while.

"What's that?"

"Today's my birthday. I'm a teenager."

"Happy birthday," I said.

"I almost didn't make it," he murmured. "Hard to believe, but I almost didn't make it."

Then he was quiet. The artillery had stopped, I noticed. I could hear someone shout an order, the creaking of wagon wheels in the courtyard. Not much of a birthday, I thought. But it could have been worse. I closed my eyes, and the next thing I knew it was dawn.

CHAPTER 22

Kevin was already awake. "Let's go," he said. "Before someone ships us off to Coolidge Palace or wherever."

"Okay, okay." I got up to my feet and used the chamber pot. The room was freezing. I put my shoes on, then the preacher's coat. "Ready," I mumbled.

"One thing," Kevin said. He looked a little nervous.

"What?"

"I want to get our own clothes."

"Huh? You mean, from our world? I don't even know where they are."

"They're probably in Lieutenant Carmody's room. Peter gave them to him after he gave us these clothes, remember?"

I remembered. "But that's crazy, Kevin," I said. "The lieutenant is the one guy we want to stay away from."

"He won't be there," Kevin replied. "Peter said he mostly stays at the palace now."

"But why take the chance?"

"Because it'll be easier walking with our sneakers on."

"Sure, but is that worth the risk?"

"I don't know," he said. "I want my clothes. I want to wear them when I go home."

I was about to argue some more, but I looked at him and decided he wasn't fooling; he wasn't going to leave without his clothes.

I shrugged. "Fine," I said. "Whatever."

We went downstairs. I wondered if Professor Palmer would be in his room. I had another pang, thinking about how I'd abandoned him. Could we say goodbye to him? But what if he decided to stop us? He'd certainly try. It was risky enough going to the lieutenant's room.

We found it halfway down the corridor.

"You knock," I whispered, although I didn't really know why we should bother knocking.

Kevin hesitated, then tapped softly on the door. We waited. No answer. He turned the knob, and the door creaked open. We walked inside.

The room was small. The bed was neatly made. A small window looked out on the courtyard. In front of the window was a wooden desk with an oil lamp and a few papers on it. Next to it was a bookshelf. On the floor was a pair of shiny black boots. By the closet door was a dresser with a comb, a brush, and few coins on top. Kevin opened the closet, and we saw a neat row of uniforms hanging along a pole, with more shoes and boots on the floor.

This felt creepy. We didn't belong here. Kevin started opening the drawers of the dresser. I just stood by the bed. "Come on," he whispered. "Look."

"Our clothes can't be here," I said. "The place is too small."

"We don't know till we've searched." He finished opening the drawers, then went over to the closet. "Under the bed," he said. "Check under the bed."

Reluctantly I got down on my knees and took a look. On the floor I spied a large black trunk and, next to it, a canvas sack. I pulled the sack out, looked inside, and sighed with relief. "Got 'em," I said.

Kevin came over and pulled the clothes out. Cap, t-shirt, jeans, sneakers…"Let's put them on," he said.

"Huh?"

"Under these clothes. It's gonna be cold out there. We can leave the stupid shoes."

He started unbuttoning his shirt. Again I wanted to argue, but I figured it'd be easier and quicker to just go along. So I put on the two layers of clothes—my "old" clothes underneath, and my "new" clothes on top. Wearing two pairs of pants felt pretty clunky, but it was great to have my sneakers on again. Kevin put on his Red Sox cap.

"You sure you want to wear that?" I asked.

"Why not?"

"People'll think you're strange, like when we first got here."

"So what?" he demanded.

I couldn't think of an answer. It was odd, but the cap seemed to make him look happier. Like putting it on brought him one step closer to going home. "Let's go," I said.

Apparently Kevin didn't have any more bright ideas, because he just said "Fine."

We went downstairs, and I could smell food from the mess. That could be the last meal we'd have in a while, I thought. I was hungry, but I didn't suggest stopping, and neither did Kevin. We went outside into the gray morning.

There was less activity in the courtyard than there had been last night—probably everyone had already left to take up their positions for the battle. The air was bitter cold. The artillery rumbled in the distance.

We hurried out of the courtyard and onto the street. And there, wouldn't you know, was Peter driving the lieutenant's carriage up to the entrance. "Mornin', lads!" he called out, coming to a halt next to us. "Larry, people've been worried. Where've you been?"

"Nowhere special," I said. "Gotta go."

But before we could get away the carriage door opened and Lieutenant Carmody was staring at us. It was the same stare I remembered from the first time we met him. He was only a lieutenant, but it was the gaze of someone who knew how to make people obey him.

He looked at Kevin's cap, then down at our sneakers. He understood what we had done, and what we were up to. "Planning on going home, lads?" he asked. "Your portal's a long ways off, and the Portuguese army's in the way."

"It's time," Kevin said. "Time to go home."

Lieutenant Carmody shook his head. "Believe me, you'll be much better off staying with us than trying to go anywhere today, of all days. Hop in, lads. We'll take care of you."

Kevin looked at me for a second, and then he took off. I hesitated for another second, then took off right behind him.

"Peter!" I heard the lieutenant shout. "After them!"

We headed for a side street. The carriage clattered behind us. I thought: Peter wouldn't shoot us, would he? We made it to the side street, then Kevin dodged into an alley, and I followed. We hopped over a wooden fence and cut through a yard to another street. After a minute I looked back over my shoulder: no carriage. We kept going for a few more minutes, then hid in another alley and tried to catch our breath.

"Think we're safe?" Kevin gasped.

"Lost 'em for now," I said. "And they can't chase us all day, can they?"

"Hope not."

Kevin didn't look so good. He was hunched over, still gasping for air. Maybe this was going to be too much for him. "You okay, Kev?" I asked him.

Kevin managed to nod. "Yeah. Kinda out of shape, I guess. Just give me a minute."

I thought about Lieutenant Carmody. He was right, of course: this was a stupid day to try to get back to Glanbury. But I had a feeling Kevin was right, too. The lieutenant probably didn't want us to go home at all. Maybe he had never really been our friend. We were just a way of helping to win the war. And making him look good.

"Let's go," Kevin said finally. "Which way is the camp?"

It took me a minute to get my bearings, but I figured it out—I was really getting to know the city. We start walking. The streets were surprisingly crowded—with people from the camps, I realized.

"What's happening?" I asked an old man with a burlap bag slung over his shoulder.

"Soldiers are gone," he said. "Need to find some food."

"Were you in the Fens camp? Are people still there?"

"No more camp," he muttered as he wandered away. "Thank God, no more camp."

Kevin and I looked at each other. "I was afraid of this," I said.

"What should we do?"

"Might as well go check out the camp. My family might still be there."

Kevin agreed, and we kept walking.

It turned out we weren't far from the park where I had seen the preacher. I pointed it out to Kevin as we went past. "Sure would be good to ask him a few more questions," Kevin said.

"No kidding."

"But you know what?"

"What?"

"I really don't care all that much. I'm sick of portals and sick of this world. I just want to go home."

And that was all Kevin had to say about the preacher.

We kept going. There were no policemen in sight, no soldiers. I tried to spot familiar faces in the people we passed, but I didn't see any. Everyone looked exhausted. Where did they think they were going? They wouldn't find food in the city. It must have felt good to finally get out of the camp, but really, there wasn't anyplace better. Some people had already given up and were just sitting by the side of the road, their eyes dead, waiting—just like they had waited in the camp.

The crowds were thinner in Cheapside. I don't think people wanted to stop there. I got nervous, but no one bothered us, except for a couple of kids who shouted out comments about Kevin's cap. He didn't seem to mind. We just walked on.

As we got close to the camp we could see smoke billowing into the air, and we could smell the odor of charred wood. The sun was up now, but there wasn't much sky to be seen.

All the military buildings had been set on fire: the barracks, the mess, even the food warehouse. Some were still burning, others were smoldering rubble. Beyond them, the gates to the camp stood wide open; the fence had been wrecked. There was no sign of any soldiers.

"Geez," Kevin muttered.

There wasn't much to say. We headed into the camp.

A few people were left, but not many. Old people who looked too weak to go anywhere. Nasty-looking men who were scavenging among the stuff that had been left behind. And animals: a pair of mangy dogs, thin as skeletons, were barking furiously at each other; an equally skinny horse gazed mournfully at them. Ahead of us a wagon lay on its side, its wheels shattered. Everywhere there was trash—books, kitchen utensils, broken toys, a single shoe.

We wandered through the camp. It was clear that my family wasn't there, but I guess we didn't know what else to do. Finally Kevin pulled at my sleeve and pointed. About twenty yards away from us a body lay face-down on the trampled earth. I shivered. We went over to it. It was an old man, with one hand stretched in front of him as if he were trying to reach for something just out of his grasp. But there was nothing there, just dirt. He lay motionless except for a few wisps of gray hair blowing in the wind. He was dead. "Should we bury him?" Kevin asked.

I shook my head. "We have to go," I said. There was a lump in my throat. My family was gone. Lieutenant Carmody was chasing us. The enemy was about to attack the city. Everything was falling apart.

We had to go, but where? We weren't returning to headquarters. And, like the lieutenant said, the Portuguese army stood between us and Glanbury. But we'd made our plan, and I couldn't think of a better one.

"A lot of people are going to die today," Kevin said, looking down at the corpse. "Maybe us."

"I know," I said. "Still, we've gotta go."

He nodded. We were silent for a moment, standing in the ruins of the camp. And then we walked out of the camp and headed south, towards the battle.

CHAPTER 23

For a while it didn't matter which direction we were heading. People were going everywhere, and I suppose no direction was particularly safe. But the further south we got, the louder the artillery sounded, and the more dangerous our journey started to feel. People going the other way kept telling us to turn back, turn back, you'll get caught in the battle. And they had all sorts of rumors: the battle had started, we were losing, we had already lost…

But there were some people heading south along with us, and they had the same idea we did. "Win or lose, we just want to go home," one woman said to us. "There's nothing left for us in Boston, and we were lucky to get out of that camp alive." She had a couple of little children with her, and a half-dead donkey carrying their possessions. The face of one of the girls was pitted with smallpox scars; she looked curiously at Kevin's cap. The woman offered us a couple of hard rolls they had gotten somewhere, and we accepted gratefully. It was our first food of the day, and we didn't know when we'd get our next.

We pressed on ahead of the family after a while, staying on the main road so we wouldn't get lost. I recalled details of the road from our journey into the city with the Harpers so long ago. I knew we were getting close when we passed by the remnants of another refugee camp on marshland. I remembered how Mr. Harper had scorned the people staying in such an unhealthy place. I wondered if they'd ended up worse off than anyone else. There were still some people there, with their wagons and makeshift tents. Probably they thought we were the fools, heading towards the battle.

"Should be a big military camp up ahead," Kevin said. "And then the fortifications."

"Think they'll attack along the main road?"

"No idea. There's a lot of territory to defend."

I recalled the discussion in President Gardner's office. The electric fence wasn't powerful enough to replace all the fortifications, so they'd try to trick the enemy into thinking the fence was a weak spot in their defenses. Would that work?

The road curved inland after a while, and up ahead we saw a crowd of people. When we reached it we asked a woman what was going on. "They won't let us pass," she said. "Say it's too dangerous."

"Has the battle started?"

"I don't think so. Someone said when the artillery stops, that's when they'll attack."

I looked at Kevin. Had we gone as far as we could go?

"What would happen if we went off the road?" he asked me.

"I don't know," I said. "What good would that do?"

"I dunno. Maybe we could sneak through the fortifications somewhere else. Or go around them. Maybe over by the ocean."

"And have both armies shooting at us?"

Kevin shrugged. "Let's go see what's happening," he said finally.

We made our way through the crowd. There were just a couple of soldiers standing guard at a barrier in the road. It wasn't anything like the scene at the Fens camp yesterday. Nobody looked like they wanted to go any further; they were happy to let the army do the fighting.

One of the soldiers looked familiar. It was Benjamin, our jailer. He was still fat, although not as fat as when we first saw him. I don't think he remembered us at first, but he recognized Kevin's cap. "Ah, the lads with the ciphering machine," he said. "What are you doing here?"

"Just trying to get home," I replied.

"Where's home?"

"Glanbury."

He laughed. "Good luck to you, then."

"Has the battle started?"

"Oh, you'll know when the battle's started. We're all waiting for the battle to start."

He seemed grateful for someone to talk to. It occurred to me that he was scared. He was sweating, despite the cold, and he flinched every time there was a particularly loud explosion. No wonder they'd stuck him back here, well behind the front line.

Suddenly someone rode up on horseback. It was Corporal Hennessy, who I'd talked to in the courtyard at headquarters the other night. "I need one of you immediately," he said to the two guards.

Benjamin looked like he was hoping his partner would volunteer. The other guy was tall and skinny and kind of dopey-looking. Neither of them said anything.

"All right, you, Benjamin, report to Sergeant Hornbeam," the corporal ordered. Benjamin looked like he wanted to protest, but instead he just sighed, as if he'd expected this all along. Then the corporal noticed us. "Hello, lads," he said. "You two reporting for duty?"

He was serious, I realized. Was he asking us to fight? Kevin and I looked at each other. And I decided: it's our war, too. "What do you want us to do?" I asked.

"Go see Sergeant Dryerson, over at the ammunition depot," he replied. "He needs some extra hands. Let's hope you've developed some muscles since you were at the food warehouse." Then he galloped off.

Benjamin looked at us glumly. "Should've stayed out of it, lads," he said.

"Which way to the ammunition depot?" I asked.

He gestured to his left. "Not a good place to be, I think. Fare you well."

And then he sighed again and trudged off. The other guard let us pass, and we headed into the camp.

"Why?" Kevin demanded.

I looked up at the balloon—the balloon we had helped invent—hovering in the air. I thought of Professor Palmer taking a bullet for us on the river. I thought of my family, somewhere in the city, trying to survive—my father over by the Charles, getting ready to fight the Canadians. I thought of all the soldiers who had treated us well. "Because it's the right thing to do," I said.

He shrugged. "I suppose so."

The ammunition depot was about half a mile away, well back from the fortifications, which had been built out a lot since we first came into the city. In some places there were now long, high walls of earth; in others there was a wooden fence supported by sandbags. The pathway we walked along was crowded with soldiers on horseback and wagons hauling stuff. Everyone looked tense. Cannonballs kept coming in, but they landed short of where we were.

The depot was another one of those makeshift buildings that looked like it had been put up overnight. It was filled with cases of ammunition, which soldiers were loading onto small wagons they called caissons. Sergeant Dryerson was a big, burly guy with a droopy mustache. "Always happy to have more assistance," he said when we introduced ourselves. "You," he said, pointing to me, "help old Augustus over there. And you,"—pointing to Kevin—"go with Quentin."

Kevin and I exchanged a glance. "We—we'd like to stay together," Kevin said to the sergeant.

"Then go off somewhere and play with your toys," he replied angrily. "I've no time for such nonsense. Keeping you separate doubles the odds one of you'll survive. Consider that."

We weren't going to argue, so we did as we were told. "Stay safe," Kevin said to me before we split up. "I don't want to spend another day like yesterday."

"Me too. Meet me back here after we win."

"Okay."

Augustus was a short old soldier with a white beard and a messy uniform. He talked nonstop while we were loading his caisson, mostly about the "idiot generals" who were losing the war for us. When we it was full, we hopped up on the bench and drove off. We were headed toward an area called Sector 7, which was somewhere to the west along the fortifications. Meanwhile the bombs kept falling. I wondered what would happen if one fell on our cases of ammunition. I wouldn't live to tell about it, I knew that.

"Idiot generals spent all their time designing them floating airships and then don't use 'em," Augustus said, pointing up at the balloon.

"I think they're being used for reconnaissance," I said. "Spotting the enemy's position and stuff."

Augustus shook his head. "What's to find out? The enemy's on t'other side of the wall, and he's coming. Soon. And look over there—idiot generals left a gap in the fortifications, and all they could find to fill it with is that wire contraption."

Sure enough, there was the electric fence. And sure enough, it looked like a weak spot where the enemy could just march through. I spotted Professor Foster, standing by some equipment connected to the fence and gesturing wildly at a group of men. I sure hope this works, I thought.

And this was Sector 7. We were bringing extra ammunition to soldiers in place behind the fence. They were quiet, staring at the fence. Waiting. "Hurry, lad," Augustus said, as we unloaded our boxes. "Don't want to be caught here when it starts. The Portuguese are just going to come pouring through that hole."

It was dangerous to be anywhere near the fortifications. A cannonball landed about twenty feet from us, kicking up a huge cloud of dirt and gravel and causing our horse to rear back in fear. "Idiot generals," Augustus muttered, as if they were responsible for the cannonball.

Back at the ammunition depot, there was no sign of Kevin. Augustus and I set to work filling up the caisson again, when suddenly something changed. Strangely, it took me a couple of seconds to figure out what had happened. There was silence. No more artillery. Augustus paused and shook his head.

"It's starting," Sergeant Dryerson said. "Let's go, men. This is it. This is the war—right here, right now."

I thought Augustus might complain about going back to Sector 7, but he didn't. We worked faster to fill the caisson—I had gotten stronger since that awful day in the food warehouse—and then we headed out again. We were silent now as he steered through the waiting soldiers. We were still on the way when we heard a huge, prolonged shout. It wasn't a cheer, it was more like the roaring of animals. Animals getting ready to attack each other.

We made it to Sector 7, not far back from the fence. Just where Augustus didn't want to be. I caught a glimpse of Professor Foster standing by his generator, looking terrified. How many Portuguese were out there? I wondered. How many soldiers were charging towards the fortifications right now, determined to kill us all?

And then I saw them: a huge blue wave approaching, ready to break over us. Someone must have given a signal, because our soldiers all fired at the same time. Some of the Portuguese fell, but more kept coming. They were firing too as they ran, and I heard the screams of agony as New England soldiers were hit.

We had finished unloading the caisson. I turned to Augustus. "Should we go?" I shouted.

But his eyes were glazed, and he was holding onto his stomach. A dark stain appeared around his hands, and he pitched backward onto the ground. I knelt next to him. He motioned to me to lean closer.

"Idiots," he muttered in my ear, and then his head fell to one side, and he didn't move.

I looked around, but no one was going to help. We were in the middle of a battle. I got to my feet and stood behind the caisson. The sounds of the rifle fire and the shouting and the screams were overpowering. The earth was shaking. I was surrounded by dust and smoke. It was a few seconds before I could make sense of anything.

Then I saw that the first Portuguese soldiers had reached the fence. They grabbed it, ready to push through. And then they were knocked backwards. Every single one of them. I heard a roar of triumph from our side. The Portuguese scrambled to their feet, bewildered, but then most of them were shot down. A second wave reached the fence. Same result.

I spotted Professor Foster through the smoke. He was jumping up and down and clapping his hands. It had worked. Electricity had worked.

And then his smile disappeared, and he too pitched over, clutching his chest.

The attack slowed down. Over the gunfire I heard the sound of a trumpet from beyond the fence. "They're retreating!" someone shouted.

I expected us to go after them, and maybe some of the soldiers did, too. But officers on horseback shouted out orders, and we stayed put, instead pouring fire on the enemy as they fell back.

I sort of figured that was it, the battle was over, but the officers didn't act as if it was over. One of them yelled at me to get more ammunition. I pointed at Augustus's body. "The driver's dead," I said.

"Then go yourself, blast you," he shouted. "Come on, no time to waste."

Reluctantly I climbed onto the bench and picked up the reins. I had done this with Susie a couple of times at the professor's house, just for fun. Now it was anything but fun. I gave the reins a shake, and amazingly the horse obeyed me, and we made our way through the bodies back to the ammunition depot. Meanwhile, covered ambulance wagons were being loaded with the injured, and soldiers raced every which way on horseback. It all looked utterly chaotic, but people seemed to know what they were doing.

Sergeant Dryerson just shook his head when he spotted me alone in the wagon. I told him what had happened at Sector 7.

"Old Gus saw it coming, poor fellow," he said. "Well, he'll have plenty of company before the day is done."

"What do you think will happen next?"

"The enemy'll regroup and attack again, I expect. But from what you say we gave 'em a nasty surprise, so it'll only get harder for 'em next time. No sense speculating, though. Let's just fill that caisson."

I loaded it up with the sergeant's help, and then headed back to Sector 7. There was only scattered fire now, and I started to wonder if he might be wrong. What if the Portuguese had given up?

No one seemed to believe it, though. The fortifications were quiet, except for an occasional shot and the groans of soldiers the ambulances hadn't yet reached. I didn't see Augustus's body. As I unloaded the ammunition I looked up at the balloon, still hovering over us. The soldier inside was signaling down to someone, using the semaphore system Professor Palmer had devised.

We'll know where the next attack is coming, I thought.

The officers started shouting out orders to the men, and a lot of them moved off, away from the electric fence to another part of the fortifications. I recalled how the professor had scoffed at the fortifications the army had been building out by Brighton. These were bigger than the ones there—they'd had a lot of time to work on them. But, except for the electric fence, the whole thing was really nothing more than some fences and long piles of packed earth, never more than about six feet high. In a lot of places there were long wooden poles sticking out like huge pencils to slow down attackers, but in other places cannon balls had blown pretty big holes in the earth. The fortifications would slow the enemy down but wouldn't stop them, not if there were enough of them, and they were determined to break through.

A lieutenant rode over to me as I unloaded the cases of ammunition. "Who told you to bring those here?" he demanded.

"Sir, the sergeant at the—"

"Never mind, never mind," he interrupted. "Load 'em all back up and take 'em to Sector 10." He waved in the direction where most of the soldiers were heading—west, further inland. "And hurry, boy."

"Yes, sir."

My arms were getting really tired, but I managed to load the ammunition back onto the caisson and started off.

I never found out where Sector 10 was, exactly. Before I got there another lieutenant stopped me. "Where are you going with that?"

"Sector 10, sir."

"Never mind about Sector 10. We need ammunition here."

So I stopped and did as I was told. And I started wondering how much control the "idiot generals" really had over the battle.

As I was unloading the ammunition again the battle resumed. The roar of gunfire started out further along the fortifications—in Sector 10, maybe. Our soldiers were crowded up at the earthen wall, their rifles aimed over it. I saw the lieutenant on his horse with his sword in the air. Then he lowered the sword, and the men began firing.

This time I was too busy to watch what was going on. I hauled the ammunition up to the soldiers, who were firing as fast as they could. I scurried along the wall, bent over to keep from being hit, and passed the bullets to whoever needed them.

"Steady, men, steady!" I heard the lieutenant shout after a while. "Fix bayonets! No retreat! It's here or nowhere!"

And then I saw why. With a roar, a long line of enemy soldiers clambered up over the wall, pushing against us, and suddenly the sound of rifle fire died down a little, and I was in the middle of a hand-to-hand battle.

I had waited too long to get away. Now I tried to get back to the caisson, but there were soldiers all around me, and I couldn't even see it. All I could see were blue-and red-jacketed men stabbing and bludgeoning each other. All I could hear were their grunts and screams and moans. And I was the one without a weapon.

It was awful. I've played lots of violent video games, but they're just stupid and pointless. These were real people, killing and bleeding and dying right next to me.

I managed to stay out of the way for a while. I was worried that, without a uniform, the soldiers wouldn't know which side I was on. Then one short, bearded enemy soldier spotted me and lunged at me with his bayonet, too fast for me to duck out of the way. But before the blade reached me I heard a pistol shot from close range, and the man dropped to his knees and keeled over at my feet. I turned around and saw Chester standing behind me. "Boys," he muttered, shaking his head in disgust. He picked up the soldier's rifle and tossed it to me, then turned to fight someone else.

I had never held a rifle before, if you don't count BB guns. My father won't have any of that stuff in the house. The rifle felt heavy with the bayonet attached, but I kept it raised in front of me as the fighting raged.

You kind of lose your mind in a battle. You're not thinking, you're just reacting. The adrenaline is rushing through you, and everything is kind of a blur. And you do what you have to do, because otherwise you're going to die.

So there was another blue-jacketed soldier. He was young and scrawny, with no beard, just a wispy mustache. Somehow I remember that mustache. And I noticed him coming towards me out of the corner of my eye. Looking back on it, I think he was heading for me because I looked young and scared. Like him. An easy target, maybe. He had a sword in his hand, and it was aimed at me.

I whirled, and at the same instant I pressed the trigger. The rifle recoiled with a force that almost knocked me over. And he screamed. Over all the shouting and shooting I heard that scream. I will never forget it. Then he toppled over backwards, still holding onto his sword.

And that was the last I saw of him.

I can't remember anything much that happened after that. I don't think I killed anyone else—but it's possible. I have no idea how long the fighting lasted. There just came a point when my brain seemed to start working again, and I realized that there weren't that many blue jackets still standing. Some had dropped their weapons and raised their hands. There weren't any more enemy soldiers climbing over the wall, either.

Finally my brain put it all together: We had won.

"After them, mates!" someone shouted, and everyone gave out a roar and raced to the fortifications. I looked around for the lieutenant in charge. All I saw was his horse, wandering by itself among the corpses and the wounded men. Somewhere behind us a trumpet sounded. I couldn't tell what was going on, but the men hesitated, and then stopped.

I looked out through a part of the fortifications that had been destroyed. The ground was covered with the bodies of enemy soldiers who had been shot before they'd made it inside. How many Portuguese were left? Would there be another attack? Or was the rest of their army retreating, defeated?

A captain rode up. I had seen him in the mess at headquarters, and had stood in line behind him once to wash up. He looked around, gave some orders that I couldn't hear, and then rode off. I asked a soldier what was going on. "We stay here and let 'em attack again if they're so inclined," he said. His face was grimy and spattered with blood; one arm of his jacket was ripped.

"Why don't we go after them?"

He shrugged. "Getting late. And we still have a city to defend, I expect. Might have to go fight the Canadians next."

"Do you think the Portuguese will come back?"

He shook his head. "We cut the heart out of 'em, lad. They won't be back."

I suppose I should have felt happier than I did. But all I felt was relief and sudden, complete exhaustion.

The ambulances had returned to the battlefield and were being loaded with the wounded. I found my way to the caisson and threw the Portuguese rifle into it. It was all I could do to get up onto the driver's seat and pick up the reins. The horse had survived the battle. He seemed tired too, but he perked up and slowly headed back to the depot.

And now all I could think about was Kevin. Had he survived the battle? And if New England had truly won, could we make our way back to Glanbury at long last?

CHAPTER 24

Kevin wasn't at the ammunition depot when I arrived. Sergeant Dryerson said he'd been sent to Sector 14. "Hard fighting there, I've heard. But don't worry, he'll be back. Meanwhile, you look like you've been through it. How'd you end up with that?" he asked, gesturing at the rifle.

I told him about getting caught in the battle.

The sergeant was impressed. "Hold onto the rifle, lad. It might come in handy. Grab some bullets for it, as long as you're here."

"Have you heard anything about the battle with the Canadians?" I thought to ask.

He shook his head. "But it looks like we've won half the war—unless the Portuguese decide to regroup and attack again tomorrow. That's better than some of us thought we'd do."

What good was it to win half the war, I wondered. I hung around the depot, taking care of the horse and helping to clean up. Outside, the camp was just as busy as before the battle, with wagons clattering over the dirt path and messengers on horseback galloping past them and soldiers trudging back from the fortifications. I kept looking for Kevin's caisson, but it didn't show up, and I became more and more nervous. It was getting dark out. What would I do if he didn't show up?

"Come to the mess with us, lad," Sergeant Dryerson said to me. "You need a good meal."

"Thanks, but I guess I'll stay here and wait for my friend."

This time he didn't say anything reassuring. "Do you need a place to stay the night?" he asked gently. "The barracks won't be full, I fear."

I just shrugged. I couldn't think about that right now. The sergeant went off with the other soldiers, and I sat down outside the depot, shivering in the cold, with the rifle by my side. It was starting to get dark. I wondered if my father was all right. And poor fat Benjamin, who had looked so unhappy when Corporal Hennessy told him to report to Sergeant Hornbeam. And Chester, who had saved my life, even if I was a boy. And all the other soldiers I had met. How many people died today that I knew?

Don't be dead, Kevin, I thought. It had been my idea to volunteer for the battle. He just wanted to go home. So if he died, it was my fault.

"Am I glad to see you," a voice said.

I looked up and saw a Red Sox cap heading towards me.

For the second day in a row, I was so relieved to see Kevin I thought I'd cry. I was so relieved I didn't have the energy to tell him how relieved I was. I just kind of waved. He sat down next to me. "It's cold," he said.

"Sure is."

"Think we can get something to eat?"

"They'll feed us over at the mess."

We didn't move, though. We were silent for a while. "My driver was shot," Kevin said finally. "Killed."

"Mine too."

"The caisson got wrecked during the battle, so I had to walk back. Then on the way they asked me to help out on one of the ambulances, take people to the field hospital. Surgery, they call it. What a nasty place. They don't have, you know, what's the word?"

I thought. "Anesthesia?"

"Anesthesia. Yeah. They could sure use anesthesia."

I shivered, thinking about it. "I killed someone, Kevin," I said. "I got caught in the battle, and I had this rifle, and I shot a Portuguese soldier. In the chest. He wasn't much older than us."

"Geez," Kevin whispered. "You okay?"

"I guess so. I keep telling myself that I didn't have any choice. Kill or be killed, right? Still."

"It's a war," Kevin said.

"Still." We were silent some more. Finally I said, "So why don't we go get some food?"

Kevin didn't respond. I looked over at him, and tears were streaming down his face. "I want to go home, Larry," he said. "I want to go home so bad."

I put my arm around him, and we huddled together in the cold and the dark. In the distance, I thought I could hear screams from the surgery.

Finally it got too cold to just sit there, so we got up and found our way to the mess—a long, low-ceilinged, smoky building with a big fire burning in a fireplace at one end. It was crowded but quiet, despite the victory. We didn't see Sergeant Dryerson, but we did spot Caleb and Fred, who were happy to have us join them. "You lads turn up everywhere," Caleb said. "Aren't you supposed to be back at headquarters?"

"Yeah," I said, "but everyone had to help out today."

"That's surely true. Interesting hat, mate," he said to Kevin. "'B' for Boston?"

"That's right," Kevin replied.

"Wish I had me one of those."

I noticed Sergeant Hornbeam looking at us from another table, but he didn't come over.

Caleb and Fred told us the latest war news while we ate cold mutton and hard rolls. We had held the Canadians off for today, but everyone expected another assault; that battle had been nowhere near as decisive as this one seemed to have been. Caleb thought that some troops would be left here to defend the fortifications, but others would be shifted over to reinforce the soldiers fighting the Canadians to the north.

"Maybe the Portuguese will swing around the city and join them," Fred suggested.

"More likely they got such a licking today that they won't stop running till they're back in New Portugal," Caleb countered.

All the other soldiers at the table got into the discussion about what would happen next. Most agreed with Caleb that the Portuguese were done fighting. "That fence was enough to scare them away," one said.

"What did that fence do, exactly?" another soldier asked.

"Don't know, but whatever it was, they surely didn't like it."

Kevin didn't seem interested in any of this discussion. Once he was finished eating, he immediately started asking where we could find a bed for the night.

"Not going back to headquarters?" Caleb asked.

He shrugged. "Maybe tomorrow."

"By the way, where is that ciphering machine of yours?" Fred asked. "Fellows, you should have seen that machine. It was the darnedest thing…"

But Kevin didn't stick around to listen to them talk about his watch. Instead he got up and left the mess.

"He's pretty tired," I explained.

"Don't blame him," Caleb said. "We're in Barracks B, across the way. Tell the orderly to find you lads a spot."

I thanked Caleb, grabbed my rifle, and went to catch up with Kevin. He was outside the mess. "What's up?" I asked. "I was going to ask them about who died in the battle. Did I tell you about Professor Foster? He got shot."

"Doesn't matter," Kevin said. "We've got to get some sleep and head for Glanbury first thing in the morning. Otherwise Lieutenant Carmody is going to find out we're here and grab us. Everyone in camp is gonna know about the kids with the ciphering machine before long. You think that won't get back to headquarters?"

"Okay," I said. "Maybe you're right. Do you think we can make it to Glanbury? For all we know, the Portuguese army is still out there."

"We have a better shot than we did yesterday, Larry. And we can't stay here. We can't be in any more battles."

He was shaking with emotion. He'd had enough. More than enough. "Fine," I said. I motioned towards the building with the big letter B painted on it. "Let's go over there and see if we can find a couple of beds. In the morning we'll figure it out."

Inside Barracks B a gloomy young soldier sat behind a desk. He must've been the orderly. He shook his head when we explained what we wanted. "That's not procedures," he said. "If you're not assigned here, you need an order signed by a colonel."

"Look," I said. "We've been fighting the Portuguese all day. Now we just want someplace to sleep. We're too tired to go looking for a colonel."

"That's the procedures," he explained again, as if we were a little slow in understanding. "You're not even soldiers," he pointed out.

"The rules say you shouldn't even be in this building."

"Let them have a bed, you imbecile!" a voice demanded from behind us.

It was Sergeant Hornbeam, his red mustache bristling.

The orderly looked offended. "They need an order signed—"

The sergeant was right in front of him now. "Give them a bed!" he shouted. "Do you have a casualty list?"

"Well, yes, but it's very preliminary."

"It doesn't matter if it's preliminary, now does it?" the sergeant pointed out. "If someone is listed as dead, he's not coming back to life, is he?"

"Not procedures," the orderly mumbled. "Highly irregular."

"These are highly irregular times. Now do it!"

The orderly studied a piece of paper for a second, and then stood up. "Come along then," he said, without looking at us.

"Thanks, Sergeant," I said to Sergeant Hornbeam.

He dismissed us with a wave. "Get some sleep," he said. "There are far too many imbeciles in this army," he muttered as he walked out the door.

We followed the orderly into a large hall where cots were laid out in long rows. A few soldiers were snoring away, but most of the cots were empty. "There and there," the orderly said, pointing out a couple of cots near the back.

"Thank you," I said.

He shook his head. "It's not right," he replied. I felt like we had ruined his day.

Kevin slumped down onto one of the cots. "I thought an orderly was, like, someone who mopped floors," he said.

I shrugged. "In another world," I murmured. I put my rifle down, flopped onto the cot next to him, and pulled the thin blanket over me. "The guys who slept here last night are dead now," I said, staring up at the ceiling, which flickered in the lamplight. "Kinda creeps me out."

"Everything here is creeping me out," Kevin said. And then after a pause he added: "I wonder why Sergeant Hornbeam was following us."

"What makes you think he was following us?" I asked. "Maybe he just happened to see us come in here and wanted to do us a favor."

"Whatever," he said. "Tomorrow morning we head home."

I didn't reply. Too tired. I closed my eyes and thought about the soldier who had lain on this cot last night. Scared. Excited. Maybe too excited to fall asleep. Maybe he wasn't a whole lot older than me. Maybe he thought he was going to be a hero. And now he was just...gone. Lying in the morgue. Probably be buried in the morning, in one of those big holes people like Chester dug. I shuddered and tried to stop thinking about him.

And instead I thought about that other soldier, with the wispy mustache, looking kind of scared as he rushed towards me, his sword gleaming. Where had he slept last night? What had he thought about?

I wondered what happened to the enemy dead—how did they get buried?

It had been a tough day. I just had to stop thinking.

Eventually my body must have agreed, because the next thing I knew I was riding in a wagon at top speed. The road was bumpy and I was being tossed all over the place, but I couldn't slow down. I didn't know why at first, and then I realized that Portuguese soldiers were chasing me on horseback. I turned to look at them, and one was the short bearded guy that Chester had killed, and the other was the kid with the wispy mustache, and I tried to shout to them that it was war, kill or be killed, nothing personal, but they didn't understand or didn't care, and they were closing in on my wagon, so I had to go faster, faster...

I opened my eyes. Kevin was shaking me. "Wake up," he whispered. "Time to go."

Groggily I got to my feet. There weren't any windows, I noticed. Thin gray light came in through chinks in the boards. The soldiers snored and mumbled in their cots. Had I really slept all night? We made our way through the cots and into the outer room. The same orderly was still there. He was half-asleep, but he glared at us as we walked by like we had ruined the war for him. Then we were outside. It was bitter cold. For some reason I thought about the arguments I'd had with my mom about putting on my gloves for the short walk to the bus stop. Wouldn't it be great if I had gloves?

"Now what?" I said.

"Now we go," Kevin replied.

"How far is it?" I asked. "Ten miles? Twenty?" I really had no idea how far Glanbury was from Boston. "Think we'll make it?"

"Yeah, we'll make it." He sounded like nothing in this world was going to keep him from making it.

"Well, how do we get past the guards at the fortifications?"

"I dunno. Why should they care? They're supposed to keep the Portuguese out, not us in. Let's go down back to the main road and see what's going on."

We hadn't gone twenty feet, though, when I heard a voice behind me. "Hey Lawrence, what are you doing here?"

I turned around and saw Stinky Glover hurrying towards us.

CHAPTER 25

S tinky came up to us. "G'morning, Lawrence," he said.

"Hi, uh, Julian. This is my friend Kevin."

"Hello, mate." Stinky glanced at Kevin's cap, but didn't say anything.

They shook hands. Kevin didn't look happy to see him. In our world, he hated Stinky Glover as much as I did. Stinky liked to give him purple nurples; Kevin hated purple nurples—who doesn't? But this world was different. With all the things that had been happening, had I told Kevin about Stinky saving me from those kids in Cheapside?

"We're heading to Glanbury," I said.

Stinky looked puzzled. "Now?"

"Yeah."

"Why?"

"We want to help the Barnes family," I said. "Get things ready for when they come home."

Not a very good answer, but I couldn't come up with a better one. "Didn't you tell me you were related to them?" Stinky asked.

"That's right. And I got to know them pretty well in the camp," I explained. "Mr. Barnes is in the army, so I figured they might need some help."

"But why now?" Stinky persisted. "The Portuguese are still out there north of Glanbury, I expect, even if they're in full retreat. And anyway—"

"Doesn't matter," Kevin interrupted. "We're going. Come on, Larry." He started to walk away.

I hesitated, and then said, "Well, see you, Julian," and turned to go with Kevin.

"Wait a moment!" Stinky called out. "I'll join you!"

Kevin rolled his eyes. "No way," he muttered to me.

But we paused, and Stinky came up to us again. "Do you know where the Barnes farm is located?" he asked.

"Well, no," I admitted.

"I can show you. Besides, three'll be better than two if there are dangers on the road—and I'm sure there will be."

"Why do you want to help us?" Kevin demanded.

Stinky grimaced. "I've worn out my welcome here, I fear," he replied. "I try to make myself useful, but it's been hard. Lots of folks just take a dislike to me. I don't know why. Now that the battle's over, I expect the soldiers'll throw me out of the camp rather than keep on feeding me. I'll have to return to Glanbury sooner or later and see if my master will take me back. Might as well do it now."

Made sense to me. Kevin looked suspicious, but he didn't say anything. "All right," I said. "Let's go, then."

Stinky's grimace turned into a big smile. "Let's go," he repeated.

We headed back to the main road, which Stinky said was called the Post Road. When we finally got there, I was surprised to see that nothing had really changed since yesterday: there were still guards posted, and people were arguing with them to be let through, even though it was barely dawn. "We've no food," one man was saying to a guard. "We've no shelter. We'll die if you don't let us go home."

"We have our orders," the soldier explained with a weary shrug, as if he'd explained it a million times already. "It's not safe out there. Besides, the Portuguese fired the bridge over the Neponset. How are you going to cross the river?"

"We'll take our chances!" the man shouted. "Would you rather we drop dead here in front of you?"

We had one big advantage over those people: we were on the other side of the guards. "The army'll surely change their minds today," Stinky noted. "That fellow is right—better to let people risk the journey home if they have a mind to try it. There's nothing left for them here. But this is still dangerous—we risk having the New

Englanders shoot at us as well as the Portuguese. Why don't we just wait and see what happens?"

Kevin shook his head. "You wait if you want to," he said. "I'm leaving."

Stinky looked at me, as if to ask where I'd found this strange kid with the strange hat. But I wasn't going to let Kevin leave by himself. "We really want to get to Glanbury," I said.

Stinky considered. "All right, then," he said reluctantly. "Let's keep going. I think I know a way past the fortifications, although it's awfully roundabout. And then we still have to find a way across the river."

So we kept walking. The sun rose ahead of us in the east, but it didn't make us any warmer. Soldiers were up and about; none of them paid any attention to us. After a while the camp and the fortifications petered out, with only a couple of observation towers looking out over marshland that stretched towards the ocean. "They figured the Portuguese weren't going to attack over the marshes," Stinky said. "Too hard to maneuver, too exposed. So they just put up these towers. We have to cross the marsh, and then work our way back towards the Post Road. And find a boat or a raft or something to cross the river."

"The marsh doesn't look too hard," Kevin said.

"Unless the soldiers in the watchtowers see us," I pointed out. "And decide to shoot."

That didn't faze Kevin. "Let's go," he said.

Stinky glanced at me again. "Coming, Julian?" I asked him.

He didn't seem too happy about it, but he nodded. "Keep to the left," he said. "If the watchtowers are still manned, the soldiers'll be looking south. We can circle around when we're out of range of their rifles."

"All right," I said. "Sounds good."

Kevin started off without saying a word. We hurried after him.

There was a bitter wind blowing over the marsh, and my eyes started watering. The metal of my rifle was so cold it stung. Frostbite, I thought. Stay out here too long and we'll get frostbite.

The long brown marsh grass was harder to walk across than I had expected. Every step we took, we broke through a crust of frost. And it looked like we had a ways to go to get beyond the marsh. Suddenly I felt dizzy from cold and hunger.

And then we heard the shots. "Run!" Stinky shouted.

I took a quick look back. There were soldiers in the watchtowers with their rifles aimed at us.

I started running. Kevin stumbled, and I had to drag him back to his feet. He was usually way faster than me, but the drikana must have slowed him down; even carrying the rifle I was faster now. Stinky was the slowest. He was gasping for breath right away and struggled to keep up with us. But we couldn't slow down—I could hear the bullets whistle past us, so I knew we were still in range. "C'mon, let's go!" I called out to them. I sloshed through some water and hurdled a little stream that cut through the marsh. My lungs were bursting, but I kept going, expecting any second that a bullet would rip into me.

But none did. Eventually I realized there weren't any more shots. I looked back. Kevin and Stinky were still running, but they had slowed down a lot. I could make out the soldiers in the watchtowers, but I couldn't tell what they were doing. Didn't matter, as long as they weren't shooting at us anymore.

"Think we're…out of…range," Stinky gasped when he reached me. Kevin just flopped down on the grass.

"Will they come after us?" I asked.

"Who knows? Don't even know why they bothered shooting at us."

"Maybe they're just bored," Kevin said.

"You all right?" I asked him. He was still trying to catch his breath.

"I think so."

I sat down next to him. My sneakers were soaked. My feet felt numb. Frostbite, I thought again.

"Got to keep going," Stinky said. "If we stay here, I wager they'll come out to get us."

"If we stay here, we'll be dead before long anyway," I said. I got up. "Can you make it?" I asked Kevin.

He nodded. "Just needed a breather," he muttered. I held out my hand, and he took it. I pulled him up, and we started off again.

It wasn't long before we came to the river. We stopped and stared at it, flowing peacefully out to the ocean. It wasn't a very big river, but we sure didn't have a way to cross it. I looked at Stinky. He shrugged. "Let's head upriver," he said. "We'll need to go that way eventually. Maybe we'll find a boat somewhere."

Kevin and I didn't have any better ideas, so that's what we did.

We started walking inland, with the river on our left. The path we were on twisted towards the river, then away from it. We didn't spot any bridges, or any boats we could borrow to get us across. It was frustrating, and I could see that Kevin was getting upset. Well, he'd been warned.

"Look down there," Stinky said.

We saw smoke coming out of the chimney of a shack by the river. Beyond the shack was a boat tied up at a little dock.

"Somebody's home," Kevin said. "Let's ask for a ride."

"Could be dangerous," Stinky pointed out. "If they've been living out here all through the siege, they won't be the sort who like company."

"Worth a try," Kevin said, and he started down the path to the shack. "Hello?" he called out. "Can you help us? We need to get across the river."

There was no response.

"Hello?" he repeated. Stinky and I came up behind him. There was all kinds of junk next to the house—broken barrels, wine bottles, a lobster pot—and a ton of firewood neatly stacked by the door. I could smell fish frying. I hated fish, but the smell made my stomach growl.

We saw the barrel of a rifle point out from a window. "Who are ye?" a gruff, cracked voice said.

"We're New Englanders," Kevin said. "Just trying to get home after the battle."

"Put down the rifle."

He was talking to me. I laid my weapon down on the ground.

The rifle barrel disappeared from the window, and a moment later a gnarled old man wearing a woolen cap appeared, aiming the rifle at us. "Ye're children," he said. "Where are your parents?"

"We were separated from our parents in the battle," Stinky lied. "We're trying to get home to Glanbury. Can you help us?"

"Who won the battle?" he demanded. His accent was different from anyone else I'd heard in this world—not English, exactly, just sort of old-fashioned. I got the impression that he didn't talk very much.

"New England did," Stinky said. "Have you seen any Portuguese retreating?"

He shook his head. "Saw 'em before, though, foragin' along the river. Nasty brutes. Killed a couple."

"How'd you stay away from them?"

"I know more about these parts'n they do. Take more than the Portuguese to get hold of old Bart Willoughby."

"So, can you row us across the river?" Kevin asked.

The old man peered at him. "What can you pay me?" he demanded.

We looked at each other. "I have, like, six shillings," I said. Professor Palmer had given me some money once, but there really hadn't been anything to spend it on.

The old man shook his head. "Six shilling's won't even buy a loaf of bread in these times," he said. Then he peered at Kevin. "That's an interesting hat," he said. "I'll take you across the river for that hat."

Kevin blinked. He loved his Red Sox cap. But he took it off and handed it to the man. "All right," he muttered. "Fine."

The old man grinned. He only had a couple of teeth. He took his woolen cap off right away and replaced it with the Red Sox cap. It made him look crazy. "All right, lads," he said. "Let's go."

I picked up my rifle. The old man led us down to the boat, and we all climbed in. It was a little rowboat, and our weight made it ride low in the water. But the old man was strong, and with a few powerful strokes he had us gliding out towards the middle of the river. "Bad times in the city, I heard," he said.

"Yes, sir," I replied. "Too many people, not enough food."

He shook his head. "Too many people there in the best of times. They tried to get me to go to one of them camps, but I wanted no part of it."

"You weren't afraid to be here by yourself?"

"Lad, I've lived too long to be afraid of anything."

I thought of the old man in the camp standing by the gate and begging me for help. And the corpse Kevin and I had seen there yesterday morning, its gray hair blowing in the wind. Maybe this guy had the right idea.

We pulled up to the opposite shore. "Thank you, sir," Stinky said as we got out.

"Call me Bart," he replied. Then he pointed to the cap and started to cackle. "See, lad? 'B' for Bart! Fare ye well." He maneuvered the boat around and started rowing back across the river.

"Let's go," Kevin said without even glancing back.

We found a path and headed towards the Post Road. After a while we came upon a small settlement—a few houses, a horse barn, a church. Everything looked empty, abandoned. "Do you think we can stop here?" I asked. "Maybe start a fire in one of these houses? I need to warm up."

"I'm not tired," Kevin said. But he was lying, I knew.

"It's not about being tired," I replied. "My feet are freezing. I'm worried about frostbite."

"Whatever," Kevin said with a shrug. I think he wanted to take a break, but didn't want to be the one to suggest it.

None of the houses were locked. We went into the biggest one; even it had just one large room containing a few chairs, a bed with a straw mattress, and a small table. On the wall was a shelf with an old bible on it and a bad painting of President Coolidge. We found some tinder and a flint on the fireplace mantel. Stinky and I gathered some scraps of wood outside, and within a few minutes we had a smoky fire going.

We all took off our shoes and socks to dry them. Stinky glanced at the Adidas shoes Kevin and I set by the fire but didn't say anything. And he hadn't said anything about Kevin's cap. He didn't seem like a very curious kid. How different was he from the Stinky we knew in our world? He didn't seem mean—just sort of, I don't know, pitiful. And he had sure helped me out so far.

We all lay down in front of the fire to rest and warm up. It wasn't very comfortable, but I shut my eyes, and I must have fallen asleep right away. When I opened them, the fire had died out and Kevin was putting his sneakers back on. Stinky was still asleep. "Let's go," Kevin whispered. "We can leave him here."

"C'mon, Kevin. Stinky can help. Remember? He knows where the Barnes farm is."

"I don't care about the Barnes farm, Larry. I care about the portal, and he's not going to help us find that."

"Well, I care about both," I said. "And what about food? I'm starving already, and we still have a lot of miles to cover. We're going to have to either beg for food, if there's anyone around to beg it from, or go hunting. I've got this rifle, but I don't really know how to load it or anything. And neither do you."

Kevin shrugged. "I just don't trust him. If you're a jerk in one world, you're probably a jerk in every other world."

Stinky stirred then. I reached for my sneakers and started to put them on. "That's better," he said, sitting up and stretching. "Probably been here a couple of hours," he added, gesturing at the ashes of the fire.

"Think we can make it to Glanbury today?" I asked.

"I don't know. It's a bit of a trek," he said. "Wouldn't want to be traveling after dark."

"Well, let's see how far we get," Kevin said. "We can always break into another house and stay the night."

"True enough." Stinky gave Kevin another what's-your-hurry look, but he didn't say anything more. We finished putting our shoes and socks back on and headed outside. The sun was bright, and the wind had died down now that we were off the marsh, so we weren't as cold as we'd been before. We pressed on towards the Post Road, feeling a little better.

We had only a vague idea how far away the road was. We followed a rutted, curvy path that was headed inland. There was no one else around, and that started to feel kind of spooky, after being stuck in the crowded city for so long. It reminded me of being in Cambridge with Professor Palmer, and thinking of him made me sad. He wouldn't have any idea where we were, if we were dead or alive. I sure wished I'd had a chance to say goodbye to him.

Stinky tried to make conversation as we trudged along. He had enough curiosity to want a better explanation of why we were headed to Glanbury. Did we have parents? Did they know what we were doing?

"We're orphans," Kevin said. "Just like you." Why did he say that? I tried to remember if I'd told Stinky the lie about Professor Palmer being my father.

"Then how've you been living?" Stinky asked. "Where?"

"In an orphanage," Kevin said. "Where else?"

"But you're my age, looks like. Wouldn't you be 'prenticed by now?"

"Well, we're not."

After a while Stinky gave up. And a while after that we reached the Post Road, smooth and wide compared to the path we'd been on, but just as empty. Behind us was the wreckage of the bridge over the river.

"Look," Kevin said, pointing to the other side of the road. A wagon with a broken wheel lay on its side in a ditch. We went over to examine it. It was empty except for a few pots. "Portuguese," Stinky said, studying the lettering on the back. "Says something about cooking. The wagon's pointing south. They probably abandoned it during the retreat."

We started heading south on the Post Road. Everywhere there was stuff that the Portuguese had dropped or left behind—clothing and utensils and empty bottles, even a cannon. And then we saw a blue-jacketed corpse, face-down by the side of the road. Stinky went over to it. He came back with the dead man's pistol. "Looks like a mighty disorganized retreat," he said, "if they didn't even stop to bury their dead."

In the distance we heard some shots. People hunting? Fighting? "Julian, could you show me how to load this rifle?" I said. "I've got plenty of bullets."

He gave me another look, as if to ask: who wouldn't know how to load a rifle? But he shrugged and demonstrated how to load the cartridges and cock it. "Simple enough," he said. "And we'll be needing this rifle before long, if we're to eat anything today."

We walked along. The shooting stopped. After the roar of the battle yesterday, things seemed awfully quiet—there was no noise except the crunching of our feet on the road. Some of the houses and shops and inns we passed looked like they hadn't been touched; others had been burned to the ground. None of the fires looked recent, though. The Portuguese were probably in too much of a hurry to do any more damage.

And then we saw people up ahead. "Not soldiers," Stinky said. "One of them's a woman, I'd say, from the shape of that bonnet." We quickened our pace to catch up with them. There was a woman, a child, and a mule, weighed down with baggage. "Good day to you!" Stinky called out when we were close enough.

The woman whirled around and aimed a rifle at us. "Come no closer," she shouted back, "or I'll shoot you all."

The woman was middle-aged, and had an upper-crust, almost-English accent. Stinky raised his hands. "We're New Englanders. We mean you no harm."

The child was about six, and she clung sobbing to the woman, who lowered her rifle but still stared at us suspiciously. "We've been set upon already," she said. "There are evil people about, both New Englander and Portuguese. One of them has a bullet in his chest for his troubles."

"I believe it, but I assure you we aren't evil," Stinky said.

"How did you get past the fortifications?" I asked. "Are they open yet?"

"No, but this morning they removed most of the guards to go fight the Canadians. If you've a mind to get out and have a few pounds to spare for bribes, you can leave."

"How'd you get across the river?"

"Some men have rafts down there now," she replied. "Making quite a good day's wages, too."

"We're headed home to Glanbury. Where are you going?"

"Braintree, God willing, and no more brigands attack us."

Braintree was maybe halfway to Glanbury. "Why don't we travel together?" I suggested. "Safety in numbers."

The woman continued to eye us suspiciously, but after thinking about it she said, "Very well. You're likely-looking lads."

So we joined them. The woman's name was Mrs. Gradger; her daughter was named Cecilia. Their story was familiar: They'd been stuck in the Fens camp during the siege. Mrs. Gradger's husband and two older sons were in the army, and she didn't know if they were dead or alive. Mr. Gradger was a lawyer, and the family had been well-off before the war, so for a while she'd been able to buy extra provisions in the camp. But then food became scarce and money became pretty much worthless, and now the family was just like everyone else.

Mrs. Gradger, though, was a tough woman. She had already killed one man today, and she sure seemed ready to shoot anyone else who tried to mess with her or her daughter.

Cecilia was another story, however. She was so tired she was barely able to walk, and she kept complaining about how hungry she was. She wiped her tears on her sleeve as she tried to keep up. Mrs. Gradger didn't seem especially sympathetic. "Barney can't carry any more weight," she kept repeating, as if the amount of stuff on the mule settled matters.

"C'mon, Cecilia," I said finally. "I'll carry you for a while." I handed the rifle to Kevin and squatted down so Cecilia could climb onto my shoulders. She was pretty light. "Thank you, sir," she said, wiping her face clean yet again.

"Cecilia, don't dirty your sleeve," Mrs. Gradger said. But she didn't object to my carrying her daughter.

We walked like that for a long time. It was good to have company, even if Mrs. Gradger reminded me a lot of Ms. Pouch, my sixth-grade math teacher, who everyone called Ms. Grouch. She spent most of the time complaining about the how badly the camp had been run and how completely President Gardner had screwed up the war and how uncivilized the Portuguese were. I think she was happy to finally get a chance to kill someone.

We didn't run into anyone else, although off and on we heard more shots, which always scared Cecilia. "No more bad men," she said. "I don't want any more bad men." Once we spotted a skinny dog, who stared at us for a long time before slinking off down a side street. And that somehow reminded Cecilia of how hungry she was. "Please, Mother," she said from my shoulders, "please can't we eat?"

I looked at Mrs. Gradger. Her face was hard, but there were tears in her eyes. "We'll be home soon," she said. "Now don't talk about food. It just makes things worse."

Stinky came over to me. "Have to do some hunting, mate," he murmured. "Before we lose the daylight."

The sun was low in the sky. It was starting to get colder. Miles to go before I sleep. I remembered that line from a poem we studied in English class. And then we were at a crossroads. Mrs. Gradger stopped and closed her eyes in relief for a moment. Then she snapped back into character. "Our house is along this road to the right," she said. "Cecilia, please get down. Thank you, lads, for the company."

I stooped to let Cecilia off. My shoulders were stiff, but it had been sort of fun carrying her. Then we all stood there. I looked at Kevin. I could tell he was all for pushing on to Glanbury. Not me. It was Stinky who made the suggestion. "Ma'am, might you consider letting us spend the night? In return we'll go out and shoot you some supper."

Mrs. Gradger said, "Oh no, we'll be fine, no need." And Cecilia started wailing.

"It'd be a favor to us, ma'am," Stinky pointed out. "We could use the shelter."

That was pretty clever of Stinky, I thought. Mrs. Gradger would rather grant a favor than have anyone think she needed one. "Very well," she agreed. "That's a reasonable suggestion. Come along."

Kevin looked disgusted. I shrugged. "Just one more day," I muttered to him. "It won't kill us."

"How do you know?"

But he didn't argue, and we all followed Mrs. Gradger down the road to Braintree.

CHAPTER 26

A few minutes later we were there.

The Gradger house hadn't been burned. It was bigger than most of the houses I'd seen in Cambridge, with a fancy black iron fence out front and a wide brick drive leading up to an entranceway supported by large white pillars. "We're home, Mother!" Cecilia shouted. "Home!"

But things didn't look right. The front door was open. All the windows were smashed. Staring at them, Mrs. Gradger looked like she wanted to kill someone else. We walked quickly up the drive, rifles at the ready. For a moment we stood by the door, listening, and then Mrs. Gradger strode inside, with the rest of us following.

The place had been trashed. Broken glass and dishes littered the floor. Furniture was overturned. Paintings had been taken down from the wall and ripped in half. We went from room to room—and there were a lot of them—and they were all wrecked. We headed upstairs, and it was the same there. Everything that could be destroyed had been. It was awful.

Cecilia started crying again. Mrs. Gradger didn't say a word. "I'm really sorry," I said to her. She just shook her head.

We went through the entire place to make sure it was empty, then came back downstairs. Kevin, Stinky, and I didn't have to say anything to each other; we all knew we had to pitch in. "I'll start a fire," Kevin volunteered.

"I'll unpack Barney," I said.

"I'll help," Stinky added.

We went outside. "Quite a mess," Stinky remarked as we unloaded the mule.

"Think the Portuguese did it?"

"Don't see why they'd do this much damage," Stinky said. "Same for thieves. Maybe it was servants or townspeople, settling old scores. They finally got a chance to show what they thought of the Gradgers. I bet they weren't so fond of Mrs. Gradger."

"She's not so bad."

Stinky shrugged. "Tell that to the person she shot. Let's get this stuff inside and see if we can find some food."

We talked to Kevin and decided that he would stay behind with the Gradgers while we went out hunting. Mrs. Gradger was starting to clean up the big living room, and Cecilia had lain down on a rug in the corner. Stinky and I headed out into the late afternoon.

"Shouldn't be hard to find game," Stinky said. "With no people around for months, the animals are probably nearabouts."

"Whatever we do, let's not get lost," I replied.

We were in a residential neighborhood. None of the houses were as grand as Mrs. Gradger's, but they were still pretty nice. We didn't see anyone else, so it was like walking through a ghost town. It took us a little while before we found a patch of woods behind a church. "This'll do, I expect," Stinky said.

We went into the woods. Stinky motioned for me to be silent. Once again I noticed how quiet it could be in this world, without traffic or radios or airplanes. We walked deeper into the woods, and then stopped again. I could hear the sound of Stinky's heavy breathing, the breeze moving the branches above us. It was getting dark; I hoped this wouldn't take long. And then I saw Stinky slowly raise the pistol he had taken from the dead Portuguese soldier.

I looked where he was aiming. There was a large, strange-looking bird waddling along the ground. Could we eat that? Stinky fired, and the sound was deafening. The bird collapsed, squawking, and then there was silence again. "Got 'im," Stinky said.

We walked over to it. "What is it?" I asked.

Stinky looked at me with a puzzled expression. "A turkey, of course," he said. "Don't they ever feed you turkey in the orphanage?"

"Yeah, of course. I love turkey. But to be honest, I'm about ready to eat tree bark."

Stinky picked up the bird and handed it to me, and we made our way out of the woods. "A lot of turkeys'll be shot before this winter's over," he said.

The dead bird was heavy, and it dripped blood as we walked. Nasty. But I wasn't going to complain. We made our way back to the Gradgers' house without a problem, although night was falling fast. Inside, the fire was roaring. Mrs. Gradger was hanging sheets in front of the windows to keep out the cold air. Kevin was sweeping up the broken glass; he looked relieved to see us return. Cecilia was fast asleep on some cushions by the fire.

"Ma'am, if you'll pluck this turkey, we can have some supper," Stinky said.

Mrs. Gradger didn't look happy about handling the turkey; that was probably something the servants did. But she stopped what she was doing and went out with us to the kitchen. Getting the turkey ready to eat was hard, disgusting work—chopping off the head, plucking the feathers, cleaning out the insides…Rather than get involved with that, I started a fire in the kitchen fireplace, then pumped some water out back. When the turkey had been prepared, Mrs. Gradger put it on a spit in the fireplace, and then we just had to wait for it to cook, while the aroma made our mouths water and our stomachs rumble.

The table and chairs had been destroyed, so we had to eat on the floor in the living room. Mrs. Gradger found pewter plates that hadn't been smashed and some old silverware, while the three of us did more cleanup. Finally we took the turkey off the spit, carved it, roused Cecilia, and ate. The turkey was burned on the outside, then too dry, then barely cooked next to the bone. But it was probably the best food I've ever tasted.

Mrs. Gradger ate with her fork, I noticed. It was the first time I had seen anyone do that since I'd been to Coolidge Palace. She looked stiff and uncomfortable eating on the floor, but as usual she didn't say anything.

There was a piano in a corner of the living room that had been too big to destroy. After we had finished I went over to play it. It was a good piano—better than Professor Palmer's—but a little out of tune. I played the song the professor liked so much:

Wanly I wandered
Through the world far and wide
Seeking some solace
For dreams that had died...

When I finished, everyone was silent. Mrs. Gradger's face was wet with tears. Cecilia was sitting on her lap, asleep again, and Mrs. Gradger absently stroked her hair as she stared off into the distance. Kevin got up and added a log to the fire. "We should all go to sleep," he said quietly. "We'll want to get started early."

"Maybe we should stand watches," Stinky suggested. "Just in case."

"I'll take the first watch," I offered.

"Wake me for one too," Mrs. Gradger said.

We arranged more cushions, and people visited the privy, and then everyone but me settled down to sleep in front of the fire. I sat next to a window, rifle by my side, and listened to the crackling of the fire and the regular breathing. Despite all that had happened that day, I wasn't very sleepy.

Wanly I wandered...

I thought about Kevin and how determined he was to get to the portal. It looked like we were actually going to make it back to Glanbury, and that was more than I had expected a couple of days ago. So maybe we'd find it; maybe we'd have our chance to step into it and see where we'd end up. I remembered the faint hope we'd had when we first came here that rescuers would follow us through the portal. So many dreams had died. But here we were, still alive, still struggling.

Long had I lingered/In an alien land...

I thought of my mother and father, and wondered if they were safe. Which mother and father? Both. Kevin would scoff, but I didn't think I could stand it if anything happened to the ones in this world. And I worried about Professor Palmer, who had probably been operating the electric fence against the Canadians. Would he be shot like Professor Foster? I worried about Caleb and Benjamin and Chester and Corporal Hennessy. This world, and the people in it, mattered to me now. It wasn't a dream, they weren't a dream.

I might be part of this world for the rest of my life.

It is only by setting out that we can finally return home, the strange preacher had said. But where was home?

I sat there for a couple of hours, just thinking. Outside it was utterly quiet. I got up once or twice to put another log onto the fire. Finally I started to get sleepy, so I roused Stinky, who groggily took my place. I lay down on the cushions and immediately fell into the best sleep I'd had in days. No dreams.

When I awoke it was daylight, and everyone except Cecilia was already up. Stinky was out shooting more game for breakfast. Mrs. Gradger had found clean clothes upstairs and was laying them out for Cecilia. And Kevin was waiting for me. "Let's go," he said.

"We can wait for Stinky," I replied. "We can wait for breakfast."

"Why?"

"Come on, Kevin. Relax."

Kevin brooded. I wondered if he was thinking of leaving by himself. He certainly wasn't happy with me.

We heard some shots, and a few minutes later Stinky arrived with a couple of dead rabbits. "Thought I spotted a deer," he informed us. "You'll need to kill a deer if you want to lay in a good supply of meat."

Mrs. Gradger looked thoughtful. Stinky skinned the rabbits for her, and then she roasted them in the kitchen. We woke Cecilia and again ate sitting on the living-room floor. "Mother," Cecilia asked as we ate, "when will Father be home?"

"Father is still fighting for our country," Mrs. Gradger said. "Along with Gabriel and Elijah."

"But we need them here."

Mrs. Gradger didn't reply. When we were finished eating, she sent Cecilia off to change. Kevin stood up to leave.

Mrs. Gradger raised a hand to stop him, and the rest of us. "Please," she said. "Don't go. Stay here with Cecilia and me. Just until my husband returns. I can pay you well."

Kevin shook his head. "No, thanks. We've got to get to Glanbury."

"But what's so important about going to Glanbury?" she persisted. "I can pay you very well. And my husband is an important man. He can—he can find you work, give you opportunities. You're good lads. You wouldn't regret it."

"Maybe St—maybe Julian would do it," Kevin suggested. "Larry and I have to go, but he doesn't. What about it, Julian?"

Everyone looked at Stinky. "You wouldn't regret it," Mrs. Gradger repeated. "We're all alone here. Think of my daughter. We need help."

It was hard for her to beg, I could tell. And that only made the begging harder to resist. Stinky looked pretty unhappy. But he too shook his head finally. "I'm sorry, but I've got to stay with my friends," he said. "We were glad to help, but now it's time to leave."

That was a little surprising. Why not stay? Was Stinky still grateful to me for helping him with those kids in the camp? Was he worried about his master beating him or something? Or was it just that he liked us? Anyway, Mrs. Gradger looked like she didn't know whether to yell at us or burst into tears. Finally she got control of herself and said, "Very well. In any case, I'm grateful to all of you and wish you godspeed."

We said our fare-you-wells. Cecilia came back in her new dress, cleaned up and cute. She cried when she found out we were going. "Mother, can't they stay? Please?"

Mrs. Gradger shook her head. "We'll be fine, Cecilia," she said. "Don't wipe your face on your sleeve."

It was tough, but a few minutes later we were headed back to the Post Road.

"How come you didn't stay with them?" Kevin asked Stinky.

Stinky looked puzzled. "What do you mean, 'how come'?"

It was one of those phrases they didn't quite get in this world. "How come?" Kevin repeated. "Why?"

"Oh." Stinky shrugged. "Don't know, exactly. But don't you think she'd be hard to deal with, once things got back to normal? She's nice enough now, but there's a reason people destroyed her home. And who knows what her money'll be worth—if anything. Remember what that fellow on the river said. She could pay me five pounds a week, but if a loaf of bread costs five pounds, that's still poor wages, right?"

Seemed reasonable to me. We didn't say anything more about the Gradgers. We all felt pretty bad, I think—probably even Kevin. There were going to be a lot of people in the same situation, I knew, and many worse off than the Gradgers, but that didn't make it any better.

The day was clear but cold, like yesterday. It didn't take us long to get back on the Post Road. Unlike yesterday, there were other people on it now—families in wagons pulled by half-dead horses, old men and women leaning on sticks, and a few scruffy-looking characters that Mrs. Gardner probably would have called "brigands."

We got the latest news from them. There were few guards left at the fortifications, so people were starting to stream out of the city, whether or not this was officially allowed yet. A makeshift bridge was in place. No one was sure how things were going against the Canadians—or rather, everyone was sure, but they all had different stories to tell. We had lost. We had won. We were still fighting. Reinforcements from the Portuguese front had turned the battle around. They had arrived too late. They had been sent to the wrong place and never arrived.

But people were unanimous about the Portuguese. If we were still seeing their discarded stuff on the road this far south of the city, they weren't likely to be regrouping for another attack. They must have been heading out of New England as fast as they could travel. And that was good news.

"More than halfway to Glanbury, mates," Stinky said.

A long distance in the cold, but our bellies were full and we'd had a good night's sleep and no one was shooting at us, so it didn't seem like such a big deal. Kevin was almost twitching with excitement.

After a couple of hours walking he began to look more tired than excited, but by then it seemed like Glanbury must be just around the next bend in the road. "Not far now, I think," Stinky said. "There's Lantham's Stables." Then, a few minutes later, "And there's the Weymouth Inn, burned to the ground. That's a shame." We walked a little faster.

And then, finally, Stinky gestured up ahead. "See the river?" he asked.

"Sure."

"That's the North River. Glanbury's on t'other side."

Kevin and I looked at each other. There were tears in his eyes. Glanbury. Home. At last.

CHAPTER 27

Home. Sort of. Certainly not for Kevin—he wasn't interested in this Glanbury. And it didn't look at all familiar to me. The North River was in our Glanbury, too, but I hadn't paid much attention to it. It wasn't a very big river. At least its bridge hadn't been destroyed.

We crossed the bridge. Glanbury didn't look any different from what we had already passed by along the Post Road. A few shops and houses, but mostly just woods and farmland, and occasionally a road leading off to the east or west. Just another little town. I wasn't surprised that President Gardner hadn't thought much of it.

Kevin looked around intently, trying to spot the place where we had burst out of the woods with the Portuguese soldiers shooting at us. It would be on our left—I recalled that much. But that was about all I remembered. And if Kevin insisted it was on our right, I'm not sure how strongly I could have argued the point. Nothing looked familiar to me. Kevin hesitated once in a while, but he didn't run off into the woods. I could sense him getting worried as we walked.

"How far to the Barnes place?" I asked Stinky.

"Another mile or two, I expect."

I wondered if the farmhouse was where my house was in the other world. Was that how things worked in these alternate universes? That would make it easier for us to find the portal—just look in the woods behind the backyard. But I remembered how confusing the geography of the Burger Queen world had been, and I figured we weren't going to be that lucky.

I was tired and hungry by now. Kevin was starting to look pretty worn-out too. I knew he wanted to keep searching until he found the portal. But he only had so much energy; it would only be daylight for so long. It would be tough.

"We turn here," Stinky said finally, pointing to a road up ahead on the right. "Go left and the road'll take us to town and the harbor, go right to the Barnes farm. It's a nice little place."

I looked at Kevin. He shrugged. "Let's go to the farm," he said.

So we turned off the Post Road, and then took another turn after a while, onto a small lane lined with hedges. "There it is," Stinky said. "Lucky thing, looks like the Portuguese left it alone. Probably didn't bother coming this far off the main road."

The house was small, far less imposing than the Gradgers', or Professor Palmer's house in Cambridge. The red barn behind the house was bigger than house itself was. Both seemed to be in good shape. We walked up the lane to the front door. I knocked. There was no answer.

"What do you want to do?" Stinky asked.

"Go in," I said. "Start a fire. Get the place ready for them."

"You mean just…move in?"

I nodded.

"If you say so."

The door wasn't locked, so we walked inside.

We found ourselves in a small entryway. On the left was a long, dark, low-ceilinged room dominated by a big fireplace, with heavy black pots and pans hung next to it. On the right was a smaller, brighter room with nothing in it but a table and chairs. We walked into the room with the fireplace. It led into the kitchen, where there was another table and chairs, and some shelves with pewter plates and cups on them. Next to the fireplace was a small storage area. In a corner of the living room was a spinning wheel. "Home Sweet Home" said a piece of embroidery hung on the wall to our right.

Home.

Strangely—or maybe not so strangely—it did feel like home.

Everything was where it should be, where I wanted it to be. Beyond the room on the right was a bedroom, with a Bible on the nightstand next to the bed. From there you climbed up a wooden ladder-like set of stairs to an attic, where there were a couple more beds with a curtain between them. On the floor I saw some wooden toys that probably belonged to Matthew. I wondered how Cassie put up with Matthew chattering away on the other side of that curtain at bedtime. In this world, she didn't have a choice.

We checked out back. Firewood was stacked neatly by the door. Beyond it was the well, and on the other side of the yard was the privy. Everything was simple but solid and clean. I thought about how my mother always insisted that we keep our rooms tidy. When we'd whine that the mess didn't bother us, she'd say, "There's no excuse for being a slob." There wasn't, really. I had a lump in my throat when I went back inside.

"Must be pretty weird for you, huh?" Kevin murmured while Stinky brought in firewood.

"It seems so…familiar. How are you doing?"

"All right, I guess. Pretty wiped. Do you think the portal's further south along the main road?"

"Probably. I haven't seen anything that looked familiar so far. But then again, it was so foggy, and we were running for our lives, and—"

"I know. I remember a bunch of pine trees across the road when we came out of the woods—but there are pine trees all over the place. Anyway, it can't be far. Glanbury's not that big a town."

Unless the portal had disappeared back where it came from. Unless it had moved. Unless, unless…"It can't be far," I agreed. Kevin didn't want to hear anything else.

We went and helped Stinky get the fire started. Then it was time to go hunting for our supper. Kevin stayed behind again. He was tired, and besides, he didn't care about hunting; it wasn't something he was going to do once he got back home.

So Stinky and I went out with my rifle and his pistol. We had to tramp through fields where cornstalks drooped, then climb over a long stone wall. We passed by a small body of water that Stinky was familiar with. "Amity Pond," he said. "Good fishing. We may be able to catch some trout there." And then we headed into the woods past the pond.

This time when we spotted a turkey, Stinky motioned to me to take the shot. It was a lot different from aiming at an empty Coke can with a BB gun. Sorry, bird, I thought. And I pulled the trigger.

The turkey squawked and keeled over. Stinky clapped me on the back. "Terrific," he said.

All I could think of was the soldier with the wispy mustache. Still, I had gotten us dinner.

We trudged back to the farmhouse, and this time all three of us helped prepare the turkey. It was gross, but it had to be done. Another skill worth learning in this world. Then we cooked and ate it the way we did the night before; it tasted fine, but I could tell I was going to get sick of turkey pretty soon, if that's all we could find to eat. Better than going hungry, though.

We found some blankets in the storage area and slept in front of the fire in the living room, like we had at the Gradgers; using the beds didn't seem right. We figured we were safe here, so we didn't stand watches. And in the morning the sun was shining, the fire had died down, and we had to figure out what to do next.

I assumed Stinky would want to leave, but he didn't seem to be in any hurry. "Oh, I'll find old man Kincaid when the time comes, and we'll work things out," he said, talking about his master. "In the meantime, there's plenty to be done here. Chopping wood, hunting, fishing…We can cart ice back from Amity Pond to preserve the meat. There should be a root cellar somewhere around. We can search for seed corn and make sure it's protected. That'll be important come next spring."

Kevin wasn't interested in doing chores. "What's the point?" he demanded when Stinky was paying a visit to the privy. "Let's just find the portal and go home. Now."

He was right, of course. We had done it. We had gotten back to Glanbury, and there was no one to stop us from going home. Still…

I wanted to find out what had happened to my family on this world. I wanted to make sure they were okay. And I didn't want to have them wonder what happened to Larry Palmer. Did he die in the battle? Why did he never come to see us like he promised?

But I couldn't say that to Kevin; he would've gone nuts. He was already staring at me suspiciously. "What's the matter?" he demanded.

"I'm just a little—I don't know," I said. "What if the portal doesn't take us home? We could step out into a black hole or something."

"Okay, yeah, it's a risk. We know that. But we've gotta take it, Larry. We can't stay here for the rest of our lives if we have a chance to make it home."

"Sure, but, you know, what if you bring those drikana germs back with you? We don't want to start a plague or something."

"I'm not contagious. This world doesn't know how to cure drikana, but they know when people are contagious. I'm out of claustration. I feel fine. Now let's go."

Stinky came back in. "What shall we do now?"

Kevin looked at me.

"Kevin and I are going hunting," I said. "We'll be back in a while."

"I'll come too," he replied. "If you shoot a deer, we might need the three of us to bring it back."

"No, uh, why don't you stay here, Julian. We'll be all right."

He looked puzzled and disappointed, but he didn't argue. He also didn't say anything when we went down the lane to the road, rather than back into the woods beyond Amity Pond.

I might never see him again, I thought.

Kevin couldn't have cared less. He practically raced back to the Post Road. When we reached it, we turned right and started heading south. "Give a shout if you spot anything that looks familiar," he said.

"Sure."

But it all looked more or less familiar. Or more or less unfamiliar. I peered into the woods on the left and tried to remember any details from those few frantic moments when we raced out of the woods and into the road. "Maybe there?" I suggested at one point, although I couldn't say why.

But Kevin got excited, and we tramped into the woods and wandered around for a while, waving our hands in front of us. We didn't find anything, although I spotted a deer staring at us like we were crazy. "Why did you think it was here?" he demanded.

"I don't know. Just a guess. I can't really remember anything, Kevin. But I'm trying."

"All right," he said. "Let's keep going."

We went back to the road and continued heading south. We stopped a couple of times more when Kevin thought he spotted something he recognized, and we went through the same routine, walking around in the woods, hoping we stumbled onto the portal. We weren't just looking for a needle in a haystack, I thought. We were looking for an invisible needle, and we didn't even know which haystack it was in.

But I wasn't going to say that to Kevin.

Finally we reached a deserted building called the Wompatuck Inn. I didn't remember the inn, but Wompatuck was the town just south of Glanbury. We looked at each other. Kevin sat down on a hitching post. "I don't know," he said softly. "I thought…I thought I'd spot something. I thought we'd get lucky for once."

"We can keep looking, Kevin. We've got time."

"Until Lieutenant Carmody tracks us down. He knows we're here looking for the portal."

"He'll think we're gone."

"He won't be sure. He'll check. You know he will."

"Well, it's got to be here somewhere."

"No, it doesn't," he replied in a tired tone. "We don't know anything about it—where it came from, how it works. We're just a couple of stupid kids who did a really stupid thing. And now…"

I didn't know what to say. Finally Kevin stood up, and we started walking back. He didn't suggest looking in the woods. "We should do some hunting," I said after a while.

He just shrugged. We had seen plenty of game besides the deer. When we got near the farm I went back into the woods; Kevin didn't join me. Within a few minutes I had shot another turkey.

"I'm sick of turkey," he muttered when I brought it out of the woods with me.

He was not going to be great company, I decided. "Tomorrow," I said. "We'll search again tomorrow."

"Okay," he replied. "Whatever."

When we got back to the farmhouse, Stinky was cooking up fish that he'd caught. If he was curious about why we'd taken so long just to shoot one turkey, he didn't say so. It wasn't hard to tell that something was wrong, but he didn't ask what it was.

So it was a quiet night. Kevin just stared into the fire; he barely touched his supper. I ate enough for two, even though I didn't like fish. Stinky talked about all the chores he had done, and it made me feel guilty. We went to sleep early, huddled in front of the fire.

I thought about my family—my "real" family—and how annoying they all could be, how rotten my life had been, with the "real" Stinky bugging me and Nora Lally ignoring me and my stupid teachers at The Gross boring me to death. What if I didn't have a choice—what if we couldn't find the portal and I had to stay here? No toilets or computers or TV, sure, but I was already used to not having that stuff.

What if I had to stay?

I fell asleep with that thought in my mind.

The next day was cold and raw. Stinky and I did some chores while Kevin moped. "What's the matter with your friend?" Stinky finally asked me while we were in the barn.

"I don't know," I said. "I think the battle bothered him. He saw a lot of suffering."

"We've all seen a lot the last few months," was all he replied.

Eventually I got Kevin to go searching again. Stinky didn't offer to come with us this time. I think Kevin was really starting to bother him.

We had only seen a couple of travelers yesterday. Today there were a lot of people on the road, all making their way south. We found out from them that no one was being stopped from leaving the city now; in fact, the army was encouraging it. The travelers had the usual variety of rumors about what was happening with the Canadians, but no one said they had defeated us, and that was a good sign.

This time we headed north, back towards Weymouth. We spent most of our time in the woods. What was the point of walking along the road if we had no clue where to look?

After a while it started to snow. "Great," Kevin muttered. "Now we won't be able to recognize anything."

But it wasn't like we were recognizing anything to begin with.

We made it all the way back to the North River. We watched the snow flecking the gray water for a while in silence, and then Kevin said, "Let's go back before we freeze to death out here."

"I'm sorry, Kev."

He shrugged. "Let's just go."

We turned back. The snow was heavier now, and there were fewer people on the road. We trudged along in silence, with our hands jammed into our pockets. The snow was light and fluffy—not good snowball snow, but we were in no mood to throw snowballs. For once I wished I was wearing those big old shoes from this world instead of my sneakers.

After a while I started looking for where we turned off the Post Road. Visibility wasn't that great anymore, and I sure didn't want to miss the turn and keep on walking in the snowstorm. Kevin didn't look like he was going to be much help. Up ahead I could make out a wagon, moving slowly along the road. We got closer. Suddenly the squeaking of the wheels stopped, and I heard a voice. "This is Town Road, I think."

It was my mother.

I started grinning and ran up to the wagon. "Mrs. Barnes?" I said. "It's me—Larry Palmer!"

She was sitting on the bench with the reins in her hand. Matthew sat next to her. "Larry?" she whispered. "Sweet Lord, it is."

There was something about the way she said it. There was none of the excitement and surprise I had expected; it was as if she could barely bring herself to speak. I looked at Matthew; his eyes were red with tears. "Larry, Cassie's dead," he said. "Our own soldiers shot her, damn their eyes."

I stared at my mother, and I knew that it was true. A tear leaked out of her eye and fell down her cheek, mixing with the snowflakes. I came closer and looked in the back of the wagon. There, in the middle of all their snow-covered possessions, wrapped in a sheet, was the outline of a body.

"Oh, no," I cried. "Oh please, no."

Mom reached down and touched me on the arm as I, too, started to weep.

CHAPTER 28

K evin and I walked alongside the wagon as Mom made her way through the snow back to the farmhouse. She didn't say anything; she didn't ask who Kevin was or why we were there in Glanbury. Even Matthew was quiet, except to complain about how hungry he was.

"We have food," I said. "We'll take care of you."

Stinky saw the wagon drive up the lane and came out to meet us. "Julian?" Mom asked, with a puzzled look on her face.

"Just staying with Lawrence, ma'am," Stinky replied. "I hope you don't mind."

She didn't respond. She and Matthew got down from the wagon, and we took them inside and had them sit in front of the fire. In the kitchen, I explained to Stinky about Cassie. "Terrible," he said. "To live through it all, and then at the very end…"

I nodded. "They're going to need all the help we can give them."

Stinky had already cooked the turkey I had shot yesterday. We carved it up in the kitchen and brought some out to them. Mom looked like she didn't want to eat, but she was too hungry to resist. Matthew wolfed his food down. "We've had almost nothing to eat for two days," he said between bites. "And we don't know where Papa is or if he's alive, and Gretel got lame and we thought we might not even make it home, and it's been terrible, just terrible."

Mom put her hand on his arm. "We're all right now, Matthew," she murmured. "Try not to eat too much. It might make you ill."

He leaned back against her, but kept eating.

Mom stood up when she had finished. "We can't leave her out there," she said.

Did she want to bring Cassie's body inside? I thought stupidly. No, she headed out the back door to the barn. I followed her. Inside, she found a pick and a shovel. "Three days she's awaited a proper burial," Mom murmured. "She can't wait any longer."

"I'll help," I said. "We'll all help."

She stopped and gazed at me the way she had in the camp— puzzled, like she was on the brink of understanding who I really was. "Thank you," she said. "Thank you, Larry. Finding you here is—is the only good thing that's happened to us in a long time."

I took the pick and shovel and followed her back out front. I set the tools down by the wagon and went inside to get Kevin, Stinky, and Matthew. Then we all followed behind the wagon as Mom drove it around the farmhouse to the edge of a little patch of woods beyond the barn. Matthew was sobbing. Kevin glanced at me a couple of times, but he didn't say anything.

Mom got down from the wagon and led us into the woods. We came to a small clearing after a while, and in the middle of the clearing a few crosses stuck up through the snow. My head started spinning as I stared at those crosses. Kevin gripped my arm. Mom pointed to a spot in the snow. "Cassie needs to go here," she said. "Beside her brother."

I looked at the cross next to where she was pointing. Two words were crudely carved on it:

Lawrence Barnes

I was staring at my own grave.

"That's the boy who would have been just about your age," my mother was saying to me. "My baby."

I think maybe I forgot to breathe for a while. "It's okay, Larry," Kevin whispered to me. "Take it easy."

Kevin and I'd had talked about what would happen if we ran into our other selves in this world. Would we both explode, or destroy the fabric of the space-time continuum or something? Stupid. We never talked about this.

Nothing happened, of course, except that I was as spooked as I could possibly be. But I didn't do anything. I just stood there in the snow. I was alive, the earth kept spinning, and that other me—the baby who didn't make it—was still at rest in the cold ground.

And now we had to lay his sister—my sister—to rest, too.

We took turns using the pick and shovel to dig the hole in the frozen, rocky soil. I did most of the work, though—Kevin still didn't have all his strength back, and it wasn't the sort of task Stinky enjoyed. It seemed to take forever. It grew dark, and my muscles were screaming with pain after a while—the most digging I'd ever done was a little bit of snow shoveling, and I'd usually complain about having to do that. But we kept at it, and at last the time had come. We lifted Cassie's body out of the wagon, then slid her down into the ground and covered her up. After that we stood around the grave as darkness fell and said some prayers, while I felt sorry for every mean thing I'd said to her in every conceivable universe.

"Thank you all," my mother said at the end. "God bless you."

And then we made our way slowly back to the farmhouse. Stinky took care of Gretel, and Kevin and I hauled in the few possessions Mom and Matthew had brought home in the wagon.

With her duty done, Mom seemed to relax a little. She looked even older, more worn down than she had in the camp. But she didn't cry much, just a few tears. Mom wasn't a crier; she was the one who gave comfort, not the one who needed comforting. She put Matthew to bed—she let him sleep in the downstairs bedroom with her—and then came out to join us in front of the fireplace.

And she asked the questions I knew were coming: "Larry, what happened? How did you get here?"

As usual I hadn't thought through my answer, so I just blurted something out. "My father died, and I had nowhere else to go."

"Oh no, Larry, what happened?"

What happened? "He was—he was working with the army. He had invented this electric fence that would, like, give the enemy soldiers a shock when they tried to climb over it. He was operating it at the battle with the Portuguese. And it worked great but—but they shot him. He died instantly." I remembered Professor Foster dropping to the ground, killed in his moment of triumph.

"Oh my poor sweet boy. Is there no end to these horrors?"

"I didn't really have anywhere else to go, so I came here," I continued. "I hope you don't mind."

"Mind? Of course not. Stay as long as you want. And your friend—"

"Kevin. He's, uh, an orphan. He lived with us. And Julian—we met him at the army camp, and he helped us get here. We couldn't have done it without him."

I glanced at Stinky. He didn't say anything about how a couple of days ago Kevin had told him we lived in an orphanage. Did he remember? Of course he did.

"You're all welcome to our home," Mom said. She leaned back in her chair and closed her eyes. Stinky threw another log on the fire.

"Can you—can you tell us what happened to Cassie?" I asked.

"Perhaps another time," she said wearily.

"Sure. I understand."

But after a moment she said, "I suppose it might help. There's been no one to talk to—just Matthew…" She paused again, and then began. "You were there in the camp that last day, Larry. You saw how wild things were becoming."

I nodded. "I barely got out. Soldiers were firing at people by the main gate."

"Yes. We'd endured for so long in the camp, but then—we knew it was ending soon, and it seemed to drive some people mad."

"Cassie wouldn't come out of the tent," I recalled. "She wouldn't listen to anyone."

"Yes, that was Cassie." Mom's eyes got a faraway look, and I imagined she was thinking about all the ways in which Cassie had caused them problems. Or maybe it was just the opposite. What do I know? "Cassie just couldn't stand it anymore," she went on. "Not another day, not another minute. We all heard the shots by the main gate. We weren't sure what had happened. Twenty people dead, someone said; someone else said a hundred. And there were other rumors: the gates had been stormed and the guards had fled. The Canadians were already in the city. There was a drikana outbreak in the camp. The wildest things. Cassie begged me to leave. But even if I had wanted to, there was no way we could get out of the camp in that madness with a horse and wagon and all our possessions. 'Leave them behind,' she insisted. 'It's all worthless anyway.'

"But I wouldn't do it. 'Let's wait for the morning,' I said. 'Everyone says the soldiers will be gone by then.'

"She wouldn't listen to me, though. She was never—she was never easy. Not bad, no, but…she knew her own mind. Perhaps if I had tried harder to understand…"

Mom paused then, as if she were thinking about how she could blame herself for Cassie's death. "Then what happened?" I asked softly.

"She ran away," Mom answered. "She didn't argue, she just ran, as if she couldn't stand it another moment. I told Matthew to go stay with the Lallys and I went after her, but it was so difficult. It was dark, and all the paths were crowded with people and wagons, and no one would get out of the way. She didn't head toward the main gate. She went to the water station. I don't know why—perhaps she thought it wouldn't be guarded at night. Perhaps she'd heard that the fence had been torn down, and there was just that little stream to cross. Or perhaps she had met the guards there and flirted with them, and she thought they would let her pass.

"I almost reached her. I called out to her, but she just kept going. I was near a soldier, and he was very young, and I could tell he didn't know what to do. Someone else called out 'Halt!' She was in the middle of the stream by now. She paused and looked back. She saw me, and I called out to her again. But then she turned and kept going. And then I heard the shot."

Mom paused again and stared into the fire. I wasn't going to say anything this time. If she wanted to talk about it, she'd do it when she was ready.

"Cassie went down," Mom continued at last. "I kept going after her, through the stream and onto the other side where she was lying. So why didn't they shoot me, too?"

I thought she wanted an answer, but I couldn't think of one. I guess she was just asking herself, though, because she repeated the question softly, and then went on. "I held her in my arms, but there was no bringing her back, no bringing her back. I noticed that the young soldier was standing next to me after a while, and he was crying and saying, 'Didn't she understand? All she had to do was stop. Why wouldn't she stop?'

"Because she's Cassie, I thought. Don't you see? She didn't think she had to stop for anyone.

"I didn't want to move, but I couldn't stay there. The soldier helped me carry the body back to our wagon. And then I had to get Matthew and tell him what had happened. And then…"

Mom put her hands to her face. Maybe this wasn't such a good idea, I thought, making her relive all this stuff.

"If she could have just waited a few more hours," she said. "A few hours later, all the guards were gone, heading off to the battle. It must have been midnight when I heard that, and it wasn't a rumor this time. The gates were open, the guards had disappeared, and people were pouring out into the city. Not that they had anywhere to go in the city. Not that I cared. Some of our friends were sitting with me, helping me grieve. They wanted me to leave with them, but what was the point? This was where Cassie had died. Why should I go anywhere else?

"They couldn't wait finally. Everyone was leaving. The camp was emptying out. But then near dawn Matthew awoke—despite everything, he had finally fallen asleep—and I knew that I had to leave too, I had to get him home if I possibly could. So I packed the wagon and hitched up Gretel, and we left."

"Kevin and I were in the camp a little after dawn that day, looking for you," I said. "It was pretty empty."

Mom nodded. "It was a dismal place, and we were all so tired of it. People looted the army buildings during the night, then set fire to them. I think they might have shot the guards if they had found any of them.

"But the city streets were no better—worse, really, because the other Glanbury families were gone, and I had no one to talk to, no one to help me. That first day I stopped at a church, and the minister took pity on us and gave us a little food. He offered to bury Cassie in the church's graveyard, but I couldn't leave her there—she had to go home too. Then I tried to get out of the city, but Gretel went lame—poor girl, she'd had no exercise for months. It's a wonder she's still alive. I don't know what I would have done if she hadn't recovered. Matthew was frantic. He wanted us to go find his father, but Henry was fighting the Canadians, and we have no idea where he was, or if he was even alive.

"Finally at dawn this morning we started out, praying that Gretel would make it. She did, thank the Lord. And now we're home. Now we're home."

I reached over and put my hand on her arm, the way she liked to do. She smiled at me and squeezed my hand. "I never thought I'd see you again," she said. "But under such awful circumstances…"

"I'll help you," I said. "We'll all help you."

"Thank you," she whispered, and fell silent.

Mom went and joined Matthew in bed a little later. Stinky fell asleep by the fire. I was still wide awake.

"That was weird," Kevin remarked.

"What? The graveyard?" I said.

"Yeah. I thought you were going to faint."

"It did make me a little dizzy," I admitted. "But in a way, it's weirder thinking about Cassie."

"Sounds like she was kind of—you know—the same in both worlds." Kevin said.

"A pain, you mean. 'Difficult,' my dad says."

"Yeah, I guess. Not that she deserved to die."

"For going nuts in that camp?" I said. "No, she didn't deserve to die for that."

"Your mom and Matthew—that's weird, too. They look just like, you know…"

"You see what I mean?" I pressed him. "They aren't different people. They are my family. They're just…here."

Kevin stared at the fire. Thinking about the portal and getting home, I supposed. Thinking about how he had no one here, no Albright family to welcome him.

"We can keep looking for the portal," I said. "It's gotta be out there somewhere."

"Yeah," he said. "Maybe." Then he lay down and wrapped the blanket around him. "Let's just get some sleep."

And then there was just me awake in the silent farmhouse. I had found my family again, but things hadn't exactly turned out the way I'd wanted them to. Poor Cassie. *I know she can be difficult,* Dad had said to me once, *but she's family. And that's the most important thing. Someday you'll realize that you love her.*

I didn't know about that. But I couldn't help thinking about Cassie. And, difficult as she was, I couldn't help wishing she was still alive and giving us all a hard time. No, she didn't deserve to die. And my mom sure didn't deserve the heartache her death had brought.

I didn't want to bring her any more heartache.

CHAPTER 29

Then for a few short weeks my life took on a new rhythm, as I hunted and fished and did chores, and later helped neighbors who had returned to homes that had been burned or ransacked. It was great to be with Mom and Matthew, but every moment was shadowed by thoughts of Cassie's death and worries about the future. Was Dad all right? What was happening with the Canadians?

And where was the portal?

Kevin kept searching, but his heart didn't seem to be in it. And I was too busy. After a few days I think he started trying to get used to the idea that he was staying in this world, but it wasn't something he wanted to talk about. Maybe talking about it made it more real somehow, and he didn't want to give up hope entirely. I guess I couldn't blame him.

And there were lots of awkward moments. Like Mom asking me about my family and my future. "You really need to go back to the city and settle things, Larry. I'm sure your father had a will, and he may have named someone to be your guardian. We can find a lawyer to help you."

"Yes, ma'am," I replied. "After the war we'll figure it out. As soon as it's safe."

If she thought it wasn't safe to go to Boston, she'd never let me go.

And then there was our clothes. She insisted on washing them— we must have stunk pretty badly. So Kevin and I peeled down to reveal that we were wearing another whole layer of strange clothes underneath our regular ones.

"Where in the world did you get those pants?" she asked.

"China," I said. "My father knows a professor in China. He sent them to us. Did you notice this thing? It's called a 'zipper'. It's really different."

"But why do you wear the Chinese pants inside your regular pants?"

"We don't like them all that much—we don't want to look weird. But we didn't want to leave them behind. They're supposed to be valuable."

I didn't like lying to Mom, in either world. It was easy to get her to believe you, and that just sort of made it worse. When she found out about your lie she would tell you how disappointed she was, how much she had trusted you, and you ended up feeling like dirt.

"All these stories are pretty pointless," Kevin said later. "Sooner or later Carmody is going to come looking for the portal—and us. And sooner or later you're going to have to tell your mother the truth."

"But I can't tell her now," I argued. "What if she thinks we're demons? What if she throws us out?"

Kevin shrugged. "She's not going to do that," he said. "She's crazy about you. Anyway, suit yourself."

But I couldn't do it. Not yet.

And then there was Stinky. He wasn't especially annoying, except that he didn't seem to want to leave, and after a while that made everyone feel sort of awkward. "No sense in going anywhere till Mister Kincaid's back," he said, talking about his master. But then we heard from a neighbor that Kincaid *was* back, and Stinky said, "I'll just get a beating when I return, so there's no sense in hurrying." And so he stayed.

I tried to explain away Kevin's story about the orphanage, but Stinky had his own explanation: "Your friend is insane," he said. "I just stay away from him as much as I can."

That was fine with Kevin.

The best times were when I went off visiting with Mom and Matthew. Stinky never went, because he was afraid of running into his master, and Kevin usually didn't go because he just wasn't interested. But I enjoyed hearing people talk about their lives, and the war, and the rumors. I enjoyed helping them rebuild their homes and barns; I turned out to be pretty good at carpentry, even though I never did much of it at home.

Everyone was really nice to me when they found out I was an orphan, but they would have been nice to me anyway. And they all had some hardship to deal with—and not just the wrecked homes and barns. A few of them had lost a family member; lots more had brothers and fathers and sons in the army, and there was no way of knowing if they were dead or alive.

More than once I ran into Sarah Lally.

Her father was a tailor, and the first time I saw her was outside his shop near the harbor. My heart started racing. "Hi," I managed to say.

She looked really happy to see me. "How did you get here, Larry? Do you know about Cassie?"

I told her the story about my father dying, and of course she was sympathetic. She put her hand on my arm and gave it a squeeze. "How awful," she murmured. "But how kind of you to come here to help."

I felt guilty about lying to her, just the way I did with Mom. But I didn't want her to take her hand away. "How are you doing?" I asked.

She gestured behind her at the shop. "There was much damage, but we'll be all right."

"If there's anything you need, let me know," I said.

"Thank you, Larry. Oh, I've been meaning to ask you a question if I ever saw you again."

"Sure, go ahead."

"That first time you saw me in the camp—you called me Nora Lally. But you never explained: how did you know my last name?"

I had forgotten about that. I had done pretty well answering my mother's questions, and even making up something about the orphanage, but this was a tough one, especially with Sarah's wide blue eyes gazing at me. "I guess—I don't know, really."

She looked puzzled, but not angry or anything. Then her father called to her from inside the shop. "Well, no matter," she said. "Anyway—I'll see you again, won't I?"

"You can count on it."

She smiled at me and rushed inside.

I did see her again, at neighbor's houses and when we went to church—the same white church with the big steeple that overlooked the town common in my Glanbury. And she was always happy to see me and easy to talk to, and it was hard to believe how scared of her I was back in my world.

Meanwhile, the news that filtered down from Boston was pretty good, although as usual everyone who showed up in Glanbury had a slightly different version. We had defeated the Canadians, and they were retreating. They weren't retreating, but were preparing for a counterattack. They had counterattacked but hadn't been able to break through our defenses, which featured an amazing metal fence that killed anyone who touched it. The blockade had ended, and supply ships from England were landing in Boston Harbor. The blockade was still in place, but England had declared war on Portugal and it was only a matter of time...

It was pretty much all anyone could talk about, and every scrap of news was treated like it was a precious gem. But no one was going to really believe anything until they heard it from a returning soldier. And that was what everyone was waiting for.

I was there when the first one arrived. A bunch of us were working on the Wilsons' barn when a red-jacketed man strode up the lane, a huge grin on his face. It was Mr. Wilson, coming home. Everyone got down from the ladders and came out of the house and crowded around. He spent a while hugging and kissing his family, and then he gave us all the news: "We beat them Canadians," he said. "We fought 'em and fought 'em, and finally they retreated back north, and they're not coming back."

"Are you sure?" someone asked. "Is it official?"

"They're working on the peace treaty now at Coolidge Palace," he replied. "And the first thing they did was lift the blockade. I hear food supplies'll be moving down the coast any day now."

"The other soldiers—when are they coming back?"

"Hard to say. They're letting the volunteers go, but not everyone at once. Don't know how I got to be among the first, but I'm not complainin'."

And then the questions really started coming. Have you seen my husband? What about my son—is he all right? There was good news and bad news for the people there. And for a few there was no news at all. Mom waited till the end. "Henry—have you seen Henry?" she asked.

Mr. Wilson shook his head. "Not lately, Emma. But that doesn't mean anything. There were thousands of soldiers. He could've been anywhere along the front. I'm sure he'll show up any day now."

Mom forced a smile. "Of course. I understand. I'm sure you're right."

So some people left the Wilsons' place happy that day, and some in tears, and some—like us—were just as worried as before.

Anyway, then things started to change.

For example, Stinky finally decided to leave. He knew it was only a matter of time before his master found out where he was, so he figured he didn't have much choice. He looked very depressed when he told us his decision.

"You've been great, Julian," I said. "We wouldn't have survived without you."

He turned red and looked down at the floor. "Don't thank me," he said. "I'm just—I'm no saint, that's all. Anyone would have done what I did."

"I'm not so sure about that," I replied. It was hard to believe, but I knew I was going to miss him. I had almost stopped thinking of him as "Stinky." I shook his hand, and then watched him as he said goodbye to the others. He looked like he was holding back tears. Even Kevin seemed sad to see him trudging down the lane away from the farmhouse. "Not one wet willie from him," Kevin said afterwards, which was about as close as he could come to saying something nice about Stinky.

And then the food arrived, just like Mr. Wilson said. A ship showed up in Glanbury Harbor filled with emergency supplies, and we all went down to the docks to get our share. Beef, potatoes, flour—even sugar and molasses. People couldn't believe their eyes. It was like a gift from heaven.

That was the day the town decided to have a victory celebration at the church hall. The date was set: December 24th. Christmas Eve.

It was the first time I'd thought about Christmas. "They don't celebrate it, do they, Kevin?" I asked.

Kevin shook his head. "Not in New England. It's just another day here. I read about it at Professor Palmer's. The Portuguese do all sorts of things for Christmas, but New Englanders say it's just a pagan tradition. Can you imagine, no Christmas?"

One more reason for Kevin to feel homesick. Me too. I remembered how excited Matthew got, so he could barely sleep a wink the night before, and he kept me awake too, of course, the two of us finally sneaking downstairs early to see the presents, Cassie coming down later and complaining about everything she got…"Doesn't seem right," I said.

"It's a different world, Larry. It'll never be your world, no matter how much you think you can make it yours."

"Okay, okay," I grumbled.

The end of the war had started Kevin looking for the portal again in earnest. "Now there's nothing stopping Lieutenant Carmody from coming down here and finding out what happened to us," he pointed out. And he was pretty upset that I wasn't interested in helping him, so he didn't pass up any chance to let me know how stupid I was being.

I saw his point, but walking around in the woods looking for an invisible needle in the haystack just didn't seem all that useful to me, when I had so much to do helping Mom and Matthew and the rest of folks in Glanbury.

And, to tell the truth, I was worried about what would happen if my father didn't return from the war. The days went by, and more and more soldiers returned home, but no Henry Barnes. And no news of him either. None of the returning soldiers remembered seeing him shot or bayoneted or captured, which was good, but none could say for sure he was alive, either, and by now we were desperate for some news. Matthew looked out the window during the day, and after dark he listened for footsteps in the lane. "He's coming home soon, Mama, isn't he?" he asked. "He'll be here for the celebration on Christmas Eve, won't he?"

"I'm sure of it, Matthew," she replied.

But her eyes were anxious, and I knew she was as worried as any of us.

"You could go in the wagon to Boston," I suggested to her finally. "Ask for him at army headquarters. They must have lists and stuff. You'll probably find out, one way or the other."

"I suppose that makes sense," she said. Then she brightened. "And we could see a lawyer and start getting matters resolved about your father."

Oops, that wasn't what I had in mind. "Well—" I began.

"Don't argue with me, Larry," she interrupted. "It's time, and you know it. We'll do it tomorrow."

"But tomorrow's Christmas Eve. Tomorrow's the celebration."

"We'll get an early start. If we miss the celebration, that's fine—I don't really feel like celebrating."

Of course I got no sympathy from Kevin when I told him.

"Just tell her the truth," he said. "Get it over with."

I couldn't see any way out. "All right," I said. "Tomorrow, for sure."

I must not have sounded all that convincing, because Kevin started in on me again. "You're still dreaming, Larry. But it's time to wake up. You can't just be this substitute kid for them. And you can't live in a substitute world. It's not going to work."

"Shut up, Kevin," I said. It was all I could think of to say.

At supper Mom told Matthew about how we were all going to Boston, and we might not make it to the celebration, and that got him depressed. And he finally understood that Kevin and I might not be staying forever, and that got him really depressed.

And that got me really depressed.

If I told Mom the truth, what would happen?

After supper I went outside to think about it. It was a clear, moonlit night, the kind where you don't seem to mind the cold. So I stood there, listening to the silence. Was Kevin right? Was I dreaming? Probably. But he was dreaming too, wasn't he? Dreaming that there was a way back home, when by now it was clear that there wasn't, that the portal was gone and we were stuck here for the rest of our lives. We were both entitled to our dreams.

Then I heard something—footsteps in the snow. Too loud for an animal. I looked up, and saw a man in a dark coat walking up the path towards the house. He was carrying a rifle and a satchel. His coat was red, I realized. A uniform.

"Dad!" I cried, and I ran to him.

He stopped, and then I stopped too, realizing what I'd said. We stared at each other.

"Larry?" he asked, staring at me with a puzzled expression. "Larry Palmer?"

"Yes, sir," I replied.

"What are you doing here?"

"I'm just, you know, helping out. You're family's inside. They've been waiting for you for a long time."

"I expect they have," he said, breaking into a grin.

That grin hit me like a blow. I couldn't think of what to say, so I just stepped aside. He patted me uncertainly on the shoulder. "Well, then, we'll talk," he said. Then he walked past me and went into his house.

And I stayed out there in the cold as he greeted Mom and Matthew and learned the awful news that awaited him.

CHAPTER 30

I stayed outside; I didn't want to intrude. Kevin came out to join me a couple of minutes later. We sat down on the front step. "Pretty emotional in there," he said.

"I bet. How did he take the news?"

"He cried. I don't think I've ever seen a grown man cry like that before."

"Did he say where he'd been—why it took him so long to get here?"

"He was helping to scout the Canadian retreat—you know, make sure it wasn't some kind of trick. He didn't exactly say it, but I think the officers really liked him—they wanted him to stay in the army. But he wouldn't."

We were silent for a while. Then I said, "I called him 'Dad' when I saw him—it just slipped out."

Kevin nodded. "He looks different with the beard, but yeah—he's your dad. Think he noticed?"

"My dad notices everything."

Then we looked up at the stars until the door opened. "Come in, boys," Mom said softly. "You'll get a fever staying outside in the cold."

We got up. Her eyes were shining. "This is a wonderful night, isn't it?" she said.

"Yes, ma'am," I replied. "It surely is."

We followed her back inside and sat by the fire while she rejoined Dad and Matthew in the kitchen.

Matthew was sitting on Dad's lap. Mom had poured cups of tea and put out some food. There was a jar of jam on the table—Dad must have brought it back from Boston. He looked at me and said, "Mrs. Barnes has told me all you've done for us, Larry. I want to thank you from the bottom of my heart. And I'm very sorry about your father's death."

I just managed a nod in return, then I got up and threw another log onto the fire.

"Tell us about the battle, Papa," Matthew begged him. "From the beginning."

"Your father is very tired, Matthew," Mom put in. "Perhaps tomorrow."

"It's all right, Emma. He's been waiting for this story, I think, and it's time he got it. I was stationed at the Brighton fortifications, Matthew, and the orders were to hold them at all costs. The artillery fire was fierce before the battle. I couldn't believe that we weren't all killed. The sun rose at some point, but we couldn't see it for all the smoke. Our lieutenant gave a speech about saving our homeland and so on, but I don't think any of us paid much attention. We just wanted to get through the battle. And after a while we got tired of the waiting and just wanted the thing to start. Finally we were moved north along the line about half a mile. We assumed those airships helped the officers decide where the assault was going to come. There had been some kind of strange, thin fence rolled out, as well. None of us could figure out what it was for."

"That's the fence that killed everyone," Matthew said.

"Not that I could tell," Dad replied. "Anyway, when we got to our new positions, the artillery fire had stopped, and it was very quiet for a few minutes. Then we could hear them coming. A little while after that, we could see them."

He fell silent for a moment. It sounded much like the battle with the Portuguese.

"Were there a lot of them?" Matthew asked.

"Too many," he replied.

"And did you kill 'em?"

"Yes, Matthew, some of them. I took no pleasure in it, but this was war, and killing is what you do in a war. It was a fierce attack. That fence just slowed them down a little, as far as I could tell. We shot many of them, but there were many more we didn't have time to shoot. They breached the fortifications, and then we were fighting them hand-to-hand. We knew that we couldn't let them past."

"And they didn't get past, right?" Matthew said. "You beat them."

"Well, it wasn't quite that simple, son. We were actually forced to retreat after a while, but we fell back in good order—it wasn't a rout. We stopped and regrouped, and reinforcements arrived—I never found out from where—so we were ready when the Canadians attacked again. I don't think they expected us to put up so much resistance. This time they were the ones who retreated, back beyond the fortifications.

"But it wasn't the end, by any means. They didn't run away like the Portuguese. And there was a rumor that their forces had broken through further west, so we were worried that we'd be outflanked. We commandeered whatever houses we found nearby and spent the night in them. We were cold and hungry and exhausted, and some of us had wounds that weren't being treated. We were happy to have survived, but we knew that tomorrow was likely to be even harder."

Dad paused to sip his tea, and Mom put a hand on his arm to comfort him. "Was there another battle?" Matthew asked.

"There was, but not the next day, as it turned out. I don't know if the Canadians made a mistake by not attacking immediately. Maybe they were in as bad a shape as we were and also needed time to regroup. But in any case, nothing happened. Except more reinforcements arrived—the soldiers who had defeated the Portuguese south of the city. That helped us immensely, knowing we had more comrades, and knowing there was just one army left to defeat.

"And then the generals started maneuvering. We marched here and there over the next few days, without any of us having a clear idea of what we were doing. We were getting very nervous. Even with the new troops we were still outnumbered. And most of us weren't professional soldiers, after all, and none of us had had enough to eat for months. We couldn't wait forever to fight, but we couldn't afford to fight with the odds against us."

Matthew was getting bored. "Tell me about the next battle, Papa," he demanded.

Dad nodded. "All right, the next battle. The final battle. Our lieutenant said to get ready, it was coming, and it would be different from the last one. It would be much bigger, and it would be on open ground, instead of fighting from behind the fortifications. Our position gave us a slight advantage—we held the heights in Brighton—but they had more troops, and probably more ammunition. The main difference this time was that we were the ones who would attack.

"So we woke up before dawn and got ready and said our prayers, and before we really had time to think or worry or be afraid we were charging down towards the enemy, and they were firing back at us. I don't know how I survived. People were dying all around me. I just tried to stay alive and do my job, which was to kill as many of the Canadians as I could.

"It was a terrible battle. Matthew, I know war sounds exciting, but I tell you, I never want to see another day like that one. And I was lucky—I was cut and bruised and punched and kicked, but I wasn't seriously wounded, I wasn't left for dead, like a lot of soldiers I knew. And I didn't end up with a leg amputated, a cripple for the rest of my days.

"Well, in the end the Canadians retreated. It didn't exactly feel like victory—again, they didn't turn and run, we didn't slaughter them. But by sunset they were gone and we held the field.

"At first we didn't know if it was going to be like before, and they were planning to fight again. I don't think we could have survived another battle. But it turns out they decided they couldn't survive one either. They retreated. And as I said, some of us just followed along after them—not to fight, but to make sure they were well and truly gone. We stayed on their heels for upwards of a week. They must be back home by now—and good riddance to them."

"We won!" Matthew said.

"Yes," Dad replied softly, "we won. At such a cost."

"You've done a lot of soldiering, Henry," Mom said.

"Too much, Emma, too much. This war did no one any good."

"I'm glad you're home, Papa," Matthew said.

"So am I, Matthew. So am I."

They all fell silent in the kitchen. Matthew leaned back against Dad and closed his eyes. Dad kissed the top of his head. After a while he carried Matthew up to the attic and put him to bed.

Mom came in to us. "Good night, boys," she said. "There's jam in the kitchen. Help yourselves."

"Thank you, ma'am," I replied.

She smiled at us; she looked so relieved. Then we heard Dad coming back downstairs, and he and Mom went off to their bedroom and left Kevin and me alone. I heard them murmuring to each other while we sat by the fire.

"Want some jam?" I asked him.

He shook his head. "No trip to Boston tomorrow," he remarked.

"I guess not."

"But you'll still have to tell them. Calling him 'Dad'—"

"Yeah, I know. After the victory celebration, for sure."

Kevin looked skeptical, but he didn't say anything. He lay down on the floor and pulled his blanket around him.

I stoked up the fire and lay down next to him. "It wouldn't be so terrible staying here," I murmured. "Even if Lieutenant Carmody finds us. We've made a lot of friends. We know how to get along in this world. We'd be okay."

I didn't think Kevin was going to answer, but after a long time he said, "We'll never be able to say 'okay' in this world. People will never understand us when we ask 'How come?'. They'll always look at us funny when we eat with a fork. There'll never be a Christopher Columbus or a Mark Twain. They'll never know who the Red Sox are. We'll never ride our bikes again."

Will it matter? I thought. When we're twenty, or thirty, or forty— will any of that matter by then? We won't say "okay"; we'll never think about the Red Sox. So what? We'll be what this world made us. But I didn't say anything. There was no sense getting into an argument with Kevin.

Instead I fell asleep, grateful that my father was home, and ready to celebrate the victory that we had helped win.

CHAPTER 31

Christmas Eve. It was a strange morning. The family was so happy; it was so sad. After breakfast Mom and Dad went to visit Cassie's grave, and they spent a long time there. Matthew, meanwhile, wanted to know if Kevin and I were staying.

"We'll certainly stay for the celebration tonight," I said.

"But you can live here forever," he pointed out. "Don't you want to?"

"I don't know, Matthew. It's complicated. We'll see."

Matthew didn't look satisfied.

When they got back from the grave, Mom said Dad would take her to town so she could help out with the preparations at the church hall. "I understand you were going to Boston today," Dad said to us. "I think it's wise to handle that business as soon as possible. Perhaps we can take you tomorrow."

"Thank you, sir," I said.

He gave me kind of a puzzled look, and I knew he remembered what I'd said to him last night. But he didn't say anything. Instead he went to hitch up Gretel while Mom got ready to go to town. Matthew decided to go with them, so after they left Kevin and I were by ourselves for a while. I went outside to chop some firewood, and Kevin joined me. The day was cold and gray, and it felt like snow was coming. A white Christmas, maybe. I was nervous, although I couldn't exactly say why. "Something's going to happen," I said to Kevin. "You feel it?"

"Yeah," he replied. "Maybe we should look for the portal. If there's a blizzard, who knows when we'll have another chance."

"You go ahead. I want to finish chopping this wood."

Kevin just shook his head and continued to sit on a stump while I worked.

When Dad and Matthew got back, Matthew was worried, too. "We don't know where Julian is," he told us.

"He said he was going back to his master," I said. "You know, Mr.—uh—"

"Kincaid," Dad said. "We met Kincaid at the church hall. He hasn't seen Julian since they were in the camp."

"Well," I said, "I don't think he liked Mr. Kincaid very much. Maybe he just decided he wanted to do something else."

"Kincaid's a hard man," Dad pointed out. "He'll have the law on Julian if he tries to leave his apprenticeship."

"I miss Julian," Matthew said.

I did, too. I didn't know why, but finding out that he'd disappeared made me even more nervous.

In the afternoon Dad went around the farm in that deliberate way of his, taking stock of what needed to be done. "You boys have helped a great deal," he remarked afterwards. "I was very concerned about how Mrs. Barnes would make out by herself. It seems that I needn't have been so worried." Dad wasn't much on handing out compliments, so that was a big one, coming from him.

"We were happy to pitch in," I said.

He nodded. "Still, it's strange that you decided to come here when your father died. Now how did you say you were related to Mrs. Barnes?"

Dad was a lot harder to lie to than Mom. "I didn't, sir," I said. "I'm really not sure."

He nodded again, and I felt like he saw right through me. But if he didn't believe me, he certainly couldn't imagine what the truth was. Anyway, he didn't interrogate me any further, and pretty soon it was time to get ready for the celebration.

Matthew slicked back his hair and put on his best blue shirt. Dad trimmed his beard and wore a white ruffled shirt and a long dark coat. Kevin and I just had our usual clothes—but at least they were clean.

I wondered what Sarah Lally would be wearing.

There were a few snowflakes falling when we started out. Dad shook his head. "Hope this doesn't get any worse," he murmured.

Matthew was so excited he started to sing.

The church hall was stuck onto the back of the church, up on the little hill overlooking the town center. When we got there, wagons and carriages were already lined up in front of it, with the horses shifting and stamping their feet in the cold. We left our wagon with the others and hurried inside. The place was blazing with light—I hadn't seen a room so bright since the first time I'd been to Coolidge Palace. In one corner, musicians were playing a violin, an accordion, and a piano, and in the middle of the floor couples were doing one of those complicated dances where everyone's moving around and switching partners and ducking in and out of lines. Ribbons and flags hung from the ceiling. There was a roaring fire in the big fireplace, and the mantel over the fireplace was decorated with pine boughs and holly; the boughs made the room smell like Christmas, even if that's not what we were celebrating. Along the far wall were tables piled with turkey and venison and ham and vegetables and loaves of bread and cakes…It was amazing.

Mom was behind one of the tables, helping to serve the food. She waved to us when we came in. Other people started coming over to greet Dad, and Matthew ran off to join his friends. Sarah Lally was dancing, but she spotted me and waved too. She was wearing a bright green dress and had a green bow in her hair, and she looked gorgeous. I grinned and waved back.

"Great music, huh?" I said to Kevin.

"I thought Matthew said Stinky was missing," he replied. "Look, he's right over there, stuffing his face."

Sure enough, Stinky was standing next to one of the food tables, eating from a very full plate. When he noticed us, his eyes widened and he put the plate down. "That's odd," I remarked. "Let's go find out what's up."

The music stopped just then, and I was thinking I'd rather go talk to Sarah than to Stinky. And that's when I heard a little voice behind me say, "Look, Mama, the boys from the woods."

The voice sounded familiar, so I turned, and I found myself staring into the faces of the Harper family.

The Harper family—Samuel and Martha, with their little boy and girl. The family that had saved Kevin and me from the Portuguese when we stumbled out of the portal so long ago. The ones who had driven us into Boston when we were friendless and clueless in this world, and I was still worried about the piano lesson I was missing.

It was the little girl who had spoken—was her name Rachel?— the one who thought Kevin had been in the navy because he was wearing an Old Navy t-shirt. They were all looking at us, though. And so was my father, who must have been talking to them.

"Bless the Lord," Martha said, "I'm so glad you boys are safe. I've often thought of you since that day we took you to Boston."

"I never did understand where you came from," Samuel said, still grumpy at us. "First your family was murdered, then they weren't murdered…Where did you say you were from? America, was it? Never heard of the place."

"I don't understand any of this," my father put in. "What woods? What murder?"

"Where's your watch?" the boy asked Kevin. "Do you still have that watch?"

Kevin shook his head sadly. And then his face lit up—you could almost see the light bulb going off over his head, like in the comics. "Do any of you happen to remember," he asked, "when we came out of the woods and you picked us up on the Post Road—where was that, exactly?"

Samuel and Martha looked at each other. "It was just past Joshua Fitton's place, wasn't it, Martha?" Samuel said.

Martha nodded. "Yes, certainly it was. I remember seeing the smoke from the house, and we heard the Portuguese soldiers shouting to each other in the woods, and we were sure we'd left too late and be captured. And then you two boys came running out of the woods on the other side of the road. We didn't know what to make of you."

"Thought you were pirates, or spies," Samuel said. "Those strange clothes. Those accents. You don't have so much of an accent now."

"The Fitton place," Kevin repeated.

"Yes, about three miles past the Barnes' farm along the Post Road," Samuel said. "You know where it is, don't you, Henry?"

"Of course I know the Fitton place," Dad said. "But what the deuce is this all about?"

"I can explain," I said softly.

Everyone looked at me.

"Well, um, I need to talk to Mr. Barnes—and Mrs. Barnes—in private."

Dad nodded slowly. "I believe that would be a good idea."

I turned to Kevin. He looked so happy. He didn't care about anything except the Fitton place. He knew exactly where to look for the portal now. "Want to come?" I asked.

"Sure. Whatever."

We started to walk off with my father, but all of a sudden Stinky was standing in front of us, still looking upset. "Larry, we need to talk," he said.

I had more important things to do now than talking to him. "Later, Julian. I'm kind of busy."

"But it's important," he insisted.

I shrugged. Nothing I could do about it.

"I'll talk to him," Kevin said. "You go on with Mr. Barnes."

That worked for me. Stinky still looked upset, but he went off with Kevin. Dad and I made our way to the food tables. Mom smiled at us. "Look at this food," she said happily. "Two months ago, could you ever have imagined it?"

"Emma," Dad replied, "Larry would like to speak to us in private."

Mom's brow furrowed. "Is anything the matter?" she asked me.

I shook my head. "Nothing's the matter. It's just—we need to talk."

"Oh." Mom set down the platter she'd been holding and looked around. "Yes," she said. "Well, then. Why don't we go into the church?"

She acted as if she had been expecting this conversation.

I followed them through a door and along a short corridor that connected the hall to the church. The church was cold and dark. Through the tall windows along the sides I could see snow falling. Mom lit a lamp while Dad threw a couple of logs into an iron stove. The walls were plain white, and there was a simple pulpit at the front. I sat in the first pew. Mom and Dad sat opposite me, on the steps to the pulpit. Waiting.

I wished I had Kevin's watch. That would at least give me a way of starting, something they could examine and touch and use. It had worked with Professor Palmer and Lieutenant Carmody and General Aldridge, and it was the kind of thing that would work with my Dad. But I had nothing, if you didn't count my sneakers and my pants with their amazing zipper. Nothing but my words.

What words could I use?

"There are other worlds," I began. "Not just this one. And these worlds have other Bostons in them, other Glanburys. I don't understand why or how, only I guess—if God could make one universe, why couldn't He make lots of them? The thing is: Kevin and I come from one of those other worlds. It's a lot like this one, but, you know, different—sometimes in little ways, sometimes in big ones. Like these sneakers and our clothes—they're not from China, despite what I said. They're what we wear at home. In this other world."

Here's one thing I like about my Dad: he takes you seriously. Matthew will start explaining one of his stupid ideas about why we have hair or who invented checkers or something—just to hear himself talk, I think—and Dad will sit there and listen and nod and occasionally ask a question, like Matthew is some sort of expert on hair or checkers. He might smile a little bit, but he never tells Matthew to put a sock in it. Same thing with Cassie when she starts complaining about how awful her life is. Afterwards she complains that Dad never does anything to solve her problems, but just listening is a whole lot more than I'd do when she starts up.

So I guess I shouldn't have worried that he'd laugh at me or something when I started the explanation. Instead he nodded like I was making perfect sense and said, "You're not talking about heaven and hell, I take it. You're talking about, er, real worlds."

"Right. As real as this one."

"And why don't we know about these worlds?"

"Well, because you don't know how to travel between them."

"But you do."

"That's right," I said. "Or, well, somebody does. Kevin and I just happened to—see, we found a—a device, a machine. We call it a portal. We don't know who made it or why—it's probably not even from our world. It was just sitting there in the woods behind my house—except, well, it's invisible. Anyway, we got in it and just kind of like stepped through it, and we were here. By mistake. That's when the Harpers saw us—we'd just gotten out of the portal, and the Portuguese soldiers were chasing us, and we couldn't get back to it. So we sort of ended up, you know, stuck here."

"An invisible machine," Dad said. Again, not sarcastically, but like he was just trying to understand.

"And that's what Kevin is looking for when he goes off walking along the Post Road by himself?" Mom asked.

"Yes, ma'am," I replied. "He's trying to get home."

"And this other business," Dad said, "about your father being a professor and dying in the war—you made all that up?"

"Well, yeah. Except there really is a professor." And then I explained some of what happened to Kevin and me after the Harpers brought us to Boston. I left out about Kevin's drikana. And I left out the—well, the complicated part, about why I was talking to them about all this instead of anyone else in this world. Not that I was going to be able to avoid that part for long.

Dad kept nodding, as if this was the sort of thing kids told him every day. "So you're responsible for those airships and that fence— is that what you're saying?"

"Well, more or less. On our world there are inventions that are much more amazing than those things, but there wasn't time to figure out how to build them here." I didn't really want to talk about computers and telephones and stuff like that—it would just make things more difficult to believe.

"But this still doesn't make sense, does it?" Dad said. "Why did you come to the Fens camp? Why were you looking for us?"

That was the complicated part. But strangely, I didn't have to explain. Mom understood. "Larry hasn't really finished describing his world," she said. "Have you, Larry?"

"No, ma'am."

She was staring at me hard, the way she had in the camp when I first gave that confusing lie about who I was. And then Dad got it. "'Dad', you called me last night," he said. "Not a word we use much in these parts. But I've heard it. I know what it means."

I nodded. "Some people exist in both worlds. They're different in lots of ways—different jobs, different homes. But they're basically the same."

"And you're saying that—that we're there in this other world?" Dad said.

"Yes. And Cassie, and Matthew. And me—I was part of the family too. And that's why I went looking for you in the camp. And that's why I was so happy to find you. I had found my family."

I fell silent and waited for a response. Dad couldn't just act like he was taking me seriously; he had to make a decision. He had to believe, or not believe. He's logical; he's a computer programmer.

Professor Palmer had talked about Occam's Razor—I could almost see Dad struggling to use it on my story. "Larry," he said finally, "this is very interesting and, well, moving, but you'll have to admit it's a bizarre tale. You're saying that—that you're the son we buried as an infant. Still alive, grown up to be a young man."

"Yes, sir, that's what I'm saying. I'm your son on another world, where medicine is better, and they can cure fevers and consumption and smallpox. I didn't die of whatever killed me here. I'm just a regular boy who goes to school and has an older sister who complains too much and a younger brother who talks too much. And a wonderful mother who worries about all of us all the time."

"Well frankly, I don't see how you can expect us to—"

As he spoke I realized that he wasn't the one I needed to be talking to. "Do you believe me?" I asked Mom.

She was gripping Dad's arm now. A single tear worked its way down her cheek. "Of course I do, Larry," she whispered. "Of course I do."

Dad turned to her. "Emma," he said, "I know how grateful you are to Larry, but—"

She shook her head. "No, that's not it. I know him, Henry. I *know* him. I couldn't understand it—couldn't understand this feeling I had when I looked at him, when I talked to him—but now I do. He's our son. He's my baby. I don't understand anything more, and I don't need to."

We were silent again. I could hear the ticking of the clock on the rear wall of the church, and the distant sound of the joyful music from the church hall.

"I suppose we'll find out the truth of it soon enough," Dad said to me. "If this—this portal is still there by Joshua Fitton's farm, we should be able to find it, invisible or not. And then you can use it go home."

Home. All those conversations with Kevin, and now the moment had arrived.

"Well…I don't know," I said.

"What do you mean?" he asked. "What don't you know?"

"See, I was thinking of staying. You know, to help you out. There's a lot I don't know about farming and stuff, but I can learn. I can be part of this family too. I feel like—like I already am."

I hadn't known I was going to say that. I had thought about it a lot, but I hadn't ever really decided. Now, there it was.

But instead of acting all happy, Mom was shaking her head. "You have to go home, Larry. I love you, but you can't stay here."

"Trying to go home could be dangerous," I pointed out. "We don't even know if the portal will take us home. We might end up in some universe where the Earth doesn't even exist. Kevin is willing to take the risk—he doesn't have a family here. But I have you, and I don't want to give you up."

I could tell the idea of the danger bothered Mom, but it wasn't enough to change her mind. "If—if I'm there, too, imagine how much I miss you. Every moment of every day, Larry. Wondering where my baby went."

So I guess I hadn't really thought it through. I thought maybe they wouldn't believe me and I'd have to convince them, but once they were convinced they'd be happy to have me stay. I could see now how stupid that was. In reality, Mom loved me so much that she had to let me go.

But she couldn't force me to go. If I stayed here, she might feel guilty, but she'd get over it. And for all I knew, maybe we could figure out how to come back here in the portal, and I could be part of both worlds. It was possible, wasn't it?

"I don't know," I said. "I don't want to leave you, now that I've found you."

"I understand, Larry," she replied. "I don't want you to leave either. But you have to. And I'm sure you know it. Take some time to think it over." She stood up. "For now, why don't we go back to the hall?" she said. "Really, we have much to celebrate."

"Do you mind if I stay here for a while?" I said. "Maybe I do need to think about things."

Mom shook her head and put her hand on my arm. "That is very wise, Larry."

Dad stood up too. "I certainly want to talk more with you, Larry," he said. "But perhaps this is enough for now."

I nodded and watched the two of them as they walked out of the church. Then I leaned back in the pew and closed my eyes. Now what? Kevin would want to head off to look for the portal as soon as possible—he'd do it right now if he could. So should I obey my mother and go with him? Go back to a world where I didn't matter, where our family argued morning and night and the schoolbus was a nightmare and I never learned or did a single thing that was really important, that really made a difference?

Where my mother missed me every moment of every day?

I tried to pray. I've never been good at praying, but now seemed like a pretty good time to ask for help. So I did.

I don't know how long I sat there. When I finally opened my eyes, the lamp was burning low and I knew I should get back to the church hall. I stood up. And that's when I heard the noise behind me.

It was—well—it was a quiet noise. A rustle, a breath. I wasn't really sure I had heard anything. But I turned, and in the dimness I saw the outline of a figure standing at the back of the church.

My heart started thumping. "Who are you?" I whispered.

"I really could use that coat back," the figure replied. And he took a step forward.

CHAPTER 32

S oft voice, black beard, glittering eyes.

The preacher from the Burger Queen world, from the park in Boston. The guy who had left his coat behind for me. The guy who had told me it was all his fault.

"Who are you?" I repeated, more insistently. I moved a little closer to him. He was wearing a ragged brown coat now. His hair was wet from the snow.

"A traveler, like you," he replied, still standing in the doorway.

"What do you want?"

He shook his head. "A better question might be: What do *you* want?"

"I want to know why you're following me. I want to know what you know that I don't."

"I wouldn't say that I'm following you," he said. "It's more that…our paths have crossed."

"Whatever. The portal—is that your machine?"

"'Portal'—is that what you call it? Kind of clichéd, don't you think? Couldn't you come up with something more original? 'Cosmic gateway'—what about that?"

I was starting to get angry. "You didn't answer my question— you're not answering any of my questions."

He smiled sheepishly. "I know," he said. "It's kind of a habit. We're not really supposed to answer questions."

"Who is 'we'?" I almost shouted.

"Okay, okay," he said. "Just calm down. I guess I can make an exception for you. You've had a tough time of it. And it wasn't like you meant any harm. You were just, you know, stupid."

I was so upset by now that I thought I might go over and start pounding him. But I managed to stay quiet, and he kept talking.

"So no, the portal, or the cosmic gateway, or whatever, isn't mine, and it isn't exactly a machine—at least, not in the way you think of machines. I just borrow it for my travels. Like you, except not so stupid. Didn't your mother ever tell you not to set foot inside invisible gizmos from other universes? That would be, like, rule number one if I were a parent."

I ignored the insult. "So what is it?" I demanded. "Where does it come from?"

"Okay, that one I really don't know the answer to. There are lots of universes, right? You know that now, of course. Actually, there are probably an infinite number of universes. Imagine one where people have advanced way beyond anything you can imagine, if that makes any sense. Maybe they're not even people, in any sense that we understand. But they develop these portals. And then they disappear. At least—none of us know has a clue where to find them."

"Portals—there's more than one of them?"

"Uh-huh. Or maybe they're all manifestations of a single underlying entity. Who knows?"

I had no idea what that last part meant, but I had another question. "You keep saying 'we', 'us'—are you from my universe? Is there more than one of you?"

"No, I'm from a different universe—although it's not all that different, and I've visited yours from time to time—yours needs a lot of help, if you ask me. Anyway, there's a group of us who use the portal. You might call us a priesthood."

"Priesthood? You're part of a religion?"

He tilted his head and thought for a moment. "Not in the way you'd think of it," he replied. "We don't have a set of beliefs. We're not trying to convert anyone. We just want to impart some wisdom."

"So you just, like, travel around to different universes and give sermons and stuff?"

He looked insulted. "Well, yes," he said, "but—"

"Don't you help people? I mean, like, this world. What if you could cure drikana? Would you do it?"

He shook his head. "It's forbidden. Simply coming to a world, simply crushing a blade of grass underfoot, is interference enough. We don't tell anyone who we are or where we come from. We just say what we have to say, and then leave."

I thought of giving President Gardner the Heimlich maneuver. If someone's dying, you try to save him. "But that's crazy," I said. "That's—immoral."

"If we save one life, why not save all of them?" he argued. "We're just visitors. Who are we to decide who lives and who dies? It's a small step from that to teaching people how to build better bombs— or electric fences. Look, what's most important is for us to guard against the corruption of power. That's something we face every day. Any of us could become ruler of a run-of-the-mill world like this—we could be worshipped as gods—by using a tenth of what we know. Does that make any sense to you?"

I supposed that it did, but I had more important things I needed to learn from him. "How did you know who I was?" I asked. "Even on that other world it seemed like you could tell I was—I was an outsider. You knew I had come there in the portal. Didn't you?"

He smiled. "Sure. It's not really that hard, after you have some experience. What's obvious to us may not be at all obvious to anyone else, of course."

"So more people use the portals than just you guys?"

"Yes, unfortunately. People like you. Random travelers. And observing the bad results of their interference has made us develop our own rules."

"So am I in trouble or something? I've broken your rules."

He shook his head. "Not at all. We live by our rules. Others do as they please."

That was a relief. But I still hadn't gotten to the really important question. "Can you tell me—can we get home in the portal?" I asked. "We've been looking for it, and now we think we know where it is. But we don't know where it will take us."

"Do you want to go home?" he asked.

"I don't know," I admitted. "This is home too, sort of. But maybe it'd be easier to make a decision if I wasn't worried that we'd end up on a world where we'd be eaten by dinosaurs or something."

"I understand," he replied. Then he was silent for a long time. "Listen," he said finally. "I'm not trying to make things difficult for you—really I'm not. I shouldn't have left the portal in the woods like that in your world. It was too close to an inhabited area, I admit it. If kids find invisible cosmic gateways, they're going to use them. We know that. So I'm trying to help you out. But I'm just not supposed to answer stuff like that. So here's the best I can do: If you want to go home, the portal will take you home."

I couldn't tell if that was an answer or not. So I said, "You once said: It is only by setting out that we can finally return home. Were you talking to me when you said that?"

He shrugged. "I was talking to whoever would listen."

"Well then, what should I do: Should I stay here, or should I go back to where I came from?"

"Ah," he said softly. "Now there's a question I can answer. Sort of. The answer is: Listen to your heart. And only to your heart. It'll tell you what to do."

I should have known that was the sort of thing he'd say.

"One final thing," he added. "The portal? I don't really think you know where it is. I moved it across the road. Too many people in the woods near the Fitton farmhouse. I'm trying to learn my lesson."

Then I heard a door open behind me. I turned and saw Kevin standing in the doorway, looking upset. "Where have you been?" he demanded. "Who are you talking to?"

"I've been right here," I said. "Talking to—" I turned back to the preacher, but of course he was gone. The front door to the church was open. I went outside and looked around, but I couldn't spot him. There were tracks in the snow. I followed them, down the walkway to the street. "Come back here!" I shouted into the night. "You can't just leave like that!"

I tripped and fell, and when I got up I couldn't find the tracks, and I couldn't find him. "Come on!" I shouted again. "Please help us!"

Kevin came up behind me. "What the heck is going on?" he asked.

"The—the preacher—the stupid preacher—" I was too mad to explain.

"Doesn't matter," Kevin interrupted. "You've gotta come with me. Right now."

"Why? What happened?"

"Stinky's a snitch—he's been a snitch all along. He went back to Boston and told the lieutenant where we were, and Carmody's coming to get us. Let's go."

Swell, I thought. What else could go wrong? I followed Kevin back into the church hall.

CHAPTER 33

"We have to get out of here," Kevin said as we hurried along the dark corridor to the church hall. "We have to get to the portal before Carmody finds us."

"Well, we might have a problem there."

"I don't care if it's snowing, Larry. I don't care if it's a hurricane. We finally know where the portal is. We're going."

We entered the hall, which was almost overpoweringly warm and bright after being in the church and outside in the snow. The musicians were taking a break. Stinky was standing by the fireplace, looking guilty. We went over to him. "What's going on, Julian?" I demanded.

"I'm sorry, Lawrence," he said. "Really I am. If I'd known, I never would have done it."

"I don't understand. Start at the beginning."

He took a deep breath. "Well, see, it started with Sergeant Hornbeam," he said.

"Hornbeam? What about him?"

"You remember how I did favors for the soldiers at the camp? I was just trying to survive, you know—get some extra food once in a while. There wasn't anything bad about it."

"I remember. What about Sergeant Hornbeam?"

"Well, one day he asked me to look after you. He said you were important to the army—he wouldn't say why—and you'd started showing up at the camp. He wanted to make sure nothing bad happened to you."

"Wait—so when you rescued me from those kids who stole my coat—"

"Hornbeam had told me to follow you," Stinky admitted. "But I was glad to do it! Then I didn't see you again until the morning after the battle."

"That was on orders, too?"

He nodded. "After the battle I talked my way past the guards to get into the army camp. I was just looking for a meal and a cot. I had no idea you were there. But I ran into Sergeant Hornbeam again, and he told me to stay with the two of you and keep you safe. He said if I did a good job he'd see to it that I got out of my 'prenticeship so I could join the army.

"And I did do a good job—didn't I? I kept you alive. I got you to Glanbury. And it wasn't just a job—I liked you. You became my mates."

"Gimme a break," Kevin muttered.

Stinky gave Kevin a look that suggested they were no longer quite so matey. "So why did you leave?" I asked.

"Well, you know how it was. The war was over. I couldn't stay with you forever—my master was in town and searching for me. I surely didn't want to run into him. So I made my way back to Boston and started looking for Sergeant Hornbeam. I found him finally, and he brought me to a lieutenant at headquarters—"

"Carmody," I said.

Stinky nodded. "And he was awfully excited to find out you were alive. But he seemed worried that you'd escape again. I heard him talking to the sergeant, and he said, 'Why haven't they found it?' or something like that. 'We've got to catch them before they get away for good.'"

Stinky looked at me pleadingly. "Lawrence, I don't know what you fellows did and I don't want to know. There's a lot I don't understand. I never really believed the stories you told me—about being orphans and such. But I never meant to hurt you. So after I spoke to the lieutenant, I decided I couldn't stay in Boston, even though Sergeant Hornbeam said he was going to take care of me. I came right back to Glanbury to warn you—got a ride from a peddler part of the way, and I walked the rest. I figured I'd find you here."

"So when is he coming?"

"I don't know," Stinky admitted. "But I don't imagine he'll delay."

"It doesn't matter what he imagines," Kevin said to me. "We have to go."

"I've never had many friends," Stinky said. By now he looked like he was about to cry. "When I met you, I thought perhaps—"

"It's all right, Julian," I said. "Really. I'm grateful you came all the way back here to warn us."

"If there's anything more I can do…"

"You've done enough. Thank you."

We left him and went to find my parents. "Don't see why you were so nice to him," Kevin muttered.

"Don't see why you treated him like a jerk. But listen. The preacher showed up—that's who I was chasing after. The thing is, he said he moved the portal."

"What?"

"Just to the other side of the road—but that might explain why we never found it. But I don't know—talking to him is like talking to Yoda or something. Everything's a riddle, except when he's calling us stupid kids."

Kevin looked like he wanted to shoot somebody. "Your parents," he said. "Did you explain to them—?"

"They know about us and the portal," I said. "They don't know this last bit, though."

My parents were talking to each other across the room. We made our way over to them. "Things are getting complicated," I said. I began by summarizing what Stinky had told us.

Dad was outraged. "No one can force you to stay here," he said. "That lieutenant can't just kidnap you. This isn't New Portugal. There are laws. If you don't want to stay, you don't have to."

I was pretty sure he underestimated Lieutenant Carmody's power, but still it felt good to have him on our side. "The thing is," I said, "we need to find the portal before he stops us."

"Well, the snow isn't going to help, but the Fitton place isn't far."

"I know, except the portal might not be where we think." And I explained what I'd learned from the preacher.

"This is baffling," Dad replied. "What do we do?"

"We need to go home right now and figure this out," my mother said.

That seemed like a pretty good idea. "Very well," Dad said. "I'll go fetch Matthew."

He went searching for Matthew, and while he did Sarah Lally came up to us, looking flushed and happy. "It's such a wonderful party, don't you think?" she said.

I hadn't had a second to enjoy it. But I said sure, it was great.

"I was rather hoping you'd ask me to dance, Larry," she murmured, looking down at the floor.

Nothing would have made me happier, but Kevin would have killed me if we delayed leaving so I could dance with her. "I'm so sorry, Sarah," I replied, "but something's come up, and we all have to go home."

Her eyes crinkled with disappointment. "So soon? No one's ill, I hope?"

"No, it's just that—" I didn't know what to say, so Mom jumped in.

"Actually, Mr. Barnes is quite tired," she said. "He's just back from the war, you know."

"Oh, of course," Sarah said quickly. "Forgive me. Perhaps you'll come visit me later this week, Larry?"

"I'll try, Sarah. I'll try."

She reached out and squeezed my hand. I squeezed back, and then she walked away. "It's wonderful having you here, Larry," she called out over her shoulder.

I smiled at her. "Get a grip," Kevin said to me.

Meanwhile Dad had grabbed Matthew, who was really upset about having to leave so soon. "Can't we stay for a half hour more?" he pleaded.

Dad shook his head. "We have to go now. I'm sorry. Let's get our coats."

A couple of minutes later we had said our goodbyes and were outside, climbing into the wagon. The snow was coming down even harder now, with a strong wind swirling it all around us. Mom put her arm around Matthew, who buried his face in her coat. We had a lantern, but its flickering light didn't penetrate far through the storm. "Travel won't be easy," my father muttered. He flicked the reins, and Gretel set out.

This is all going way too fast, I thought. I needed more time to think things through, but I wasn't getting any. I looked at Kevin, who was sitting next to me, nervously glancing around as if he was expecting Carmody to appear out of the darkness.

I thought about telling him the one good thing the preacher had said: that the portal would take us home.

Except even that wasn't very clear. If you want to go home, the portal will take you home. That would work for Kevin, certainly. But what about me? What if the portal read my mind or something and decided I didn't really want to go home? Would I end up somewhere else? Back here? Why wouldn't the guy give me a straight answer? For someone who traveled to different universes handing out wisdom, he sure didn't seem to have a whole lot of social skills.

"I don't know, lads," my father called out. "It'll be all we can do to get back to the farmhouse in this weather."

He was right. We could barely see the road now, and Gretel was straining to make her way. How much worse was it going to be after a few more miles of travel? And how were we going to find an invisible portal in the woods in this mess? I looked at Kevin again. He just looked glum and stayed silent.

"Mr. Barnes can take you at first light," Mom said.

"Where are they going?" Matthew asked.

"We'll explain later," Mom replied.

At least Lieutenant Carmody was going to have as much difficulty in the storm as we were having, I thought. It was hard for my father to find the turn into the lane leading to the farmhouse. But Gretel seemed to know the way, and finally we pulled silently up toward the house.

"Did you leave a lantern burning, Henry?" Mom asked.

"Of course not," Dad replied.

We all stared at the light shining in the window. As we got closer, we saw a horse and carriage tied up by the front door. "Let's get out of here," Kevin said to me, and he got ready to jump out of the wagon.

"Don't, lad," Dad said. "You won't survive in the storm."

"He's not going to capture us," Kevin replied. "Come on, Larry."

"Who's not going to capture you?" Matthew demanded. "What's going on?"

"That's not the lieutenant's carriage," I pointed out.

Just then the door opened, and a single figure stepped out into the night. I breathed a sigh of relief and joy.

It was Professor Palmer.

CHAPTER 34

I jumped from the wagon, ran up to the professor, and hugged him. Kevin was right behind me.

"Hello, Larry," he said. "It's good to see you. And you, too, Kevin."

"We missed you," I said. "I'm sorry we left like that, but—"

"I understand. I'm just so glad you're both alive."

"We're glad you're alive, too," Kevin said.

Then my parents came up with Matthew, and the professor said, "You must be the Barneses. My name is Alexander Palmer, and I beg your pardon for entering your home uninvited. I rode down from Boston this evening in the utmost haste, and the weather—"

"Of course, sir," Dad replied. "You're most welcome. Larry has told us about you. Let's all go in out of the snow."

We went inside, although Dad went out again almost immediately with Matthew to put Gretel in the barn. Kevin stoked up the fire, and Mom heated some cider.

"I'm afraid I'm here with some distressing news," Professor Palmer murmured to me. "Would it be better if we talked in private?"

"Not really. I've explained about who we are and the portal and everything. So, is this about Lieutenant Carmody coming after us?"

He raised an eyebrow in surprise. "You've heard?"

I told him a bit about Stinky Glover.

"Interesting—so that's how Carmody found out where you were. Yes indeed, I did come to warn you about him."

"When's he coming?" Kevin asked. "How much time do we have?"

"He's coming as soon as he can, as far as I know. But the storm may delay him, obviously."

"How'd you find out?" I asked.

"And how'd you get here before him?" Kevin added.

"I found out because he told me, Larry. He has always assumed that I would be eager to have you boys kept here, even against your wishes, in the interest of science and the advancement of knowledge. How little he knows me, after all these years. As for how I managed to get here before him—as soon as I found out I spoke with General Aldridge, and he urged me to leave immediately; he was as outraged by this plan as I was. Carmody had to stop at Coolidge Palace before making the journey."

"Why? To see the president?"

"That is correct." Mom handed the professor a cup of hot cider. He bowed and thanked her, then continued. "The president is less of a fool than he looks, I fear. And the lieutenant is more of a schemer than I expected. He has decided his opportunities are greater if he sides with the president against General Aldridge. He explained about you boys to Gardner, and convinced him that you are vital to New England's survival, and possibly more. With the knowledge you bring, why couldn't we conquer our enemies? I rather think he believes there's no one we couldn't conquer, in fact."

"That's stupid," Kevin protested. I thought of the preacher talking about how easy it would be to rule a run-of-the-mill world like this, and I wondered just how stupid the idea was.

"Well, that was their thinking," the professor went on, "—if they could find you, if you hadn't already left. But that raises the question: Why are you boys still here? Have you not been able to find the portal?"

"That's right," I said.

"I'm very sorry to hear it. But I fear that staying in Glanbury will not be an option, unless you want to be part of what Carmody and Gardner are planning. Perhaps you do. I'm sure you'll be treated well. But if you don't, we must move quickly to get you away from here. Despite the war, I have many academic friends in Canada, and I'm sure—"

"We're going to try to find the portal," Kevin interrupted. "As soon as we can. We have an idea where it is."

"Ah. That's good, then. You'll have to hurry, though." The professor looked a little disappointed. "I only wish I had a little more time to spend with you. I was so happy to find out you were all right, and now—"

Kevin's eyes lit up. "You should come with us!"

"You mean—into the portal?"

"Sure—why not? Think of all the stuff you asked about and we didn't know the answer to. Imagine what you'd learn if you came to our world and got to talk to real scientists—people as smart as you."

Now the professor looked confused, flustered. "But—but if I left, I couldn't come back."

"We don't know that for sure. Anyway, so what? You don't want to be around here when they find out you helped us escape. President Gardner doesn't like you anyway."

"True, but—"

I suddenly thought of the most important reason for him to go. "There's no smallpox in our world," I pointed out. "Your wife and son may be alive."

That stopped him, and I could see my Mom react, sitting by the fire. "They may never have existed on your world, as I understand it," he pointed out. "Or they may have died of some other disease. Anything is possible. Correct?"

"Only one way to find out."

"Well, I'll consider it," he replied. "It would certainly be…quite an adventure."

Dad and Matthew came back in the house then. "We pulled out the sleigh and got it ready," Dad said. "We can leave as soon as the snow let's up."

"You're going away," Matthew said to Kevin and me accusingly. "Dad told me."

Kevin nodded. "It's time," he said.

"Matthew, take off those wet clothes and have some hot cider," Mom said.

Matthew reluctantly changed his clothes and sat on Dad's lap next to the fire. The rest of us also gathered around the fire, although Kevin kept getting up to check on the snow. People talked—about the portal, about the war, about Carmody's treachery—but I didn't pay much attention. It just felt so good to be there, with my family and Kevin and the professor, with the fire blazing and the snow coming down outside. If only I could have captured that moment forever…

After a while I closed my eyes. And, in the middle of everything, I had a dream about grilled cheese sandwiches and tomato soup.

That was our regular Sunday night supper. We complained occasionally, especially Cassie: Why couldn't we get takeout? Why couldn't we have real food? But Mom wouldn't relent. The meal was cheap and easy, and she liked it. Besides, it was what she'd had on Sunday nights growing up, and if it was good enough for her, it was good enough for us.

So I'm sitting in my usual place at the kitchen table, across from Cassie. I slurp down some of my soup, and then I happen to look over at her. She's one of these people who can get angry at you just for looking at them. Just for breathing the same air, really. So she says to me, "What are you looking at?" And I say: "Nothing." And she says: "I'm not dead, you know. That's just in your stupid dream."

And I say: "That's not a dream. This is the dream."

And she says: "You're so stupid." And she turns to Dad: "Isn't he stupid? Isn't this the reality?"

And Dad smiles his leave-me-out-of-this smile and says: "One person's dream is another person's reality."

And then we're both mad at him for not agreeing with us. But he says: "It really doesn't matter. No matter what the dream is, it's time to wake up."

"What if I don't want to wake up?" I say.

"It doesn't matter. Wake up. Wake up!"

I opened my eyes, and Dad was staring down at me, but he had a beard, and it wasn't Sunday night in my world, it was Christmas Eve in a very different world.

"Wake up, Larry," he repeated. "Someone's coming."

"In the closet," Mom said, gesturing to the storage area to the right of the fireplace. "Quickly."

She had pulled out the blankets and some other stuff that they kept there. I got up, and Kevin and I jammed ourselves into it, and then she pushed the stuff back in and closed the door.

Kevin and I knelt down, cramped and in darkness except for a sliver of light through the door. It wasn't really a closet like in our world; it was only about four feet high, but it extended back a few feet, so we couldn't stand up, but we could stretch out a little bit. It's Carmody, I thought. He was bound to look in here. And that would be that.

There was a loud rapping on the door. I heard footsteps, then muffled voices, then a lot more footsteps—boots moving across the wooden floor, this time coming towards us. And then Lieutenant Carmody's voice, just on the other side of the closet door from us: "Professor Palmer, how interesting to meet you here."

"Hello, William."

"Didn't you trust me to find our young friends?"

"I couldn't wait to see them. I was overjoyed to learn that they survived the battle."

"As was I. Wretched weather, though. Peter had a devil of a time getting us down here. Now Mr. and Mrs. Barnes, we're looking for a couple of lads named Larry and Kevin. We have information that they are living with you."

"*Were* living with us," my father responded. "They have returned where they came."

Silence. I tried to imagine what Carmody was doing, how he was reacting. He wasn't happy, I knew that. I was sweating. My back hurt. The blankets were making my nose twitch, but I willed myself not to sneeze. I could hear Kevin's breathing—why couldn't he be more quiet? "What does that mean, exactly—'returned where they came'?" Carmody asked finally.

"They finally found the portal that would take them home, as I understand it. And they're—well, gone."

"Excuse me, Mr. Barnes, but I think that rather unlikely. Our information is that they were here a couple of days ago, and that they'd been unsuccessful in finding the portal."

"That's true, sir, but something happened."

"And what is that?"

"They met the family who picked them up that day coming out of the woods," Dad replied. "Name of Harper. They remembered where that was."

"Ah, I think the boys mentioned that family to me. And where is the portal? Did you see them leave?"

"They said it was in the woods near the Fitton farm—about three miles south on the Post Road. I didn't see them leave—it was rather emotional, sir. My wife and son have grown quite attached to the boys. We brought them to the woods, they went in, and they didn't come back out."

I didn't realize my father was that good a liar. There was another silence, and then I heard more footsteps. "Well?" Carmody demanded.

"I checked the barn. Nothing there. A sleigh's been moved out, though." It was Peter's voice.

"Any footprints leading away from the house?"

"None that I noticed, sir."

"Search the house. Sergeant Hornbeam, find the stairs to the attic and look around. Peter, search down here."

"There's a little boy sleeping up in the attic," my Mom said. "Please don't wake him."

No response. Footsteps again. So all my father's lying would be in vain, once Peter opened the door to the closet. And he'd probably get in trouble, too.

"Nothing in the kitchen," Peter reported.

"Check that closet over there," the lieutenant said.

"Yes, sir."

I braced myself. The door opened. The blankets moved. Then Peter was leaning in and staring at us. He paused, then slowly winked and put the blankets back where they were. "Nothing in here," he said as he closed the door.

"Nothing in the attic," Sergeant Hornbeam added.

"Very well," the lieutenant said. "Can you show me where you dropped off the boys?"

"Not in the dark," my father replied.

"Yes, yes, in the morning," Carmody snapped.

"All right."

"Alexander, do you want to come with us? I understand there's a reasonable inn on the Post Road."

"Mr. and Mrs. Barnes have invited me to stay here, William," the professor replied. "I've had enough of traveling for this day, I think."

"Would you like some hot cider before you leave?" That was my Mom, speaking for the first time. Did she have to be so nice? Why didn't she just let them go?

"No, thank you, ma'am," Carmody said. "Sorry for the intrusion. These were interesting lads, as I'm sure you understand."

"Indeed we do."

"One thing more: You're not to speak of this portal to anyone. Understood?"

"Yes, sir." That was my father again.

More footsteps and muffled voices, then a door slamming. We waited, and after a minute the closet door opened and the blankets and junk were pulled away. Kevin and I crawled out. Everyone was grinning. "I thought surely you'd be discovered," my mother said.

"We were," Kevin replied. "But Peter kept it to himself. I always liked Peter."

"Thanks for making up that story," I said to Dad. "It sounded great."

"I don't approve of what that man wants to do," he said. "You've done nothing wrong, and he has no right to try to keep you here against your will."

"I agree," Professor Palmer said. "But what do we do now?"

"If I understand correctly, he won't find your portal when I bring him to those woods by the Fitton place," Dad said. "Will that make him suspicious? Or will he give up and go back to Boston? In which case the boys can just hide out until he's gone."

"I think it unlikely he'll return to Boston without doing a thorough search for the portal," the professor replied. "Even without the boys, he and the president will be interested in what they can glean from the device itself—although it will be precious little, I imagine."

"If the lieutenant stays here, he's bound to find out that we were at the celebration tonight," I pointed out. "Everyone saw us there. So he'll know Dad's story was a lie."

"We have to look for the portal," Kevin said. "Right away, before he comes back. If we wait around we'll get caught. I just know it."

Looking for an invisible needle in the dark. In a snowstorm. Good luck to us, I thought. "We'll have a better chance of finding it if we wait till dawn," I said.

"Larry's right, I'm afraid," Dad replied. "Even finding the Post Road won't be easy right now."

Kevin looked like he was ready to go off through the snow on foot, but he calmed down. "All right," he said. "Dawn." He went over to look out the window.

I felt really sorry for him. Even in daylight, what were the odds we'd find the thing, with what the preacher had told me?

Mom brought us some cider, and I sat back down by the fire. I wasn't sleepy anymore. It was time to get this over with, one way or the other.

No one wanted to talk now. The professor nodded off once in a while, but the rest of us stayed wide awake. It didn't seem very long at all before Kevin said, "It's brightening out there." Dad went over and checked, nodded his agreement, and said, "I'll hitch up Gretel."

Kevin stood up. "Let's go home," he said to me.

CHAPTER 35

Kevin and I put on the clothes from our world, then our coats. Professor Palmer was coming with us; Mom was going to stay home with Matthew.

"Please be careful, Larry," she said. I knew she'd say that.

I went over to her. She pulled my coat tight around me, and then touched my arm. "If you don't come back," she whispered, "I will always see your face in my mind. And I will always be grateful that you came into my life." She kissed the top of my head and hugged me. "Now go, and be good to your mother. She worries about you every minute."

"I don't want to go," I said. "I love you."

She just shook her head and turned away. I ran up to the attic and kissed Matthew, who stirred but didn't awaken. When I came downstairs, I took a quick look around, and then followed the others out of the farmhouse.

Outside, Gretel was already hitched up to the sleigh. Dad got up on the bench to drive. Kevin and I sat on one of the facing seats; Professor Palmer sat on the other. "A one-horse open sleigh," I said to Kevin.

He didn't bother answering.

The snow had mostly stopped. The air was cold; the sky was brightening. Dad picked up the reins. Mom waved to us from the doorway; her cheeks were wet with tears. We all waved back, and then we started off.

It was slow going at first, as Gretel got used to her burden. The world was silent except for the shooshing of the sleigh's runners over the snow. Silent and beautiful, with the snow weighing down the branches of the trees. I spotted a deer gazing out at us from a stand of pines.

"If we find the portal, will you come with us?" I asked Professor Palmer.

"I can't decide," he replied. "What do you think?"

"I don't know." I thought about the preacher's advice. "Listen to your heart," I said. "It'll tell you what to do."

"Yes," he murmured, "I expect it will."

I thought about my own heart. What was it saying? There was something that Kevin had said about hearts once, long ago...but I couldn't quite remember it. Finally I let it go.

We were on the Post Road now, and going faster. Three miles to the Fitton place. And then what? How would Kevin react if we couldn't find it? How would I react?

"Oh, no," Kevin said after a while.

Behind us we saw a dark shape on the road.

Kevin looked around at Dad. "How much further?" he asked. "I think we're being followed."

"Around this bend, then a bit beyond. If it's Carmody, he won't catch us in a carriage."

"Still, can we go any faster?" he pleaded.

Dad flicked the reins, but Gretel was pulling a lot of weight through the snow, and she just didn't have the strength to speed up. But Dad was right, the shape behind us didn't come any closer. I was pretty sure it was the lieutenant's carriage, though.

"Let's go!" Kevin cried.

We rounded the bend in the road. Nothing looked familiar to me. How much further?

To our right was a small slope, and at the top I saw someone standing in the trees. "Stop!" I shouted.

Dad pulled on the reins. I got out and started running up the slope. The figure disappeared back into the trees. I turned and saw Kevin behind me, and Professor Palmer struggling through the snow behind him. And I saw the carriage pulling up behind Dad's wagon.

I reached the trees. Where was the figure? I kept going into the woods. A pine bough slapped me in the face and drenched me in snow. I was out of breath; my feet felt numb. Where did he go?

Then I saw him, standing in a small clearing. The preacher.

He looked cold.

"I didn't mean to leave like that last night," he said. "But I wasn't supposed to be talking to you, never mind your friend. I seem to be breaking rules left and right, though. So what's one more?"

"Is it here?" I demanded.

"I wasn't standing out there for my health," he replied—a little crossly, I thought. "Look, here's some final wisdom, not that you're in the mood for it. Don't think badly of me. It is difficult to find one's way—in any world. We—all of us—can only do our best." He took a step backwards.

"Wait a minute!" I called out.

"And remember," he said, "it is only by setting out—" But that was all I heard. He had disappeared.

"Who was that?" Kevin asked, coming up beside me.

"The preacher. He was waiting for us, to show us where he put the portal. He just stepped into it."

Professor Palmer joined us, trying to catch his breath. "They're right behind us," he gasped. "I think you boys should—"

Kevin didn't have to be told what to do. He headed into the middle of the clearing, but not soon enough. Lieutenant Carmody crashed through the trees and came up beside the professor. He took out his pistol and aimed it at Kevin. "Good morning, lads," he said. "And Professor Palmer. Not exactly where I was told the portal was, but no matter."

We stood there. A few seconds later Sergeant Hornbeam and my father showed up; the sergeant was holding a pistol to my father's back. "Morning, all," he said. Behind them came Peter, looking unhappy.

"You know everything we know," Kevin said to the lieutenant. "Keeping us here won't help you. Please let us go home."

The lieutenant shook his head. "President Gardner wants you to stay. And so you'll stay." He paused. "I'm the one who is to go."

"What?"

He shrugged. "Did you think we'd have this device in our possession and not try to use it? You may be right that we've learned all we can from you. So I'm go to where you came from and return with those marvelous things you described to us—medicines, inventions. Weapons."

"But that's nuts," Kevin said. "The portal doesn't work that way. If you go, you won't be able to get back."

"Perhaps. But you boys are hardly experts on the portal, now are you? The president thinks it a risk worth taking. And I agree."

"William, about the boys," Professor Palmer said. "I beg you to reconsider. We owe these lads an enormous debt. Without them, we'd have lost the war. And I can assure you that my interrogations of them have been complete and exhaustive. They have nothing left to give us. Surely we can let them go home."

"They'll be treated well," Lieutenant Carmody said. "My orders are clear. This is where they are to stay."

"What if you keep me and let Kevin go?" I asked him. "You—or Sergeant Hornbeam—can just say you didn't catch him in time. That's almost true, after all. If you'd been ten seconds later, he'd have been gone."

"I'm afraid not," he replied. "I have my orders. The president wants you both. He has a personal affection for you, Larry, of course. He was quite amused when he found out you had made up those stories about your experiences in China. But Kevin has a somewhat better knowledge of the science of your world, in my opinion. Come along, lads."

I looked over at Kevin. I could tell what he was thinking. Should he just make a run for it? Dive into the portal and hope for the best. Maybe the lieutenant wouldn't really shoot him. Maybe he'd just be wounded and could still make it home.

"Please don't, Kevin," I said.

"Why not?" he replied. "Why not?" There were tears in his eyes. To be this close…

And then I heard a familiar voice behind me. "Damme, it's too early in the morning for this sort of nonsense."

I turned. It was General Aldridge. He was unshaven, and his uniform was the usual rumpled mess. "Thank you for the information about the lads, Alexander," he said to the professor. "I came as soon as I could, though this snow was a nuisance. I believe I missed a turn back there somewhere, but no matter. Everyone I was looking for is here. Give me the pistol, Sergeant," he ordered Sergeant Hornbeam. "And Lieutenant, kindly set yours down."

Sergeant Hornbeam obeyed immediately. But Lieutenant Carmody said, "I believe an order from the President of New England would supersede an order from you, General."

General Aldridge sighed. "Sergeant, you have no direct orders from the president, I take it?" he said.

"No, sir."

"Then kindly take the man's pistol."

Sergeant Hornbeam hesitated this time, but finally went over to the lieutenant and held out his hand. "Sorry, sir," he said. "We should go back and sort this all out."

"By then there'll be nothing left to sort out," the lieutenant muttered. But he handed his pistol over to the sergeant.

"That's better," General Aldridge said. "Now, I take it this famous invisible portal is somewhere in the neighborhood?"

"Yes, sir," Kevin said. "Right over here."

"And you lads want to go home?"

"Yes, sir."

"The lieutenant wants to use it too," Peter said, speaking for the first time. "Why don't you let him?"

The general looked at Peter, then at the lieutenant. "Is that true?" he asked.

"Yes, sir," the lieutenant replied. "To bring back the knowledge from the other world, if possible. As requested by the president."

The general scratched his chin. "Seems very risky."

"I'm prepared to take the risk."

"Very well, then—go ahead."

The lieutenant hesitated. "Now?"

"No, let's stand here for an hour or two and freeze to death. Of course now."

"What about the boys?"

"You can leave them in my care, Lieutenant. Who better to carry out the president's orders than the leader of his military?"

The two men stared at each other. Finally Lieutenant Carmody stiffened and saluted the general. "As you wish, sir."

General Aldridge casually returned the salute.

"Kevin," the lieutenant said, "can you show me where the portal is exactly?"

Kevin walked forward to where the preacher had disappeared. He reached out his hand, and it too disappeared in mid-air. He pulled it back, and it reappeared. Then he moved it forward again—gone. "Here," he said.

"Extraordinary," the general muttered. "Are you ready, Lieutenant?"

We waited. Finally the lieutenant nodded and walked over to the portal. "I wish no one unhappiness," he said. "Please believe me. I only seek to do my duty."

"Thanks for everything you did for us," I said.

"How do I—"

"All you've gotta do is step in," Kevin said, "then just, you know, step out the other side."

"Very well." He looked around at all of us then—and, I think, at the trees, the snow, the sky—everything there was to see on the cold Christmas morning. Then he followed Kevin's instructions.

He was there and then he wasn't, vanishing into invisibility in a split-second. None of us moved, as if we expected him to come back if we stayed still long enough. But he didn't return. He was gone.

Professor Palmer went over and reached his hand into the portal the way Kevin had done, then took it out again and shook his head.

Kevin walked back to General Aldridge. "Are you going to let Larry and me go, sir?" he asked.

"Of course," the general replied. "Speaking of duty—you've done your duty here. More than your duty. President Gardner will be disappointed, but he'll get over it. If you happen to see Lieutenant Carmody in your world, send him our regards and tell him to come back soon."

"Professor Palmer is going to come too," Kevin said. "Is that all right?"

"Really? Doesn't anyone want to stay here? I know the weather's been unpleasant, but it's rather nice in the spring." General Aldridge turned to the professor. "You wish to leave us, Alexander?"

The professor was looking at the portal. "I—" he began, and then he shook his head. "No, I don't wish to leave." He turned to us. "I can't go, boys. This is my home. You've given me much to think about, much to learn, but I should learn it on my own. And, you know, General Aldridge is right: it's lovely here come springtime."

"Okay," Kevin said. "I understand. So it's just you and me, Larry."

Everyone turned to look at me.

I couldn't move. I couldn't speak.

Listen to your heart, the preacher had said.

It is only by setting out that you can finally return home.

"Larry," my father murmured softly. "You have to go. We love you, but you have to go."

And then I remembered what Kevin had said about hearts—back in our world when I brought him to the portal. *I wonder what happens if, like, one half your heart is in this world and the other half is in the other.*

Just a stupid little comment—the kind of thing Matthew would say. But it made a different kind of sense to me now. This is the way it was going to be for me, no matter what choice I made. There wasn't a right answer or a wrong answer—it was just a question of which half of my heart I was going to leave behind.

I hugged my father—something I never did at home—and he tousled my hair. He was weeping—something he never did at home. I was starting to cry too. Then I said my goodbyes to the rest of them: Peter, who had saved me more than once, and General Aldridge, who had rescued us from the lieutenant, and Professor Palmer, who had been our other father in this world. I hugged them all.

"We will miss you terribly," the professor said. "But you're doing the right thing. Fare you well." His eyes were moist too.

"Good luck to the Red Stockings," the general said to Kevin.

I figured I'd better do it before I changed my mind. I looked at Kevin. "Ready?"

"Are you kidding?" he said. "I've been ready for months."

"Then let's go." Like Lieutenant Carmody, we took a last look around, at the faces so familiar to us now, at the world that had been our home, and then we stepped into the portal and left them all behind.

CHAPTER 36

Into the interior of the portal, filled with clouds, like a bathroom after a long shower (which I hadn't taken for months). Heart pounding, scared beyond anything I had felt before.

If *you want to go home, the portal will take you home.* That's what the preacher had told me in the church. If only I could be sure what he meant...

Vague shadows to the right and left. One, two, three steps, then out of the portal.

Into warmth and bright sunshine.

No, I thought. Not right. Not on Christmas.

Was it the wrong world? I looked at Kevin. He was blinking his eyes against the sunlight. "Where is this?" he asked. "When is this?"

We looked around. The leaves on the trees were green, but fading a bit. That oak tree looked familiar...

It felt like a warm September afternoon.

"Well..." I said. My heart was still pounding, but with a different kind of excitement from what I'd felt a minute ago.

"When you went into the portal before," Kevin said, "to the Dairy King world—when you came back—how much time had gone by?"

"I don't know. I didn't stay all that long." But then I remembered coming out of the portal—how Stinky had been waiting for me, right where I had left him. As if no time had passed. "Do you think—?"

"Could be? Why not? What do we know about time? What do we know about anything?"

I looked down at my coat—the one the preacher had given me. It looked really shabby in the sunlight. I took it off. Were we back home—and back when we had left? Had this all happened, like, in the blink of an eye? "Let's find out," I said.

"Wait a minute," Kevin said. "What about Lieutenant Carmody?"

We looked around again. No sign of him. Was he here? Or had the portal brought him to some other world? "Doesn't matter," I said. "What's he going to do to us now?"

"You're right. Let's go." Kevin took off his coat too, and we raced through the woods. Yes, I thought I recognized these trees, this path. In a few minutes we saw what we were hoping to see. There was the old swing set in my back yard. There was the garage, with Kevin's bike next to it.

And there was my mother standing on the deck by the kitchen door. "Larry, would you please hurry up?" she called out when she saw us. "We're going to be late for your piano lesson."

Kevin and I ran through the backyard and up to her. She looked younger than the mother I had said goodbye to less than an hour ago; but she was the same woman. I went to hug her, but stopped short as she made a face.

"Look at the two of you," she said. "You're filthy—and soaking wet! Larry, your new sneakers—you've ruined them! What have you been up to?"

Kevin and I looked at each other as we caught our breath. I didn't think about my answer, really. It was just a reflex. "We didn't go far," I said. "We just like…slipped in a puddle. Sorry."

Mom shook her head. "Honestly, Larry, sometimes you have no consideration. What were you thinking? And Kevin, you should know better, too. Your clothes are like rags."

"Sorry, Mrs. Barnes." But Kevin didn't look sorry. He was grinning like crazy.

"I don't see what's so funny, Kevin," Mom said. "Now run along home. Larry, go in and change. Quick! We're never on time for Mr. Rosen."

I stood there next to Kevin. "Well," I said to him, "I guess—that's it. See ya, Kev."

"See ya, Larry. I'll call you later."

"Okay," I said.

He smiled at the word. "Okay," he repeated, still grinning. Then he went over and got on his bike.

"I don't know why his mother doesn't make him wear a helmet," Mom said.

"Beats me," I replied.

So, why didn't we say anything?

Well, would you want to tell your Mom you'd stupidly stepped into a portal or a cosmic gateway or whatever and gone off to an alternate universe for over three months and fought in a war and been shot at multiple times and exposed to deadly diseases? I didn't think so.

Of course, we could prove our story, more or less. Show her the portal. Get scientists out here to examine it. We'd become famous, be interviewed on TV, make a million dollars.

But I wasn't really thinking about any of that. It was just: We were back, and that's all that mattered. I didn't want scientists or TV shows. I wanted to eat supper with my family. I wanted to sleep in my own bed. I wanted to see Cassie again. I went past my mother and inside the house.

Cassie was in the kitchen, eating crackers, probably so later at supper she could say she wasn't hungry and demand to know when were we going to get some good food around here. She stuck two fingers in her mouth as I approached, making like she was going to puke. "You smell like raw sewage," she said. "Haven't they taught you how to use deodorant in middle school?"

I smiled at her. I thought about kissing her, but she probably would've whacked me. "It's so great to see you, Cassie," I said instead. "Really it is."

"You're retarded," I heard her mutter as I left the kitchen.

Upstairs, Matthew was playing a video game. One of my video games, I realized, when I saw the guilty expression on his face. "I thought you were at your piano lesson," he said.

"Still here," I replied. "It's okay."

"What's okay?"

"Playing my game You can play it all you want."

"Really?"

"Sure? Why not?"

"Thanks, Larry," Matthew said. But he looked suspicious. What was I up to? I wasn't up to anything. I just put on some deodorant and changed clothes. Before going back downstairs, I went into the bathroom and stared at the toilet. I flushed it once, just for fun. Things were going to take a little getting used to.

"Larry!" my mother shouted up to me.

"Coming!" I left the bathroom and went to my piano lesson.

I don't remember anything about the lesson; my mind was too filled with other stuff to concentrate. There was just so much more of everything. More noise, more sights, more smells—although none of the body odor that Cassie had objected to, and that I had gotten so used to. I was a little overwhelmed. The car went way too fast—and on the wrong side of the road. The radio was just too loud. I remember asking Mom if I could turn it off, and that got her worried. "Are you feeling all right, Larry?" she asked. "You look pale. And you're talking a little strangely. You're just not yourself somehow."

Not myself. Had I developed an accent, along with everything else? "I'm fine," I said.

She didn't look convinced. That's what I always said. "What exactly were you doing back there in the woods?" she demanded.

"Just goofing around," I said. "Really."

Later Dad came home—beardless, and not as strong-looking as the soldier/farmer I had left behind a few hours ago, but still my dad. We sat down to supper, and I had my first mashed potatoes in months, and my first fresh vegetables. The milk was way colder than any I'd had in the other world, but nowhere near as good-tasting. And it was strange watching everyone use a fork instead of a knife to eat. As we ate my father asked his usual question: "So, what did you do today, Larry?"

And I gave my usual answer: "Nothing."

And then I started to laugh.

Kevin called later. The phone was something else I'd have to get used to all over again. "You say anything to anyone?" he asked.

"Nope. You?"

"No. You going to?"

"I don't know. Your parents suspicious or anything?"

"Mom can't understand why my hair is so long," Kevin said. "But I mean, what's she gonna say? I went over to your house for a while, then I came back. And that's it. I was gone, like, two hours, max. How much can your hair grow in two hours?"

"Well, should we say something?"

"I suppose so, but—I dunno. I don't feel like it. Not right now, anyway."

"I know what you mean."

"I was wondering," Kevin said. "How can we be sure this world is exactly the same as the one we left? Maybe we'll go to school tomorrow, and Stinky won't exist. Or he'll be just a little bit different. Maybe we won't be able to tell what's different."

"I don't want to do any wondering for a while, Kevin."

"Yeah, okay, just a thought. Any sign of Lieutenant Carmody over there?"

I had forgotten about him. "No. I hope he's all right. He wasn't that bad."

"I suppose. If he's not here, we'll never find out where he is."

"I guess not."

Cassie came in and glared at me for hogging the phone for three whole minutes.

"Gotta go," I said. "Cassie wants the phone."

"Cassie. Geez. Cassie's alive again. And you know something else? I'm twelve again. I lost a birthday when we came home. Anyway, it's good to be back."

"Did you flush a toilet?" I asked him.

"You bet I did. And took the world's longest shower. See ya."

Cassie had heard my last question, and made a face at me like I was too weird for her to even contemplate. I just gave her another smile.

I tried watching TV after I hung up, but it jangled my nerves like the car radio, and besides, it was way too stupid. I did like getting into my bed and feeling that comfortable mattress beneath me; I wouldn't miss those straw mattresses and hard floors. I wasn't tired, though. For all the excitement of the day, it hadn't been that long since I'd been dozing in front of the fireplace and dreaming of grilled cheese sandwiches. So for once I really enjoyed talking to Matthew. He was happy about my letting him play Final Fantasy so he was even chattier than usual. After he'd been yakking for a while I decided to bring up a topic of my own, which I figured was just the kind he liked to talk about. "Matthew, what if there are millions of universes, each one just a little bit different from all the others? What if we each have millions of different lives? In some of them we're rich, in some of them we're poor, in some of them stuff like cars and computers haven't even been invented. In some of them we might be dead, or maybe we never even existed. What if we could go to another universe and see how we lived there? Wouldn't that be cool? Wouldn't we learn a lot? Matthew?"

No answer; he was asleep. For once I had out-talked him.

There's no place like home.

That's what the movie says. Now I was home. So I should've lived happily ever after, right? No more fighting with Cassie. No more getting mad at my Mom or annoyed at Matthew.

That lasted less than a day.

Cassie yelled at me in the morning for being in the shower too long. Well, she was the one who complained that I smelled bad, wasn't she? And Mom wanted to drive me to the bus stop—she was still worried about that pervert in Rhode Island she'd read about. It's so dangerous nowadays, she told me. You can't be too careful. *I'll tell you about danger!* I wanted to shout at her. I'll tell you about cannonballs falling all around you and Portuguese soldiers charging at you with swords and bayonets. I'll tell you about Canadian soldiers trying to decide whether to kill you, and New England soldiers shooting at you from watchtowers…And I survived it all.

But I didn't say anything about that. I just got into a stupid argument with her and almost missed the bus. Nothing had changed—except me. And how had I really changed?

Well…

Take Stinky Glover. He was still here, despite Kevin's fantasy. On the bus the next morning he gave me a purple nurple instead of a wet willie. Same difference. He still thought the name "Lawrence" was incredibly funny.

But, you know, I didn't really mind. On that other world, he had helped me, maybe even saved my life—saved me from an enemy soldier, anyway; taught me how to hunt; showed me the way home, even if he had finally snitched on me. Maybe on some other world he was a good guy whose master didn't beat him. Maybe on some world we were best friends. I let it go.

And Nora Lally. Before English class I decided, what the heck, and I went over to her. "Hi, Nora," I said. "Listen, I was thinking—I'm a pretty good writer, at least that's what Ms. Nathanson tells me. If you want someone to, like, take a look at your compositions before you turn them in, I'd be happy to. Just for, you know, spelling and grammar, that kind of stuff."

Pretty lame, huh? But she smiled—just the way Sarah Lally smiled—and she said, "Thanks, Larry. That'd be great."

It couldn't be that easy, right? But it was. I smiled back, and we sat down to find out what Ms. Nathanson had to say.

And the piano. I might not have had a good lesson that first day back, but still…I found myself playing more than I ever had before, just for the fun of it, the way I had at Professor Palmer's.

And one day Mom asked, "What's that piece, Larry?"

I realized I had been playing that old song Professor Palmer liked so much:

Wanly I wandered
Through the world far and wide
Seeking some solace
For dreams that had died.

Long did I linger
In an alien land
Till tears finally left me
As I stood on the strand.

And there was the final verse that I had tried not to think about in the other world. But now it seemed okay to remember it:

Then homeward I hastened
To friends I'd forgot
And found where I'd left it—
The joy that I sought.

"I don't know," I said. "Just something I picked up."

"It's very lovely," Mom said. "I don't think I've ever heard it before."

It was lovely, and I was glad I had learned it. I was glad of a lot of things that had happened to me.

* * *

Long did I linger
In an alien land…

I kept thinking of Kevin's stupid remark about your heart being in two worlds at once. Because that's how I felt sometimes. I was glad to be back, glad to have plenty to eat and no one shooting at me. But half my heart was still in that other world, with the professor, with my family, with Sarah Lally, even with General Aldridge and

President Gardner and Stinky Glover. What were they doing right now? How was New England making out after the war? How was the Barnes family making out, with Cassie dead and me gone and no harvest to keep them through the winter? Was Professor Palmer all right? Was Stinky in trouble with his master? I would never know, but that didn't mean I would ever forget.

And found where I'd left it—
The joy that I sought.

I don't know about joy. But whatever it was, it had always been here, right? And it just took a little growing up to find it. I couldn't keep smiling at Cassie when she insulted me, but I could remember her in the camp, unhappy and desperate, and I could feel a little pity for whatever was going on inside her.

And my mother. Was it so hard now to see the overpowering love that was behind her fears of every danger that lurked in wait for us? In how many worlds had she lost me because she hadn't been vigilant enough? In how many worlds did I lay buried in the family graveyard, and she had to spend her life mourning what might have been?

Finally, there was the mystery of the portal. Kevin and I talked about it endlessly, and he was fascinated when I told him the preacher's story, fascinated by the idea that some mysterious race had built the portal and then disappeared, and this other race used it just to go preaching, without really understanding it. But mostly he was fascinated by the idea that the portal always brought you home, if that's what you wanted. "Wouldn't it be great," he said, "if—every time your life started to suck—you could step into the portal and just come back when you're ready?"

"Uh, Kevin, you're skipping over the parts where you get shot at and come down with a terrible disease. Who was the one that was desperate to get back here?"

"I know, I know. But still…"

Still…

Then there was the day Kevin came over with a copy of the Glanbury Mariner. "See this?" he asked.

He pointed to an entry in the police log, which the paper prints every week.

"2:17 a.m. Fowler Street resident reports strange man sleeping

*in tool shed. Man fled when approached. Described as medium
height, wearing red jacket, carrying old-fashioned pistol.
Cruiser dispatched, searched neighborhood. No one found."*

It was dated the night after we had returned home.

"So he made it," I said.

"Looks like."

"What should we do?"

Kevin shrugged. "I don't know what there is to do."

But eventually it became too big a secret to keep. The portal was
just too important not to talk about it, especially if Carmody was
around. I figured my father was the one to tell. He'd know what to
do with the knowledge, and he'd know how to keep Mom from
getting too mad at me when she found out just exactly what we'd
been up to back in the conservation land where we weren't supposed
to be. Kevin agreed. "Let's not say anything to your dad until he sees
the portal for himself," he said. "Otherwise he'll think we're just
making everything up."

So on Saturday when Mom was out shopping Kevin and I told
Dad there was something we wanted to show him out in the woods.
"Found some buried treasure?" he asked.

"Not exactly."

"You know your mother doesn't want you wandering around too
far back there, right?"

"Yeah, I know, but anyway—this is going to be pretty
interesting."

So he followed us out into the woods. Kevin kept looking at me
like, this is really gonna be something. And he was right. It wouldn't
just shock Dad, but everyone in the world. It would change the way
people thought about everything—science, religion, history. And we
were the ones who found it.

And what if the scientists figured out how to use it, and we could
return safely to our other world?

I knew the way pretty well by this time, although Dad kept
bugging us by explaining stuff and pointing out the names of trees
and the birds. Everything was an education to him. Well, we were
about to give him an education. Kevin and I stopped when we
reached the clearing.

"It's right here, Dad," I said. "Watch this."

Kevin and I went over to it and reached out our hands.

They didn't disappear. We looked at each other, and then started walking around in the small clearing, waving our arms. "It's gotta be here," Kevin muttered.

But it wasn't.

"May I ask what you're doing?" Dad asked. His arms were folded, and he was looking at us like he was trying to figure out if this was some kind of middle-school joke that he didn't get.

"Is it the wrong place?" Kevin asked me.

I shook my head. "It's gone."

I felt like I'd been punched. It couldn't be true, but it was. The portal was gone.

"Well?" Dad asked. "I could use some help raking, if we're done here."

"Sorry, Dad," I said to my father. "There was something here, but now it's gone."

"Do you want to tell me what it was?"

I looked at Kevin, and he just shrugged. "I guess not," I said. "It doesn't matter. Sorry we bothered you."

Dad just shook his head. "Larry, you sure have been acting strange lately."

"It's a phase," I replied. "Like Cassie. Could you like—give Kevin and me a minute?"

"All right, but don't get into any trouble back here. You know how your mother worries. And grab a rake when you come back."

He turned and walked away from us.

"Figures," Kevin said, kicking at a rock.

I noticed something else. "I took off the preacher's coat when we got out of the portal. It's gone, too."

Kevin looked around. His coat was still there, lying on the ground where he'd dropped it. "The preacher moved the portal," he said.

"Didn't want stupid kids taking it for any more joyrides, I guess."

Kevin sighed. "Oh, well. It would've been something, wouldn't it? The look on your Dad's face…"

"Yeah. Still, this is okay."

"It's okay," Kevin agreed, sighing again.

And we walked slowly back out of the woods.

This is okay—this life, this world. But one thing I remember is the preacher telling me how easy it was for him to spot another traveler—someone who didn't belong, someone from a different world who was just passing through. Are there a lot of those travelers, or just a very few? Sometimes I find myself trying to see if I can spot them, too: scared kids like me or soldiers in red coats or wandering preachers with black, glittering eyes…

And I find myself wondering: What if I do spot one? Another stranger, say, talking to a small crowd in a park or on a street corner, telling them to how to live and love and appreciate the universe…? Would I run from him as fast as I could? Or would I say, *Please, show me where the portal is. I don't care about the risks. I want to go back to that other world again—just for an hour, just for a minute. And if I can't go back, let me try for a new world, a new adventure.*

And I think about what the preacher had said to the people in the Boston park: How can you know what is in you unless you have struggled, unless you have been asked to do more than you thought you were capable of doing?

What better way to do that, than to find a new world?

I really don't know what I'd do if I spotted a traveler.

But I'd like to find out.

ALSO BY RICHARD BOWKER

SCIENCE FICTION SERIES
The Last PI Series
Dover Beach, Book 1
The Distance Beacons

The Psychic Thriller Series
Summit
Marlborough Street

Replica
Forbidden Sanctuary

THRILLER/SUSPENSE
Pontiff
Senator

Turn the page for an

excerpt from

TERRA

The Portal Series
Book 2

———◆———

Richard Bowker

Again a wave of homesickness came over me. I shouldn't be here, wearing this stupid robe, lying in this uncomfortable bed.

Like the night before, I must have fallen asleep eventually. And like the night before, I awoke to see someone standing in the doorway.

But this time it wasn't Palta staring at me. This time it was Gratius, and he was holding a gun.

"Don't be afraid," he whispered. "We must rescue Affron and Valleia."

I poked Carmody, who was instantly awake.

Gratius repeated what he had said. He motioned with the gun. "We must go. Now."

"Where are they?" Carmody asked him.

"In prison. In the palatium. Come."

"I suggest we obey him, Larry," Carmody said. "What have we got to lose?"

We quickly got out of bed and put on our sandals. In the moonlight coming in through our small window I got a better look at the gun. It was strange—the shape wasn't quite right. It didn't seem to have a trigger, and the barrel was a little too thin. And the metal glowed a soft blue in the moonlight.

Was this the weapon Valleia had told Carmody about?

When we had our sandals on, Gratius led us out into the atrium.

...just in time to see a lamp come on in Hypatius's cubiculum. He appeared in the doorway a moment later. His hair was messy; his robe was rumpled; his eyes were bloodshot. He set the lamp down on a table in the atrium and stared at Gratius—stared at the gun.

"Oh dear," he said. "Oh my."

He and Gratius started talking to each other in Latin. Gratius gestured with the gun; Hypatius shook his head.

"I forbid it, my friend," Hypatius said finally in English. "It cannot be done. It isn't right. I know that this business with Affron is not proceeding the way you would like, but you will destroy us all."

It was at this point that I noticed Palta, her arms folded, standing in the shadows of the atrium just outside her cubiculum. Gratius had his back to her, and Hypatius didn't notice her because Gratius was in the way. She was listening intently to their conversation.

And then she started walking slowly forward, towards Gratius.

I stared at her. Should I say something? Should I try to stop her? She glanced at me, and then looked back towards Gratius.

She was staring at the gun in his hand. In her own hand was a small knife.

The argument between Gratius and Hypatius lapsed back into Latin and continued. Gratius looked upset. Hypatius looked frightened. Gratius began to speak...

And then Palta leaped forward and stabbed his hand. Gratius yelped in pain and dropped the gun. She grabbed it and scampered back away from him, brandishing it at us. She said something to Gratius and motioned to him to move aside. He did as he was told.

She aimed the gun at Hypatius.

Hypatius extended his hands and spoke to her in Latin—gently, as if explaining to her the mistake she was making. His face was sweating; his hands were shaking.

"Diabolus," she hissed. And then there was a brief low hum, an even briefer flash of light from the barrel of the gun, which turned a deep blue. Hypatius's body glowed a brilliant white for a moment, hands outstretched, mouth open to reply....

And then his body disappeared.

There was a bitter smell in the air. On the tiled floor of the atrium where Hypatius had stood was a small heap of ashes.

He was gone. Totally gone.

———◆———

Terra
available in ebook and print

Richard Bowker is the author of *Replica*, *Senator*, and other novels. He lives near Boston with his wife and two sons.

You can contact Richard through his website: www.richardbowker.com

www.ingramcontent.com/pod-product-compliance
Lightning Source LLC
Chambersburg PA
CBHW030958260626
47169CB00002B/600